BEYOND
THE WIDE
MISSOURI

JAMES J MCLAUGHLIN

GUILDHALL PRESS

First published in April 2008

Guildhall Press
Ráth Mór Business Park
Bligh's Lane
Derry, N Ireland, BT48 0LZ
T: (028) 7136 4413 F: (028) 7137 2949
info@ghpress.com www.ghpress.com

The author asserts his moral rights in this work in accordance with the Copyright, Designs and Patents Act 1998.

Front cover image of Medicine Bow Mountain, Wyoming, courtesy of Margo Clark, Dubois, Wyoming, from www.windrivergearshop.com
Internal images courtesy of St Louis University and Nevada Historical Society.

Sponsored by John Donnelly of SDC Trailers and JOC Management Consultancy.

 Trailers Limited

 John O'Connor
Management Consultancy

General Editor: Paul Hippsley
Typeset by Kevin Hippsley
Copyright © James J McLaughlin/Guildhall Press
ISBN: 978 1 906271 11 4

A CIP record of this book is available from the British Library.

ACKNOWLEDGEMENTS

My thanks must go to Barbara Meyer, teacher and local historian from McLaughlin, South Dakota, for putting me on the right 'trail' in my search for Patrick McLaughlin, and Michael Maher, librarian, Nevada Historical Society, Reno, Nevada. Also to John Waide, archivist, Pius Xll Memorial Library, St Louis University, Missouri; Helga Chapman, Royal Norwegian Embassy, London; and Fr John Walsh, whose great grandfather was a hotelier in California in the gold rush days and who brought the story back to Maghera. And to John McGinley, a friend from schooldays, whose knowledge of the overland trails was of immense value to me.

My eternal thanks must go to John O'Connor for the many miles and hours he devoted to driving me and helping in my research in Northern Ireland. It was through his determination and dedication that this book was finally published. I will be forever indebted to him for making my dream a reality.

Thanks also to Rosella O'Connor, Beryl Knox and Rose Sargeant for their successful search for books long out of print and to Loretto Bradley for ancient Celtic songs. To Tamasin Gough for her research in Oslo. To Matthew Gittins, ornithologist, for sharing his knowledge of the birds of the area. To Graham Mawhinney of Ballinascreen Historical Society for his valued editorial contribution. To all at Guildhall Press for their professional input, advice and support. And finally to my wife, Eileen and our son Dermot, for without their help I would have achieved little.

I am very grateful to John Donnelly of SDC Trailers whose generous sponsorship made this publication possible. Also E O'Connor Estate Agents for supporting the book launch.

If I have forgotten anyone who assisted in the research or production of this volume, I seek their forgiveness. And if any discrepancies – factual, temporal, linguistic or otherwise – have circumvented my scrutiny, then I freely accept full responsibility and hope they do not mar your enjoyment of this amazing story.

ABOUT THE AUTHOR

No one could be more qualified to have written this book than James J McLaughlin. Maghera, the mid-Ulster market town lying at the foot of the Sperrin Hills, is his hometown as it was of the two main characters in the story – Willie McKay and Patrick McLaughlin. Like them, James has fished the same mountain rivers with his father, and in his youth he followed  in their footsteps with his dog and gun. Like the heroes he has resurrected through these pages, James was an enthusiastic rover from an early age. As an airman and sailor, he has travelled far and wide and has had many years' experience as a pilot of powered aircraft and sailplanes. He now lives with his wife Eileen in the south of England.

INTRODUCTION

Beyond The Wide Missouri is an historical novel presented in a semi-fictional format. It is based on extensive research carried out by the author into the lives of Willie McKay and Patrick McLaughlin from Maghera in Ireland's Ulster Province.

James J McLaughlin set out in 2004 to learn what light, if any, could be thrown on the story of the two young men who left the verdant hills and valleys of their hometown in the mid-nineteenth century in search of adventure and fortune in the untamed lands west of the Missouri and the Mississippi rivers to the Pacific seaboard. He was to discover one of the most absorbing and fascinating stories ever to emerge from the pioneering days of the Wild West.

Was he, the author, of the family line of Patrick McLaughlin, the gold prospector from Maghera, also the author's hometown? Was young Willie McKay the sole survivor of a fierce battle with a band of renegades and subsequently adopted by the Sioux?

Eoin Walsh, a lawyer and historian, had published a short story titled *Willie McKay* in the early 1950s which was a brief account of a chance meeting on the prairie between the prospector and the Sioux warrior from Maghera. It was this little narrative that, years later, prompted James J McLaughlin to investigate further. His diligent research took him down old trails of historical interest, many never before chronicled.

Like the wild Missouri river before it was tamed and harnessed by man, *Beyond The Wide Missouri* flows, at times powerful, even brutal; always uprooting pieces of history long forgotten, like "Old Muddy" itself unveiling its secrets – sometimes tranquil but never stagnant, ever flowing, ever changing. It is a unique story of adventure and courage, sacrifice and achievement, and reveals insights into aspects of native-American culture and spirituality that even today are lessons for us all.

FOREWORD

Easter week 2007 brought me a delightful surprise. My old school friend John O'Connor presented me with the manuscript of *Beyond The Wide Missouri*, lovingly researched and written by James J McLaughlin. John said it had been inspired by a short story my late father Eoin had published when we were both children. He suggested that it was a very good read. And so it is. In fact, it is a cracking read!

The tale begins in pre-famine Ireland. Our two protagonists, Willie McKay and Patrick McLaughlin, grow up together in the foothills of the Sperrin Mountains in the north of Ireland, the author's native heath – and mine. Theirs is an idyllic world, a land where milk and honey flow.

The story then moves with Willie to the New World of 1841. We find ourselves in a plush New Orleans hotel; aboard a Mississippi steamboat; inspecting wagons; stocking up in a wholesaler's; discussing firearms; learning about horsemanship; on a wagon convoy trekking across Missouri; under attack from renegade marauders; and being 'adopted' by a tribe of friendly Sioux.

We catch up with Patrick in 1859. The author introduces us to the world of the gold prospector. There are sheer gold nuggets of information in this section of the book also. We learn, for example, the history of the famous Comstock Lode, the world's richest goldfield. We hear about panning for gold and the staking of claims. A young German miner's injured foot teaches us about medicine and doctoring in the Wild West. And all the while, the narrative gathers pace. Then, suddenly, the book reaches its climax. But I cannot be allowed to spoil a fabulous story.

I congratulate Jim McLaughlin. Irish people love words. Our author is no exception. No amount of exposure to satellite television or text messages can empty our vocabulary of its richness. We love the sound and the feel of words and hold a story full of engaging facts and well-turned phrases a story worth hearing. I wish this absorbing book great, great success.

John R Walsh
Buncrana, County Donegal
April 2007

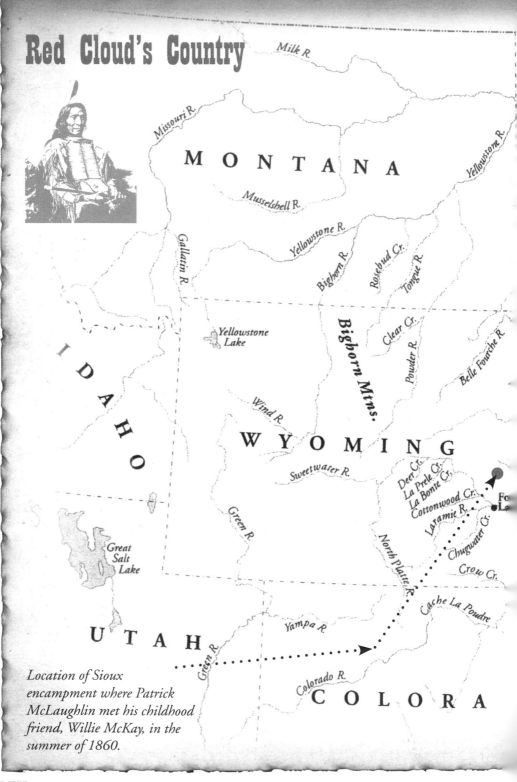

Red Cloud's Country

Milk R.

Missouri R.

Yellowstone R.

M O N T A N A

Musselshell R.

Gallatin R.

Yellowstone R.

Bighorn R.

Rosebud Cr.

Tongue R.

Clear Cr.

Powder R.

Belle Fourche R.

Yellowstone Lake

Bighorn Mtns.

I D A H O

Wind R.

W Y O M I N G

Sweetwater R.

Deer Cr.
La Prele Cr.
La Bonte Cr.
Cottonwood Cr.
Laramie R.

Fo
L

Chugwater Cr.

Crow Cr.

North Platte R.

Green R.

Great Salt Lake

Yampa R.

Cache La Poudre

U T A H

Green R.

Colorado R.

C O L O R A

Location of Sioux encampment where Patrick McLaughlin met his childhood friend, Willie McKay, in the summer of 1860.

N

NORTH

DAKOTA

Souris R.

Sheyenne R.

Red R.

Heart R.

onball R.

Grand R.

Moreau R.

SOUTH

DAKOTA

Medicine Cr.

James R.

White R.

Missouri R.

e R.

brara R.

North Loup R.

Elkhorn R.

Middle Loup R.

ue Cr.

NEBRASKA

South Loup R.

Prairie Cr.

latte R.

atte R.

MINNESOTA

Mississippi R.

Big Sioux R.

Minnesota R.

Des Moines R.

IOWA

Platte R.

Big Blue R.

MISSOURI

Republican R.

KANSAS

Smokey Hill R.

0	70	140	210 Miles
0	112	224	336 KM

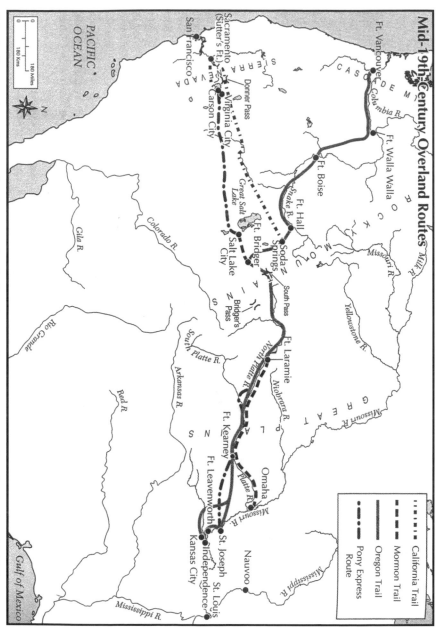

Map indicating the various overland routes taken by frontier travellers, prospectors and traders in the mid 19th century.

To my wife Eileen, family, friends and the people of Maghera.
And to those early Irish pioneers who displayed great courage and a sense of
adventure to seek a new life in the land of opportunity.

St Patrick's Church, Glen, Maghera, in the
nineteenth century, as it was when McKay and
McLaughlin were baptised and where, as boys, they
sang in the choir.

CHAPTER 1

'In Nomine Patris et Filii et Spiritus Sancti.'

The priest's voice was barely audible above the scream emitted by the infant as the cold baptismal water was poured over his forehead. The open window above the font gave vent to the cry. In the near distance, a farmer culling rabbits on his land discharged a shot stirring the sleeping rookery that nestled atop the stand of tall elms that bounded the little parish church. The raucous cry of the angry parent birds mingled with the screeching of the nestlings.

'William John McKay, I baptise thee in the name of the Father and of the Son and of the Holy Spirit.' Another application of water to the forehead, followed by yet a louder scream and a cacophony of sound which rose to assail the peace of that spring morning in 1815.

Young Willie McKay grew up on his parents' farm in Ulster. Like all farmers' sons of that period, Willie had his chores to do and learned the skills required to do them. He could milk the few cows they had by the time he was twelve years old. And as soon as he was big enough to walk behind a horse-drawn plough, Willie was doing a man-sized job.

School attendance was not compulsory at that time but local authorities and church bodies made every effort to ensure that the children in those rural communities attended class as often as possible and, in the little schoolhouse in Falaleigh, Willie received a good basic education. From early schooldays his best friend was Patrick McLaughlin. Little is known of this boy's family background;

perhaps he lived in the nearby town of Maghera. If that were so, the boy may well have had to walk a total of four miles each day he attended school – not an uncommon endeavour in those days. Anyhow, Patrick was almost always there, sometimes rain-soaked, when the assembly bell was rung.

The McKay farmhouse was a long single-storey stone building with a thatched roof and the ubiquitous whitewashed exterior. Many of these remained as dwelling houses well into the twentieth century. The front faced south-east, commanding a panoramic view of the Moyola Valley and the little market town of Maghera – that is, when the mist was not rolling down from the hills behind. The farm's arable acreage lay in that direction, all of it within view from the front of the house. Behind the dwelling house was the yard, the central point of the farm's activity, with all the usual outhouses around it. The nearby road, suitable only for the traffic of the day, the horse and cart, tailed away to a mountain track into the Carntogher Hills.

Running south from Magilligan Point on the Atlantic shore for some twenty miles and then south-west for another ten miles are the Sperrin Mountains, which divide the county of Londonderry into north and south regions. Carntogher is a section of that range. Its bulbous head, known as the Snout, is one of the high points of the Sperrins and a landmark for miles around. Today this area is visited by many walkers who enjoy the two paths set out for them on the Carntogher Way, giving them access to an area of outstanding beauty. Mountain tracks have long since given way to modern roads and the Glenshane Pass is now part of the main road linking Belfast and Derry.

Work was labour intensive on all small hill farms in those days and at harvest and turf cutting, even the women were not exempt from work in the fields or on the mountainous turf banks.

From early boyhood the turf-cutting season was Willie's delight; riding on the cart with his father Jim and two older brothers, Willie holding the reins, "in charge", the big horse plodding steadily upwards, the dogs running close by. Here and there small fair-weather clouds would sail overhead. They seemed closer now and Willie would watch them as they drifted over the valleys below like squadrons of ships in full sail bound for some distant shore. The skylarks rose vertically all around them from the heather.

On arrival at the turf bank, Jim McKay would unhitch the horse from the cart and leave her to graze placidly until daylight was almost over. The boys would bundle the provisions for the day into the wheelbarrow, while Jim took charge of the special turf-cutting spade for safety's sake. Cutting the oily black sods was Dad's work. The two older boys' detail was to stack them in the wheelbarrow and, each one taking his turn, wheel them well away from the face and stack them into little stooks to be left for the wind and sun to dry.

Patrick would join them sometimes, and on such occasions Willie and he, with the two dogs, found plenty of occupation. Prince, the Border collie, was a working sheepdog and enjoyed his days off romping in the heather with the boys and the lively little black and tan Lakeland terrier called Screen. This was little Willie's own dog, given him by an uncle when it was a mere bundle of fluff. The benefactor lived in the neighbouring district, or parish, of Ballinascreen and someone decided Screen would be a fitting name. Screen and Willie were inseparable; a boy and his dog growing up together.

In the late afternoon, as the sun was dropping over the horizon, the day's work over, their dad, or Pa as he was known, blew the whistle for their return. It was the whistle he carried for Prince's instruction when gathering the sheep, and here it served a dual purpose. The two young ones were away on a hillock above the workers foraging for blueberries that grew in abundance among the heather at that time of the year. They didn't hear it for a wind was rising and blowing away in the direction of the others. Prince heard it and made it known to the boys with much barking and pawing.

'I'll race you down,' said Patrick.

'Come on then,' said Willie who, having noted the wind direction, pulled his jacket over his head, holding the ends high, and took off in full sail, half in flight and half bounding with Patrick flying beside him. The dogs, bouncing on ahead, would occasionally glance behind almost smiling as if to say: 'You have wind and sail to help you but we are ahead of you.' An exhilarating new game had just been discovered. Those were long carefree days on that mountainside; they were their halcyon days, never to end.

And in the snugness of the little farmhouse when the day was ended, with the soporific aroma from the glowing peat fire in the open grate, sleep came easily to two small boys and one small dog bundled in a heap in Willie's bed.

'Dad would like you to come fishing with us, Willie.'

'I can't. I'm no good at it and anyway, there is always something for me to do here.'

Patrick's disappointment showed. He had always come to the farm, lending a helping hand and occasionally staying overnight. He felt he was the one doing all the running. To his knowledge, his pal had never been further south than the little schoolhouse or the new big church built from cut granite, dwarfing the little chapel now standing almost abandoned. St Patrick's was three years in the building. 'But, Willie, Dad said he would teach you. It's good fun and, Willie, if you get good at it you will be able to bring home some nice trout and they taste good.'

Mrs McKay, who had just finished preparing a batch of dough, washed her hands and, drying them with her apron, turned to her son saying, 'Pat is right; you have two older brothers capable of helping your father. It is time for you to see the town and meet some other people and learn things as well as farming.

You're growing up, so go off and enjoy yourself.' Turning to Patrick she asked, 'Pat, where does your father go fishing?'

'The Mullagh, Mrs McKay.'

She thought for a moment. 'The Mullagh! But that is a small river – sure it's only a wee stream – I wouldn't think he would find much there. Now I would have thought he would have to go to the Roe or the Grillagh.'

'He does, Mrs McKay, he fishes them when he can get away for two or three days. At times he stays in one of the cabins they have up there and takes with him people, fishing people who want to learn the rivers.'

'Your father must be well up in it; it would be nice for Jim if he could do something like that now and again. The only thing he brings in is the odd rabbit. All the guns he has about the place and never gets time to go out in the mountain for a day. Look,' she said, pointing to the double-barrelled smooth-bore above the door and another two resting on blacksmith-turned hooks affixed to the fire breast close to the low ceiling, 'there's enough here to arm a platoon of soldiers. Fort McKay you might say.' A hen, emitting a low clucking noise, high-stepping its way through the open door onto the flagstone floor of the living room-cum-kitchen, head moving from side to side with an air of superiority, caught her eye. She shooed it out, closing the door. 'As I was saying, Pat, we have a fine armoury here, but no fishing rods or that sort of thing.'

Patrick turned to her, smiling at the impertinence of the egg provider. 'That's all right, Mrs McKay, Dad has three or four good rods, lines and all that kind of stuff. Willie can borrow whatever he needs. Mam will pack us up a good lunch. She even wraps up a towel and soap so we can wash our hands before eating. I don't like handling the bait, but you get used to it.'

'That's settled then,' said Mrs McKay. 'When will you be going?'

'I'll ask my dad,' said Patrick. 'Maybe Saturday, the day after tomorrow.'

'Good. I hope you have a successful day on the Mullagh,' smiled Mrs McKay.

The Mullagh river, its source somewhere in the Sperrins, flows lazily through the flat meadow lands that lie to the west and to the south of Maghera to join the larger Moyola that empties into the north-western shore of Lough Neagh. It is a docile little river, its course taking it through some of the most beautiful arable farms, plantations and meadows in all of Ulster – a kaleidoscope of constantly changing scenery. Down the years, the river and its banks were well maintained. Workmen never appeared to be present, to be doing anything, yet it was always pristine clean and orderly, a parkland. On either side a variety of trees lined the ramparts – elms, sycamore and weeping willow – their roots binding the ramparts and giving them strength against the floods of winter. In winter seasons, when the rain was persistent and heavy, the river would have its way and the Mullagh was no wee stream but a raging torrent flooding vast areas of meadowland on either bank.

This was the Mullagh in the days when Patrick McLaughlin and his son fished there, when its waters were teeming with trout and grayling. No licence to fish was required, no questions asked. One just took up the rod and went fishing or strolled on summer evenings along its banks. That was the status quo and remained so well into the twentieth century.

Willie enjoyed his first day fishing and returned home in the evening the proud owner of his first fishing rod of bamboo cane which broke down into three parts, one battered old canvas bag with several nice fat trout and two medium-sized eels. Screen was up quickly from the fireside to investigate the bag and the strange smells emanating from it. The catch tasted good and Willie was hooked on angling. And there were the other rivers running through the Sperrins, the Roe and the Grillagh, where not only trout and grayling were plentiful but also salmon.

Over the next few years, with Prince and Screen for company, the pals would spend many happy hours along those rivers, often walking long distances to reach the best fishing, always learning from the experienced men they would meet along the banks as well as from Patrick's dad. Often the dogs would raise a hare or a flock of partridge. Now and again a snipe, startled by the probing nose of a dog by the riverbank, would suddenly take off from its heather camouflage and fly away in that zigzag manner characteristic of the bird before settling down to level flight prior to landing at a safer spot. The whole Sperrin Mountains seemed to abound with wild life; plover, pheasant and grouse, hares and rabbits too numerous to be counted and foxes proliferated and roamed at will for no one bothered them. Only when a fox ventured down onto one of the farms was it in any danger and Maurice O'Neill, a local trader in Maghera, always paid well for a fox fur complete with head and tail. Willie McKay was no stranger to guns. His father had taught his three sons the use of the double-barrelled twelve-bore from an early age, knowledge necessary on the farm in those remote areas.

Safety with firearms was of paramount importance and the boys were taught well. 'Do you think you could handle a shotgun, Pat?' asked Willie, as little Screen bounced across their path in the heather.

'I'm sure I could; why shouldn't I? I never fired a shot or even handled a gun but I'm sure it's easy.'

'Do you see that wee dog of mine over there bobbing up and down enjoying himself?' said Willie, pointing at Screen.

'Aye, what about him?' Patrick asked.

'Well, if you had a gun in your hand and that wee dog were to spring up in front of you as he just did, he could be dead, mistaken for a rabbit. When you have a gun in your hand you wait until you are sure what is in your sights. We're bringing the guns up here, Pat, and you are going to learn how to handle one.'

'That would be fun, Willie – this is a hunter's paradise.'

'When you are ready, you can get a bit of practice in around the farm. After you've learned how to carry your gun with safety and had some practice at a target that we'll set up, we might find a few rats for you around the haggard.'[1]

'Will your dad not object to me using his gun?'

'So long as he knows you are safe with it he should be all right. We can share the cost of the cartridges as we go along.'

And the floods came. Late in the winter following Willie's introduction to fishing on the banks of the Mullagh, the ramparts in places submitted to the river, covering several hundred acres of meadow land by three to four feet. The Moyola, its parent river, also spilled over the good rich farm land but caused little damage.

Frustrated, McLaughlin with a few of his pals viewed the devastation. 'If only we had a boat, what fun.' East of the flood area the land rises considerably and was not subject to flooding. This was grazing land supporting large herds of stock (beef cattle). On the high points of these large fields, feeding troughs were placed. These were sturdy things of wood construction and some fifteen feet long, three feet in width at the top and dished in the centre. Running the full length of the base at equal distance were holes of a quarter-inch diameter; these would allow rainwater to drain off thus leaving the feedstuff to remain dry. The free-standing troughs stood about two feet off the ground on two trestle legs integral to the whole unit.

The gang stood leaning on the cut-granite parapet of the bridge gazing down into the swollen river beneath them, longing for the impossible, a boat. McLaughlin, in a pensive mood, spoke after several minutes in silent thought. 'I think we might have ourselves a boat.' Turning his back to the bridge he pointed: 'That field over there where the ground rises. Come on.' And before any questions were asked, he was leading the little gang up the road and through the iron gate into the field and straight to where two troughs were. They stood contemplating them briefly.

'But it won't do,' Sammy Woods cut in. 'It's got holes in it, it'll sink.'

'It's too heavy,' said another.

---

1 Haggard: small field near a farmhouse where hay and farm equipment are stored.

'And those big heavy legs,' complained a third.

'Well, for a start,' said McLaughlin 'you're speaking in the singular: no, we are having these two here, look,' and he swept his hand across the fields. 'There are plenty more around and the cattle won't go without.'

'What about the legs and all those holes?' asked Jimmy McKenna.

Patrick paused for a moment and thought. 'Look, the McKay boys are coming into town tonight; we'll leave it until there is enough muscle to move the two of them and under cover of darkness we'll get them down to the water's edge and hide them in the bushes. Leave the legs and holes to me.'

With the requisite tools, wood and nails from his father's workshop, McLaughlin put in a full day's work, cleverly concealed under low-hanging branches at the edge of the flood water. The drainage holes were easily taken care of. Sturdy straps of wood with a nail at either end and driven into the "gunnels" at equal distance served as seats. Oars were quickly and easily improvised and before nightfall, vessels and crews were ready for sea.

The flood water was slow to recede that season and the moon waxed and waned, throwing ghostly shadows across the watery landscape where oaks stood tall above the water. Courting couples strolling along the narrow road some little distance away may have heard the battle cries and witnessed the eerie sights of great naval battles being enacted in miniature on those calm moonlit waters. And in the tradition of honourable naval gentlemen, when the waters receded, the vessels were returned to their rightful owner. At daybreak a bemused landowner and two of his farm hands stood over two missing troughs now mysteriously returned, lying flat on the ground, their drainage holes tightly caulked with wood dowelling and the neatly amputated legs lying close by.

They were youths with schooldays well behind them and no real occupation. Willie was obliged to do his bit on the farm and was always a willing helper, but it was not income, not real income. There was a limit to the number the small farm would support and Willie gave the matter careful consideration. He would keep his counsel until the moment was right.

CHAPTER 2

Maghera in those days, and for several generations thereafter, was essentially a market town. It was central to a wide community. Two main roads crossed at the town centre, the premier one running from Belfast to Derry in the north-west. Well sited for trading, it was also unfortunately a focal point for the marauding armies that ravaged that land over the centuries.

A long-established market was held each Tuesday. Main Street became alive, regardless of the weather. Stalls, hastily erected, lined almost the entire length of the street: stalls with fresh fruit and vegetables, stalls with coloured beads and a multitude of other decorative bric-a-brac, second-hand goods and others with new and more upmarket items – and fish, always two or three fish stalls, their owners doing a brisk trade selling their local, freshly caught, freshwater herring, or pollan as it was and still is known. Pollan, a native fish of Lough Neagh, is perhaps the only freshwater herring on the planet.

In addition to the weekly market, the fair was held on the last Tuesday of each month. This was really the farmers' day, the cattle market. Often chaos reigned while the cattle were being herded through the streets to their various enclosure points. Occasionally, a stall must have been upended as the poor noisy beasts were driven through the narrow streets leaving their telltale evidence in their wake. Horses and other farm stock would be traded at the monthly fair. There was lively barter among traders and much slapping of each other's hands when deals were made. Bars and other refreshment establishments all must surely have shown handsome profits. At the close of day, the noise, the clatter of horses and carts, the jostling of crowds would have melted away. Stalls would have vanished as magically as they had appeared in the early morning before many of the townsfolk had arisen. A scattering of drunks would have huddled together in little groups here and there wailing out an Irish ballad before each made his weary way homeward and the curtain of night came down.

Willie rose early and dressed in his best. He had slept little throughout the night. The cockerel in the yard heralded the morning, his crowing in full volume setting off a donkey on a neighbouring farm. Willie hastily prepared a frugal breakfast and a large mug of hot sweet tea and sat down to enjoy it. Having washed up he went back to the bedroom, put some money into his pocket, took a small notepad and pencil from a shelf above his bed and returned to the kitchen. Quickly he scribbled a short note, left it on the table and put the notepad and pencil in his breast pocket and went out closing the door quietly behind him. The note read: "I've got some business in town. Hope to see you all there later." He buttoned his jacket against the chill morning air and set off at a brisk pace to cover the three miles to Maghera. The eastern sky promised well for the day ahead.

Some market traders were beginning to erect their stalls, their merchandise still on their wagons or in large untidy bundles on the pavements when he arrived. Others were only coming in. The streets were still clean. Maghera was not yet awake. He had come in too early. If only he had stayed in bed another hour, but then the rest of the family would have been up; the cows had to be milked. He had to get away early and keep his plan to himself.

He was beginning to think that his actions may have been selfish. Were they not all coming into town today? And he had deprived them of a pair of hands. His absence would now leave the others late. Milking, feeding the livestock, a score of important things to do. And the people he had particularly come to see may not arrive for another two hours or more. Moreover, he was feeling hungry and the shops and cafés would not be open until the sun had well risen. If only he had had a good breakfast of bacon and eggs and his mother's home-made bread – but the smell of cooking would have stirred them. No, he had salved his conscience; he could not have planned otherwise. And would they not be pleased for him when they learned what he had done?

The street traders had little time for small talk at that hour. They had to work fast to get their stalls put together and their horses stabled. Time may have been on Willie's side but not theirs. There was still time to kill so he would go for a walk through the woods and along the riverbank and when he would return, one or other of the cafés would be open where he could have a good hearty breakfast and be set up for the day. And after all, this was an important day. This was the most important fair of the year, the May Fair, and his life was about to change.

In the café, Willie took a small table by the window overlooking the main street and ordered a large plateful of bacon and eggs with all the trimmings. Most of the tables were empty but that would soon change. From his vantage point he could see quite a large stretch of the street below. The usual traders were there, and more. Across the street two gentlemen with turban headdress, men from a far-off land, were already engaged with customers. Food stalls, candy stalls, an organ grinder with his monkey dressed in a little green jacket and red trousers holding up his master's cap for pennies. Jugglers and tumblers were arriving. Entertainers of all kinds, musicians and magicians, card sharpers and cheapjacks filled the street. People with English and Scottish accents, professionals who toured the provinces, all for one day coming together, attracted by the Maghera May Fair.

The May Fair was known locally by some as the Hiring Fair. It was the day when wealthy owners of the large lowland farms would come into town with the express purpose of engaging young people, boys and girls, for a half-year employment with the option of renewal by mutual consent. Boys would be engaged to work on the land and girls in a domestic capacity. The farmer, having assessed the suitability of the applicant, would state the terms, such as the type of farm, whether the land was arable or supported cattle and whether dairy or stock herds or a combination of both. This would allow the young man to come to a decision. Perhaps he was a good herdsman but had no experience with a plough. Much depended on the size and workings of that farm. If the applicant could not accept the terms he was free to move on to the next man and listen to what he had to offer. Usually there was not much to choose between them. The bottom line was free board and lodgings, little remuneration, long hours and hard work, with the farmer always holding the ace card: never anything in writing, just a firm handshake and the contract was settled. This was the world Willie was about to enter; a world for which he would leave home and avoid being a burden on the rest of the household, at a wage insufficient for a contribution to his hard-pressed parents.

Willie left the café and stood off a little way, his back against a wall, keenly weighing up in his mind the scene before him. He could see a line of work-hardened, middle-aged to elderly men, each standing before a small table and with a chair beside him. On some of the tables there would be a water jug and a glass; on others an extinguished pipe, a box of matches and a pouch of tobacco – no evidence of any paperwork or pen. It occurred to Willie as he listened to these men how embarrassed they could be if suddenly presented with a document and pen and asked to 'sign here'. Perhaps it was just as well for them to keep such material away. Each farmer had a little group of young men around him. Some girls were listening in and occasionally a hand would be raised and a question asked but not always answered. One burly fellow with a large red nose and receding ginger hair, interrupted in full flow by a tiny female hand, glanced past it to catch sight of young Willie's muscular frame and thought, *there's a likely lad, I could use him on my land.* The girl never got her question in. The man nodded to Willie and the nod was returned. Eye contact had been established. Willie moved away from the wall and as he approached red nose's little group he felt a tap on the shoulder. He swung round quickly and found himself looking into the grinning face of Patrick McLaughlin. 'What are you doing here, Willie?'

'I'm just thinking—'

'Of hiring yourself into slavery? For Christ's sake, Willie, come away from there!'

'But—'

'No buts, man, come here!' Taking him by the sleeve, Patrick pulled him away a few paces from the little group before confiding in him. It was just as well for red nose, and Patrick, that he had left his shotgun at home for if not, Patrick would have been dead and red nose on a murder charge.

Patrick led his pal away and across the street, weaving through horse-drawn vehicles towards a café. 'Come in here, Willie, I've got news for you and I'll tell you about it over a cup of tea and a bun.' At the table, Patrick glanced around to ensure he was not being overheard then relaxed. 'Listen, Willie, I've got a job and something else.' He paused, giving Willie time for it to sink in. 'I've got one for you as well, a real job.' He paused and sipped his tea.

'What is it? What are these jobs?' enquired Willie.

'You know that bakery at the other end of the town, the one that opened up six or seven months ago?'

'Aye,' answered Willie.

'Well, I've got a job there firing up the ovens, setting out bakery trays, lots of work. There is some night work, too, but we all take turns at it. I start on Monday next.'

'And where do I come in?' asked Willie.

'The manager is a Scotsman, a Mr McBaine. I've told him all about you and he would like to see you.' Willie was about to speak but Patrick raised his hand. 'Listen, the bakery is expanding and they are in need of more staff. They are shortly to start a delivery round, I mean rounds, four of them, as soon as they get the new bread vans in from Belfast. They're in the making now and the horses have been ordered from Scotland – Clydesdales I think they are called.' The picture was taking shape in Willie's mind.

'Clydesdales, they are beautiful horses, big and powerful,' said Willie. 'I could work from now till doomsday with horses like that.'

'It looks like you'll be doing just that. I told Mr McBaine that you are a good man with horses and that's why he would like to see you.'

'When I do go to see him, you'll come with me I hope.'

'Of course, Willie, I'll have to introduce you. What about tomorrow? The sooner the better.'

'All right, Pat, I'll call for you at your house about nine in the morning. This is great, Pat, I'm obliged to you.'

They finished their light refreshment. Patrick left the money for it on the table and moved towards the door, waving a thank you to the girl behind the counter. On the street, just as they were going their separate ways, Patrick called after him, 'Will you be at the céilí[1] tomorrow night? Plenty of girls, and there is a top band coming in from Magherafelt.'

'I'll be there.' There was a moment's pause. 'And, Pat, I won't ever forget this and I swear that one day I'll make it up to you.' On that they went their separate ways, Patrick for home and Willie to wander around town in the hope of finding the rest of the family amongst the carnival crowds. He spotted the trap[2] tightly packed between others, guessed it would be several hours before they would get away, and having no further interest in the carnival, he set off for home on foot.

Mr McBaine was a dapper little man somewhere in his mid-fifties – the epitome of neatness in a brown overall coat, his expensive brown leather shoes well polished. He was courteous to the tall youth he was showing around his bakery with the confidence of a man very much in charge. Willie was given a brief tour of the bakery and was shown how it worked, getting a smile and a wink from one or two of the girls as he passed through, a little distraction not missed by Mr McBaine. They moved out through the rear doors and into the yard. Here the manager turned and faced Willie.

'This will be your domain, Willie: here is the loading bay all new, all roofed over and large enough for four vehicles to be backed in here alongside each other. You will be responsible for collecting your bread, buns and cakes using the trays you will have left from the previous day with the orders you had taken. Is that clear?' It was certainly clear that Mr McBaine had been an army man for a good number of years.

'Yes, Sir,' Willie answered.

'It may all look a bit confusing now but it is quite simple, you'll see. Now over there,' Mr McBaine continued, pointing to a storeroom behind a large door, 'that is where all the groceries will be kept. There you will find your

---

1 Céilí: dance or house party.
2 Trap: light horse-drawn buggy.

daily orders such as tea, sugar, jams, that sort of thing. Later you will get a list of all we carry.'

Willie did not expect to become a grocer and was having doubts at this point. To drive around the country behind a Clydesdale doling out a loaf of bread here and there was fine, but to be a travelling grocer, well, that was a vocation he was not prepared to undertake. 'You see,' continued Mr McBaine, 'over and above your wages there is a small bonus on bread and cake sales, but on victual – that is what we call them – the bonus is good. The more you sell, the more you earn. And remember, all our rounds will be out-of-the-way districts where there are no shops. This is something new. We will be bringing the shop to the people. You are the first lad in, Willie, and, if you feel you can fit in you could have a job for life.' Any negative thoughts that may have arisen soon vanished – this sounded good. Willie *could* fit in.

He was shown the building where the vehicles would be housed and the stables a short walk away. 'I have been told by your friend you are a good hand with horses.'

'I love horses,' said Willie. 'They are wonderful animals.'

'You will have charge of a Clydesdale – the Scottish draught, the giant among horses, big gentle creatures. They have been working the land in Scotland for many years and have been drawing drays, and the same vehicles that you will be driving soon, around the streets of Glasgow and Belfast for a long time now. They were first developed to carry armour in the battlefield; marvellous creatures, you will get on with your Clydesdale.' He took his watch from his breast pocket and noted the time. 'Well, Willie, as soon as all is ready I'll get word to you through Patrick and we'll soon get you going.' He held out his hand; Willie, shaking it, thanked him, parted company and went off to the McLaughlin home in a state of euphoria.

CHAPTER 3

A year and four months had passed since the inauguration of the bread delivery by the bakery. Four delivery vehicles, each supplying two rural districts, eight rounds in all, were now established. It was a boon to many outlying homes. In those homes, delivery day became something to look forward to.

Willie's two rounds took him into the townlands of Ballinahone, the Moyola Valley area and Tirkane, in the high hill district lying below the Sperrins, his home ground. The rounds were serviced on alternate days; Ballinahone, in the valley and close to Maghera, proved to be the shortest and he could be finished by mid-afternoon leaving him more free time. But one day each week at the end of this round he would set aside an hour or so to oil the harness equipment and polish the brasswork including the ferrules on the shaft ends. Nellie, the big Clydesdale mare, always had Willie's attention.

Willie brought more than much-needed fresh bread and groceries to the people in those off-the-beaten-track farmhouses and cottages. He was part of the community, this affable young man. He made friends with all and did good trade. From the older people often there would be a word of advice: 'You should be away in America, a young fellow like you, making your fortune.' And the old lady who had spent some years in America and now lived alone in her little cottage surrounded by her roses, would kindly suggest to him that he should be in London or New York 'having that tenor voice trained' and how the world would be his.

Willie had a good voice and often sang as he drove through the countryside. No need to have it trained, whatever that meant. That did not mean that he was perfectly contented with his life. True, he was in very agreeable employment, earning money and he was saving. Unlike Patrick, who now had a steady girlfriend and would no doubt marry and remain in the community all his days, Willie sought wider horizons. Although a little restless, life was treating him well at the moment; he would bide his time.

Sitting on that little seat atop his van, driving along lonely roads, he had time to think, to plan. Mr McBaine had as good as promised him a job for life. Fine, but without land a man had no roots and being the youngest of three brothers he would not inherit his father's farm. This was by custom, if not by law, in Ireland in those days. Idyllic as things were, all this could not continue. At some time he would have to make a change.

In America, Willie had learned, land was there for the asking, especially out west. Perhaps he better not leave it too long; if he were to get over there and stake a claim, the sooner the better. After all, many were emigrating almost daily from Ireland, in fact from all over Europe, all heading for a new life in the New World. There was the land of golden opportunity. What fortune or fate would await him? And then there was Charles Thomson from Maghera whose father, John, after the death of his wife, emigrated to America with his six children. John died almost within sight of land, leaving six orphans to be put ashore and adopted by a blacksmith and his wife. Charles Thompson, still known in Maghera as Charlie, grew to become one of America's leading scholars and a personal friend and confidant of George Washington. He also had a major role in transcribing the Declaration of Independence of the United States. Would he ever become as famous as Charlie Thompson?

Many were the thoughts and daydreams that raced through his mind as he travelled the country alone. Or was he alone? Did it not occur to him that his best friend was sitting on the seat beside him? How could he part from little Screen? No, that would be unthinkable; he would put the whole idea on hold for a few years. After all, Screen was an old dog now. Yes, that was it, he would wait.

Fate was to take a cruel hand in Willie's dilemma and made the decision, for within a few weeks Screen got distemper and died shortly after. Over the next few weeks Willie's life was as empty as that part of the driver's seat on his right which Screen had made his own. He was moody, sometimes snappy, and his customers made allowances and always had a word of sympathy, and when the old lady from America invited the "poor boy" in to have a cup of tea with her, he burst into tears. Willie was in mourning for his lost pet, his closest friend. At the end of each round he would just hurry home and get into work about the farm and was left to get on with it. His parents, in their wisdom, knowing it was the healing process, gave him space.

Prince was an old dog now, retired and replaced by a young dog just trained, enthusiastic and eager to work the sheep, indifferent to old Prince, now slow and stiffening a little in the hind legs. And watching him, Willie reflected with sadness on the years they all roamed the hills together.

'How long ago since we've had a day's fishing, Willie?'

'I don't think we've been out this season. We just don't seem to get the time,' grumbled Willie.

'We'll make time, McKay. Look, it's Thursday night; we are both off on Saturday. Let's try the Altkeeran – it's no great walking distance and the trout should be jumping for the bait.' *Just the diversion,* Patrick thought, *to pull his pal out of the miseries.* Willie sat in thought for a moment, gazing at the big open grate with its turf fire burning brightly, giving off its particularly pleasant smell. He lifted the tongs, played with the burning turfs, placing them here and there on the fire, then looked up.

'Aye, that will be all right, Pat; Saturday morning early. The weather looks like it will hold.' He turned to his parents and brothers as if saying, 'Are you sure you won't need me?' But unanimously they agreed he should go.

'I'll make sure you're both well provided for and bring home a good catch, both of you,' said his mother.

They sat around the fireside until late into the night, sipping tea from large mugs, talking idle gossip and teasing Patrick about his new girlfriend; just light good-humoured banter punctuated occasionally by the crashing sound of the door latch as another neighbour would amble in and place himself by the fire and join in the chat.

This was the accepted way of life in those parts. Some homes were an open door, their congenial atmosphere and attraction a magnet to like-minded friendly neighbours. McKay's was such a house, often burning the midnight oil, and that in the literal sense was true, for two whale-oil-filled lamps mounted on wall brackets strategically placed on opposite walls and augmented by the cosy glow from the big turf fire were the only illumination that the room had or required.

Patrick reached the farmhouse as the rising sun's first ray targeted its four windows, momentarily setting them aglow. He walked round to the back door where he was greeted by Prince. The door was open and he walked straight in. Willie had his tackle lying in a neat bundle on the kitchen floor and was preparing breakfast for them both. The smell of the bacon and eggs frying with hot pancakes on the hob was inviting. One of Willie's brothers had gone with the young dog to bring in the cows for milking, otherwise the farm was not yet awake. The boys had little conversation at breakfast and what few words were spoken were kept in a low tone in respect of those still asleep. That extra hour in bed when it came around was a luxury.

Sitting at the table in front of the large window Pat McLaughlin had an unobstructed view of the whole valley below. Away down there and over to the left was his town and he reflected on the distance he had just walked with the weight of gear he had carried. If the catch would be a good one at the day's end that would add more weight on the reciprocal journey but at least it would be downhill all the way. To the right, veiled in a thin morning mist, lay the whole picturesque parish of Ballinascreen with Slieve Gallion beyond and, further to the right, Crockmore, mountains he had only ever seen in the distance, and he wondered how Willie, sitting here at the table, could wake up each day to this beautiful scenery with such disregard.

They walked the Tirkane Road, fortified with a good breakfast. When they came to the Tullykeeran bridge they dropped down the bank to the river's edge. A startled woodcock rose up in front of them and flew off in fright, making a high whirring sound. They both instinctively gave the spot a wide berth, taking care to avoid the nest with its four creamy-white, blotched with light brown and grey, eggs. Having assembled the rods and lines and baited up the hooks they moved upriver a little way in search of a pool where the water would be placid and, if anything, a little deeper.

The Altkeeran's source in the Tullykeeran Mountain firstly flows away to the north through steep rocky ground and turns east almost at right angles where the ground levels off and the water slows down in its course. From the bend to the bridge was always known to be the best fishing area, not so fast and plenty of pools among the rocks. This was the stretch of the river they chose and selecting a nice large pool they dropped the baited hooks, secured their rods by digging the ends into the mossy ground and then angled them on forked willow rods. Having done all that they sat down to relax and chat. A young heron wading among the shallows a little way upstream was a good indicator that fish were about.

'You know,' said Patrick, turning around to rest on his elbow, 'if we don't catch one single fish today, just sitting here enjoying the scenery is worth it all. This is paradise, Willie.' Before Willie could answer, they were interrupted by a splash, like a huge plopping sound, followed by what sounded like a dog shaking off water. Both of them simultaneously leapt to their feet to see an otter settling down on the opposite bank to enjoy his catch.

'That's unusual,' remarked Willie, 'otters don't normally eat during daylight hours.'

'Then he is stealing from us,' joked Patrick. They watched the little animal, fascinated by his antics, flicking the trout around. Then it stopped and looked at them and when he had finished eating he turned, lay on his back and cleaned his face with his forepaws, looked again at his audience and with one leap and a splash was gone. 'That is the first otter I've ever seen,' said Patrick. 'Charming little fellows.'

'They kill a charming amount of fish, too,' Willie replied. 'When one otter gets into a school or shoal, call it what you like, it can all but clean it out in a night. If only they would take a fish and eat it but they don't; they just snap off that juicy bit behind the head and go on for the next one. That's the charming wee otter.'

After such commotion it would have been a brave or foolish trout to venture out of hiding for any bait, however enticing, so they picked up rods and stakes and moved on upriver. Willie stopped suddenly, dropping his free hand on his pal's shoulder, and pointed ahead of them to the middle of the river.

'What is it, Willie?' Willie motioned for quiet.

'Can you not see it?' He gave Patrick time to focus his eyes. 'There, just among the rocks, mid-river.' And standing statue-like on one leg, head down and peering into the water, was the heron, his colouring blending with the rocks. 'Wait,' whispered Willie. 'Wait and watch.' Patrick marvelled at the keen eyesight of his pal. Suddenly and mechanically the bird's head dipped into the water and returned with a large, wriggling, silver-bellied trout in its beak. It rose clumsily and slowly into the air, leaving a thin trail of spray in its wake, with its live cargo firmly held. As it gained altitude, slowly at first, its long legs and neck streamlining for optimum aerodynamic effect, Willie made an observation that could nearly have been a prediction. 'You know, that trout could be well over a pound and a half in weight and for its size, that is a light bird; now why can't man build a contraption to lift him into the air like that?'

They watched the heron change direction and fly off to the west in slow regal silence. Today, if those two boys were standing on that same riverbank looking up into a cloudless sky, they would see the vapour trails of larger, man-made birds, moving in the same direction, for Maghera and the Carntogher Hills lie directly under the flight path of the airliners out from London's Heathrow and Gatwick bound for New York's JFK and other major United States and Canadian cities.

McLaughlin suggested they move upriver to its source and work it down, a suggestion readily taken up by McKay. They each picked up their belongings and trod the heather around the river's bend and upwards, steadily upwards. The going was heavy in the mid-morning sun.

Startled larks took off vertically and fluttered above them, filling the mountain with their melodies. Whether their sounds were warning cries to others of their species or whether it was just their nature to break into song was of no importance – they were pleasant to the ear. Further ahead of them, a kestrel in search of food held position against the breeze, its tail angled in a downward curve and wings pulling a considerable degree of negative reflex, hovering, sharp eyes scanning each inch of ground below. It moved away a little in sideways flight, hovered again and having selected its prey, dropped and was lost among the heather. To some little creature death came swiftly on a glorious spring morning.

'Is this your first time on the Tullykeeran?' Willie asked.

'First time,' Patrick assured him.

'Look,' said Willie, 'it doesn't matter a damn if we go home empty handed. Let's make the most of the day. We'll leave our rods, bags, bait and everything just here by the river's edge, all except the refreshments, and we'll climb to the top and have a good look around and by that time we should be ready for whatever mother has prepared for us.'

'Now where did an Irish country bumpkin learn to speak like that? Did you hear yourself? "Whatever mother has prepared for us,"' taunted McLaughlin. 'Frightfully English I'd say.'

'I can lay it on when I like,' snapped Willie. 'Now shut up and let's go. I'll race you to the top.'

It was not the tallest of the Sperrin Hills. There were peaks aplenty everywhere around but the Tullykeeran did not peak; it was flat, a plateau, but on that clear morning the view it offered was wonderful. Fields and meadows away below them stretched to the horizon, all of a deep rich green, all marked out and bounded by neat hedgerows contrasting with the stone walls of the hill country. Mile after mile of stone walls: how the ground could give up so many stones and the labour involved was mind bending. And McLaughlin was well aware that his pal standing beside him often had a hand at building and repairing these hill walls.

'Let's eat and enjoy the scenery, Pat.' And without further ado, they knelt down and began setting out the packages: home-baked kibble wheaten bread heavily laden with butter from the churn, hard-boiled eggs, cheese, chunks of ham and two bottles of fresh buttermilk, the by-product of that batch of butter.

'Willie, we'll have to turn up with a good catch for all this.'

'We better,' said Willie.

'I think we'll change the bait on the way down. I think we should use the grub and less sinker.'

'If you say so, Pat.'

Patrick, scanning the horizon to the south-east, pointed and asked, 'Willie, that water away out there, is that Lough Neagh?'

'That is just the north-west tip of the lough, that wee neck of water that empties into the Lower Bann. That's all you see of the largest lake in the whole British Isles. If we were on top of Crockmore or Slieve Gallion we would see a lot more.' Willie paused to eat then continued, 'When the Vikings invaded this part of the world they made Lough Neagh their inland harbour. Hundreds of their longships sailed round the Atlantic coast to the mouth of the Bann at Coleraine and they rowed their ships all the way up the Bann.'

'Willie, Willie,' interrupted McLaughlin, 'we both listened to the same lesson in school, remember?'

'Aye, we did, sorry.'

'That must have been some sight,' remarked Patrick. 'Hundreds of their ships tied up along the shores of the lough.'

'They must have been a fearsome sight,' said Willie, 'with their axes and shields and horns on their heads; anyone who dresses up in that kind of way must be daft.'

'They must have caused awful damage with their plundering and rape.'

Willie continued, smiling, 'Could be we are all the result of a Viking night ashore.'

'You've got a bad mind, McKay.'

'Who knows, McLaughlin? Many a true word was spoken in jest. Who knows?'

They finished eating, bundled up their bottles and containers and pushed everything into the canvas bag and started downhill to where they had left their fishing tackle. It was now early afternoon and no fishing had yet started. They baited the hooks with grub and reduced the amount of sinker. In the drop of the "young" river, worm, grub or whatever would not come to rest on the bed. They spaced themselves out and slowly walking downwards they "played" the river and did not have long to await a result. Soon their lines became taut, the rod ends bowing to the weight. The bait was taken and lively big rainbow trout wriggling on the lines were landed and bagged.

'Looks like we could be in for a few hours' fun!' called a smiling McKay.

'Don't holler like that, McKay, or you'll frighten them off.'

They continued playing the river slowly downstream. As quickly as they could bait up and drop the lines back in the water they were getting bites, the little ones thrown back for another day. Their run of luck would not last and they knew it, so they made the most of it while it was there. 'I could live here for ever,' said Patrick as they took a break to review their catch.

'So could I,' said Willie, 'but I'm not going to,' and noting the questioning expression on his pal's face he motioned to sit down and revealed his plan. Patrick was neutral in expressing his comments, wished him luck, glanced at the position of the sun and suggested they make a move for it was a long way to the Tirkane Road.

'Willie, it's a nice still evening and as yet early. When we get to the bend where the river widens out I might have a try with the fly.'

This was a skill Willie had not yet achieved. 'Have a try if there is enough light left when we get there. I'll just watch.'

A honk, honk sound above them caught their attention. A skein of wild geese, in line astern, were homeward bound. At the river's bend it was decided to head for home. As they walked as fast as the uneven ground and the catch and the equipment would allow, the mantle of the night was closing in, giving prominence to the sounds of nature: curlews with their sad plaintive cries and all around them the sound of crickets among the heather and further, out of sight, two snipe spiralling and diving in an aerial display of courtship, the drumming of their wings and tails emitting harsh sounds somewhat like the bleating of sheep.

On their trek home that evening they could not have guessed how soon their way of life would change. And on they tramped through the dew-laden heather, blissfully unaware that through all their green years the whole Sperrin range, with her dark granite crags and her wild mountain streams, was their training ground and that a strange hand of fate was wielding the hammer and the bulbous Cairn Snout where they oft-times sat with their dogs and their guns was the anvil upon which the soft malleable metals of the young McLaughlin and McKay were being beaten into shape.

CHAPTER 4

The reception area of the St Charles Hotel in New Orleans was abuzz with activity that Sunday afternoon of 21 March 1841. Porters were working fast, under the direction of the head porter, to clear the mountain of luggage from the foyer to the respective rooms. Some of the regular guests, taking tea or just sitting reading in the adjacent restaurant, displayed a slight irritation at the sudden disturbance of their peace.

Ten new guests milled around, idly waiting for the leader of the party to walk through the door. He and one other were with the carriage drivers attending to the expenses. Twelve men in all, they had just disembarked from a Norwegian vessel out from the port of Bergen. Adverse winds had delayed their arrival by more than three weeks, a delay which would alter their schedule somewhat.

Andur Oskarsen and Einar Andersen, having discharged their responsibilities with the drivers, walked into the foyer, discussed the question of the luggage with the head porter and joined the others at the reception desk. They were not the usual "run-of-the-mill" cotton traders or theatrical people who frequently stayed at the St Charles and St Louis Hotels, nor were they of the immigrant population landing at the port in huge numbers in those days to join the westbound wagon trains at Westport. They were well heeled and well in command with an air of professionalism. The guest list was impressive and there were those in Washington who were not unaware of their arrival.

Andur Oskarsen, leader of the group, was a certificated Master Mariner. Andur's claim to fame was that an ancestor, on his mother's side of the family, had sailed with the Danish explorer Captain Vitus Bering on the *St Peter* when she and her sister ship, the *St Paul,* were commissioned in

1740 by Tzar Peter the Great to chart the Alaskan waters. Oskarsen's eleven companions were:

Einar Andersen – Ship's Officer, Master Mariner
Ola Hansen – Novelist and Freelance Journalist
Kristoffer Eriksen – Medical Doctor (Edinburgh)
Anders Lein – Civil Engineer
Arild Holtop – Geologist
Morten Olsen – Mining Engineer, Roros Copper Mines, Norway, and Kongsburg Silver Mines, Norway
Stig Brevig – Civil Engineer
Truls Gundersen – Metallurgist
Brunduif Lillegard – Explorer and Writer
Oskar Haug – Cartographer
Harald Seter – Mining Engineer, Roros Copper Mines, Norway, and Kongsburg Silver Mines, Norway.

They would be staying at the St Charles until Wednesday morning when they would board one of the scheduled passenger-cargo steamboats for St Louis. In that year, over 2,000 steamboats operated on the Mississippi, many of them being two-way packet-line operations carrying passengers and cargo on regular schedules.

Having signed the guest list, ten of the party went off to their rooms leaving Andur and Einar with the receptionist to take care of a few details. After the discomfort of ship life, hot baths were uppermost on their minds. 'The captain of the *Fjorden* and his officers will be joining us for dinner this evening,' said Andur. 'That will be nineteen in all. Will that pose a problem with the seating?'

'I'm sure not, Sir, but I'll ask the head waiter to have a word with you if you will be kind enough to bear with me for a moment.' At a signal from him, a bellhop disappeared and in what was less than a minute, perhaps, the manager had joined them.

'Please excuse my absence on your arrival, gentlemen, I was unable—'

'That is quite all right,' cut in Einar, 'your staff were most courteous and helpful; we were well taken care of.'

'Indeed we were,' Andur confirmed.

After the handshakes and polite formalities, Andur repeated his request to the manager regarding their intention to have extra guests for dinner and was assured that all stops would be pulled out and there would be no trouble seating the party. 'It is "Dinner Adieu", a rather important little occasion, and it was my suggestion that we should hold it ashore, away from the confines of the ship,' said Andur, 'and if you would be kind enough to ask the wine waiter—'

The manager raised his hand in reassurance, 'I shall attend to that myself, gentlemen, be assured.'

'Thank you, Mr . . .'

'Johnston, forgive me, my name is Johnston.'

'Thank you, Mr Johnston, that is reassuring. I wish our St Louis' problems could be solved so easily.'

Mr Johnston raised an eyebrow: 'Problems?'

'Yes, as you—'

The manager stopped him there, pointing to the lounge seats in the corner by a window. 'Gentlemen, please be seated.' When the two men were comfortably seated and Mr Johnston sitting facing them across a coffee table he began. 'What problems have you got with St Louis, may I ask?'

Andur did all the talking. 'As you know, the *Fjorden* is the best part of a month late docking.'

The manager nodded in agreement then politely interrupted. 'Excuse me,' and turning to a passing waiter called, 'trois thés vite, s'il vous plaît.'

'It is unusual to hear an Englishman speaking French,' remarked Andur, 'and with an accent.'

'I am a Londoner,' said Mr Johnston. 'My mother was Parisienne. I was educated in London and Paris. It was in Paris I did my hotel training. As you were saying, about St Louis – you are having difficulties?'

Andur began: 'Since its conception more than three years ago, preparations for our little expedition have been in progress here in America and in Norway. It is part of our plan to cross Missouri by ox-drawn wagon train.' The tea tray arrived and the waiter quietly went about his business serving it. Andur continued, 'It has long since been arranged with a firm of wagon builders in St Louis to build ten wagons. Three of them will only be for spares and equipment, six for travelling and sleeping accommodation for twelve men, and one is to be, as they say in America, the "chuck" wagon, quite an order.'

Mr Johnston nodded with a little smile. Andur continued, 'There is a body dealing with all this and all the ancillary equipment, rather like a ship's chandler. They are also responsible for providing guides. Eighteen months ago I travelled as a passenger on one of our ships to spend time in St Louis arranging all these things. The office in Oslo – not our shipping office, this is an entirely separate entity – has been in regular communication with St Louis and, upon Mr Andersen's advice and my own, before leaving Bergen we should have arrived in St Louis over four weeks ago, allowing for overnight stops, breakdowns of the riverboat, and so on. Now, with what could be another two weeks, they may well have decided that the entire project has fallen through and with such a demand for wagons, we could arrive there to find them sold on together with the oxen and equipment.' The waiter brought a pot of hot water, replenished the teapot and moved quietly away.

'Your frustration, gentlemen, is that you have no way of informing your people in St Louis of your whereabouts and that you are on your way, is that correct?' They both nodded in agreement. 'Now,' continued Mr Johnston, 'since you last travelled the river, Mr . . .'

'Oskarsen.'

'Mr Oskarsen, forgive me. Since you last travelled the river, several of the two-way packet lines have been running an express mail service between here and St Louis. They ply between the two cities non-stop, except for refuelling, and the competition is quite fierce. They have got the time down to something like three days. It has been done in just sixty hours. I know one leaves every evening at seven o'clock, which means, if you were to send your message from the reception desk here to catch the seven o'clock boat I shall ensure it is delivered to the line post-haste and it should arrive in St Louis about the time you are boarding on Wednesday morning.'

'That is excellent,' exclaimed Andur.

Einar Andersen added, 'No doubt our contact in St Louis would allow a reasonable margin of time but this will allay our fears. Now we can all enjoy a few days in New Orleans and a leisurely trip on the Mississippi.'

Andur agreed and, feeling relaxed, noted, 'And perhaps we may all have time to fit in a show at one or other of New Orleans' theatres.'

Mr Johnston was a curious man. A puzzle was a thing to be unravelled and here was a puzzle: twelve men embarking on an expensive adventure from half way across the world to travel a wagon trail across Missouri; twelve men all qualified in their own professions, he knew, for his sharp eye had scanned the guest list before he sat down with Andur and Einar. And, he gathered, authorisation for this expedition stemmed from on high in Norway; and why Norway? The two seafaring gentlemen sitting with him seemed to be in charge and after all, they had been taking their ships into New Orleans for some years but that was bringing passengers in and taking cotton out. Could these two be the prime movers in this, and if so, what information could they have got from the hinterland as to warrant such a move across the prairie?

Andur, sitting opposite him, allowed himself the faintest smile as he sipped his tea for he anticipated the question about to come from Mr Johnston. 'So you are about to follow the wagon trails westwards, gentlemen?'

Einar drew out his pocket watch and flicked it open, a gesture that could have indicated time was getting on. He said, 'Yes, it is just a little adventure we all dreamed up some years ago and at last it seems to have come to fruition.'

Mr Johnston got to his feet, saying, 'Well, if you gentlemen will excuse me, I have an important dinner to arrange,' then paused for a moment and made a suggestion, unprecedented in all his years as the manager of St Charles. 'Perhaps, gentlemen, you would like to join the head chef and myself in his office and we can all have a hand in selecting your courses.' They readily agreed and after dispatching an urgent message at the reception desk they all alighted on the head chef in his tiny office.

The group had two full days and nights to enjoy the city, just to wander about at their leisure and enjoy the Creole food in one or two of the restaurants and visit the French Quarter with its rows of bars and restaurants which offered foods of many cultures. If time permitted they might even see an opera. For the two seafarers all this was familiar ground and they could take pleasure in giving their companions a guided tour.

Those were the days of the cotton boom and New Orleans was the centre of that industry; everywhere King Cotton prevailed and ships from many nations, trading not just in cotton but in so many other commodities, put into New Orleans. Large three-masted vessels, their sails furled, were being manoeuvred alongside the docks and others were being towed out into the estuary where they would unfurl and set course for the open sea, all this managed by efficient steam-driven tugs, their horns sounding night and day, every day of every week. And everywhere throughout the city, the fancy-dress carnivals and the negro musicians – all true citizens, which pleasantly surprised the liberal-minded Nordic visitors. The multicultural society of New Orleans pulsated with life and the only regret the Norsemen had was that time was limited for they could have tarried longer in that carefree place.

The carriages were on time, all waiting in line in front of the main entrance and the numerous pieces of luggage being manhandled by cheerful porters. Bills were settled and later, when the guests were gone and the gratuities shared among those of the staff assigned to the party, none would be displeased. If the twelve were leaving New Orleans a little heavy hearted it would be tempered by the anticipation of a long and leisurely journey, punctuated by many interesting stops, in the comfort of a steamboat along the majestic Mississippi river. Mr Johnston, dressed in suitable morning attire befitting his station, was present for their departure. He was still none the wiser as to the purpose of their mission and if he had any misgivings as to its outcome he kept them well hidden. He thanked them for their patronage and bade them farewell and Godspeed.

The St Louis-built *Iolanthe* was one of the latest vessels plying the river. A 160-foot side-wheeler, port and starboard, drawing a draught fully laden of no more than six feet; well balanced and well suited to working the river. All the steamboats on the Mississippi were fuelled by wood, mostly cottonwood. The smaller stern-wheelers would use between 25 and 30 cords per 24 hours or approximately one cord[1] per hour. A boat of the *Iolanthe*'s size would require up to 40 cords per 24 hours. Fortunately, wood – especially cottonwood – was in abundance. There were established refuelling stations along the river with timber fetching about three dollars per cord.

On the Missouri river, however, this service was not so well organised and steamboat crews often had to rely on "woodhawks" for their supplies. These enterprising fellows, a mixed lot of Indian, part-Indian and white traders, living cheek-by-jowl with the Indian communities, cut and sold the wood along the riverbanks for up to eight dollars a cord with these prices rising even higher further along the river. Woodhawking, as it was known, had its hazards for they were constantly exposed to the not-infrequent war parties – one reason perhaps for the high premium on their merchandise.

The year 1812 saw the arrival of the first steamboat in New Orleans and within nine years 287 steamboats were putting in at that city. By 1825–26, New Orleans saw some 700 vessels but a large number of these were employed as tugs with the demand for more as more shipping arrived. When vessels of the *Iolanthe* class came into service, around 1839–40, well over 2,000 steamboats were working the river.

Throughout the cruise, Andur Oskarsen was a constant source of information to the rest of the party – like a headmaster with his pupils – and he was enjoying it. He was, in fact, a natural teacher. From their leaving the dock he was pointing out to the newcomers standing around him on the afterdeck all the places and things of interest, such as the speed of the vessel. She had just left port with a clear run and would be steaming, at a guess, at about six knots.

Andur's guess of a vessel's speed would leave little margin for error. At six knots, without stops, St Louis would – and how he wished it – be soon reached. But the speed of a steamboat on the Mississippi was determined by many factors and if a calculation was to be taken on arrival, the overall speed may be as little as three to three and a half knots. Like Einar Andersen, he

---

1 Cord: a measure of cut wood of 128 cubic feet or 3.62 cubic metres.

knew the geography of the Mississippi basin, its flood areas and the dark alluvial soils deposited over thousands of years around the delta by the Mississippi and the Yazoo rivers and their tributaries.

The Mississippi countryside from March until early November is nature's garden. Everywhere is aglow with aster, azalea, honeysuckle, pink primrose and much more, and everywhere the magnolia, the state tree, many of which come into flower twice in the season. Huckleberry, hazel, redwood and dogwood all added to the magnificent view along the riverbank. Those who sailed the Mississippi in the heyday of the steamboats, and the indigenous people before them in their canoes, would have seen fauna such as bison, bear and beaver, wolf, wildcat and cougar; everywhere wild turkey and many species of waterfowl.

Despite the bends in the river and the volume of river traffic, the *Iolanthe* made good steaming to their first stop at Baton Rouge. It would be a short stop. The mariners would be on deck watching the docking and pulling away from the quay, for their interest in steamboats was growing. The docking was straightforward but once the gangway was pulled in, the *Iolanthe* wasted no time in getting under way. Both wheels slowly turned a few revolutions astern, easing the bow away from the jetty, then a few more revs on the port to bring the bow around and then forward on both wheels and she was under way. The two sailors looked at each other, amazed at the ease and speed of the manoeuvre.

'I would say,' said Einar, 'sail has had its day.'

Andur nodded in agreement. 'Yes, I would say it has.'

The noise from the engines was disconcerting to those not accustomed to the sound and the vibration, especially when the steel door would be flung open by an engineer coming up from the engine room or on his way down. Midship, and just aft of the saloon, was the recreational room, its only furniture being tables and chairs made fast by a chain from the bottom of each item which clipped to a steel ring anchored to the deck. The chain was in two sections with a turn-buckle for applying or releasing tension. A few pictures of sailing ships on the high seas and one of vessels of all types in New Orleans harbour hung from the bulkheads. Only one form of recreation was obvious: this was the poker players "pit" with all but the case-hardened, cigar-smoking, players being repelled by the noxious fumes. For'ed of the accommodation and above was the wheelhouse, reached by an outside ladder, with the chartroom behind it, and on the bulkhead above the chart table was the ship's clock, its brass casing highly polished. This private domain of the skipper and his wheelhouse watch would undoubtedly be visited a few times in the course of the trip by two deep-sea captains.

*Numerous merchants supplied the steamboats and the wagon trails as the pioneers
ventured west to explore the new territories and search for gold.*

The next docking, not as perfunctory as the previous one, was Natchez, where several passengers disembarked and some joined. Natchez, perhaps the most thriving of the cotton ports on the river when cotton was king, is now one of the major centres of the paper-manufacturing industry.

Stores had to be taken on board – much of it being "chained" hand to hand by slave labour, the work lightened by the harmony of their chant – galley supplies, deck and engine-room supplies, stores that would see her into St Louis. Huge bales of cottonwood were swung over the afterdeck, where a hatch was opened and the bundles lowered down, tons of it to feed two avaricious boilers. Water was taken on for the boilers from a crude pumping station and, separate from it, the domestic supply was pumped aboard. Docked fore and aft of the *Iolanthe* were barges being loaded with bales of cotton, manhandled also by slave labour, all bound downriver to New Orleans and the waiting ships. Andur reflected on the times he conducted the loading of his ship, an unwilling party to a nefarious system.

Some minor repairs had to be done to the vessel, which would allow passengers ashore for as much as five hours. Those ditherers still ashore by the sailing time would be summoned by three sharp blasts on the whistle at intervals of one minute. With so many whistles and foghorns constantly blasting on that river port, one required a special hearing to pick out the salient sound.

Vicksburg, Tallulah, Helena and Cairo, with even smaller stops, still lay ahead but these were just passenger stops. Cairo would be the last major port of call but no more stores were to be taken on except for fuel and water and at an average of five knots steaming she was doing well for time.

In the mid-morning of 7 April, when *Iolanthe* put alongside the quay at Cairo, fore and aft heaving lines were thrown and each caught by a waiting longshoreman, who dragged the attached hawser ashore and made it fast to the bollards. That done, two other hands jumped ashore and were thrown a rope by which they dragged out the gangway. Passengers, most with luggage, disembarked to join waiting relatives. Newsboys charged on board with their bundles, the latest off the St Louis presses; cabbies, their horse-drawn buggies on the quay, got in the way of long ox-drawn wagons loaded with cotton bales. Messenger boys were there, too, with all kinds of information for the captain and his crew. One messenger boy in particular with a sealed official-looking envelope called out: 'Captain Oskarsen, message for Captain Oskarsen!' adding to the chaos.

Andur intercepted the boy as he dashed around the deck reciting his message and took the envelope to the privacy of his cabin to open it. The letter read:

Dear Captain Oskarsen,

We are in receipt of your message of Sunday 21st of March 1841 received by special courier and for which we thank you.

Upon your arrival in St Louis you will be met on the quay by our agent, Mr Beamish, who will bring you up to date with what has and is being arranged regarding your wagons, supplies and other ancillary equipment. We vouch that the building of your wagons has been completed some weeks ago and await your inspection. Regarding the oxen, these you must purchase at auction. Tuesday and Friday of each week are established auction days. We have arranged through our associates that you be provided with a guide who Mr Beamish will introduce to you. He is a young man of twenty-six years. We advise you do not find any problem with his youth. What he may lack in years he certainly makes up for in experience. Furthermore, he will not do your bidding nor will he fetch and carry for you. His remit is clear; he is charged with your safety and to expedite your passage as uneventfully as possible across a hostile land. Not only is he your guide, he is your captain engaged by you.

Also, he will travel fully provided for the journey and will at no time be dependent upon your food and other supplies. We have every confidence in him and we have no doubt you will find him a cheerful and competent young man. His name is William John McKay.

I am, Sir,
Yours faithfully,

Matthew F. Clement 24.3.1841
for R.J. Morgan – Chandlers & Forwarding Agents
Old Market, Front Street Wharf, St Louis, MO.

CHAPTER 5

St Louis was no different from any other city in the rain. Tied up at the levee on Friday, 9 April 1841, the *Iolanthe*, her decks rain swept and deserted, rose and fell gently on the river's swell. There would be no movement from crew or passengers before an amelioration of the downpour that was holding the city's movement at a standstill. At half past four on this Friday afternoon, the whole length of Front Street Wharf, which would normally have been a hive of industry, was deserted save for a few hackney cabs that had been dropping off their passengers before being caught suddenly in the downpour that now lashed the city.

Since leaving Natchez, unceasing rain had confined the passengers to their cabins and dining room. Now they waited impatiently, their luggage all packed and neatly stacked, ready to be put ashore. Most had assembled in the dining room for a last cup of tea or coffee from the steward. The two captains together with Truls Gundersen and Dr Kristoffer Eriksen, the youngest member of the party, were in conversation, cups and saucers in hand, by the windows that faced west. They were remarking upon the inclement weather now holding them on board and generally on their bad luck with the weather since leaving Bergen. Looking through the rain-spattered window, Einar Andersen remarked, 'Looks like this front is moving through,' pointing with cup in hand to the long thin break in the cloud away to the horizon.

The front moved through with another close behind but the short respite was welcomed. The gangway was lowered and made fast with much noise. The skipper and his crew became alive again. Cabs and porters appeared on the quay. Mr Beamish, taking one stride to the average-sized man's two, cleared the gangway and bounded into the saloon introducing himself and apologising for the unusual bad weather.

'Gentlemen,' he exclaimed, addressing the assembly, 'I am not going to detain you now with long-winded explanations; all I wish for at the moment is to get all of you and your luggage off the vessel and to the recently opened Planters Hotel. We have arranged everything for your stay there and I have no doubt you will be made very comfortable. Nothing will be happening over the next two days, Saturday and Sunday, which will give you time to settle in, relax and, weather permitting, see something of St Louis.' As he was speaking, porters and cab drivers were hastily moving the luggage to the cabs and the group, escorted by Mr Beamish, got off without any further delay to the comfort of their hotel.

Monday mid-morning, the skies were blue, and the winds were fair. Everywhere, like the daisy in the meadow opening to embrace the morning sun, the young St Louis on the Mississippi was fresh and alive. To the west, on common land where the city had not yet encroached, Mr Beamish and the twelve fledgling pioneers assembled in a large enclosed area. Within the enclosure stood three enormous sheds of wood construction. Above the open door of the largest of the buildings which stood in front of the other two were black sign-written words on a white plaque: JAMES HARVEY & SONS, WAINWRIGHTS. Underneath was an artist's drawing of a covered wagon beneath which were the words: MANUFACTURERS OF CUSTOM BUILT WAGONS and the address, CHOUTEAUS POND, ST. LOUIS, MO. Stacked around the corral fencing were huge quantities of machined timber, wheel hubs, spokes and sections of wheel rims and wrought iron shaped in all forms for wagon assembly.

Between the two rear buildings was a man-made pond, round with a diameter of some fourteen to sixteen feet and about two feet deep, the water being supplied from the nearby Chouteaus Pond. The artificial pond was filled with finished wheels, the purpose being that the soaking over days or even weeks would expand the wood against the metal rims thus providing a tight and often lasting fit. On the trail, in wet or muddy conditions, the wheel rims usually remained secure, but in long dry spells rims would often become sloppy due to the wood contracting, and, where possible, the wheel would require changing and the unserviceable wheel be carried spare until water was available. Within the buildings and the compound about fifty skilled men were busily employed.

'Let's all go inside,' Mr Beamish suggested, 'and have ourselves a conducted tour.' They moved towards the door of the main building but Mr Harvey, who was expecting the party and was watching them arrive from his office window, greeted them at the threshold. Pleasantries exchanged, they were invited to the office for coffee before proceeding on a factory tour. At this point Mr Beamish suggested he would take his leave and would return for his party in two hours' time.

Coffee over and preliminary matters discussed, James Harvey took his customers through the full length of the main shed, through the rear open door which was almost as wide as the front one and into No. 3 shed. At the furthest end was a group of wagons tightly stored and ready for delivery.

'Here, gentlemen, are your wagons,' declared Mr Harvey turning to the group. 'As you came through the factory you will have seen vehicles in various stages of construction and you may observe that most are larger than these here, as are those over there,' pointing to others parked in neat rows for optimum use of space. 'Now, firstly, let me take you to one of the larger vehicles. This wagon is known as the Conestoga. It was designed in Pennsylvania by a German group who needed large, bulky wagons for their freight. If you care to take a look inside you will see that the floor slopes to the middle and is slightly raised front and rear. The purpose of this is that barrels would tend to settle towards the middle and the slight elevation front and rear prevents the cargo sliding out when the wagon is climbing or descending a hill. These wagons are built essentially for freight. We get quite a demand for the Conestoga. Over here, this wagon is built for the overlander. Similar in design but with a flat floor, it is slightly smaller and lighter. With the first, as many as twenty-four oxen or mules would be used and a second wagon hitched behind the first. This is known as backaction – all heavy stuff and fortunately for you, gentlemen, they will not be necessary. Now let us go back to your little consignment.'

Ola Hansen, novelist and journalist, and Oskar Haug, cartographer, got busy on their sketch pads, others taking down notes. No one as yet had any questions to ask. James Harvey continued. 'Here we have a sturdy little vehicle just half the size of the Conestoga. Light, strong and with all the comfort of the larger model. She will get you to your destination in less time than that one,' pointing to the last one they had been viewing. 'Teams of only four to six oxen would be necessary to draw one of these or six to ten mules. Yours, of course, will be oxen and considering your numbers and supplies, four beasts to each wagon will be sufficient.' He paused briefly, then continued, 'This little wagon is known as the Prairie Schooner. Designed and first manufactured by two young brothers by the name of Studebaker, it is now being built and marketed by several companies under licence, including ourselves.

'Prairie Schooners are the most numerous wagons going westward today.

The old Conestogas were considered too heavy and many oxen and mules died under their weight.' He paused for reflection. 'Not a pleasant situation to be in.' Then, pointing to the nearest Schooner, he continued. 'This little lady became the answer to quite a few problems. Now, before I go further, let me firstly point out that your order was for ten of these wagons. Captain Oskarsen and I thrashed this out some time ago.' The captain nodded his agreement. 'Here you will find eleven. Let me explain. You need only accept the original ten. The extra one we can sell on very quickly. We just cannot build these things fast enough. If only we had twice the size of premises and twice the manpower.' He shook his head in exasperation. 'But, let us consider the advantages of a spare wagon. Firstly, should you lose a wagon due to damage beyond repair then you just abandon it and carry on but more importantly – and this was brought to our attention by the young man who is to be your guide – should any of your party fall ill on the trail with some fever or other, and this does happen, then this becomes your isolation ward while still moving.' He paused to allow his point to sink in. Dr Eriksen readily nodded his agreement. Captain Oskarsen put it to a quick vote, reminding them that the cost of the extra oxen would also be added.

'Well, we all appear to be in agreement,' said the captain, 'but in our absence, will you raise this with our office in Norway?'

'Yes, of course, we can take care of that,' James Harvey assured them. He then continued, 'Do remember that on your return to St Louis, having conducted your survey, you can trade in your experienced vehicles to us or to any one of a dozen other merchants in the city.' The phrase 'having conducted your survey' was the first reference to the party's intended expedition into the wilderness made by an outsider since their arrival in America. How much information was James Harvey privy to or was it just an educated guess?

Harvey checked the time from his watch and continued. 'Let me take you through the Schooner quickly before Mr Beamish comes for you. The weight of this wagon is 1,300 pounds empty. Most of the parts can be dismantled easily and repaired en route. Again I emphasise that considering only two men to each wagon and with your amount of equipment, you will get away with four oxen per vehicle, and remember each one of you will walk a considerable part of the way.' Then he added with a chuckle, 'Nothing like walking for a healthy life.'

Returning his attention to the wagon, Harvey pointed to the canvas cover: 'This we call the bonnet and it is held firmly in position by these hardwood bows,' pointing to the U-shaped ribs holding the canopy in place. 'The timber for these comes to us in large quantities. We machine it into rods of the requisite thickness, soak them until they become pliable, then they are bent and held fast in shape until they are dry. It is important that the tension is just right for if they are slack the canopy, or bonnet, will be slack and if they have too much tension the oscillation of the wagon over rough terrain will cause them to spring and this would result in the bonnet being ripped. Many of the migrants, to save costs, use homespun cotton doubled over for waterproofing but we use good-quality canvas. Here we have the sideboards; note they are bevelled outwards so the rain will run off, rather than into the wagon from underneath the bonnet. Note how the bonnet is angled at front and back. This gives added protection to the interior. In front we have this large box fastened to the front board. This is the jockey box and serves a dual purpose: firstly it is the tool box and secondly it serves as the footplate for the driver and passenger, or, if you like, shotgun rider. Incidentally, all the tools necessary for the repairs of any part of the wagon you will find supplied in that box but please check them against the list when taking delivery. The brake lever here on the side, when operated, applies this block, known as the brakeblock, to the wheel rim. Quite elementary. Now, gentlemen, we come to the most important feature of our Prairie Schooner. Let's look inside from the rear.'

He lowered the rear board and pointed out the two elongated black boxes on either side, running the full length of the wagon and two feet square. 'This,' he said, pointing to one of the boxes, 'is known as the Yankee Bed. Made from hardwood to prevent shrinkage and sealed with tar and with the self-sealing top firmly secured, the Yankee Bed is designed to float when crossing deep-water rivers. Your seats by day, bed by night and a watertight locker for bedding and clothing and other valuable possessions. And lastly,' again noting the time, 'we come to this long tapered pole with the crossbar on the end. This is what we call the falling tongue,' he explained, lifting the end up and lowering it in demonstration, 'and the crossbar here is what we call the neck yoke and, at the rear, the singletree and doubletree. All this your guide will explain in greater detail when he teaches you how to "yoke up". Any questions, gentlemen?'

All seemed quite satisfied except for one question put by the journalist, Ola Hansen: 'Yes, Mr Harvey, could you explain the reason for those canvas sheets that look something like hammocks attached to the underside of each wagon?'

'A very good question, Sir,' said James Harvey with an amused smile that might predict a funny story. 'On the vast grasslands of the prairie, of firewood there is little, but of buffalo there are many. Their droppings when baked dry in the sun make excellent fuel. When dry they are simply called chips. This hammock, as you aptly call it, is referred to as the chip basket. Your young Irish guide, whom you will be meeting in a day or so, can be somewhat more prosaic. He calls this the shit basket.' Mr Beamish arrived just in time to enjoy the joke.

CHAPTER 6

It was just known as common land, or common fields, the land lying west of St Louis. The young thriving city had not yet grown into it. South of Chouteaus Pond and over to the west where the prairie began, the scene was anything but common. It seemed the world and his wife had come together in one enormous ragtag rabble here on the south-western flank of the city. Scenes like it were also happening in Independence, Missouri, and Westport. These were the transit stations for the great migration westward. Here they would muster in sometimes appalling conditions to kit out for the five or six months' hazardous trek across the wilderness, many to the fertile land of Oregon, others to the future goldfields of California and others taking the safety of the wagon trains only to get off at places like St Joseph or Council Bluffs. All in search of that new and better life.

It was into this melting pot of humanity that Mr Beamish had led his party in what he referred to as an educational tour. 'You will witness near-panic activity here today,' said Beamish, marching along at the head of the column. 'There are two or three large-sized trains to be on the move soon and all seem to be behind schedule at present. The general opinion held by the wagon masters is to be on the move around mid-April, so the animals can have fresh grass across the prairie. Any later, and for a good part of the crossing the grass is scorched. Leave after mid-May and the train can be held in the snows of the high mountains.'

'Mind how you tread here,' he called, addressing the group. 'The place here is so muddy.' One of the group remarked how distressing it must be for the womenfolk trailing so much mud on the hems of their skirts. Wagon wheels, oxen, mules and horses chewed the rain-soaked earth.

'Now, where were we?' continued Mr Beamish. 'Yes, as I was saying. To leave late and get snow-bound for the winter in the mountain passes is serious. It has cost the lives of many and no doubt will again. Oh! Here is someone I would like you gentlemen to meet.' He paused and pointed to a man demonstrating to a group of novices the technique of "yoking up". 'That man over there is one of the most experienced wagon masters on the plains today.' Reasonably satisfied that his pupils had got the idea, the man in question left them to move on to others in need of his helping hand when Mr Beamish called out, 'Charlie!' and attracted his attention with a wave of his hand. 'Charlie, if you can spare a moment, I have some fellahs here I'd like you to meet.'

'I'll be right over there with you, Alistair, jest as soon as I see to the lady strugglin' with that barrel.' He walked the length of two wagons to where a woman was having difficulty rolling a barrel of fresh water. Charlie took her wrist and led her gently back a few steps and with no effort at all lifted the thing into the cradle provided on the side of the wagon and lashed it down. He then turned to the lady, touched his hat, saying, 'Ma'am,' and walked at an easy gait towards Alistair Beamish and his party, leaving the woman wiping her brow and smiling her thanks. Charlie was no giant. He was a wiry little man, a terrier, who amazed the Norwegians by the ease with which he had lifted that heavy barrel. As he approached them, he spat and the colour of the spittle was the same as the mud it joined. Charlie's vice was obvious for all to see: he chewed tobacco.

'Gentlemen,' said Mr Beamish, 'I would like you to meet Charlie Roach.' And turning to Charlie again, 'Charlie, I am sorry to distract you and I know how busy you are, but—'

Charlie cut in with a bit of his ready-made philosophy, 'Alistair, the busy man has always got time for an old friend and the stranger. It's the idle son-of-a-bitch that jest ain't got time for nothing.'

Alistair Beamish introduced Charlie Roach to each and every member of the party with a short résumé for each man and to the Norwegians an account of the colourful life of this experienced frontiersman. Charlie had already learned something about the little group and was keen to know more.

'I've got charge of over eighty wagons, near on ninety,' Charlie told his audience, 'and I have to get them rollin' soon. This spell of wet weather has slowed everything down. And what's more, they're nearly all Conestogas. Big heavy brutes. The goin' is sure gonna be tough along the Santa Fe. You boys all got Prairie Schooners?' He was assured that was so. 'You're headin' north-west; I guess you're makin' for them Black Hills?'

This was a very direct question. Overlanders were mainly en route to California or Oregon. On the Oregon Trail, the trains passed through the

Dakotas but all circumvented the Black Hills. Charlie, on learning that some of the party were mining engineers and such, assumed they were gold prospectors and was intent on pursuing that line when Alistair stepped in and diverted his line of questioning. Neither Alistair, nor the company he represented, was privy to the nature of the Norwegians' expedition and an embarrassing situation had to be prevented.

Charlie Roach was true to his statement for, despite his workload, he stood talking at length to his old acquaintance and answering with enthusiasm all the questions put to him by the strangers from overseas. They found him a sincere and interesting man with a marvellous sense of humour. Charlie had made a good impression without even trying.

It was a short walk from the Planters Hotel on the following day to the office and warehouse of RJ Morgan at Old Market on Front Street Wharf, and Andur Oskarsen and Einar Andersen decided that a little exercise in the fresh morning air was what they needed. No need for any of the others to come along as there was nothing they could do to be helpful at this point anyway. The captains were old hands at ordering supplies.

Alistair was in his office on their arrival and, having introduced his secretary, suggested that coffee would be welcome. She disappeared into what was the kitchen, while Alistair made his guests comfortable and produced stores lists for each of them.

'One for you, Einar,' handing a sheaf of papers to Einar, 'and one for Andur.' They were all on first-name terms now since their previous meetings. 'Before you leave I'll give you a copy for each of the others.' Alistair took a tray from the girl and got to work with it on a small table by a large window while the two men scanned over the lists.

'This is quite a comprehensive list,' remarked Andur.

'It is,' said Alistair. 'All you will need and more.'

'Tell me,' asked Einar, his finger underlining the salient word on the list, 'what is saleratus?'

'I don't know the word in Norse but in English it is baking powder. I think saleratus is only the American word. In other words, aerated salt.'

'Ah! I understand,' and looking towards Andur. 'I do not think we shall be needing any aerated salt.' It was evident Einar Andersen's knowledge of baking was limited.

'Indeed you will be carrying quite a large quantity of flour, most essential, and let's hope someone in the party knows something about cooking,' informed Alistair.

'In the months ahead, Einar, we will all learn,' Andur predicted, and after a thoughtful pause added, 'we will learn a whole new way of life.'

'Let us talk about armaments,' Alistair began. 'Presumably you both are familiar with firearms of some kind?'

'We have both used rifles and smoothbore in Norway,' said Andur, 'and we each have a Colt revolver which was ship's officer issue but we are short on ammunition.'

'You have Colts?' Alistair asked, surprised. 'That is excellent. We can easily replenish your depleted stocks of ammo but our stock of Colts is low. Certainly we can supply but so much to the good. The Colt revolver has only been in production for four years and they don't appear to be coming off in any large numbers yet. What have you been using your ammunition on, mutinous sailors?'

'I don't think either of us ever fired them until we were travelling passengers from Bergen,' said Einar.

Andur continued, 'We thought it time we got in a little practice, shooting at bits of flotsam that we could throw over the aft end. It's an excellent piece of American engineering.'

'Indeed it is,' agreed Alistair. 'We have a few in stock at twenty-five dollars apiece. You will find your guide has got one, and Charlie, but I can't recall seeing it on him yesterday. Where did you come upon yours? Not in Norway?'

'Oh no,' said Andur, 'we bought ours in New Orleans over a year ago. Before our Colt it was just a single-shot pistol, not a great help if one ever found oneself faced with a mutinous charge.'

'Anyhow,' continued Alistair, 'you are to be armed but you may well find that the least of your dangers will come from the Indians. It is possible you will cross the prairie right to the Platte river without even seeing one and if you do they will more than likely be Cheyenne who, if you pass on your way, will not bother you. Where the Platte empties into the Missouri is Pawnee country. Could be a bit touchy.' He held out his left hand and wiggled it from side to side to emphasise his point. 'Thereafter you will be in the land of the Sioux. I beseech you my friends, tread carefully.

'Early in 1804 two army captains, Meriwether Lewis and William Clark, set out from St Louis here with an expedition of army volunteers and the blessing of Thomas Jefferson to chart a course all the way to the Pacific seaboard. It was Jefferson's dream that the Missouri joined the Columbia and if that was so, what a prize that would be for the US government – a direct waterway to the Pacific coast. They made it to the coast and back but not all by canoe. The Bitterroot Mountains got in the way. It seems they insulted the Sioux by offering their chiefs pieces of trinketry for presents whilst at the same time displaying a cannon mounted on the bow of their keelboat – a "take this or get that" diplomacy. They passed through the Sioux territory, concealed their keelboat and carried their canoes over Bitterroot, a prodigious effort, but the Sioux were waiting for them on their return trip and some unpleasantness resulted.

'It must have been galling for poor old Meriwether and William to discover that the English and the French, coming up the Columbia and down from Canada, had for some years, quite happily, been trading guns and ammunition with the Sioux in exchange for pelts. I am sure I would be aggrieved if someone walked onto my land without permission, offering a fistful of brass buttons and some coloured handkerchiefs. Anyhow, the Lewis and Clark expedition were not tops when it came to diplomacy and the Sioux are still bristling from their intrusion. So, take care, my friends, when you go beyond the Missouri.'

It was obvious to the captains that the late Lewis and Clark were no heroes for Alistair but they took a mischievous delight in how he tactfully delivered his cautionary lecture through the misdeeds of the tactless army officers. 'This word pelts,' asked Einar in his Nordic accent, 'what is pelts?'

'Furs, Einar, the skins of beavers, and so on; a very lucrative trade then and still is.'

Alistair glanced at the clock on the wall and raised his empty cup to his secretary who smiled her acknowledgement of the signal and quietly gathered the cups and saucers to the tray. 'Do you think you could find some cookies for three hungry men while you are there, Ann?'

'I'm sure I can,' replied Ann.

'And don't leave yourself out of it. It's time you took a break.'

'Yes, I may have something in the kitchenette and catch up on my reading.' She swept away silently and minutes later was back with fresh hot coffee and a stack of cookies, served it up and was gone.

'Right, gentlemen,' exclaimed Alistair, picking up the store and equipment lists, 'let's take the foodstuff first, most essential.' The others simultaneously picked up their lists and produced pencils from their breast pockets. 'Originally this victual list was compiled and recommended by a panel of experts, including several doctors in Pennsylvania, for migrants travelling the length of the continent, a journey that took the best part of a year,' he explained. 'The list we have here has been scaled down to suit the pockets of those leaving from Westport or St Louis. From Independence, less again would be required, I guess. Bearing in mind weight and space factors, the overlander must exercise prudence when loading his wagon. However, ships' masters are au fait with all this so we can move on. This is the list as prepared for each adult travelling the California or Oregon Trails.' Alistair called out each item and price and the captains ticked them off:

150 lbs. of flour	@ 2 cents per lb		$3.00
20 lbs. of cornmeal	@ 5 " " "		$1.00
50 lbs. of bacon	@ 5 " " "		$2.50
40 lbs. of sugar	@ 4 " " "		$1.60
15 lbs. of dried fruit	@ 6 " " "		$0.90
10 lbs. of coffee	@ 10 " " "		$1.00
5 lbs. of salt	@ 6 " " "		$0.30
½ lb. of saleratus	@ 12 " " "		$0.06
2 lbs. of tea	@ 60 " " "		$1.20
5 lbs. of rice	@ 5 " " "		$0.25
5 lbs. of lard	@ 5 " " "		$0.25
½ lb. of pepper	@ 8 " " "		$0.04
15 lbs. of beans	@ 6 " " "		$0.90
1 gal. of vinegar	@ 25 " " gal.		$0.25
	Total		$13.25

'Remembering you have a return journey, let's double that and add about one-third for time on site, four dollars and forty-five cents, in all thirty dollars, ninety-five cents each. Times twelve will make a grand total of three hundred and seventy-one dollars and forty cents. Are we agreed, gentlemen?'

'The guide, Alistair,' said Andur, 'let's put thirty dollars worth towards the guide's fare.'

'A generous gesture, Andur, which will make it four hundred and one dollars and forty cents. Shall we say four hundred even?'

'Agreed.'

The guns and ammunition department was strategically situated at the furthermost end of the huge warehouse, away from the doors. Windows presented no problem for they were all high. Nevertheless, it could not be classed as an armoury for nothing was seen to be locked away and staff and customers handled the arms with the same ease and indifference as those at the kitchen and tools section.

Dealing with ships' chandlers was no new experience for either man, but here in the offices and warehouses of RJ Morgan the pace was different from anything they were accustomed to in Oslo or Bergen or on the London river or Antwerp. But that was the Old World, moving at its interminably slow pace, steeped in legal restrictions. This was the New World on the very edge of the frontier. Where else could they witness a woman walk up to the gun counter in a large store and ask to see the shotguns, measure a few for comfort to her reach, break one expertly at the breech, point the barrels at the light of the window to inspect them and, having satisfied herself of the merchandise, say to the assistant, 'I'll have that and three boxes of cartridges.'? Having made her purchase, she turns to her children, telling them to take the items to the wagon and wait there. She immediately goes to the footwear department where she will spend the best part of an hour trying on several pairs of high-buttoned shoes only to walk away dissatisfied.

Above either end of the long gun counter were two white rectangular boards displaying in bold black letters the items on sale and against each item its price: "Rifle (Hawken) 15 dollars, Shotgun 10 dollars, Musket 10 dollars, Colt revolver 25 dollars, Single-Shot pistol 5 dollars. Shot sold by weight 5 dollars per pound. Powder 1 dollar per pound. Hunting knife 1 dollar. Smooth-bore cartridge 3 dollars per box."

The gun counter was crowded with eager customers all talking at once above the noise of the breaking and snapping shut of gun breeches and the metallic chatter of bolts being opened and slammed shut in quick succession. Alistair piloted his two special customers through a side door at the end of the counter by the wall and into a large gun room. The windows of this room were heavily barred. There was little or no ventilation and the smell of castor oil, one of the best gun lubricants of that time, assailed the nostrils. Only a few members of the staff, going about their business, were present and talking was easy.

In one corner, sagging against the walls, were three experienced easy chairs that had been found somewhere at some time and taken out of retirement. After a cursory inspection to ensure that no oil or dust might adhere to his or his guests' clothing, Alistair sat down and beckoned the others to follow. The armaments list was discussed and agreed and Andur asked, 'I have never heard of this Hawken rifle; can you tell us more about it?'

'I can and more,' said Alistair as he rose from his seat and walked across to the far side where a long line of rifles was stacked in racks against the wall. He took one from the rack and returned with it to his seat where he displayed it, showed how it could be taken apart for inspection and cleaning, then handed it to them for their approval. They were impressed.

'A résumé of the Hawken rifle,' continued Alistair as Einar passed it back to him. 'In 1750 three brothers, Niclaus, Christian and Wolfgang Hacken, arrived in Philadelphia from Switzerland. They were gun makers. Their descendants, Jake and Sam, now Hawken, set up a gun-making business right here in St Louis shortly after the turn of the century. Their workshops are not far from this very building and if you have time this trip I'll take you along and introduce you to the two elderly brothers, Sam and Jake. If not, we can make a point of it on your return. Two very interesting men. Their engineering is par excellence.' The captains both nodded their agreement. 'We only stock the Hawken rifle. If a customer requires any other make we can order it up but no one has ever had cause to complain about the Hawken.'

'Your Hawken will suit us, Alistair,' said Andur, 'and yes, we would like to meet the Hawken brothers but it will have to be on our return.'

'Fine,' said Alistair, 'and after lunch we can look at the pots and pans and many other accoutrements essential to a wagon train.'

CHAPTER 7

I t was upon the advice of Alistair that Captain Andur Oskarsen had his little "crew" assembled in the afternoon of Tuesday, 13 April, on the muddy fields just north of Chouteaus Pond for the auction.

The sweet smell of the fresh prairie grass carried over hundreds of miles on the soft westerly breeze fused with the warm pungent odour that is always associated with cattle. Oxen, many oxen, were being herded through open gateways into the requisite pens by ranchers expertly cracking long whips with the skill that comes with practice and makes it all seem so easy. Once in their allotted pens the riders with reins in one hand would skilfully bring their horses around and away from the open gate where two waiting cowhands would close them. Once secured in the pens, a gang of men, some with paint pots and brushes and others with apron-like garments with a large pouch, similar to that worn by carpenters, would immediately climb over the corral fence. Those with the pots and brushes would daub the backs of each animal with a coloured vegetable-based paint to indicate their ownership whilst the others with the pouch aprons smartly glued a label on their backs with a lot number.

The air was filled with the plaintive mooing of cattle and the trample of a thousand bovine hooves, the incessant cracking of whips, the neighing of horses and ranchers calling to each other and the occasional curse when something did not go as it should. These were prisoners, born to the lash, their only purpose to serve the will of man, always docile, always acquiescent. Many would never reach the trail's end. Of those that would not make it, most would collapse under the heavy yoke, their hearts having given out. Others would go mad from thirst and plodding monotonously forever across hot and arid lands, their wild pitiful roaring and maniacal kicking swiftly quelled by a bullet in the head lest the others in harness became infected, their flesh sometimes butchered to augment a dwindling food supply.

There were milk cows, too, going under the hammer at up to seventy to seventy-five dollars apiece. Families joining a train would often take with them a cow and sometimes two. After the initial outlay the cow travelled "rent-free", providing the family with milk and butter while the grass lasted; on the deserts, however, there could be a problem. Those families who could afford to bring a cow along would inevitably have a milk churn lashed to the right-hand side of their wagon. Travelling west, that was the side sheltered from the sun. A good milk cow cost more than double that of an ox and seven times that of a mule but dividends thereafter could well outweigh the initial cost. She could produce milk morning and evening, more in the morning since travelling by day did not permit much time for grazing. Any surplus milk would be put into the churn and the constant oscillation of the wagon throughout the day would, by evening, have provided the family with butter to spread on freshly made bread.

The little group of Norwegians were feeling uncomfortable and somewhat conspicuous in a crowd that was totally foreign to them. Alistair had not yet shown up and they wondered what might have happened to him. They decided time would be better spent wandering away from the crowd and walking slowly across an open stretch of ground towards the pens where the mules were being marshalled. Mules are more lively creatures, each with a mind of its own and more interesting to watch.

Outside the office of James Harvey & Sons, Wagon Builders, a chestnut gelding was standing at the hitching rail, his reins thrown loosely over the rail and passed casually through the loop. He threw up his head and emitted a low rumbling noise from his throat as his master and pal appeared in the doorway. It was not a neigh, just a low throaty sound. In the language of the horse world it is the sound that says, 'Glad to see you again; I was bored waiting.'

The man in the doorway stopped to read what may have been instructions on a sheet of paper he was carrying, then folded it, put it in a breast pocket and walked to his horse. He gave the chestnut a friendly pat on the head and stroked his neck saying, 'There, Chuck, I'm back. Were you getting worried, boy?' He slipped the reins from the rail and sprang easily into the saddle. He had bought Chuck five years earlier in Independence from a livery stable proprietor who acquired him in settlement of a debt. At the time he was a scout with Charlie Roach and had just lost his horse as a result of an unfortunate accident. The chestnut responded to the name of Charlie but it was soon discovered that Charlie, the horse that is, had a predilection for what the chuck wagon could offer whenever the train would stop for meals, and Chuck, being the abbreviation of Charlie, his new name was established.

Chuck was steered away from the factory and turned north at walking pace past the conglomerate in their final preparation for the long trek westward, the rider's sharp eye scanning the caravans. He rode with the easy sway of a man who is at home in the saddle, insouciant, slightly detached from all around him, yet sharply aware of everything that moved. Leaving the wagon site and moving towards the ox pens that were ahead of him and to the right, his attention now focused on a small group of men walking away from the ox enclosures and towards the mules. Maintaining his slow pace, he and they, if they continued, would meet when their paths crossed. He had reckoned right.

Twelve men now stood facing rider and horse feeling guilty of trespass. They thought the man leaning forward over his horse's ears seemingly about to speak was some sort of marshal intending to admonish them. The rider seemed to read their thoughts and before he spoke, a twinkle of a smile appeared. Tipping his broad-brimmed hat back slightly he spoke, not with the accent of an American, the part he looked, but Irish and distinctly Ulster, as Andur detected, for he was accustomed to putting into those north Irish ports.

'Howdy,' the rider called down to them, 'I'm your new guide; my name is Willie McKay.'

To the ear, his Christian name sounded like Woolly due to a minor speech impediment from the day he first spoke his name. He was the epitome of the plainsman. His tunic and trousers were buckskin, the tunic sleeves fringed. The trousers came over brown leather boots with raised heels to give security to the boots on the stirrup plates. Brown leather gauntlets protected his hands from the constant chafing of the reins. Around his waist he wore his gun belt fully loaded with ammunition but the holster was empty, as was the rifle or saddle holster. From mane to hooves, his horse was immaculately groomed. The Norwegians could not but observe the highly polished leathers including the boots that could well have been those of a cavalry officer on parade. His ease of manner and movement was infectious.

Willie threw his right leg over the empty saddle holster and horse's head and slipped effortlessly off the saddle. His spurs jangled as he touched the ground and stood before his novice overlanders. He was perhaps two inches taller than civil engineer Stig Brevig, the tallest of the party. First to speak was their leader, Captain Oskarsen, who introduced himself and then the rest of the party to their new leader. From that first meeting they were all on first-name terms.

'Tell me,' said Andur, 'how did you find us so easily?'

And a smile broke over Willie's face. 'I was told by Alistair Beamish to ride over to the corrals and find a band of twelve dudes all rigged out in spotless new buckskins.'

'What are dudes?' asked geologist Arild Holtop. And peals of laughter reverberated above all the noise of that market place when Willie explained to the twelve newcomer Norwegians the West's slang word, dude.

By the mule pens were several rows of makeshift livery stables and here Chuck was left. Willie guided his charges through the crowds to an advantageous position at the stalls, enquiring of them as they jostled through the crowd exactly how many wagons they had bought and were they all Prairie Schooners. The sheet of paper in his breast pocket perhaps had it all anyway but he liked to hear it for himself. He explained to them that having made their purchase, the oxen would be corralled and a rental charge imposed until their departure. With all the information collated, Willie was ready to undertake the bidding for them.

When they were all seated on the terraces with the captains on either side of him, Willie took the sheet of paper from his pocket, studied it briefly and turned to Andur on his right saying, 'The price of a single ox outside auction is between thirty and fifty dollars. Here they go in lots which makes them cheaper per head. They can go for as little as twenty-three dollars apiece, but let's say ours work out at twenty-five dollars and we have eleven wagons,' he glanced at his paper and continued, 'and all are Prairie Schooners which weigh when empty 1,300 pounds, that is half the size of a Conestoga. They are brutes and I pity the oxen that have to draw them. All in all, yours are light and four oxen per wagon should be enough. That is forty-four beasts in all and you will need a few in reserve. Often on the trail, if an animal shows any sign of weakening we take it out and put in one of the reserves. After a day or two just walking behind the train it is often back on form. These poor things, like anything else, ourselves included, need to rest once in a while. And it can happen that one or two may die. So, if I can get them a job lot at the right price, would you agree to six spare making it fifty in all? Should it happen that there is a lot of that number or near it, then the overall price will be better still.' Andur did not speak but with an affirmative nod and a friendly slap on the back it was agreed. Why waste effort above such noise when sign language will suffice?

Auctioneers took up their positions. Whips cracked and a collection of bewildered bovines surged into the ring above which the auctioneers stood or sat at their desks, their ushers close in attendance. It was as if all hell had broken loose. Willie sat with his sheet of paper rolled into the shape of a baton, the implement to catch the eye of the auctioneer.

'It looks like they are going in lots of four and eight today,' said Willie. 'That's not unusual. Eight is the maximum number per wagon. They're auctioning off to the individual waggoner. If it is a family who has two wagons then he must bid twice if he only needs twelve, that is six to a wagon.

We could be lucky here, six lots of eight which would do but I would like to think we had six in reserve, so over there in that last corral' – he pointed with his rolled paper – 'they are sold as to your needs at a bit over the odds.'

As Willie kept the captains informed, they in turn passed on the reports over the din of the proceedings. Regardless of the excellent command of English that each of the Norwegians possessed, not one could understand a word that rolled off the fast-moving tongue of the auctioneer; nevertheless, the atmosphere was a new and exciting experience and one they were thoroughly enjoying. Andur and Einar, conversing across Willie, reflected on the many times when their vessels had been tied up in the port of New Orleans, their holds being loaded with cotton, how it never entered their heads to visit a cotton auction. Six times Willie's paper baton caught the auctioneer's eye and six times the gavel came down and each time eight big docile beasts would be led from the ring.

They walked slowly away from the corral area, to the west, not far, just enough to get upwind of the hot odour of cattle. The cool breeze carrying with it a score of perfumes off the Missouri grasslands was refreshing.

'Tell me, Willie,' asked one of the party, and perhaps he was asking the question for all of them, 'are these auctions held through the year?'

'No,' said Willie, 'they were set up only two or three years ago when people started moving west, most for Oregon and California. Then others started heading for places like Montana and Colorado. This year is seeing the biggest movement yet and it's my guess that it will get bigger. And there is word that Washington has a big hand in it. Last spring that place back there was only a shack with a few pens and over there,' pointing to the transit area, 'just ten or twenty wagons coming out of Harvey's factory, and look at it now a year on. Harvey can't expand fast enough. But all this is not answering your question. No, they don't take place all year round. This is about the busiest time. Wagon masters like to be rollin' by the middle of April if they can. If after—'

'We believe it has something to do with the grass,' interrupted Morten Olsen, mining engineer. 'Considering there is so much preparation yet to be done, are we not going to leave our departure a bit late?'

'Relax,' said Willie, 'the rain we have had over the last few weeks, the heaviest and longest for a good many years, will keep the grasslands growing well into the Fall. Good lush green grass all the way to the Rockies. Plenty of sugar in grass like that, you'll see. Watch the animals put on weight instead of losing it. And don't worry, we will be rollin' before the weekend.' Sugar in grass? Several of the group turned without speaking to Kristoffer Eriksen for confirmation and the doctor answered their question with an affirmative nod of his head.

Willie left his party by one of the three chuck wagons that provided refreshments for the multitude. The fare was limited to hot sweet coffee, flapjacks and freshly baked cookies and scones. Flapjacks were served with a helping of molasses syrup. The aroma that emanated from these wagons was inviting. No need for the entrepreneurs of these little gold mines to cross far and dangerous lands to improve their lot. They were making it here and now.

At the mule pens Willie was deliberating over the purchase of a pair of mules he would need as pack animals for the forthcoming expedition. He was bent over with an animal's hind leg lifted by the fetlock when a familiar voice behind him spoke in jest, 'Look at the tooth before the hoof.'

He dropped the hoof and straightened up to find Charlie Roach standing behind him. Charlie was smiling but he was not in any good humour; he was in fact in a foul mood, spitting streams of chewed tobacco and "goddamning" everything that was wrong with the world.

'Charlie, you old rattlesnake,' exclaimed Willie as they shook each other by the hand. 'It's been a long time since we met up. How are you, Charlie?'

'The better for seeing you, Willie. I've got the biggest train goin' outa' here that I can call to mind and I'm left to do all the ass kickin'. I've got three scouts and I could do with as many more. All big heavy wagons. Eight beasts to every yoke and not a goddamn reserve. They just can't afford an extra animal. Ah tell you, Willie, I'm gonna lose a few beasts this trip.'

'Where are you headed, Charlie?'

'California.'

'I thought so; a long way.'

'With luck it will be a year and maybe three months before I hit St Louis again, and then, Willie, I'm gonna settle here. I'll celebrate my sixtieth birthday on the trail this time, only there ain't gonna be no celebrations. When a man reaches that milestone in this work, he keeps it to hisself. If my reckonin' is right it ought to come about a hundred miles west of Independence, about three hundred from where we're standin'.' Willie let Charlie talk away. It was winding him down. 'Mention of Independence,' Charlie continued, 'I'm losing a third of my train there; yes, Sirree, thirty wagons jumpin' off at Independence. That'll lighten my load a bit.'

'Now that *is* something you ought to celebrate,' said Willie. 'I'll tell you what you'll do, Charlie; you'll get yourself a bottle of the best, like the kind we had in a bar in that same town when we celebrated my bargain at finding Chuck. You celebrate your birthday and the lightening of your load and remember to have a good quaff for me.'

Charlie was feeling good now, relaxed. 'That's just what I'll do, Willie, doggone if I don't.'

He took a part bar of tobacco from a vest pocket and a small knife, cut off a plug and as if it were the thing to do, reached it to Willie who held up a hand saying, 'No thanks, Charlie, I'll be all right.'

Charlie, without further thought, slipped the plug into his mouth. Willie never succumbed to the tobacco habit in any form. Never thought about it. 'Where are you aheaded with them there Viking boys?' asked Charlie, a twinkle appearing around the sides of the eyes. 'They ought to be wearin' horns on their heads. When you've knocked down a few buffalo maybe you can provide your guests with some fancy headdress. That ought to impress the Pawnee!' Charlie was a man who enjoyed a joke; he revelled in his own and his laughter was somewhat between a chuckle and a cackle.

Willie left him laughing until he ran out of steam. 'Charlie, you cunning auld dog. Why did you ask where we were headed when you already know we are going north-west of here?'

'I said nothin' about north-west.'

'You did, Charlie, you spoke of the Pawnee; not hard to figure out. You're fishing, Charlie, but I wish I could answer your question. I just don't know where we are going. I have asked Captain Oskarsen and all he told me was he had "Sealed Orders", some kind of navy jargon.'

'I'll tell you, Willie, Alistair introduced me to them boys and I reckon they are after gold. They're headin' for them Black Hills. I always knew there was gold in them Dakota Hills. And I'll tell you somethin' else, Willie.' He spat to emphasise the point he was about to make. 'I reckon the government is tied up in it. There's big money goin' into this little expedition and it ain't all private money.'

Willie gave the mule a pat on the neck and sat on the corral fence. He was listening. Charlie was a man worth listening to. Willie knew that more than any man. He was Charlie's protégé. Charlie went on, 'Twelve men, every goddamn one an expert in his own field and two of them minin' engineers. If you need a minin' expert you turn to Europe. This nation just ain't got many of them fellahs yet. And there's another one of them makes maps. I tell you, Willie, them fellahs are hell-bent on somethin' big and I'd bet my bottom dollar Washington's got a hand in it.'

'It adds up,' admitted Willie. 'It all seems to add up.'

'And, Willie, you take some advice from an old timer,' and he poked a finger at Willie's chest.

But before he could continue, Willie interrupted, 'Charlie, I've always taken your advice.'

'Well, listen and take some more now. You keep well in with them boys and if they find that yellow stuff some of it is bound to rub off on you. I tell you, young fellah, you could be a very rich man. But I tell you another thing,' and he paused for a moment to take his watch from a vest pocket and glance at the time, 'they're all greenhorns to the ways of this land, they're all goddamn greenhorns and I wouldn't undertake what you are about to do without a troop of US cavalry. Them two seafarers could well prove themselves in a tight spot but they have never faced a war party. And that young doctor fellah; what's he goin' into the wilderness to see? That's jist a waste of good education. A man needs no doctor out here. Here if you live, you live, and if you die, you die. That young fellah ought to be at home tendin' sick people and expandin' his medical knowledge. Well, I guess I better be rollin', and, Willie, you keep them fellahs well away from war parties or you'll be on your own.'

'I'll do my best,' Willie assured him. They shook hands and said their farewells.

When he was just a few paces away Charlie turned back to Willie and, in an emotional outburst, threw his left arm around Willie's shoulder and grasping his hand with his right hand said, 'You take good care of yourself, son.'

'And you, too, Charlie. Thanks for all you've done for me.' And as Charlie walked away he called after him, 'And don't forget Independence.' Charlie waved in reply but did not turn his head for Charlie Roach must not be seen to shed a tear.

Willie watched him walk away until he was lost among the overlanders and their wagons: a small indestructible man with quick jaunty steps on bowed legs, a relic of a lifetime in the saddle. An eerie feeling, a premonition, stole over Willie, and perhaps it was also with Charlie, that neither man would cross the other's trail again. Sadly, this prophecy was to come to pass.

CHAPTER 8

The year 1841 saw the start of the Great Migration westward. It would continue over the following twenty-five years until the coming of the railroad. In the beginning, most set out from St Louis and Westport and by 1844, wagon trains were also setting out from St Joseph, Bellview and in ever-increasing numbers from Independence. Often trains leaving St Louis and Westport or Independence would join up along the trail thus swelling the size of the convoy. All manner of trades and professions were represented.

On Thursday morning, 15 April, Charlie Roach and his three scouts were mustering their convoy of ninety wagons bound for California via Independence. On the same site Bruno Lohmann, of German parentage, was making ready for departure a train of some seventy wagons, their intended destination the rich arable farm lands of Oregon. Bruno would travel with Charlie's train as far as Independence where fresh supplies would be taken on and families for Independence would "jump off". Thereafter he would take his caravan of mainly German and Dutch farmers and their families on a hazardous trail over a land where roads did not yet exist, where rivers were to be crossed when safe fording places were found. Beyond the grasslands would stand the Bitterroot mountain range, the most challenging and foreboding of all. Bruno was a trailblazer: one of the first great guides to establish what was soon to be known as the Oregon Trail, a distance of two thousand miles from Missouri to Oregon.

The following day, eleven Prairie Schooners trundled out from the compound of James Harvey & Sons and turned north-west towards the open prairie. They would trek 800 miles on a heading of 315 degrees with a latitude of one degree. They would cross the Missouri river in North Dakota twelve miles north of what is presently known as Mandan where fording sites are plentiful. Place of location for the crossing was 47 degrees latitude, 101 degrees longitude. Here they would change course to 275 degrees, five degrees north of due west, with a plus or minus of one degree. On this course they would trek 545 miles across present-day Montana to map reference 47 degrees latitude, 112 degrees longitude, a place known as the "Gates of the Mountain's Wilderness". This course was plotted by Captain Andur Oskarsen, Captain Einar Andersen and cartographer Oskar Haug, and approved by two United States officials in Oslo two months before the expedition boarded the *Fjorden* at the port of Bergen.

They walked either side of their lead animals; the purpose was two-fold: it lightened the load on the oxen and walking in the crisp morning air could only enliven them after their little farewell party in the Planters Hotel the evening before. Most, if not all, with the exception of Willie, were feeling sorry for themselves and wondering if it was all worth it. This would be their mode of transport over the next 1,300 to 1,400 miles and then there would be the return journey.

Willie on Chuck would occasionally canter to the head of the column where he would stop and watch how his fledglings were doing, for their training had been basic. What was lacking in knowledge must come with each new day's experience.

And Willie would also be learning for he, too, would soon be treading unknown territory. He was yet to meet the Pawnee or the Comanche or the Sioux, and when he would one day come face to face with the warriors of the Crow nation it would be in a way he could never have contemplated.

Before noon on the first day, Willie halted the column at the request of Captain Oskarsen. From the lead wagon, that of the mariners, Andur and Einar, each took some leather cases containing instruments, followed by Oskar Haug with a rectangular table, a tripod and over his shoulder another case with more instruments. Having placed these items carefully on the grass he returned to the rear of the wagon and fetched a large roll of parchment. The plane-table was set up on its tripod and the parchment, the ends of which were affixed to heavy rods that held it open when unfurled, was laid on the table. At high noon Andur and Einar took sightings with their instruments. Willie remembered such an instrument being used by the officer of the watch on his passage to New Orleans. This ritual would be performed at noon of each day and at other times, mainly morning and evening.

The three Norsemen, speaking in their native tongue, were engrossed in their work and Willie, although interested, refrained from interrupting and in any case this was not his department. He solicited the help of others to release the animals to rest and feed. Kristoffer Eriksen and the two civil engineers, Anders Lein and Stig Brevig, got organised in the chuck wagon. Kristoffer, his medical expertise not much in demand, had volunteered to undertake the duties of chief cook, with others lending a hand on a rota basis. Chuck wasted no time in presenting himself at the rear of the chuck wagon and Kristoffer, with great presence of mind when ordering up the stores, ensured there was an additional supply of dried fruit and oats for his newfound friend. A good routine was quietly falling into place.

When the midday meal was over and the instruments stowed, Willie suggested that only one should walk at the head of each team and the other ride in the wagon and change over every hour or so. Later on, when they would get to know their oxen and how best to handle them, there would be more time to relax on the move, but now there was something else to learn. He drew from one of his saddle bags a pack of target-practice cards which only Willie could have remembered to bring. He took six from the pack and placed them against a little rise in the ground, a distance of some twenty-five yards away. They had a talk on safety precautions, on loading and how to present the rifle to the target and on maintenance of the rifle. Thereafter each man had some practice with generally good results which pleased Willie. Everyone had praise for his Hawken rifle. Next, the revolvers and single-shot pistols. Those with revolvers passed them around so everyone had a try. Andur and Einar, with their Colts, were excellent shots, but for the rest of the party the results could have been better. They enjoyed their practice but it was one that had to be curtailed for the ammunition supply was not inexhaustible.

Before leaving St Louis a meeting was held regarding security on the march. Priority was given to nightly stopping (making camp). Circling the wagons was always the first consideration with wagon masters. It was standard procedure, but wagon masters invariably travelled with large trains in their charge. Wagons could be placed close together for fortification and yet leave enough grazing space within the circle for a considerable number of animals. Also, the trains carried many men all trained in the use of firearms, all armed, with women and many of the bigger children behind them, all practised in reloading and a good many of the women quite proficient in firing the rifle and shotgun.

This little band of thirteen men, most with only the most basic firearms training, had none of these advantages. The best they could hope for was good diplomacy and good luck. So it was acknowledged that in order to provide grazing for fifty-three animals – fifty oxen, two mules and one horse – within the circle, eleven wagons would be so widely spaced as to leave serious breaches in their defences. It was concluded that the only course left open was to rope these areas off by running two lengths of light hemp rope between the wagons, the first length about two feet from the ground, the top one somewhere level with a horse's breast. The ropes would be made fast to appendages from the wagons and stretched taut. Not much defence against a war party (and Willie had seen a few warrior bands on the move) but there was always good diplomacy, good luck and a prayer.

Captain Oskarsen would be in charge of the watch duties and no man, including himself, was exempt except Willie – and his presence would always be about. On the trail he often made do with little sleep and rarely ever accepted an offer to rest in a wagon, preferring instead to bed down in his roll with a blanket over his saddle for a pillow. Often when rain threatened he would seek shelter under a wagon with the light canvas sheeting that he always carried attached to the wagon wheels on the windward side.

On their first night of making camp, some difficulty was experienced in positioning the wagons for the oxen handled awkwardly in the hands of their inexperienced masters. It was a tiresome experience and one fraught with considerable danger as their metallurgist, Truls Gundersen, discovered when one of his oxen threw a kick at him, narrowly missing his kneecap. He cursed the bovine brute, reflecting on what he had given up for this: his family and lovely home in a picturesque area on the outskirts of Oslo.

After the wagons were finally positioned and the animals secured, the mariners prepared to take their celestial sightings and Oskar Haug set out his plane-table and upon it the chart and compass, protractor and other measuring equipment. A high cloud formation made it impossible to take any accurate sightings that night. Only Venus made brief intermittent appearances with a faint Jupiter hanging low over to the south-east. They contented themselves with rough calculations and hoped for a break in the cloud before dawn.

After the noon sightings and midday meal the following day, Andur called a meeting and when the entire party was seated as comfortably as possible on the grass he took from a small black valise a sealed envelope. Opening it, he produced an official-looking document together with a smaller envelope, also with the wax stamp of officialdom.

'Gentlemen,' he began in English, 'we are now "at sea", as it were, and as it is my duty I shall now inform you of the purpose of this mission and why we are travelling in this direction. Willie,' he continued, looking directly at their guide sitting in the middle of the ring, 'raised an admirable point before leaving St Louis. He suggested that, for security reasons, we tag onto Bruno Lohmann's train to a point 100 miles past Fort John where Bruno would turn off west into the South Pass, at which point we would turn north. I would dearly have loved to have accepted Willie's advice and chosen that route, but for reasons that will become evident, I had to disagree.' He paused for a moment, then holding up the letter of instruction he continued, 'The content of this letter of instruction has, until now, been known to a very small group of men – myself, Captain Andersen,' nodding towards Einar, 'our cartographer and two senior officials in Washington. There is one other gentleman who is privy to this forthcoming undertaking, Martin Van Buren, eighth president of the United States who has just left office. Towards the close of our meeting I shall pass this document around, firstly to Willie, who will pass it on while he and I have a little chat.'

Willie was getting the feeling that he was rapidly becoming surplus to requirements – but without indignation. The style of leadership and charm of this Norseman, with such a command of the English language, was disarming. This would be an easy ride – no crude methods of navigation with a pocket compass and peering occasionally into the night sky to ensure Polaris was still there. *What a lucky break, and on the payroll as well,* he thought. He was soon to learn otherwise.

'This letter of instruction, together with the content of the smaller envelope which I have carried with me from Oslo in this valise, lays down specifically the route we must follow to our destination, and sealed in this envelope are our instructions when we arrive there. Now, Willie, would you care to read all this – no need to rush – and when you have finished it, pass it on? The last man to read it will return it to me. Meanwhile I am going to help myself to another cup of coffee.'

Shortly after, Captain Andur, pitching the dregs of his coffee onto the grass, called, 'Willie, are you ready?'

Willie almost snapped, 'Yes, Sir,' with an involuntary leap to attention as he had so often witnessed in the army posts he had passed through, but he braked himself in time from making a fool of himself to the others and the embarrassment of Andur. 'Aye, I've read it, Andur. You'd like a word with me?'

'Yes, would you come over here with me?' Willie followed Andur to the plane-table, out of earshot of the others.

'Willie, I have seen you taking an interest in our sextants.'

'Your what?' asked Willie.

'Sextants.'

'Ah! That's what they're called. When I was a passenger on the ship crossing the Atlantic I would see a man at certain times each day with one of these and it wasn't hard to figure out what its purpose was. I guessed it was an instrument to do with sailors but I was surprised to see it being used on dry land.'

'Quite,' said Andur. 'The man you would have seen on that part of the deck we call the quarterdeck was the Officer of the Watch. Among several of his duties is the navigation of the vessel. After the captain, who is often known as the ship's master, there are three navigation officers or "mates" as they are more often called. There are three mates for there are three watch systems. We have first, second and third mates and their seniority is in that order, the first being second only to the captain. He is the chief officer and carries a master's certificate, the second officer will carry a chief's ticket and so forth. The reason being that, if the captain is taken ill or dies at sea or for whatever other reason is unable to continue, there is a qualified officer to take up that position. Anyhow, let us not digress.'

'Willie,' said Andur, looking up at him intently, 'we have a long road to travel together so let us start out as we intend to continue.' Here he paused, giving his words time to sink in. *This is the let down*, thought Willie. *No need for me among this crew with their highly technical instruments and their charts. One thing for it, I'll turn round and hightail it back to St Louis – Chuck and my mules and me. That will stump them. They will be left high and dry.* And on reflection his blood drained to his toes. Deserting the client in the wilderness; the captain leaving his ship and his crew. He would be fired immediately with no prospect of signing up with another outfit.

Andur cut in on his negative thoughts. 'What Einar and I have in mind is to teach you the rudiments of the sextant and its complementary instrument, the chronometer.' This was more uplifting news to Willie's ears. 'The sextant,' continued Andur, tapping the leather case in which it was enclosed, 'is a complicated little instrument to master but not impossible for anyone of reasonable intelligence and a will to learn. Once I have explained the parts and their functions and shown you how to take a reading the rest is practice, practice, practice, and you will learn how to align your map with those features on it relative to the compass points, true north and magnetic north, and quite a lot more. Are you interested?'

'You bet I am.'

'Good,' said Andur. 'We can start as soon as you like and when we return to St Louis we can have a search around for some equipment for you, and failing to find it in St Louis, no doubt I will get it in New Orleans and have it sent on to you care of RJ Morgan. I guess that's enough for now so we better get back to the party.' Willie thanked him profusely and as they turned from the plane-table Andur remarked casually, 'And Willie, if our mission proves successful your life may take a different course but your navigation training will still hold. It may come in useful on your own yacht.' He gave Willie a knowing wink and walked ahead leaving him to think, and think he did. *You auld dog, Charlie, how right you were.*

On rejoining the others resting on the grass, Andur called out, 'Have you all read and digested the content of the letter?' All nodded in the affirmative and Harald Seter, mining engineer and last to read, handed it back to Andur who returned it to the valise, took from it an old and well-handled map, with many omissions and inaccuracies, and held it up for all to see saying, 'Here, gentlemen, is the route we are to follow. It may be off what is becoming the beaten track but our orders are that we travel alone. From here we travel 800 miles on a heading of 318 degrees with a plus or minus of two degrees to a position of 47 degrees latitude 100 degrees longitude where we will turn west for 540 miles to our place of location 47 degrees latitude 112 degrees longitude. On arrival there, this second envelope will be opened. And now, Willie, if we are all ready, please prepare to move us out.'[1]

---

1 In 1841 three presidents held office. Martin Van Buren: eighth president, from 1837 to 1841, left office in March having finished his term. William Henry Harrison: ninth president, died on 4 April, shortly after taking office. John Tyler: tenth president, from 1841 to 1845. Since the expedition was first planned in the spring of 1838, President Van Buren, though his signature was never put to any known document, was obviously the one informed.

CHAPTER 9

In the cold light of dawn on 18 April, with their oxen yoked up on this first Sunday "at sea", Captain Andur Oskarsen, with his little group assembled closely around him, read a short passage from the pocket-sized English Bible and concluded with a short hymn familiar to most men who go down to the seas in ships:

O Trinity of Love and Power
Our Brethren shield in danger's hour;
From rock and tempest, fire and foe,
Protect them where'er they go;
And ever let there rise to thee,
Glad hymns of praise from land and sea.

All joined in singing the hymn except Willie, simply because he did not know the words. He would learn them soon and be ready to give full voice next time, for did he not sing in the choir at Glen Chapel when he was a schoolboy, and at Falaleigh school all those years ago?

And truly they were at sea, for when the sun behind them peered over the horizon there opened up before them a tranquil green sea of grass, the undulating waves coming towards them, made by the ever constant westerly breeze. And with the gentle roll of the wagon, a sailor could not but be at home in such a setting.

So far there had been no sighting of buffalo nor of any of the Indian population, but come early afternoon that would change. At high noon Willie would have his first lesson on the purpose of the sextant from the master. The mercury read 1,028 millibars, blue skies with little puffs of fair-weather cumulus. Ahead of the lead wagon small bluebirds rose from the grass, already taking on a deep rich hue, enhanced by the rains of March. And borne on the breeze that emanated a thousand miles away was a potpourri of magnolia, coming into its first flower, of many species of wildflower mingled with the scent of fresh grass and the budding hawthorn that would be adopted as state flower of Missouri. 'In a land like this,' remarked Ola Hansen, novelist and journalist, 'a man could live for ever.'

They were holding well on course with the Mississippi a few miles north of them. Willie, shading his eyes with his hat brim, studied the sun's position. It was nearing midday so time to call a halt and giving Chuck a gentle touch on the flanks, he cantered him to the head of the caravan and held up his hand. Having attracted the captain's attention he pointed to the sun then pointed to something ahead, turned and cantered off in that direction. He had obviously spotted something of interest. It was a river a few hundred yards ahead, the first of many to be crossed on their journey. He returned at a canter and reported the river ahead, suggesting it was an ideal place to stop. The river was quite shallow, slow flowing and the water sparkled. The animals were all impatient. Willie slipped the saddle off Chuck and pointed him downstream. Chuck and the mules following were capable of looking after themselves. 'Keep them all downstream,' called Willie to the ox handlers. 'We must keep the water clean for our own supplies.'

'If you can leave your horse and mules for a moment, Willie, would you come over here and watch what we are doing?'

'Coming, Andur,' called Willie, and he wasted no time for it was obvious there was some hurry.

Andur and Einar "shot the sun" directly as it reached the noon-day position, the ideal position for a reading, and Oskar entered some calculations on the chart, and all three men checked their findings. Andur then turned to Willie who was anxiously keeping an eye on his horse and mules, and said, 'I doubt if you will take in much instruction on these instruments at the moment, you are much too busy for that. All I would like you to see is the position that we have just fixed on the chart here. This evening I shall explain more fully how we arrived at it. Here we have a river. That is an established feature. On this chart which Oskar is drawing up we have these lines,' pointing to the vertical and horizontal lines drawn on the parchment.

'Yes,' said Willie, 'the latitudinal and longitudinal.'

'Good,' replied Andur. 'No further need to continue along those lines,' admitting a faint smile at his little pun. 'From the sightings Einar and I have taken and cross-referenced, we place ourselves here, latitude 39 degrees north and longitude 91 degrees west with a plus. This line here which Oskar has drawn,' he pointed to a distinct line zigzagging down from the north and turning slightly south-east, 'is the same as is on this old map here,' and unfolding another even older-looking map he continued, 'and this one here continued on over to our starting point, St Louis, where it then zigzags south is—'

'The Mississippi,' cut in Willie.

'You are right with me,' said Andur, 'and this thin line which Oskar is drawing in now – and note that it is absent from both these old maps – is a tributary of the Mississippi. Now here comes the finer point. Oskar, would you excuse us for a moment please while we get a little closer to the scale and legend?'

To the right-hand lower section of the chart he pointed to some small figures. 'Down here on the bottom right-hand corner, Oskar, you will note, has drawn this rectangular box into which he has penned some notes and symbols which we can come back to later, but just at the moment I would like you to note this line of figures here.' He indicated to 1:1000000 and looked at Willie. 'That, Willie, is the scale of the map we are working on which means this is a very small-scale map. Basically, the smaller the scale the larger the area the map represents. One inch on this map represents sixteen miles on the ground.' Willie showed enthusiasm and made all the right noises. 'Now,' continued Andur, picking up a divider set, 'let us place this here on the Mississippi and open them slightly until this leg points here on the thin line that Oskar has just drawn and now we will return to the box, place our dividers on this line here against these figures which are calibrated to represent distance on the ground, and we read off two miles. So, William, we have discovered that we are standing on the east bank of a tributary two miles south of the Mississippi and if you look closely at the river here on the map you will see a hairpin bend just there.'

'Yes, I see it,' Willie agreed.

'Now,' said Andur, 'look to your left and just behind you.'

'My God,' exclaimed Willie in amazement as he turned to a smiling Andur.

Before Willie could utter a further word, Andur drove the point home, 'And all this would not be achieved without understanding these gadgets here,' indicating the sextant and chronometer.

Where Willie had his first lesson in the finer points of navigation and cartography was just two miles south of what is now Hannibal on the banks of the Mississippi, and in a humble cabin close to the opposite bank a lively six-year-old, Samuel Langhorne Clemens, was growing up to enjoy a happy and adventurous boyhood in that idyllic playground. The world would later know him as Mark Twain.

'Captain Oskarsen will be taking you off to sea as his chief officer,' jested one of the mining engineers, Morten Olsen.

'Don't give it a second thought,' called back civil engineer Anders Lein, as he walked towards the coffee pot hanging over the fire from a wrought-iron tripod. He replenished his mug, spooned a little sugar and returning to his place on the grass, continued, 'He is known to be a hard taskmaster. Once you have signed Articles to Oskarsen your fate before the mast is sealed.' Lein was a droll character whose sense of humour was in the lack of it. Rarely did he burst into laughter but when others were enjoying some hilarious situation or joke he would permit a wry little smile with a twinkle in his eye, the smile emphasised by a row of strong, slightly prominent teeth, the view Willie got of him as he returned to his place opposite him. A wise and intelligent man drawn a little within himself. After his profession, or perhaps before it, Anders Lein had one passion: he was an accomplished violinist and there was talk that at some time in his life he was lead violinist of an orchestra of some note in Stockholm.

'I may surprise you all on our return,' said Andur with a smile. 'I may let Willie have my ship in return for his Chuck and the open plains.'

'And I may have a better idea,' said Willie, rising from the grass and pitching the coffee dregs from his mug. 'I think we should get tidied up and replenish our water supplies.'

Just then a fish jumped for a fly, making quite a splash. Someone remarked that it must have been a big one and how he could do with some fresh fish. His wish was about to be granted. From somewhere around the hairpin bend voices were drifting towards them. They were all now on their feet and some looking a little anxious. Willie placated their unease. 'Don't worry, it sounds like a small group of Osage, probably out fishing. Better open the tobacco store, we may have some bargaining to do.'

Almost as he finished speaking came four tall Indian men, two walking either side of the river. They were carrying nets it would seem, and a large amount of fish in hide bags. Willie greeted them in their own tongue. 'Hey, American boy,' called one of them, 'you like fish?'

'Yes,' called Willie, cupping his hands to his mouth, 'we like plenty fish.'

Again the first man called back in not so loud a voice as they were drawing nearer, 'We have plenty nice fish; you have plenty tobacco, yes, we make good business.'

Kristoffer was starting off to the supply wagon when Willie turned and whispered, 'Bring some of each, plug and flake, but not too much to start.'

The four men laid their bags on the grass and began shaking hands with everyone. The man with the most English asked, 'You all American, yes?'

'No,' Willie told them, 'these men are Norwegian.'

'Nor . . .'

'Nor-weg-ian,' explained Willie, dragging it out.

'Ah, Norwegian.' He had caught the sound and repeated it. 'Norwegian, that is good,' and pointing a forefinger at Willie, 'and you, wagon boss, you American?'

'No, I am Irish.'

'Ah, Irishman, that is good. I Irishman.' And he indicated with a wave of his hand towards his colleagues. 'All Irishmen, all drink whisky.' And a cunning smile prefaced the question that was coming. 'You have whisky? We have plenty nice fish, still living, look,' and he pointed to the movement within the bags.

Willie assured them that they had no whisky but could supply them with nice Irish tobacco in exchange for their fish, just as Kristoffer arrived with the merchandise.

'He Irishman, too?' he asked of Willie, and Willie assured him that Kristoffer was Norwegian, and they all shook hands with Kristoffer, telling him they were all Irishmen and, looking in mock disgust, informed Kristoffer that he, Willie, was the first Irishman they had ever met without whisky.

There was a quick repartee among the four in their limited English mingled with peals of laughter. The Norwegians enjoyed the Indians' sharp wit and sparkling sense of humour. Willie volunteered the information that Kristoffer was a doctor and the man with the best broken English bent over holding his back, claiming it was damaged from carrying heavy sacks of fish. This act was again followed by roars of laughter from all. They were an entertaining quartet but it was time to barter and move on.

That evening at dusk the thirteen enjoyed an excellent meal of fresh brown pan-fried trout with a delicate hint of garlic and some carefully selected herbs. The helpings were ample with some to spare. As a fish cook, Dr Eriksen excelled himself. It was asked if it might not have been improved even further had it been fried over a buffalo-chip fire. Willie assured them that buffalo-chip fires certainly did something to enhance the flavour but that was yet to come. For now, their fresh fried brown trout with their mugs of Hochheimer Wein was all a man could ask for. The few miles they had lost on the trek today would be gained tomorrow. They had all worked so hard and this night was for relaxation.

Following the fish course came a compote of fruit preserved in syrup, served up by the good doctor's lily-white hands. The camp fire was stoked higher and the soot-blackened coffee pot hung from its tripod. The night drew a purple veil over the prairie and the stars shone. Out there somewhere a sharp, harsh sound pierced the darkness, somewhere between a bark and a howl. Someone asked if it was a wolf and Willie told them it was a coyote and that they would hear more of them in the nights ahead, and wolves, too. And they would soon learn the different sounds.

From his makeshift seat propped against a wagon wheel, Anders Lein rose and walked slowly towards his wagon with a characteristic little stoop, for Anders was slightly round shouldered. He clambered inside and returned shortly with his most cherished possession, his violin, and a mischievous toothy smile.

Anders had sailed with these men across the Atlantic from Bergen on what was a protracted voyage. At their Dinner Adieu in the St Charles Hotel, New Orleans, what could have been a more fitting and memorable farewell for officers of two vessels of the line to part to than the strains of "Auld Lang Syne" from the deft fingers of a master? And on the steamboat on the Mississippi where music was constantly being enjoyed by passengers and crew alike, Lein's violin lay mute. Had he forgotten entirely that he had brought it along and had now just remembered, or was he saving it for this very occasion? Whatever was in his mind, Anders Lein, on this informal occasion, under a prairie sky, would entertain.

No one spoke or moved. They just sat watching Anders as he tweaked at the strings for a moment, tensioned a string or released another, then placed the instrument to his chin and with the bow produced a few tentative notes followed by more adjustments. Strangely it was an unprepossessing little instrument: no glossy surface or evidence that it was ever taken from its case and occasionally wiped over with a wax-impregnated cloth. Its case, lying open on the grass beside him, reflected a much-travelled piece of hand luggage.

Mugs were recharged so no one would need to move during the recital. Anders glanced around the ring to ensure everyone was comfortably seated. Someone had just stoked the fire and sparks leapt and crackled and faded out. A myriad of moths and other flying insects homed in from out of the darkness and buzzed the flames with death-defying audacity.

The violinist began with some light classical stuff and drifted away into a medley of Scottish airs. What heavenly sounds could be produced from this mundane little piece of craftsmanship, the product of some old master craftsman in a dimly lit and ill-ventilated basement workshop in Vienna or Italy. Could it have passed through the hands of Antonio Stradivari himself? Who knows? One thing was certain: Anders Lein was not going to tell.

There has always been an affinity between the Scottish and Norwegian peoples and nowhere is this more reflected than in song and dance. Robbie Burns is as much revered in Oslo as in Oban or Orkney. And if any Indian had been within a mile of the camp that night he would have heard twelve rousing male voices calling Bonnie Charlie back again, accompanied by a sound from some strange and wonderful instrument.

After the rousing airs, Anders paused and fixed himself some coffee while it was still hot. In the interval, conversation was lively and questions were put to Anders. It transpired that he was drawn to music from an early age and could read it before he had mastered his own Norse. His father was a civil engineer and strongly felt that his son should equip himself for a professional career other than the risky life of a musician. A doctor friend of the family suggested medicine but at the time those in Norway seeking to enter that profession would, more often than not, have to find a place to study, mostly in Scotland. Anders chose to follow in his father's footsteps and remain in Norway where he had more opportunity to follow his music as well. He was now in his early forties, well established as a civil engineer and widely sought for his musical talent. Having finished his coffee he picked up his violin and bow and slipped away into his own world.

He led off with a racy selection of military march tunes then slipped into some lively national dance music from his homeland and floated without pause into the lilting Scottish airs that he seemed to love. From the Highland dances he drifted again into the gentle and sombre air of "Ye Banks and Braes O' Bonnie Doon". Willie picked up his saddle and moved beside Anders and hummed a while to pick up the note. The tenor voice of the Irishman harmonised: 'Ye break my heart ye warbling birds that warble on the flowery thorn, thou mindst me o' departed joys, departed never to return.'

The others sitting around the ring must have been grateful for their wide-brimmed hats to cover their eyes.

The fire had reduced to smouldering embers and pipes had long been extinguished. There would be other nights like this one, many others on their long trek north by north-west. And they would feast not just on trout and salmon, caught by their own hands, but on deer and antelope and turkey, and, yes, juicy tender steaks from young buffalo, helped down by good rich Burgundy. And Anders would be joined by Brunduif Lillegard, explorer and writer, with his melodeon, and Truls Gundersen, the metallurgist, with his harmonica – but this night belonged to Anders.

The fire was grey and white ash now and the air chilled. At first light they would be up and making ready to move out.

CHAPTER 10

It is their eleventh day into the trek. It is early morning and the mist has not yet started to rise off the prairie. If at the end of the day their progress has equalled that of the previous ten, they will have covered 220 miles or so from leaving St Louis. Light is beginning to filter through and soon they will be able to move into their normal pace which will maintain their twenty miles per day average. The oxen make low mooing sounds and begin to act out of character and refuse to move forward. Visibility on all sides can only be measured in feet. The two mariners at the head of the lead oxen, holding their compasses close to their faces, check their readings. Their heading is right. The feeling within the animals is now getting to the men; not that of fear but that of "stand still, you cannot move".

From the rear wagon Willie called to those in front, 'Don't move and stay still, we are in a herd of buffalo. No need for alarm, just wait; pass my message down the line.' Those relaying the message were obliged to work their vocal chords harder for the saturated air inhibited the travel of sound. It was an eerie and silent world in which they found themselves encapsulated. Only the muffled sounds of grazing and the occasional scratching of a hoof against the ground betrayed the animals' presence, yet strangely, beyond that white wall, the men could feel a sense of weight – disturbing but not frightening. Willie in the chuck wagon called out another message to be passed along the line: that everyone must get into his wagon and remain there until the weather lifted and make as little noise as possible. *And how was Willie aware that the buffalo were out there?* was a question on most of their minds.

In the lead wagon Einar recalled an experience of some years gone by when he was a junior deck officer – an experience at sea with similarities to the situation in which they now found themselves. The ship was making for Fredericia in Denmark with – what was fortunate for the vessel and her crew – a cargo of marble from Naples which placed her well down in the water and with a good centre of gravity. Off the northernmost point of Denmark, where the Skagerrak meets the Kattegat, they got fog-bound as was to be expected at the time of year. They could only drop anchor and wait for it to lift by midday. What was not anticipated – and its presence had possibly brought about the fog – was ice: an ice floe pressing on her port side. Had she been carrying a light cargo, Einar may not have survived to tell the story. Like the unseen buffalo outside the wagons, so was the ice hidden by the fog, but its threat was felt.

'Yes, those waters can constantly throw up surprises,' remarked Andur. Peering out of the wagon, he tapped Einar on the shoulder saying, 'Look.' And there, through a lifting mist, was a wall on all sides of huge dark bison gently getting on with enjoying the sweet dew-laden grass. Willie on Chuck, whip in hand, moved cautiously between them and the wagons, tentatively at first and then, when sufficient space was secured, a few cracks of the whip and a wheel or two from a trotting Chuck and they began to scatter. The way ahead was now cleared.

About 170 miles to the south and a little westward, Charlie Roach was about twenty-five miles east of Independence. Charlie, with his heavy Conestogas and delays due largely to the lack of maintenance by his clients, was reckoning a day and a half, but if he kept a steady pace for the day he should have his train within ten miles of Independence by sundown. Bruno, with fewer unnecessary stops, had pushed on. He should now be clear of Independence and heading on towards the Platte river with a smaller train. So far it had been an irksome trek. And today would be unusually hot for the time of year. It was an unwritten law that the speed of a wagon train is determined by the speed of the slowest wagon, and Charlie covering just fifteen miles a day, or so he said, had a few slow wagons. Now, with any luck, he should have his train in Independence by noon on the morrow, have a good freshen-up and drink a good glass or two to the health and safe return of Willie McKay.

At noon, before they settled down for the midday meal, sightings were taken and the maps drawn up. Before they stopped, Andur and Einar at the head of the lead wagon had shot two young antelope. After the meal and a short rest, Willie would supervise the skinning and butchering. Tonight there would be fresh meat on the table. Willie, studying the northern skyline, suggested that a few volunteers should gather in the chips before the rain came. The suggestion of handling the chips provided a joke or two and a few sniggers. 'It is a duty and a pleasant one to collect fuel,' snapped Willie. 'My old friend Charlie Roach calls it harvesting.'

'And we have learned,' retorted Arild, 'that Willie McKay calls it shit.'

'All right, Mr Holtop,' declared Willie when the laughter abated, 'you're on skinning and butchering duties.'

'Yes, Sir,' answered Arild with a snappy salute, 'and who speaks of rain on a hot day like this?'

Einar pointed to a long line of heavy black clouds away to the north: 'See all that up there? By nightfall that will be upon us and that is much rain, just believe me. That plainsman there,' pointing to Willie, 'knows what he is talking about.'

By early evening of the same day, Charlie Roach decided to stop his train. They had had an uneventful day despite the premature hot weather and the train had made good progress. Independence lay less than ten miles ahead. They were all travel weary; mothers and children were tense and irritable. They would all have a quiet evening, relax and be freshened up for Independence by midday tomorrow.

Had Charlie received a formal education, refrained from chewing tobacco and gone to West Point, he may well have risen through the ranks to that strata where the air was rarefied, for he was a born leader and natural strategist on the field of battle. With a large train, ninety wagons, it was Charlie's policy when stopping for the night to split up the number of wagons and form two circles, leaving a distance of 200 or 300 yards between them, his train of thought being that should a war party attack the train it would have not one circle to deal with but two. Circling this larger area would necessitate spreading their forces and were the warriors to enter that area between the circles they would almost certainly ride into a dangerous crossfire.

Charlie had many rules for the safety of his charges and often he would come up with a new one if he felt the occasion warranted it. Where firearms were concerned he was a disciplinarian, a martinet. No child was going to have its head blown off as a result of a loaded shotgun left carelessly on the bunk of a wagon as was known to have happened. Before setting off on trek, Charlie's charges would have learned what was expected of them. Men would have firearms practice and women would be practised in loading the weapons, and those wishing to learn to shoot would be encouraged. But Charlie was not trigger happy; all life to him was sacred. Somewhere deep within him was a religious man, and like the military training in his youth, it had stood him in good stead.

As they circled their wagons that evening before the sun had set, they need not have concerned themselves about the possibility of a war-party attack. The indigenous people of the plains had more important concerns. They had attached importance to the rise in temperature and the restlessness of the otherwise placid buffalo. The migrants from the eastern cities would have paid little or no attention to these things or the long line of huge black clouds rising away on the northern horizon, their anvil-like shapes and the bursts of cloud through the flat tops of the "anvils". How could they have known that those towering columns of cumulonimbus clouds building up along the northern plains was the front line of a battle about to begin, a battle of the elements, one more ferocious than man could devise?

Far to the south from the rain forests of South America and the warm waters of the Gulf of Mexico trillions upon trillions of miniscule vapour droplets, rising towards the sun, were caught in the upper air currents and carried northwards where they would meet an equally huge mass of dense cold air moving from the far north. Where these giants collided in the sky an awful atmospheric battle would erupt.

One of Charlie's Indian scouts saw the foreboding signs and, taking him aside, warned him but his philosophical reply was, 'We are here: we can do nothing about it but trust in God and hope the storm will pass us.'

It was in the early hours of the morning of the next day when it came. From a dark and laden sky there came a crack like that of a colossal whip with a flash that illuminated land and sky for many miles with a simultaneous rumble which meant that the storm had broken directly above the wagons. Horses and mules squealed and some broke their tethering, and the oxen emitted sounds foreign to their character, milling around their improvised compound. The wagons shuddered on their wheels. Infants shaken from their sleep shrieked and women prayed. Men dashed through the deluge trying to quieten the frightened animals.

But the worst was yet to happen. From the north-west over a radial of some twenty miles, illuminated by persistent lightning, were five behemoth serpents spiralling down from the sky and moving south-eastwards in a grotesque malevolent dance. 'My God,' a man could be heard to shout, 'it's all coming our way.'

Some of the funnels would dissipate and others would appear but they were still a long way off and they could play themselves out before reaching the camp. And that is what happened. One by one they faded out and the migrants breathed sighs of relief. Others stood in the downpour, lightning flashes revealing the tension on their faces, as they prayed in thanksgiving for their deliverance. But a perverse and cruel twist of fate was dealt them, for directly north of them at no more than a mile away another funnel snaked down from the low cloud base, struck the ground with awesome force, sucking up everything in its path, and within moments had carried away five wagons and all those frightened people sheltering within to their deaths. Had that tornado started further away and had more time to increase in speed and dimension it would have certainly taken away the complete circle of wagons and all life within it, but as it was it had sliced away only a small section of the circle. No animals were killed or maimed but they all scattered in wild panic.

A heavy morning mist blanketed the prairie. People huddled in their wagons, too shocked and too cold to do otherwise. The dank ambient mist pervaded the interior of the wagons compounding the misery and the hopelessness. It was to be hoped the heavy mist would prevent the animals from wandering too far but until it lifted, the dead would lie out there among the wreckage.

The sun had well cleared the eastern horizon before its rays began taking effect but as it become lighter people began to move and mustered in little groups within their camps. Those within the circle west of the stricken camp could not see or hear anything. Looking to the north – and indeed it was difficult to determine any compass point without the instrument – visibility was only a few feet, but to the south it was lifting with a steady improvement of vision. It was out there somewhere that the victims were lying. And it was from that direction that seven horsemen riding abreast appeared from out of the mist. They stopped short of the ring of wagons circled to the west.

Silhouetted against an early sun struggling to penetrate the mist, they sat motionless in total silence; they were a ghostly apparition. A woman cried out, 'My God, no!'

The metallic and menacing sound of a dozen rifle bolts chattered almost simultaneously, and Charlie Roach's voice bellowed out the order, 'Hold your fire, goddamn it, hold your fire!' The rattle of the rifles made no impression upon the Indian horsemen: they conveyed no fear, no emotion.

Although he wore no ceremonial headdress, the man in the centre gave the impression of being their chief, but this was no ceremonial occasion. Or was it? He was clearly holding a bundle across his forearms, something like a doll in a white nightdress with indistinguishable red markings. He dismounted in the way Willie would often do, by throwing his right leg over the horse's head and sliding to the ground, the bundle still lying across his forearms. As he walked towards the puzzled group with the slow stately manner befitting a chieftain, a woman screamed and sobbing ran towards him. He did not smile or speak in sympathy, and almost ceremoniously he handed over the broken body of a small girl. Then he bowed and turned towards his horse. Charlie, his scouts and now a large assembly of migrants watched dumbfounded as the seven horsemen faded back into the mist as they had come. In that fleeting moment two peoples, light years apart, came together in a common bond.

Before the mist had fully lifted, two parties were organised, one to round up the animals and the other to search for the victims and salvage whatever possible from the wreckage. The women hurriedly prepared soup kitchens and whatever other improvised meals they could put together. Rounding up the animals was the least difficult of the tasks. The heavy mist had seen to that. They were found not too far away, banded together in their own groups. Finding the dead was a traumatic experience: the identification of close friends and loved ones who had set out with them on what was to have been a once-in-a-lifetime experience with the prospect of a better life at its journey's end.

They all should have been in Independence now. It was early afternoon. Instead, they were toiling through the wreckage of a wild and wind-scattered night. Small groups of men with picks and shovels began organising grave digging. Others had sawn falling tongues and neck yokes from the wrecked wagons to improvise crosses. Charlie would have none of it. He was the wagon boss and he would give the orders. They were less than ten miles from Independence and the bodies would be taken there where they would be officially recorded and afterwards given a Christian burial. On his orders, all wreckage was cleared up and any material that could be of use was salvaged. All canvasses recovered were turned into shrouds. Long timbers, such as base frames and falling tongues, were used as travois to be drawn by the now spare oxen.

All that could be burned was burned and the site left as tidy as possible. Charlie was always aware that the land he was passing through was Indian land and it was his policy to keep a good rapport with his fellow man.

Before noon on the following day, Charlie Roach, on horseback, led his followers to a site by the river just east of Independence. The help and kindness that went out to them was overwhelming. Among those bound for California there was a growing feeling to remain. Kansas City was growing. The outfitting post of Westport offered work for many – opportunities here were as boundless as the land itself. It was put to a vote and the majority decision was to remain. Charlie Roach had no choice but to settle here or return to St Louis. He could continue as a wagon master working out of Westport, but in his heart of hearts he felt that his wanderlust days were over. The vote, he knew, went in his favour and after all he now knew these people. They were all strangers to the people here but Charlie was no stranger to Independence and they would all need someone to help them settle in.

The overlanders on the Oregon and California Trails had many gauntlets to run and perhaps the least chronicled by historians is the tornado. Each year there are well over 700 in America, most of which are centred on the Midwest, the very lands over which the migrants had travelled. Perhaps there were not so many then as today. The problem of atmospheric pollution was not a factor then. The most favourable time for the wagon trains to set out was mid-April. This assured the animals good grazing during the spring and early summer months. From late July to early August the grass would be scorched.

The departure time was critical for another factor: snow. On those high mountains the weather could close in early and it was important to be over the passes before the snows fell; the importance of it was often a matter of life or death. The overlanders were left with no choice but to run the gauntlet of the tornados. But of all the hazards they faced, the least came from the Indians. The number-one killer must surely have been cholera. It has often been said that in the twenty-five years or so of that vast migration a grave was dug every mile of the way for a cholera victim. Sadly, this infectious disease was passed on to the indigenous population where often whole villages were wiped out.

Charlie bought the livery stables where he and Willie found Chuck and retained the two hands who had worked it for years. They were old acquaintances. Nearby he bought for himself a modest dwelling place. Often when asked if he had considered marriage, his reply was always the same, 'Many's the time ah have thought about it but then there jist ain't no woman that's gonna put up with me and mah tobacco and ah jist ain't figurin' on partin' with mah tobacco.'

The following year he found a plot of land at a bargain price that ran along the river rampart, and with it he started a gun club. Down the years Charlie had witnessed many horrific fatalities with guns, largely due to ignorance, and had heard stories of many more. When he first found the plot for sale he immediately visualised how it could be used, for it was too near the river for much else and the high rampart was ideal as a target area. It was a long-held dream of his that people should be educated in the use and safety of firearms as well as reading and writing. Charlie's gun club may well have been the first to be established in America but since official registration was not required then for such establishments, there is no way to confirm it.

He always waited and watched for Willie to appear. It was his hope that Willie and Chuck would turn up at his livery stable. To Charlie, Willie was always a son, but Willie never came.

Charlie Roach died in 1886 at the grand old age of eighty-five. It was the year of the formation of the Union Pacific Railroad Company and the end of the wagon-train era – Charlie's era. He had seen it in and he had seen it out.

CHAPTER 11

It was a night of torrential rain, but save for the occasional flash of forked lightning with its attendant crash of thunder, Willie McKay and his pioneering Norwegians slept comfortably in their wagons. On nights like this, Willie would occupy the spare, or more correctly the emergency, wagon. He would, when using this wagon, always feel somewhat privileged for he had it all to himself and once or twice in the comfort of the bunk the thought occurred to him that his employers may have felt that his suggestion to have an extra wagon was a cunning ploy. Early in the night Chuck had got himself lodged up tight against the leeside of the wagon and if it was not enough for Willie to have his sleep disturbed by the storm there was Chuck adding to it by snorting, pawing the ground and occasionally applying his rump to the sideboards.

Before turning in, it was generally agreed that in the morning they would make a later start. Progress so far had been excellent. They had covered around 250 miles, which was, as the navigators agreed, an average of almost twenty-three miles per day. Even Willie found that difficult to believe but had to accept: when all factors were considered, this was a small caravan and all Prairie Schooners, light and manoeuvrable, and they were all fit and healthy men. Willie was all too aware that this pace could not be maintained for much longer without a heavy price. It was time to rest themselves and their animals and carry out an inspection and refurbishment of their wagons. The storm had passed in the night leaving a sodden grassland in its wake and the area had escaped the tornado activity. Willie and his companions would never know the tragedy that had befallen Charlie Roach's train to the south of them.

After breakfast the following day, which they ate standing since the ground was too wet to sit on, Willie's first duty was to Chuck and his two mules. He made a fuss of them. They were all rubbed down and all their hooves inspected and any foreign matter removed. Then a thorough check of the oxen paying particular attention to their legs and hooves. He found no evidence of any impending lameness but suggested to Andur that he should take six out of harness for about a week and put in the reserves, spreading them throughout the wagons. He supervised the jacking up of each wagon, the removal of every wheel and greasing of each axle hub. Iron tyres were checked for firmness to the wheels. Neck yokes, single and double trees, bonnets and brakeblocks were all given an inspection. This, Willie suggested, would be carried out every other week, possibly on a Sunday, whereupon Einar remarked how akin it was to a "Captain's Sunday at sea" inspection. Oxen reserves would be changed over every alternative week.

The rest of the day, it was decided, would be given over to rest and recreation. Around mid-afternoon, a hunting party was formed to augment the food supply and provide an hour or two of light exercise. There were no buffalo in sight but that was not their quarry. That necessitated skinning and butchering and this was their rest day. A deer or antelope would require less work and a couple of turkeys would make a nice change to the menu.

Chuck had, from the start, taken kindly to Kristoffer. 'I'd say you're a man who has had a bit of experience with horses at some time,' remarked Willie, seeing both of them together, Chuck nosing into Kristoffer's pockets.

'Oh yes, we have always had a horse in the family and also, the family I stayed with in Scotland when I was a medical student had an Irish hunter of fifteen hands or thereabouts.'

'An Irish hunter, eh?' exclaimed Willie and without a further word he turned around and walked away in the direction of the spare wagon.

Kristoffer turned to Chuck wondering if he had caused offence but Chuck's eye had caught something of interest and he looked away over Kristoffer's shoulder emitting a low rumbling sound. Kristoffer turned to see Willie returning with a saddle and bridle over his shoulder, the reins trailing along the grass. Kristoffer, ruffling Chuck's mane, whispered to him with obvious excitement, 'It would appear, Chuck, we are going for a ride.'

Tentatively at first, Kristoffer walked Chuck in a wide circle around Willie, turning him to the left, then to the right. Satisfied with the response from the horse, he nudged him into a little trot and, as he began to feel more comfortable and still rotating round Willie who called out an instruction or two, he eased Chuck into a canter. Chuck was the horseman's dream, lively, yet gentle, and quick to respond. Kristoffer could feel the latent power he had under him but would familiarise with him a while more before giving him his head. He slacked off the reins, placed both hands lightly on the saddle horn and let Chuck canter around Willie a few more times. A call came from someone in the watching group which sounded like Arild Holtop, the only jester in the party. 'Getting a bit cocky now,' or words similar reached his ear followed by a burst of boisterous laughter.

Comfortable now with Chuck, he trotted him over to Willie for a few final words. 'You must be very proud of him.'

'I am,' said Willie.

'Tell me,' asked Kristoffer, 'what is the purpose of two long reins?'

'A good question; in Europe you ride for different reasons, as in the eastern states of America, but here in the West our horses are working horses. In Europe you do not tether your horses to a hitching rail as we do here. It's easy and quick to throw a few coils of rein around the post and as easy to release, and if the reins fall loose to the ground while the rider is away about his business the horse will just stand. I'll show you what I mean in a moment. Here we use what is known as split reins, two separate reins of a length that if they fall they must reach the ground with some to spare. Let's say, if I were riding out on the prairie, no one near me, and I fall off my horse, I will need that horse when I get up. Now I'll leave Chuck to explain it better than I can, so get him up to a gentle canter and drop the reins.' This Kristoffer did and Chuck came to a halt.

'I get the message,' called Kristoffer.

Willie called back, 'Stay there, I'll come over.' He walked to where Chuck was standing and patted his head and neck and said to Kristoffer with a grin, 'And that's how we do it out West. Now you both seem comfortable with each other so away you go. Keep to the short grass where you can and if you get up to a gallop watch out well ahead for foxholes.' Having said that, he took off his hat and hitting Chuck with it on the rump he yelled, 'Yahoo!' and Chuck, with Kristoffer on board, was off like the wind.

On Saturday, 15 May, as the last glow of sunset dipped below the plain, they made camp. Later, when the celestial bodies would appear in the night sky, sightings would be taken but drawing up the chart and other calculations would wait until the morrow. They had agreed mutually to break their own rule on the previous two Sundays, as they had continued their journey. Tomorrow they would rest save for a cursory inspection of the wagons and animals. Tonight, under a clear and starry sky and after an evening meal of some young buffalo steaks and a good red wine, they would relax. And perhaps, with a little persuasion, Anders Lein would provide a little music, accompanied by Brunduif Lillegard with his melodeon and Truls Gundersen on the harmonica.

Since leaving St Louis they had travelled, without incident, 670 miles. Their position at noon on that Sunday, 16 May, was thirty miles north of latitude 45 by fifty miles west of longitude 98 – well into the Dakotas. Another eight days, the navigators had reckoned, would put them at the intended position where they would find fording of the Missouri river. Then it was westward across North Dakota and Montana for 525 miles.

All was going well and there was every reason to be pleased. Mr Beamish had warned them unnecessarily of a possible encounter with the Pawnee. They met none, but then Pawnee territory was mainly south of the Platte and their course took them well away from that land. Arapaho and Cheyenne they found most agreeable and were allowed to pass across their lands without let or hindrance. Much exchange of goods took place between these visitors from a distant land and their hosts, for that is what they were. The Norwegians would return to their families with fine crafted figurines sculpted from the cottonwood and depicting braves on horseback and chieftains in all their finery; also leatherwork and embroidery and buffalo robes painted in patterns of many colours. The once tough hides were worked on by the women, scraped and dried in the sun and kneaded until soft and supple. These were not tourist trinkets for there were no tourists then, but the products of a proud and colourful people which they exchanged for tobacco and coffee, commodities very acceptable to the Indian. With beans, flour and dried fruit Kristoffer was parsimonious but tobacco, coffee and tea were abundant and ample stocks were set aside especially for trading.

Dr Eriksen had proved himself not only an able cook but the ideal purser. Among the sailors of the Royal Navy, dating back perhaps to the time of Henry VIII, the word "purser" somehow got corrupted into "pusser" and remains so until this day. Captain Oskarsen, unable to leave his ship in the harbour, with a little mischief, dubbed the doctor with the soubriquet "Pusser" Eriksen.

Under the guidance of Andur, Willie was making good progress with his navigation. A naturally keen sense of direction, born in him from his boyhood days when he wandered through the Sperrin Hills and honed by Charlie Roach over the years he was with him, was to his advantage. But mastery of the sextant and chronometer and plotting charts was to the credit of Captain Oskarsen. The first principles he now had; with practice would come the skill. When they crossed the river and turned westward, he would have nearly another month of practice and there would be the long trek back to St Louis. Yes, he would find the instruments there in some chandler's store and the mariners' almanacs. He would be well equipped and sufficiently skilled when the time came to take his next wagon train across the prairie. The only wagon master ever with the skills of a mariner – how impressive that would be to his clients; and to be able to inform them of the time changes as set by GMT.

'Willie,' called Andur, jolting him out of his daydream several days later, 'I have been discussing with Einar, a moment ago, about stopping, say at noon on Monday, so we could all spend the afternoon fishing or, for those who wish, shooting.' Willie was puzzled for a moment, for there was no evidence of any rivers or streams in the vicinity. 'Look here, Willie,' said Andur, pointing to one of the old faded maps with many folds, 'a day and a half from here we should come upon this little river which empties into the Missouri here, just a few miles south of where we are to make our crossing. Where it crosses our path we can stop for the rest of the day and when we proceed we can follow it at a more leisurely pace, either on its right or left bank; that is if the river is there at all for it appears to be without a name. We don't know how accurate this map is but we have made such good progress thus far I think we can ease off now and relax a little. Don't you think so?' Willie was in agreement, but it was a decision that was to cost them dear.

Willie's little wagon train, having followed the river with no name, arrived at its confluence with the Missouri at noon on 24 May 1841. The weather was close and sultry with a gathering overcast. It was a pleasant place where the rivers met and a good spot to stop and refresh themselves and water the animals. The navigators had intended to have been at the area before noon so they could determine the best part of the river for fording and take their sightings to fix their position.

Willie, Andur and Einar walked along the Missouri north of the confluence and found a likely place some 200 or 300 yards upriver. The banks either side were low, allowing a level entry and exit, but further back from the river on the west bank the ground rose slightly with some rocky hillocks immediately to the right of the wagons' path. *What an ideal place for an ambush*, mused Willie. The river was wide and reasonably shallow with a good sandy bed that obviously built up over the years. It looked sound enough but the conclusive test was to wade in, which Willie did, taking a sturdy fallen branch with him. The branch, or pole, would serve a three-fold purpose: firstly for testing the density of the sand, secondly for depth-gauging the water, and thirdly as an anchorage for Willie.

Where the water was deepest he hacked a notch with his knife. Satisfied with his tests, Willie returned to discuss his findings with the other two. A rough measurement of the pole suggested that at its deepest the water would not rise much above the axle and if it did the Yankee Bed innovation would prove adequate in preventing water damage. The sandy river bed proved dense enough.

'What do you think, Willie?' Andur asked.

'I think it will be all right. I also think this place is a regular crossing for horses. Some hoof prints on the far side and we are in Sioux territory now. Yeh, we'll cross here and keep a sharp lookout.'

Their position then was as follows: latitude 47 degrees north, longitude 101 degrees west, about fifteen miles north of where Mandan now stands. By mid-afternoon, as the wagons were lined up and prepared to cross, the sky had clouded over and the weather become oppressive. Local electric storms were imminent. Should they go on or wait until the storm passed? If they were to wait and the rain was prolonged and heavy there was every possibility of the river rising. They decided to make haste.

Wagons and animals were assembled on the east bank at the place Willie and the captains had decided upon. Their wagon master ensured that all firearms were loaded and kept close at hand. He then placed each man to his allotted position. Andur and Einar would ride in the first wagon with the mules in tow. Eriksen would follow with the chuck wagon. As each wagon reached the opposite bank the driver was instructed to clear the area for those following. Willie stressed the importance of this drill. After the chuck wagon the other six would follow, with the last three wagons taking in tow two of the reserve oxen. The wagons would move in line astern, but spread slightly, so that the wheels of the following wagons would not travel along the ruts made by those in front. Once in the water the oxen were to be kept moving. Willie emphasised the importance of being alert. His orders on every detail of the crossing were concise. When everyone was ready, Willie on Chuck entered the water. Through Chuck he could feel the river bed give slightly but there was no cause for concern.

Overhead the black ominous cloud, unable to bear its weight much longer, was beginning to discharge its first heavy isolated droplets. Andur glanced up anxiously at the incipient storm and urged his oxen into the water. Tentatively the others followed. Their anxious wagon master charged back calling for more haste, his horse churning out sprays of water. 'Keep them moving,' Willie repeatedly called. 'Give them the whip! Move, move!'

Above, the sky gave a low rumbling growl, a warning of its impending anger. The scene suddenly got confused and noisy. The lead wagon soon made the opposite bank with Eriksen and Lein and Lillegard close behind. Three wagons safely on terra firma. The remaining five, making good headway, were somewhere in mid-river with their guide hustling them on. With his left hand resting on the back of his saddle he looked over his shoulder and, seeing five men standing on the bank, he wheeled his horse around and waved his hat in a form of salute when his smile turned to anger at their evident complacency. He spurred Chuck towards them with great urgency, spray rising in every direction, and within seconds he was with them. 'Your rifles, where are your rifles?' Olsen in the fourth wagon was just landing with the others close behind. 'Get back in your wagons,' Willie shouted, 'and get your rifles!'

Stunned by this sudden outburst and not being soldiers trained to react to sharp commands, they tarried, and those were the last furious words they heard from Willie McKay.

Overhead, jagged tongues of forked lightning ripped the heavens apart with the sound as of a thousand sheets of glass being shattered across a troubled sky, and an acrid smell of brimstone assailed the nostrils. The torrential rain came swiftly. The war cry that arose from the other side of the hill mingled with the crashing thunder and threw the pioneers into utter confusion.

If the attack had been planned to take advantage of the elements it was done with deadly cunning. It was not a large party but they operated as if they were, which added to the confusion of their victims. They came screaming in from two sides, those from the south just ahead of the group coming in from the north. The unfortunate unarmed men scrambled for their wagons. Willie spurred Chuck for the shelter of the rocks, simultaneously drawing his rifle from the saddle holster. Behind the rocks he gripped Chuck's nostrils, twisting his head towards the side as he wanted him to lie down, and speaking to him gently as possible, 'Down, Chuck, down, boy.' Chuck was trained to this drill as a foal by his first owner whom Willie had never met and to whom he was now so grateful, as he was to the owner of the livery stable in Independence for giving him a demonstration of this skill at time of sale.

Under cover he wasted no time in picking off the enemy. He could see with horror that his dear friends on the riverbank were now beyond help and those still in the water were overwhelmed. His mules, he could see, were being dragged away by a painted warrior on horseback and the oxen were being slaughtered. It was now left to him to defend himself and poor Chuck lying beside him, his sad face looking into his friend's. 'They'll never take you, Chuck,' he promised, laying his Colt revolver on the rock beside him. 'The murderous bastards will never take either of us.'

They crept up on him from behind and as he swung around to shoot them others gained ground in front and through his rain-drenched eyes visibility was blurred. Accurate reloading could not be maintained at this speed and in such conditions, and when his rifle breech jammed he continued dropping them with his revolver. It was hand-to-hand now and the last assailant he shot before the chamber emptied he met with a barrel into the Indian's face as he squeezed the trigger. The man was lifted and slapped hard against the ground by the force of the big .45 calibre bullet, the back of his head blown away.

The next man had the empty revolver smashed into his face and he threw the weapon at the next one coming, who dodged it. Willie was fighting with a madman's fury. A frightened horse scrambled heavily onto all fours and reared up on his hind legs, pawing the air with his front hooves, his rain-soaked hide seen to shine against a jagged flash of lightning. And Chuck squealed a wild and frightened squeal. A man's arm-span is commensurate with his height and Willie McKay stood six feet three inches. The man who dodged his revolver raced on at him but Willie blocked the arm that raised the club and grabbing his long plaits either side of his head, drew him towards him with terrifying strength, bringing his forehead down into the smaller man's war-painted face, and he fell like he was pole-axed with his face severely smashed.

Again, Chuck reared up squealing, his nostrils flared. Willie turned towards him and in that moment of distraction was clubbed. He was on the ground but did not feel the ground. There was a buzzing in his head and a myriad of stars danced before his eyes. He must get up but his body would not respond. He knew he was not dead and somewhere in the deeper reaches of his mind his fear was of being scalped before he died, and there was Chuck; he had to reach out to his faithful Chuck, but there was only the buzzing and the stars . . . and then they were gone.

Downriver a mile or so, a squirrel busily preening itself by the riverbank stiffened instantly into a statue-like figure to gaze intently at an object in the water which caught its attention. Bobbing in the dark swollen water, the feet touching the reeds, was the body of a man, face down and arms outstretched. Two arrow shafts in close proximity to each other protruded from his back. They had penetrated deeply into the heart and the victim had died instantly. The body bobbed and turned slowly, touching the reeds where a curious little creature sat transfixed. Then it floated away in a slow rotary movement towards the middle of the river to lodge momentarily against a sandbank and to drift away amongst other flotsam from that accursed happening. The squirrel, its curiosity sated, returned to its preening. Branduif Lillegard, mountaineer, explorer and writer, had left his last work unfinished.

The storm clouds that had hung over the place a short while before had drifted far to the east. The peals of thunder sounded like distant and random gunfire. A struggling rainbow arched the river where such a short while before a fierce battle had raged underneath a low and angry sky. The golden willows that lined the riverbanks leaned heavily towards the dark and turbulent water and their rain-laden leaves wept. Nature itself was in mourning for the innocent victims of that dastardly and fiendish act that had despoiled a picturesque and peaceful land.[1]

---

1 Despite a thorough search by the Morton County Library, Mandan, North Dakota, no record was found of such an incident on that stretch of the river. However, as it was a small wagon train and war parties rampaged frequently along the banks of the upper Mississippi and the Missouri at that time, it may not have attracted much interest and passed unnoticed. It is reasonable to assume that the attempted crossing could have been made at that point for it would have put them on a westerly course towards Montana and their intended destination, known then as the Gates of the Mountain's Wilderness, about ten miles north of what is now Helena.

In August 1805, on their homeward journey from the Pacific coast, the Lewis and Clark expedition split their party into two groups to meet up at a predetermined point further east. Lewis took the northern route while Clark went south. Unknown to Lewis, he passed within miles of one of the world's richest goldfields. Lewis and Clark were not interested in America's mineral wealth so the mountain would keep its secret for another fifty-nine years.

Had Captain Oskarsen's valise been recovered from the wreckage and the sealed envelope opened, it may well have thrown light on their intended mission and how one sea captain became the prime mover in a project that caught the interest of Washington officials.

In 1864 a small band of gold prospectors who called themselves "The Georgians", namely John Crabb, Robert Stanley and John Cowen, down on their luck from the Californian gold rush and subsequent Nevada gold and silver days, searched in vain for many months in the Bitterroot Mountains. Before returning to Virginia City in defeat, they made one last attempt at panning in Alder Gulch in a place called Prickly Pear Valley. Soon gold nuggets appeared in their pans and Alder Gulch became Last Chance Gulch. In the city of Helena, Montana's capital, the main street is aptly known as Last Chance Gulch.

CHAPTER 12

They had no eyes. Like ghosts they floated in front of him. There were men and women there, and children, whose faces would come close to him and quickly fade away. Either side a woman leaned over him. The one to his right was holding some kind of receptacle which contained cold, refreshing, life-giving water; he knew for he was aware of it, cold and invigorating, as the angel on his left applied it to his burning brow. But these could not be angels for they were Indians.

It was nearly twenty-seven years since he lay in a similar position with his head resting in the crook of someone's arm while water was poured over his forehead, but that was before recall. Was he being baptised again and into some kind of Indian heaven? Yes, that was it, there was a battle and he died and now he was being made ready for an Indian Valhalla, some celestial palace in the sky where heroes who died in battle feasted for eternity.

No, Willie McKay was not going to any happy hunting ground and he began to rise but was restrained. Then a voice broke the silence saying, 'Stop fighting, we are your friends and we are trying to help you.' The voice was calm and reassuring and he stopped struggling. The face that spoke was looking down at him. But where the eyes should be there were only two dark holes and this confused and frightened him for he was unable to shake off this strange sight.

Above him the poles of the tipi came together with the sheeting firmly secured to them, and there was a round aperture at the top where the poles met. Nearer ground level, at a height easily manageable, the buffalo hide sheeting folded back making three narrow openings of about six feet in length providing ventilation to the interior. They were placed at equal distances around the wall and through one of these vents a shaft of sunlight beamed in, splashing its golden hue against the opposite wall. He lay facing the light beam and in his confused and dazed state he could see that it crossed the foot of his bed almost parallel to the floor.

Whilst the ghostly apparitions floated around him, he began to make an exercise of it all. If the sunlight was entering at that low angle then the sun was getting low in the sky: it must be late afternoon and he was facing west. *If a man can figure out like that*, he thought, *he cannot be dead*. He must not allow himself to fall asleep. There were questions to ask. Who are these people and how did he come to be here? And he became restless again and the man who spoke as a friend gripped his shoulder in a firm and friendly grip, and he relaxed and lay gazing at the myriad of dust particles suspended in the sunbeam, together with little clouds of pale blue smoke that emanated from the burning of some heavenly scented essence that took him back to the little chapel on the Glen Road and the smell of incense at the Sunday Mass. And he drifted down into the world of sleep, to heal, with two Indian angels tending his wounded brow.

Willie was awakened by a soft gentle tapping of fingers on the back of his right hand. When he slowly came round the girl was smiling down at him, beckoning him to sit up. As he raised himself into an uncomfortable, jack-knifed position she piled several rolled-up rugs behind his back, indicating to sit up more straight, and when he did she placed another soft rug between his head and the light wickerwork bedhead. She then spread a large additional rug over his knees and tucked the edges in around him, smiled and was gone. Only then did it occur to Willie that he had seen her eyes.

Willie had been suffering from concussion, the effects of which were now easing off. He had slept a long and profound sleep which may have been due in part to some local herbal remedy administered to him the day before. His memory, too, was returning: the thunder storm, the brutal hand-to-hand fight with the fierce war-painted fiends. Yes, of course, that was how he came to be here. His friends, all dead. *And why haven't they killed me?* he thought. *They're saving me for something special, and where are they all? If I am a prisoner then why am I not bound hand and foot? No, I can't be a prisoner. The one who spoke English: he said they were my friends. They were trying to help me. Where are they now?* Willie was strangely alone, confused and frightened, and his mind, like his eyes due to a confused brain, was playing him false.

From the outside of the tipi he heard female voices approaching and two girls entered. One was the girl who had awakened him and helped him up. She was carrying a bowl and spoon and her companion had a plate or tray with what looked to Willie like chunks of bread. The bowl, spoon and plate were of carved wood. Steam, and an appetising smell, emanated from the bowl and Willie mused on the idea of a wooden bowl being well suited to contain the heat. Both the girls appeared friendly and both were smiling. The taller and older one, the one carrying the bowl, knelt by the low wickerwork bed near the patient: the other walked around and took her position opposite, just as they had when they bathed and dressed his wound. The one on his right dipped the spoon into the bowl and offered it to him. It tasted excellent and his smile and a nod expressed his approval. She smiled and said, 'Lo wota,' which meant soup or soft food and to eat it. He needed no further encouragement. He was ravenous and could not remember how long it was since his last meal, or what he had eaten.

'Good,' Willie acknowledged, nodding in appreciation. 'Buffalo, yes?' pointing to the contents of the dish.

The girls looked perplexed, then the younger one realised what he was asking. 'No, no buffalo . . . tahca.' The girls made signs by putting their hands to the sides of their heads and wiggling their fingers repeating, 'Tahca, tahca.'

'Ah, deer,' Willie called out in a voice near to a shout and he raised his hands to his head in comic imitation of the girls and, forgetting his injury, caused a minor commotion when his thumb struck the wound. Instant peals of laughter burst from the girls as they repeated 'deer'. Willie took the wooden spoon in his own right hand and his left grabbed a fistful of dark brown bread and, dipping the spoon in the soup, said, 'Deer good; tahca good, too,' and ate heartily. And he thought how long it was since he had heard the ring of girlish laughter and how refreshing to the ear it was.

When the collation was finished the girls rose to leave with the empty dishes. Willie delayed them to ask if he was a prisoner, indicating in sign language with his hands outheld as if bound. They looked towards each other for an answer, speaking quickly in their own language, and the meaning of his question became apparent. The older girl put down the empty dishes and indicated a negative reply by moving her left hand, palm uppermost, in a sideways motion, saying, 'No, no, no.' "No" seemed to be the universally accepted negative reply. Opening all, or nearly all, the lappets, she indicated the outside world and that he was free to go, and smiling she repeated the words several times over, 'No wókaške,'[1] and closing the lappets she indicated in sign language that he must sleep. It was clear that he was no prisoner; when well enough he was free to go – but where?

It was impossible for Willie to know how long he had slept or what time of day, or even what day it was. He had not as yet dwelled on the fate of his comrades or how the loss would affect his life. He had lost his mules and very likely his loyal and faithful Chuck. St Louis was a long way back and

---

1 Wókaške: prison or jail.

without his mules and Chuck and his provisions, including the Hawken rifle, it would be impossible, utterly impossible. Willie McKay was alone, further north than he had ever been and a stranger in a world not of his choosing.

Sombre thoughts veiled his mind, making any constructive thinking impossible. It was while in this state that a lappet was flung open with some degree of authority and a large buxom woman, stone faced and settled well into middle years, barged in. She walked round his bed, her eyes fixed on his, and knelt on the left side where she could see the wound. Willie was already sitting in a propped-up position and without further preliminaries she started to remove the dressing.

Willie was baffled at how this harridan of a woman could be so gentle in her ministrations. From the hide she carried, she produced a small pouch and took from it a soft spongy material with which she wiped the wound. It was cold and it stung. Following that she did something that astonished Willie. She fixed his head in a forward position and, putting one hand under his chin and the other on his crown, fixed his head so his eyes would look straight ahead. Then she put an index finger vertically by the side of the left eye and said in a manner as to indicate a question, 'Wanyanka?' while pointing directly ahead where he should be looking.

Willie, knowing it was futile to speak, nodded in the affirmative. She moved the finger into positions backwards and forwards of his eye, repeating, 'Wanyanka?' and repeatedly Willie indicated yes or no. She walked around his bed and repeated the actions with his right eye and again he answered yes or no to the question, 'Wanyanka?' Willie had learned to say "See" in Lakota. She then made him close his eyes, extend an arm full length and bring the index finger slowly to touch the tip of his nose. She carried out a series of such tests with exactness and it was clear to Willie that she was testing his coordination, but what baffled him was her knowledge of what he thought was exclusively the white man's medicine. Having concluded her checks she packed up the contents of her bag, patted him on the hand and proceeded to leave. In sign language he stopped her by pointing to the wound on his forehead and gesticulating that it may require re-bandaging, but she was not in agreement; Willie's wound would heal itself.

No sooner had the medicine woman gone than the lappet was again flung open and a young man of somewhere around Willie's age walked in. He was dressed in buckskin tunic and trousers, both fringed. On his feet were moccasins of the same soft buckskin. They appeared to Willie to be the most comfortable footwear he had ever seen. His raven-black hair hung over his shoulders and fell down his chest in two plaits which were held in place by a brightly coloured headband. He moved across the lodge noiselessly and with the easy flow and gracefulness of a mountain lion. Avoiding Willie's gaze, he moved to where a pile of rugs were and began to rummage through them.

Willie's eyes did not leave him and he thought how a body so lithe as his and in shoes as soft could sneak up on a man and kill him with ease. When the surprise visitor had selected a rug, he turned towards Willie, smiling and rolling up the rug, and came to the bedside, placed the rug on the floor and sat on it, folding his legs in front of him in an easy manner. Looking directly at Willie, he tucked the edges of the rug underneath him and when comfortable he spoke.

'How are you feeling today?'

And Willie answered, 'I feel fine, thanks to the care I have had here, but I now think I should be going.'

'Where?' asked the young Indian, and he held up a hand to Willie in gesticulation. 'Don't answer that.'

'You speak very good English, very good. Who are you?'

'You have the good fortune to have been rescued by braves of the Lakota Sioux. You are the only survivor.' He paused for a moment to allow it to sink in.

'I know,' said Willie, 'I know.'

'The renegade who struck you was too close to strike with the full force of his club and when the club struck you he was already dead.' Willie looked at him as if he knew what he would say next. And the answer came, 'Yes, I shot him through the head.'

'You saved my life; I cannot ever repay you.'

'Unfortunately we were not in time to help your friends.'

'They were good men,' reflected Willie, his eyes staring at the buffalo robe that covered him, 'great men.'

'You will avenge their deaths,' the young Sioux assured him. Again Willie looked him in the eye, a questioning look, and the Sioux answered, 'You are in honour bound, you will avenge.'

Willie threw off the soft buffalo rug that served as a blanket and walked around the lodge somewhat shaky at first. His head still ached and he felt a little dizzy. His visitor picked up a seat similar to the one he was using and bade him sit down opposite himself. When his visitor saw he was comfortable he began. 'You have remarked on my good English and you ask who I am. There is a Catholic mission far south from here in the home of the Oglala. It was run by teaching Fathers, the Jesuits. They taught us well.'

'Then you are a Christian?' Willie asked.

'At the mission we were all baptised into the Catholic faith but I still live as my ancestors lived. I am a Lakota but I learned many things at that little mission. They taught us wisely, those Fathers in their black robes, and I always try to pass on some of their teachings to my people.'

'Are you the chief?' asked Willie.

The Lakota smiled, 'No, I am not the chief; you have yet to meet him.' Willie marvelled at the man's command of English and wondered how long he had been with the Jesuits and what course took him there.

The Sioux continued. 'My name is Tateyanpa Caksi which means to fly with the speed of the wolf—'

'I like that,' interrupted Willie.

'I like it, too, but when we were baptised we were asked if we would each like to adopt a Christian name. It was our choice, we did not have to accept.'

'And what name did you choose?' Willie asked.

The Sioux smiled and held out his hand in introduction, 'You can call me John.'

'And I am William, but you can call me Willie,' and a friendship was established.

The lappet was flung open again and the intrusion could not have been better timed. Two men, evidently elders, entered through the opening, followed by the chief. John stood up and raised his right hand in salutation. Willie followed for it seemed the only thing to do. His height caused him a feeling of awkwardness and in the presence of the chief, whom he towered over, he felt somewhat embarrassed. Regardless of the difference in height, the chief was an impressive figure. His weather-beaten face was the epitome of health. It also told the story of a man who had enjoyed happiness and endured sadness. His almost black sloe-eyes seemed to Willie to pierce into the very thoughts of his mind. From a beautifully soft and decorated leather headband stood a plume of soft white feathers. Above the cloud of white down, a column of black eagle feathers, some with white tips, fanned out above the forehead and trailed away to the nape of the neck. From the temples hung two silver fox tails which reached down to his chest along with his two plaits, as black as the eagle feathers that adorned his crown. His arms and chest were bare, save for a sleeveless jacket or jerkin and armlets of soft decorated leather on his upper arms. His jerkin, trousers and moccasins were of tan buckskin. His two lieutenants were similarly attired but without the elaborate headdress.

He studied Willie for a moment, a smile playing around those sharp eyes, then turned to the others and spoke as if asking a question, which provoked some laughter. John interpreted the joke to Willie who was looking a bit sheepish. 'Chief Two Rivers asks if you talk down to the trees.' Willie smiled and felt relaxed; the man had a sense of humour.

Chief Two Rivers then looked straight at Willie and asked, 'Your name?' The reply was Willie McKay. 'McKay,' the chief mumbled, 'McKay, haw, Scotsman?' and he poked a finger into Willie's midriff.

Willie tactfully stifled the word "no" and answered in one word, 'Irishman.'

The chief paused in thought and continued, drawling the exclamation, 'Haw! Scotsman, Irishman, hawl same. Good warrior man,' and with a smile gave Willie a light friendly punch in the chest and turned to confer briefly with his elders. It was clear to Willie that he was the object of the discussion and when they had reached an agreement it was left to John to do the explaining.

In perfect English he told Willie that the chief and the elders had conferred upon him his Lakota name. 'Under a fierce thunderstorm you fought that renegade band with the fury of a mountain lion. You came, it would seem, with thunder and now your Lakota name will be Wakinyan which means Thunderbird.' Willie smiled his approval and John continued his translation. 'Chief Two Rivers and my elders are pleased you accept your Lakota name and later, when you are well again, they hope you will join with them in smoking the calumet.' Willie knew nothing of the Sioux language but he knew that the calumet was the peace pipe.

The wagons all lay on their sides; those that had reached the west bank had their canvas bonnets ripped away and their precious contents scattered and strewn along the bank. Only the downpour had saved them from the torch and disintegration to ashes, but then that may have been a better outcome. Eight new Prairie Schooners, only a few weeks in service, the proud workmanship of James Harvey and Sons, artisans, had been reduced to trash on a river fording. Small mammals and birds fed on the stale food and decomposing vegetable matter from the chuck wagon that had been Dr Eriksen's personal pride. Torn bits of carcasses, that only a few days before had been fine gentle oxen, lay putrid under swarms of flies.

Of the five wagons that straddled the river, each causing a small dam as the water built up behind and curled around them in ripples to flow on its way, little was left intact. The watertight Yankee Beds within, designed to preserve their contents, had been smashed open by axe-wielding maniacs, and their contents either strewn around the interior of the wagon or pitched into the river. The whole scene was pitiful.

'Why?' asked Willie, hunkered by the riverbank gazing vacantly into the water. 'Why?' he repeated several times, but John, standing beside him, remained silent. No words of consolation would help and he was only too aware of the pain it was causing Willie and others close to himself. But that would wait.

'They all lie west of the Missouri, over yonder.' John spoke in solemn tones as he pointed in the direction where Willie's friends lay. 'That is, those we could find; there were nine.'

'Nine?' queried Willie. 'There were twelve, three missing to the river.' John nodded in silence. 'There were five on the bank here.'

'Four,' corrected John. 'The river was rising and a body lying close to the water's edge would have slipped away.' In the heat of his battle, Willie would not have seen Brunduif Lillegard fall into the river with two arrow shafts deeply embedded in the middle of his back. 'It is small consolation, my friend, but at least the one the river took did not lose his scalp.'

Willie shot a fierce glance at John and uncoiled himself from his hunkered position like a tensioned spring that had suddenly been released. 'Scalped?'

John nodded, 'Yes, Willie, scalped.'

Willie stood staring silently at the ground for a moment. 'Scalped,' he repeated and John saw the knuckles of his clenched fists turn white. 'Captain Oskarsen, Captain Andersen, Dr Eriksen, Anders Lein, Brunduif Lillegard.' He spoke their names the way a roll of honour is solemnly called for those who have fallen in battle. And he raised his head and asked, 'Wind of the Wolf, did you kill them all?'

'Only three besides what you killed,' was the reply. 'The others fled. There are about thirty of them. They range north-west of here, towards the land of the Crow. They are mainly renegades from the Crow with a few Comanche and one or two of our own.' He paused a moment. 'What *were* our own. For more than two moons they have savaged white men and red men alike without any end purpose, just wanton destruction. With your small train, they most likely thought you were traders heading our way and their guess was they would find rich pickings. We have a party ready but it is Chief Two Rivers' wish that we wait until you are well.'

It was an invitation Willie would not refuse. He looked down at the ground with a wry little smile then at his Sioux friend and spoke softly and with menace, 'Wind of the Wolf, we will kill them all.'

CHAPTER 13

The pinto mare was not his favourite choice. She was small, not much above the pony class, and she moved at a gait uncomfortable to Willie. On her credit side she could wheel and turn quickly and respond to the rider's instruction by his body movements thus leaving the rider almost hands free – a necessity when the rider is engaged in battle. The flat thin saddle was at first peculiar but he appreciated the purpose for it and soon settled into it, or rather onto it. The one important adjustment Willie required, if he and his Indian pony were to work in concert, would be a pair of stirrups to accommodate his long legs. This was easily accomplished by two of the women. The stirrups were completely of hide – no metal whatsoever was incorporated in them – and they were designed so the rider could slip his feet free from them instantly and with ease. Another modification that was cheerfully carried out to his specification was a shallow leather pouch between three and four inches in diameter and a depth of only two or three inches. This was fixed firmly to the outside of the right stirrup with the open end facing the rider at the correct angle.

Willie McKay was no exponent of the bow and arrow nor were clubs and lances his forte. His Hawken rifle and revolver were now gone. If only he had a broadsword like those carried by cavalry officers. It was the lack of the latter and the inability to use the others with any degree of dexterity that prompted the idea for the pouch to be fitted to the stirrup.

As far back as he could remember, Maghera had always been a garrison town and some of the English soldiers stationed there often, for recreation, practised what was in Robin Hood's England a very formidable weapon for hand-to-hand fighting: the quarterstaff. The local boys could not but be impressed by this manly art of combat. The practice of this form of martial art, often conducted in the open, was impressive and entertaining: thrust and parry and block. And when the attacker would go in low to sweep away the opponent's legs, the opponent would skip over the stave with breathtaking timing and bring his in across the shoulders of his crouched adversary. Whatever hardwood the soldiers' quarterstaffs were cut from, the local youths had no problem in finding a good alternative, the ash, which grew in abundance. Young straight saplings, locally known as ash plants, were cut, stripped and polished and left to dry and quarterstaff duelling, at which Willie McKay excelled, was no longer exclusive to the British Army.

On the plain where they mustered, the scene was one of awesome splendour. Horsemen assembled from several points, moving at an easy pace towards the focal point where the chief and two elders sat motionless on their horses. Sixty, perhaps more, warriors prepared for battle, each man armed with a weapon or weapons of his choice. Most carried a short bow and a quiver full of arrows slung over their backs, others had rifles. Whether archers or riflemen, all were equipped with an ancillary weapon such as a club or lance. Every man carried a knife sheathed in a leather scabbard worn either on a belt around the waist or strapped to his bare leg. They rode in little groups, some singing, some talking light-heartedly, perhaps exchanging jokes. Here and there, a high-spirited horse would break into a little dance to the incessant drumbeat, and the rider, swaying easily on his back, would allow him to settle down in his own time when he had had his little jig.

The rising sun cast its blessing over the parade ground, bathing all in a soft light. A little distance away from where the warriors gathered, Willie sat astride his pinto. He was placed there by John and instructed not to move until he came for him. Watching the proceedings, a strange farrago of feelings gripped his senses: elation, that emotion akin to pride, anticipation mingled with a pinch of apprehension fused into one heady mixture, and a tingling sensation ran down his spine. This day he was not just watching a show being performed for his entertainment. In this performance he was a member of the cast waiting in the wings for his call. On this day he would avenge the massacre of his friends. How grateful he was to this warrior chieftain for allowing him to join the battle and also for realising that it could be the healing of his spiritual wounds. And he would remember this day always: the colourful spectacle taking place before him, the wheeling and neighing of the horses, their snortings, the smell of horse and those brightly coloured saddle blankets; the ease of the young warriors as they marshalled around their chieftain, the tan bodies further irradiated by the glow of the morning sun. Many years from now he would tell his grandchildren, perhaps back in Ireland, of the day he rode into battle with the Sioux.

This was the stuff that stories are made of and the children would listen wide-eyed but then they would not believe him for it was only a story, a good story told by an old man, and old men never go to far-off places or do exciting things; and old men were never young men!

From the assembly, one horseman broke rank and galloped towards Willie. His rifle lay across his back, the barrel protruding above his left shoulder and angled between head and shoulder; a lance resting in its scabbard hanging from the right side of the lightweight saddle stood vertically to somewhere level with the warrior's head, with a coloured pendant flowing from it. His coloured headband sported one long feather, nothing as ostentatious as that of the chief and his elders. His torso was naked except for brightly coloured leather bracelets on the wrists and upper arms, and tight-fitting buckskin trousers which came to just above the calf left the rest of the legs bare. On his feet were tight-fitting moccasins. Around his waist was a belt to which was attached a scabbard and knife. This implement was held close to the body on the right side. Unlike the renegades they were going after, he wore no warpaint nor did his fellow warriors, and Willie wondered if this was an act of respect for him or whether it was not the custom of the Sioux. A few times on the Santa Fe with Charlie Roach he had an engagement with the Navaho or Apache and they always looked fearsome with their warpaint. This man, who now pulled up his horse with great deliberation in front of him, looked no less fearsome, even with the absence of paint. Willie could have been forgiven had he thought this was a different man from the quiet-spoken educated fellow who, not three weeks before, had sat with him in the tipi.

'Follow me, Willie, and stay close,' Wind of the Wolf called over the sound of the drumbeat, that had now reached a crescendo, and the clamour of the entire gathering. Willie touched the pinto's flanks with his heels and moved up to John's left. 'We have a long ride ahead of us, Willie,' John called in a voice loud enough to penetrate the clamour. 'Have you brought enough food?' As he asked he cast a keen eye over the pouches slung across Willie's saddle. Willie assured him that his supply was ample.

'Here I have a packet with pemmican[1] and in this one jerky[2] and here is water,' tapping each in turn. It was the chief's oldest daughter who had packed his provisions and Wind of the Wolf did not hesitate to drive home to Willie that she was noticing the tall white man.

'Red Wing nice Lakota girl, eh?' and he threw Willie a knowing glance.

'She sure is,' replied Willie, 'she sure is.' And there the conversation ended for they had joined the war party.

---

1 Pemmican: meat paste, fat and other ingredients made into a paste.
2 Jerky: strips of dried meat.

John guided Willie to the front of the gathering. There they turned to face the chief and elders and when salutes were exchanged, John issued commands accompanied by signals with his right hand and they were on their way. John, or Wind of the Wolf, was evidently the officer in charge and a capable leader he appeared to be.

As they rode at a steady gait, braves would canter up to Willie to welcome him and by sign language would congratulate him on his choice of weapon. He appeared to be much at home amongst his new-found friends and was comfortable with his long pole tucked in the crook of his right arm and the end resting in the pouch by his right foot. Several of the braves would speak to him as if asking a question and when he turned to John for advice he was told they were asking his name. 'Say Wakinyan, that is your name now.'

Pointing a forefinger to his chest, Willie called out, 'Wakinyan,' and in sign language they all appeared to approve. They fell back a little to discuss among themselves this giant who was riding with them with this ridiculously long pole tucked in the crook of his arm.

Then, left to his thoughts for a while, it suddenly struck him and he said to himself, *Hi, what's all this Wakinyan? That's not my name, my name is Willie McKay, William John McKay from Falaleigh, in the Barony of Loughinsholin.* In his thoughts he made great emphasis of it, almost speaking it aloud, lest he should lose all sense of reality. Already he had lost trace of day, or time. *These guys are clever. God, why didn't I see it before? They are sucking me in; they want me for some sort of ridiculous object, a laughing stock. What was that about the chief's daughter? That's it, I see it all now. I am Willie McKay and I'll play along with their game and I'll help them out with their little war and avenge my friends and that's it, finish. Back to St Louis if I've got to walk it.*

'We should be joined by some company soon,' John called across, and before Willie could respond he had turned and was calling out orders quite incomprehensible to the Irishman. They had been riding not more than an hour by Willie's reckoning. There was a change of behaviour with the troop that disconcerted him, and spotting this John turned to him and explained. 'Our scouts have informed us that your friends and ours,' he emphasised these last words with unconcealed sarcasm, 'have strengthened their numbers, mainly Crow and some Gros Ventre, but we will surprise them with our numbers and our timing for they do not know we are coming.'

Willie had never heard of Gros Ventre. *God, how many more tribes are there in these parts?* he thought.

The land over which they travelled was not flat where the horizon can be seen in any direction. It was undulating and sometimes hilly. Ahead lay a range of these low hills through which their cavalcade must pass and lying some miles ahead of them was a break in the range to which Wind of the Wolf was leading his troupe. Still a long way off, he attracted Willie's attention and pointed to a far hill. There a puff of smoke was rising followed by another. The two men looked at each other knowingly; no word passed between them. The patter between the warriors livened, a few gave a loud whoop or two followed by the others and all began waving rifles and lances, and to the delight of the entire troupe, Willie, whooping with the best of them, brandished his eight-foot pole about his head. Willie knew how to win friends and influence people.

From an outcrop in the canyon the reinforcements charged whooping and brandishing their weaponry to be met with similar greetings from the oncoming party, and their sounds echoed around the canyon. The meeting was light and carefree, just friends having a reunion. Conflict was taken lightly by these people. Willie was being pointed out and discussed much and the new arrivals, on their horses, jockeyed for position to slap him on the back, shake his hand or jest in their language about his choice of weaponry. He would retract what he had spoken a short while ago. These people he could easily identify with. And he was growing accustomed to their adulation.

A brief council was held by the leaders and when a decision was reached the followers were informed. The renegades, according to the reconnaissance party, had been located less than a day's ride to the north-west. They were some fifty in number but well outnumbered by over two to one, and a surprise attack would prove a decisive factor. The two parties, now merged, would at midday stop for food and rest, then continue until nightfall and within close range of the enemy rest up, keeping to the south of them. With the rising sun behind them they would spring their attack from two sides. Their scouts had provided them with a good intelligence report on the local geography and it seemed they were camped by a river on the north side of some low-lying hills; it was a vulnerable position and one that little thought had been given to. If only the brigands were to remain there, this would be a gift to the avenging parties.

Wind of the Wolf and Red Hand left their parties well south of the hill. Willie, green to war-party tactics, was to remain with the main party. Only the two leaders would go on foot to reconnoitre the area to the north. If their scouts' information was correct, the renegades' encampment lay a short distance away from the slope and south of the river where it bent. They would also have to locate the position, or positions, of their horses, most of which were stolen, for it was their intention to take them all. And there was the question of sentries who would have to be taken care of. The moon, which was at quarter, was now lying well over to the west so there was no risk of being silhouetted against a southern sky. At the top of the hill, lying flat on their bellies, they had a commanding view. The entire camp was asleep and if there was a dog or two with them, which was unlikely, they, too, were asleep. 'No sentries, no dogs and camped on the north side of these hills,' observed Red Hand. 'They are as stupid as they are mad.'

'They will die as they have killed others,' Wind of the Wolf predicted, 'without a chance to defend themselves.'

Further to the north were the horses. They were in two groups of perhaps fifty, if not more, and sufficiently far away from the sleeping villains as not to be alarmed when the attack took place. The two leaders looked towards the eastern sky, then at each other and nodded; they would wait.

In the grey light of dawn a lookout lay flat to the ground atop the hill. The two war parties were assembled a short distance back on the south side. The rising sun moved over the summit, throwing its gentle warmth over the scout's back. Below, men were stirring and the shadow of night was retreating before the light beyond the bivouac. As its first dazzling rays touched the periphery of the encampment his hand went up in a signal and within that brief moment when the sleeping area became suffused in the harsh sunlight, the attack was upon them.

The two parties charged in from either side of the hill – not dissimilar to the method these outlaws used on the unsuspecting Norwegian party. Those armed with rifles went in on the first sweep, followed by clubs, tomahawks and lances and one Irishman armed with a quarterstaff, which later was credited with having inflicted a heavy toll on the enemy. The plan was cleverly executed. Wind of the Wolf's party swept in from the west side of the hill, attacking the south area of the camp moments before Red Hand's men swept in from the east to attack the north side. The short time-lag gave Wolf's party a chance to clear the area, thus avoiding collision and confusion. The riflemen and archers, having made their strikes, continued their runs for a predetermined distance to allow those employing clubs and other hand-to-hand weaponry to play havoc among a surprised and confused enemy. That was the second phase of the battle.

The third and final phase was the return of the riflemen and archers, now using hand weapons, which included some rifle butts but mainly lances. They charged in from both sides simultaneously. This was the mopping-up operation. Much shouting and whooping was encouraged throughout the attack to surprise and demoralise the enemy.

Willie's first victim went down from a blow to the chest from the end of his staff which he applied in a jousting action. With the combined weight of rider and horse at the gallop the man died instantly. What happened immediately after the blow was struck, whether by accident or intention, was a gracefully executed recovery movement and one that did not escape the sharp eyes of the Sioux warriors. Willie did not slow or stop his horse but continued at the gallop. Holding the staff at the fulcrum he allowed it to rotate freely from the body of the dead man and when clear he gave it a jaunty spin to bring it to its original position, whilst simultaneously wheeling his horse about for the next run in. It was a manoeuvre that any skilled lancer would have envied.

If the Sioux fought with ferocity, Willie became savage. Four times he caught a man by the hair (a man who was too close to his horse's flanks for him to use his staff), and dragged him along with superhuman effort until the wretch was clubbed down by a colleague. The last of these unfortunates had not been clubbed but dragged some considerable distance from that scene of carnage before Willie dropped him to turn around and finish him off with the staff. He could see the annihilation was over without contest and scalps were being taken. With a blow from his quarterstaff he killed his opponent, or in this case his victim, and without thought or hesitation he threw down the staff, dismounted and grabbed the man's hair and in one movement of frenzied anger severed the scalp from the head. Astonished at how easily it gave way to the knife, he stood frozen with horror at this action of his and he shook the blood-soaked repulsive thing from his hand like one would a venomous spider. Then he cried out, 'Jesus Christ, what am I doing?' And he ran to the river where he washed himself.

None survived the onslaught, no quarter was given. They died as they had brought death to so many innocent people. The horses were herded and taken and the two parties headed south for home. To the victor went the spoils. Among the carnage there lay one bloodstained knife and beside it a man's scalp and one eight-foot-long pole. In the lodges of the Sioux, the quarterstaff in the hands of Willie McKay would be discussed by the young braves and old men alike, but as a weapon of war it would lie where it had been discarded, on that field of retribution.

Willie sat on a boulder gazing vacantly into the noisy tributary that dashed past the encampment over its stony bed, making haste towards a more placid parent river – dancing and splashing over rocks and stones and pausing a while here and there to form a pool where trout would laze. He pondered on the soothing effect that the sparkling, clear, tumbling water could have on the mind and spirit. He remembered rivers like this, faster perhaps for the fall was steeper. The Roe and the Glenelly were rivers such as this with their deep, dark pools wherein dwelt the trout and grayling and, in the season, where the salmon would rest before their long Atlantic journey to the cold waters of Alaska. How many trout and grayling had he taken from those pools, or how often played a salmon until it exhausted itself and surrendered? And he recalled little Screen dancing and barking at the wriggling fish slapping itself against the mossy bank.

A splashing sound of something striking the water a little way off to his left snatched him from his reverie. Red Wing, the eldest of the chief's three daughters, had come to fetch water. It was Red Wing and her sister Little Eagle who had tended him when he was injured. And it was they, together with the little but well-intentioned help from their youngest sister Pretty Elk, who erected the small tipi, removed from the noise of the main encampment, so that he would get the rest he had needed for a speedy recovery. Was that exceptionally loud splash really necessary, and how much was the container of water needed as she returned with it, glancing at him with a coy smile? Smoke signals could not have been clearer.

The splash of a trout in the pool momentarily drew his attention back to the river where several more were entering the little oasis of still water. He was contemplating the ubiquity of this species throughout the West and Midwest of America and how the rivers of his own homeland teemed with them when he heard a familiar clip-clop sound coming along the hard surface leading to the river. But this was not a local horse; this horse had shoes and Indians' horses and ponies did not have shoes. Could it be that another white man had found the camp, or had the elders held council and sent out to some white men, traders perhaps, to come and take him back to his people? No, this could only be a dream, but he was not dreaming as a wet snorting nose nudged his back and Willie spun round to be reunited with his best pal, Chuck, all saddled and bridled and with his rifle in its holster, and yes, his gun belt and revolver hung over the saddle horn.

It was an emotional reunion from which the chief and John stood well back. Chuck neighed and snorted and pranced about, while Willie hugged him around the neck and tousled his mane. Having allowed a discreet time to elapse, Chief Two Rivers and John walked slowly to join Willie and Chuck. The chief selected a rock for a seat several paces away while John came straight to Willie at his horse's head and joined in making a fuss of one very excited horse.

Willie turned to John but before he could speak John anticipated the inevitable questions. 'That day as you lay unconscious, our first concern was to move you away from your horse. He was frantic and reared up so close to you that we feared those flying hooves could have killed you. We picked up your rifle and revolver from where you had thrown them. Your horse Chuck was no trouble to hold while we were taking you back here; he just followed you like a faithful dog. Since then he has been with the other horses. We moved them further away so you would not see him, or Chuck see you, until you were well again.' Willie nodded his understanding.

'When we saw the contents of those wagons we knew those men were on a peaceful journey. We have gathered some of their equipment and personal things, but it would be difficult for you to take them with you when you return to your – what the white man calls – civilisation. Their families should have them.'

'You are fine people,' said Willie. 'One day, my friend, the white man may learn that, as you have learned and as the Fathers in their robes have known, but my people fear that before understanding is reached there will be war between us.' Chuck reared his head and gave a loud neigh, pawing the ground with impatience.

Both men laughed spontaneously and the young Lakota changed the subject, patting Chuck on the head and saying with a smile, 'You have a wise horse, he is telling us to have no more talk like this.'

'I see you have saddled and bridled him,' Willie remarked.

'Your horse is ready for you to take for a long run across this open land where men are free. Go off with the wind in your face – and think.'

'Think of what?'

'When you return, let us hope you will have the answer with you.'

'Answer?'

'Whether you wish to stay with our people or return to your people. You will always be welcome among us. You could be one of us.' He turned to the chief and in his native tongue appraised him of the direction the conversation was taking and the chief replied.

'What did he say?' asked Willie.

John answered, 'The chief said he wished you were his son.'

Willie expressed his appreciation with a smile and for a moment fell silent in thought, and when he turned to John he asked, 'Is he thinking of grooming me for chieftain?'

'You are not of the blood. No, you could never be a chief of the Sioux or the Cheyenne or the Arapaho or any of the other tribes of the great plains but you could stand beside the chief and the elders of the Sioux with power and pride. In this land you could be a king,' and he added, 'but no crown.'

Willie reflected on the words of Captain Oskarsen not more than two moons ago, for he was now measuring time like the Indian people did. *And, Willie, if our mission proves successful, your life may take a different course but your navigation training will still hold, for it may come in useful on your own yacht.* But it was a dream now and a dream it would remain.

'Am I right?' asked Willie. 'Has the chief got three daughters but no son to hand the crown on to?'

'He had a son whom he lost long ago but who died recently.'

Willie inwardly marvelled at the ease and fluency with which the young Indian could express himself and he thought, *this young fellow of my own age could teach me my language – but then, I didn't learn mine from the Jesuits.*

'Lost long ago but died recently?' queried Willie, a little puzzled. *Did he die in battle? Against the Crow maybe?*

And Wind of the Wolf spoke to his chief updating him and the chief nodded in reply. 'He died with the Crow but the battle was an ignominious one. Can you remember when you were fighting for your life behind the shelter of that rock?' Willie nodded. 'Do you recall the warpainted renegade whose face you pushed that heavy revolver into,' he motioned to the weapon hanging from the saddle horn, 'and blew away the entire back of his head?' Willie nodded again and John looked towards the chief and continued, 'That renegade should one day have inherited the crown from his father here.'

'You are telling me that I killed the chief's son?'

'His only son. But have no regrets. The chief lost his son long ago when he joined that band of renegades. He defected from his family, his people.' There was an awkward moment, alleviated by the chief when he rose up and, walking towards Willie with a smile, shook his hand. The subject would never again be discussed.

The rest of the day he roamed, Willie on Chuck and in his own saddle. The world was beginning to get into order again. Everything felt good and tomorrow he would devote time to polishing up his saddle and the rest of the leatherwork and give Chuck a good brushing down. Chuck always enjoyed that and now he was looking a little neglected; and yes, his shoes, he better have a look at his shoes. It was a long time since he had a new set of shoes. That was back in St Louis when he had had him hot shod by the farrier. All Chuck's tackle was in the emergency wagon upended in the river. *Could it still be there?* Tomorrow he would force himself back to that place and retrieve some useful things, if they were still there.

As the sun was setting and he turned Chuck for home, two antelope bounded ahead of them, weaving and zigzagging and leaping obstacles in their path. Above them a turkey vulture, black against the sky, soared in a long lazy figure of eight, and higher still, small formations of Canada geese were heading homeward, stragglers from the earlier spring migration from the warm waters of the Gulf of Mexico and the Mississippi Basin.

Chuck, with energy to spare, pounded the prairie. Small clusters of little western meadowlarks rose in haste before him, their bright yellow breasts glinting against the low-lying sun. A killdeer plover, with the distinctive white bars across its throat and chest, fearing that the approaching sound was that of a predator about to steal her eggs or chicks, rose up from her nest and flew, or rather flapped, low over the grass in a wide circle with what appeared to be a broken wing, a characteristic of the bird to divert a predator away from the nest.

The graceful antelope continued ahead of Chuck. *Was it their game to have a race with the horse?* thought Willie. *Were they showing how clever they were or were they just so stupid it did not occur to them to move aside?* While the thought was in his mind they obliged him by veering off to the left, leaving Chuck to thunder on, stirring the prairie creatures from their rest. 'Slow down, boy,' said Willie, patting his horse's neck with one hand while the other applied the reins. Chuck responded with a shake of his head, blowing froth from his nostrils and gradually slowing down to a lively canter.

Willie had no appreciation of the distance that he and his horse had travelled on their outward ride and now he was a little anxious to get nearer to the camp before darkness fell. He kept Chuck at the steady canter which he knew he could maintain. He would like to be within sight of the village before sunset, for this was unfamiliar land to him, yet instinct told him that he could not be far away. His moment of anxiety vanished when away ahead of him and to the right he saw the thin line of the river with the bend. It was at this point on his outward-bound ride earlier in the day, when he reached the top of the high ground, that he looked back and saw the bend in the river and behind the trees to the left was the village of his newfound friends.

No rush now, he could relax and canter Chuck home. And home, he decided, was no longer St Louis but just over the hill. As the sun dipped below the horizon, a coyote howled away to his right and a brown speckled burrowing owl rose in fright before the horse's hooves to alight on a bush a short distance ahead, where it sat and watched with a scornful look from behind its snowy white eyebrows as the intruder passed by.

Willie needed this day to be alone to think and to make decisions. He had the offer to join them, an invitation few white men, if any, had ever had. With these people, and in a land like this, he could be free. 'A king without a crown,' that is what the man said. And the chief's daughter, Red Wing, did she not smile at him? *Yes,* thought Willie, *a man could make a good life for himself here. But once the decision was made, there would be no turning back.*

In the morning he would return to the wreckage on the river and recover his farrier equipment and horse shoes, if they were still there, and could shoe Chuck with a new set. If they were not to be found it would not matter much, for Chuck was destined to live out his life on the prairie where horse shoes were unnecessary anyway. One thing would be for certain: his favourite horse was not going to be ridden into any skirmish or hunting expedition. The Sioux were not short of horses and the pinto was better suited to that kind of work.

The bend in the river came within sight and the smell from the pinewood log fires drifted towards him. Overhead a red-tailed hawk circled leisurely.

Caught for a brief moment by the last crimson glow of the setting sun, its tail glowed as if on fire. And away to the south the sky appeared to darken as an enormous flock of passenger pigeons headed homeward to roost somewhere in the western prairie. Willie watched them in complete fascination until they had gone beyond the horizon.

That night in the chief's lodge, Willie sat in a place of honour among the elders of the village. The chief took the calumet in both hands, directed it towards the ground, then to the four corners of the earth, paused for a moment in meditation, then took several puffs and passed it around. After the smoking of the peace pipe, conversation became lively, with Wind of the Wolf translating. Willie decided that he would learn the language. He already had a good workable knowledge of the Cheyenne and Osage languages and there was no reason why he should not master the Lakota.

At first he was central to the conversation with all eyes directed at him. One old warrior, looking straight at Willie, spoke in his native tongue. He turned to John for help and was immediately put at ease. It was explained to him that the old warrior had said, 'On his first engagement he had "touched coup" four times'. And when Willie asked what touching coup meant, it was explained to him that to approach an enemy in battle and touch him physically is an act of bravery and defiance in the face of the enemy, and for him to repeat it four times as he had done merited high commendation. In the heat of battle Willie had four times grabbed a renegade by the hair with his left hand, pulling and smashing him against his horse. What the braves had not considered was the advantage Willie had, with his extra arm length and the kinetic energy of the moving horse making the deadly movement look easy. His quarterstaff and how he had used it in battle was central to the conversation for quite a while and the cause of much hilarity.

An elderly woman entered carrying a bundle of firewood and, kneeling before the dying embers in the middle of the lodge, she kindled new life into a near-dead fire, and when the flames took hold of the sweet-scented pinewood she withdrew as silently as she had come. And Willie learned that, at the turn of the century, while they were in winter encampment just north of the confluence of the North and South Platte, that lady had given birth to a son and the boy was called Two Rivers.

A little later, several younger women entered, bearing food and drink, and not least among them was Red Wing, her eyes catching Willie's across the dancing illuminations of a lively fire. And John whispered that she was his cousin and he was a nephew of the chief. The warmth and comfort within that lodge and the happy conversation took him back to other nights in the céilí houses, like his own home, in his native Ireland. And just beyond the buffalo-hide protection of the tipi lay a wild and challenging land.

Willie had never before considered the discomfort of his clothing: the combinations underwear (long johns), the flannel shirts, the heavy serge trousers and jackets, and all buttoned up. He recalled how he had so often sweated under the hot sun in such apparel, but no more: in the tipi, where he donned the light buckskin, his body was free and cool. Only a short-fitting type of jerkin, open at the front, covered his torso. A tight-fitting loincloth covered the hips and the inner surface of the legs, with two apron-like flaps at front and back and held around the waist by a thin belt, from which hung his knife in a leather scabbard. On his feet were comfortably fitting moccasins. His arms, chest and legs were bare and when he bundled up his white man's clothes and placed them in a neat pile, he picked up a lance and moved hesitantly from the tipi to receive his initiation ceremony, the first of several, into the fold.

Outside the privacy of the tipi he encountered his first audience and suffered that terrible panic known as stage fright. Facing him were the chief and elders, all in their splendour, and the many braves, old and young, and most frightening of all were the women and children behind them. And he, Willie McKay, standing before them in what was to him nakedness. His initial feeling was to run back into the tipi and he half turned to do it when a cheer that went up stopped him.

And he recalled the night in a playhouse in New Orleans when a young chorus girl, scantily clad, appeared on stage to make her debut in a song-and-dance number. And he remembered so clearly how she froze on that stage before an all-male audience. The scurrilous uproar, whistling and foot-stamping that greeted her appearance could easily have ended her career before it got started. That frightening feeling, mingled with guilt, was now laid at his own feet for he had been among the foot-stamping, whistling hooligans. He recalled how she stood her ground and gave her tormentors a long icy stare, then with her little black cane with the round silver handle, she tipped the back of her hat and went straight into her number that merited not three but four curtain calls and a standing ovation.

And it came to mind how four roughnecks, one William John McKay amongst them, fired by her beauty and professionalism, spontaneously sprang onto the stage and carried her shoulder high among the audience. And raising his lance aloft, he threw back his head and emitted a loud uncontrollable roar that echoed around the hills beyond. And when it trailed away another arose in anguish and in anger – in anger at a God who could permit this irreversible situation – and in emotional exhaustion he fell to his knees and in the depth of his depression, two pairs of sturdy hands raised him to his feet. And from the throats of a hundred Lakota braves a resounding cheer went up, for a Celtic warrior had come amongst them.

CHAPTER 14

It was June 1859 in Nevada. On a hillock overlooking the plain that lay to the west, the Shoshone watched them from afar: two small dark dots on the horizon dancing erratically behind the haze of the midday heat. Slowly the dots enlarged as distance closed. Shading his eyes with his hands he glanced at the sun hanging at its zenith, then looked away towards the two dots, mentally making a rough calculation of the distance and time the riders would take to reach him. Under the noonday sun they would be travelling slowly. *They would not stop,* he thought; *nothing for them here.* He was curious and he would watch and wait.

Slowly through the shimmering haze the dots took shape and where two were, four now appeared, two pairs. To the Indian this could only mean one thing: two horsemen, white, with pack animals. They held a steady course across the plain and it became clear to the Shoshone that they were heading for the range of hills that lay behind him and away to the north. They must pass close to him. Keeping abreast of each other and sitting straight in their saddles, with an air of purpose, they simultaneously nudged their mounts into a canter with parade-ground precision, only to be pulled up by their pack mules reminding them of their loads. They would find what they were coming for and what they were to find would, a few years on, be paramount in determining the outcome of a nation's war and influencing a president's decision.

The riders stopped at the foot of the knoll where the Indian sat, looked up at him and talked for a while between themselves. Then one of them took a map from the saddlebag and spread it haphazardly across the saddle. The stoical Shoshone sat motionless, watching the strangers in council over the large sheet of paper lying across the horse's back. They looked directly up at the Indian, then one hurriedly gathered up the map, pointed to the hills lying to the east and walked up the slope towards him, map in hand. The tall stranger looked down at the squatting Indian and asked if he spoke English. The Shoshone nodded and replied, 'Some.'

The stranger then pointed to the range of hills beyond and asked, 'Is Six Mile Canyon over there?'

The Indian smiled and rose to his feet with the ease of an athlete and to the surprise of the horseman he was almost as tall as himself. The Shoshone people were usually of a small stature, unlike the Osage and Arapaho. He indicated towards an area of the hills, saying, 'Six Mile Canyon over other side; nothing there.'

The man looked at his map and again to the areas where the Indian had indicated, smiled and said, 'You could be very right, thanks for your help,' and turned towards his companion holding the horses at the foot of the hillock. He uncorked his flask, took a few sips of water, replaced the cork and folded the map. 'Peter,' he said after a pause, 'we appear to be right, the Indian says it is over there on the other side of that line of hills.'

'An hour and a half ride from here,' suggested Peter, 'and if we go around that low area and get over easily to the other side we ought to find plenty of shade, water our horses and stretch our bones and wait for the sun to drop down a bit. Two hours altogether, would you say?'

'I would say you're about right and my guess is there are plenty of streams over there, cool clear water; let's go.' They mounted and rode on, raising their hats in salute to the Shoshone as they passed.

Patrick McLaughlin and Peter O'Reilly had ridden 250 miles from San Francisco through the western territories. This was Shoshone country where white folk were not very thick on the ground, not yet. Only a scattering of hastily erected dwellings, the homes of prospectors, dotted the land west of the hills. 'Peter, I have a feeling we could be luckier here than in California,' said McLaughlin as they rode side by side. 'I feel somehow that I am coming home.'

'How come?'

'That range of hills out there, where we're heading, is very similar to where I grew up. It is called the Sperrins.'

'The Sperrins,' cut in Peter, 'I've heard of the Sperrins often, they are about as well known as the Mountains of Mourne.'

'Just about,' said Patrick. 'Those hills sure remind me of home,' and, pointing to a particular area, 'and there is Carntogher, one of the high points. My home town, Maghera, lies a few miles to the south of it.'

'I have heard of Maghera, too,' replied O'Reilly. 'Isn't that on the Belfast–Derry road?'

'That's right. What is the name of that hill in Tipperary where you did some mining in your youth?'

'Slieve Kilmalta. Silvermine Mountain they called it. Not much silver left by the time I got there, plenty of zinc. You know, they were mining silver out of it by the ton when the Romans were in Britain, then it was closed for centuries. When it was opened again it never was worth much. I would say the Romans had the best of it.'

'What happened to it?' asked Patrick. 'Did they come and take it?'

'No, they bought it. Shipped it back to Rome. They put a high value on the quality of Irish silver.'

'I would have thought,' said Patrick, 'that with the armies they had they would have come and taken it.'

'The Romans never invaded Ireland,' said Peter. 'They traded with her. Agricola was the longest serving commander in Britain. Four years was the term the commanders served away from Rome. Agricola did seven in all, in Britain. When asked once by an Irish chieftain why Rome never invaded Ireland, Agricola replied, "I could take your country with one legion but I could never hold her. Better we trade with you."'

'Pity the English didn't think that way,' was McLaughlin's caustic reply, 'they might have saved themselves a whole lot of trouble.'

They were nearing their destination and there was a rise in the ground. The hills no longer looked like Patrick's Sperrins. They lacked the height and ruggedness and there was an absence of heather. A small band of Shoshones on their ponies watched them from some way off. As of one movement they raised their hats to them and the Shoshone returned the salute in the tradition that was their own. The mules brayed and pulled on their leads. 'Water around somewhere,' remarked Peter.

'And there it is,' said Patrick pointing across the neck of his pal's horse to a sparkling stream about 200 yards away. They turned towards it, dismounted, left the animals to it and refreshed themselves.

McLaughlin and O'Reilly were of the many. They had been the latecomers to the Californian gold rush. Not that even if they had arrived with the first rush of 1849 would they have been any more successful. First in was no guarantee of success, nor was experience, but it helped. In his youth O'Reilly had worked the silver mines in Ireland. There he learned his trade. McLaughlin had no such knowledge. It was a chance meeting in a bar in San Francisco one evening in late 1856 that brought the partnership together. McLaughlin had just arrived in California to try his luck. For the previous five years he had been riding for some of the early ranch owners in Texas, herding longhorn cattle. He was one of the pioneering breed, later to be known as cowboys. Meeting up with a fellow countryman, almost on arrival in town, and a miner at that, must have seemed a good omen to him.

O'Reilly had arrived in the goldfields three and a half years earlier and, not knowing the country, wisely signed up to work for a mining consortium. There he remained and had done modestly well. Patrick was also not short of a dollar. Riding the range for a few years for some early ranchers and being a man of temperate habit he had put a bit by, unusual for a man in his trade. It took little persuasion for O'Reilly to get him to sign up with the company, work with him as a paid unskilled miner and learn the tricks of the trade. There they would work for a year or so, pile up a few dollars and then move on.

The fire that gripped the hearts and minds of those who sought riches when someone first shouted, 'Gold!' in California was now cooling. Seams were running out and mines were closing but there would still be enough of the "noble metal" in the ground to hold many in its grip for another few years.

O'Reilly had an uncanny talent for finding the stuff. While working for the company he would often go away into lonely places in the hills to do some placer mining along the streams, better known as "panning". He had a good knowledge of rock formations. If he found "colour" (gold dust) in the bed of the stream – and he sometimes did – he would follow the stream's bed. That stream's bed may well have changed over thousands of years and what is now a small though lively stream would have been a powerful river a million years ago. The flowing water being the abrasive agent against rock would, over centuries, have the effect of emery cloth on metal. Those rocks would have been thrown up by volcanic action millions of years ago. In time, the water and frost would crack and split the rocks. The exposed quartz rock formation would be forced by the flowing water to surrender the miniscule flecks of gold to be washed away and to settle in areas of the river or stream where the particles would sink, such as in pools where the water was still. There it would remain hidden under a foot or two of sand and gravel.

The novice panner of that era – and most were novices – would work such areas and if finding nothing would move on. If, however, he were to find colour he would pan the sand or gravel using an improvised sluice until he was satisfied that he had all there was in that area. Often it was pathetically little, relative to the work he had put in. The experienced placer miner, like O'Reilly, would follow the creek back, "reading the story" as it were.

But Peter had two strokes against him: he could not afford to give up the day job and until McLaughlin came along he never found anyone he could trust. With a trusted partner, twice the work could be got through in the time available. One could be shovelling while the other was sluicing, or one could be shovelling and panning while the other was away investigating the source of a possible lode. And so it was over a beer in a bar in San Francisco that two strangers met and through an instant trust the miner and the cowboy formed an alliance to go for gold.

O'Reilly worked underground for the mining company. The miners worked in shifts, usually of eight hours' duration with frequent breaks, and with him McLaughlin was a willing and quick learner. But for a tall man accustomed to riding herd, the work was claustrophobic and back breaking. The seams were producing well and pay and bonuses were good and the growing city of San Francisco was a lively place to visit. They agreed to jointly deposit the dust from their placer-mining enterprise, after assay, and over the next two and a half years a considerable sum had accrued. When the time was right they finished with the company, outfitted themselves, saddled up and headed for the hills.

'What do they call this godforsaken place you've brought me to, O'Reilly?'

'It's called the Washoe and it might not be so godforsaken when we've looked it over.'

'Hmm, sounds like washout to me. You've had a hankering for this place for a long time. Why?'

'I'll tell you, Pat, listen. A countryman of ours, a John McKay, some years ago looked this place over with a partner. They staked a claim but nothing was ever done about it. McKay went back to California and probably is still there. Likewise the other man just vanished. Then there was another, a man by the name of James Fennimore. He had the nickname "Old Virginy" since that was where he hailed from – Virginia. Those men, I tell you, could smell gold like a hound dog can smell a fox. They wouldn't have wasted their time hanging around here if they hadn't known something.'

Patrick thought for a while rolling a cigarette, lit it, blew smoke up into the air and turned to Peter. 'If these fellows are as sharp as you say, why did they not hang around a bit longer and get the stuff out?'

'It's not always so easy, Pat – shortage of equipment, money, who knows?'

They had pitched their tent on the east side of the hill by a fast-running creek, so there would be shade and water. The grass was in plenty but not lush. The horses and mules would have sufficient for their needs without putting on weight in their idleness. That could come of pasturing on rich green grass. The sun had dropped over the hill and the first curtain of evening was closing over the plain. The horses and mules were tethered near the water. Over the fire the coffee pot hung from a collapsible wrought-iron frame – important items of equipment. They would have a light supper of brown kibbled bread with jam and sweet black coffee. When they would finally sleep, their gun belts would be at hand and their rifles well secured, but on their first night at camp they would not sleep much. They sat by the fire talking late into the night and reminisced over past happenings in each other's lives.

'Do you regret, Pat, leaving the ranch work, all the excitement of the round-up, the trail, all that?'

'Yeh, ah do sometimes and ah sure hope this pays off.' A man can leave his native land, be it Poland or Czechoslovakia, Italy or Ireland, and make his home in New York or New Orleans and retain his native accent, but if a man settles for Texas he may well hold on to that accent in part or in whole, but he will develop the drawl. The Texan drawl is as infectious as the common cold and Patrick, although his Ulster accent still prevailed, now drawled his vowels.

'What is it about the life you miss most?'

'A lot, the comradeship, no looking over the shoulder for the other guy going to put something over on you. Round-up time, the chuck wagon and the trail. A thousand head, maybe twice that, on the move. The singing around the fires at night when you have got the cattle quiet.' Here he punctuated to roll and light a cigarette. 'You know, this may sound strange but you have to work with cattle to understand; I miss the sounds of the cattle, especially at night when they are settled and you are rolled up in your blanket, that lowing sound sure can make a man sleep.' Somewhere in the night a coyote howled out. 'And that, too,' said Patrick. 'There are always plenty of those guys.'

'But it is a tough life,' remarked Peter. 'It can't all be sunshine and roses.'

'No, it's not all easy. It's often hard work. A man becomes attached to his horse and sometimes a horse will break a leg and have to be put down. To see a man crying like a child as he is taking the saddle and bridle off his dead horse, his pal, is a heartbreaking sight. And there are accidents aplenty and sometimes fatal. I will never forget one, when a young fellow, a pal, went into a bush to retrieve a steer that had wandered off from the herd. Suddenly his horse reared up in fright. It was the squeal of fright from the horse that caught my attention. I was some way off. The suddenness of it threw Jerry. He fell on top of what had caused his horse to shy, a goddamned rattlesnake. It struck him inside the thigh on that main artery – there's a name for it, it's no matter – but I tell you by the time I had galloped over to him, and I was first there, he was gone. I'll never forget those eyes and the colour of his face. Nineteen years old, that's all, a boy just starting out – left a mother and a little brother to fend for themselves. The boss took care of all the funeral expenses and provided an income for the mother and the boy for a long time after. He was very good but it just softened the blow. That kind of thing happens.'

The fire smouldered and died, leaving two tiny lights, like glow-worms, to brighten and dim in the dark as they smoked their last cigarettes for the night. At first light there would be work to do.

Mount Davidson looked closer and overwhelming in the cold morning light. The embers of their fire still smouldered and when it was rekindled they fried some thick slices of salt bacon and with chunks of coarse brown bread and hot sweet coffee they set about their frugal breakfast. It was agreed that one or the other would have to make contact with the Shoshone, if any were around, and barter for some food. Better dealing with the Indians than the white men, if indeed any of them were in the vicinity. The Indians would ask no questions.

Patrick's first consideration was to inspect the horses' hooves for flints and so on and ensure that no shoes had come loose on the trek. For the unshod mules the task was easier. The inspection over, Patrick saddled up, tied an empty pannier to the saddle horn and set off on his "shopping trip". In his absence, Peter, rifle in hand, walked the stream for some distance, investigating it for the presence of fish and more importantly for telltale signs of gold, but there was no evidence of either. Perhaps the river would prove more fruitful but that would have to wait. Some fresh fish would be very acceptable.

He found four streams in all: fast-flowing creeks tumbling down the hillsides to empty into the river below. Where each stream, or creek, merged with the river they would pan for colour, flecks of gold, and if any were found their sluice equipment would be set up. One would do the panning while the other traced the creek back up the hillside noting the rock formation. Such creeks Peter referred to as "lively".

Patrick returned with the pannier stuffed with various fresh meats and freshly baked cornmeal bread. He had travelled in a left-hand sweep for a five-mile radius and had been about to give up when he spotted wisps of smoke rising vertically in the still air away to his right. It came from a small encampment of Shoshone. He paid cash and they plied him with all he needed. Asked if they had seen any white men, they had seen none other than himself and his pal who had raised their hats to the little group they had passed the day before, which was good news. *How a little good manners can pay*, thought Patrick.

Early morning they were on the move. The equipment was loaded on the mules and they moved down into the canyon, leading their horses. They found a place near the river where the grazing seemed fairly good and there they tethered their animals, unloaded the mules and set about some serious work.

The first day's panning was unsuccessful, as was the second and third. They panned twelve to fourteen hours a day but no colour showed. They moved from site to site, lugging their equipment around. It was hard work, made the more so by its futility. At the end of the fourth day in the canyon they moved camp to a place where a lively creek was charging down the hillside, pitching its contents into a placid pool. Where the waters met, the bed was fine sand, the product of rock and silica and whatever other minerals the earth had thrown up through the ages, abraded and polished and deposited where it would rest until disturbed by man. In the morning, if this area were to prove as unproductive as the others, at least they could change the breakfast menu for they discovered fish here.

As the rising sun crossed the hill, its warmth lifting the mist and warming the dank dewy air on the canyon floor, McLaughlin and O'Reilly brought their sluice equipment to the river's edge and prepared again to pan for gold. McLaughlin was having serious doubts about his decision to join the gold rush. Over in Texas on a morning like this he could be riding herd and getting paid for it. On the road he was now taking, the terminal that was destitution loomed ahead. How many gold seekers had found their way there and how many more would? How long would it be before he and his pal would find themselves there, at rock bottom and no way back? These thoughts he kept from Peter lest he should dampen his enthusiasm; no need for both of them to be depressed.

Patrick found it easier to stand barefoot, trouser legs rolled up, in the water and shovel the sand while Peter sifted, sitting on the bank. They had not long to await results, for amongst the remaining sand in the pan, minute flecks, no larger than grains of salt, that down the eons of geological time had been entombed in the darkness, shone out in radiance to greet the morning sunlight. This was placer gold.

Patrick's thoughts of destitution quickly fled and even the more phlegmatic Peter gave vent to his feelings and, yet, in his excitement, instinctively glanced around in every direction lest they be overlooked. It was now decided that only one should continue with the placer mining and the other do a good probe of the rock formation back up the hillside along the creek. Peter asked Patrick if he would go, promising to work like a Roman slave on his own. Patrick walked over to his tool bag and took from it the following items: one two-pound hammer, one large chisel, two steel wedges, one large and one small, and a pocket magnifying glass. As he moved towards the hill, being the joker he was, he turned to Peter with a smile: 'O'Reilly, if you find a nugget among that stuff and you decide to leave before I get back, be decent about it and leave me my horse and mule.'

As the gradient got steeper, large boulders either side of the creek left him little option but to walk through the clear tumbling water. But what did wet feet matter on a day like this? He would put all his experience of the past few years into practice. No stone would be left unturned. On either side of the water there was dry grass mingled with moss and mud, baked by the sun onto the stones and into the gravel, and beyond, where the huge rock formation presented a wall, a waterline mark reached up to two feet indicating that in very heavy and prolonged rain this benign stream would become a raging force of dark muddy water. It is said that the river never alters its course and that may be true today, but before the world settled, geological forces were constantly in a state of flux. Where a river had found its course, over thousands or even millions of years, some volcanic action or huge earthquake would push it aside but the river, always searching for its lowest level, the ocean or sea, would find a new route to its destination, forever wearing down rock and anything else in its path. Many of the fissures created those millions of years ago are the canyons we have today.

These basic geological facts were known by most of the men who moiled for gold. They knew the lay of the land and how it came to be. They were geologists and mining engineers, self-taught, and for the most part their only university was adversity. Patrick McLaughlin had only three and a half years' experience but had learned well; he had the feel but, unlike O'Reilly, he still lacked the fever.

Patrick walked the rock face, tapping, looking for small fissures created down the years by water erosion and frost. Several large fragments gave way to the hammer and chisel but on inspection failed the test. Where the course of the stream rounded a bend he followed and now was out of view from Peter away below. Here he found a cavern of only four or five feet in depth. The rock face here was not smooth like the large boulders he had examined but was rugged and sharp. *At least,* he thought, *he could have a field day hacking away at this stuff.* It looked like anthracite but was not.

He found a section that could give way easily to the hammer and chisel. It appeared to have a grain, again like anthracite, not only in appearance or colour but in formation, though most definitely rock. Patrick carefully placed the chisel for maximum effect and under the first blow from the hammer it came away in one large chunk, causing him to jump clear before it dropped on his feet. He could not believe what he saw lying there before him: there in the cleaved section was a cross-section of quartz with the most miniscule traces of gold, so minute it could have been overlooked by the untrained eye. A find like this on the surface, albeit in a cavern, was more than any prospector could dare expect. Unable to contain himself he ran downstream and when Peter came into view he called, waving excitedly. Patrick was generally a phlegmatic devil and with sudden behaviour like this Peter got the message.

They both stared at the slab Peter was holding in both hands. Few words were spoken, then Peter handed the rock back to Patrick and walked into the cavern followed by Patrick who handed him the hammer and chisel. Peter did his own cursory check and picked up the same quartz seam with the same crystalline affinities. He turned, looked straight at his colleague and said, 'Pat, this is the end of the rainbow.' They sat down against a boulder, unaware how wet it was, and stared in silence at the lively water of the stream. Peter broke the silence; reaching into his shirt pocket he produced a nugget about the size of a pea, and with a faint little smile he said, 'McLaughlin, your horse and mule are still there.'

Deep in thought, they were in no hurry rolling their tobacco and lighting their cigarettes. The date was 12 June 1859. By law a claim must now be staked, and fast, and both men knew that the peace and loneliness of Six Mile Canyon on the Washoe, which they had come to know, would soon be gone forever.

CHAPTER 15

Judge Walsh arrived in Six Mile Canyon in July 1859 and legalised their claim. He was the first Californian to visit the new strike following the positive assay reports. Many more would soon follow. By the time their claim was legalised, two more names were added to the partnership of McLaughlin and O'Reilly, that of Emanuel Penrod and one Henry Tompkins Paige Comstock, whose name would be remembered long after the others. Almost three weeks before Judge Walsh had authorised the claim, the original two had agreed to give 466.5 feet, almost a third, of their entire mining ground of 1,400 feet to two fellow prospectors working another location known as Gold Hill, in exchange for two horses or mules and two arrastres, crude mills for pulverising ore.

Around three days after their discovery, McLaughlin and O'Reilly were sitting on their saddles by the stream. Their backs were to the sun and they were enjoying a meal of cooked venison and cornbread bought from the Shoshone, when a dark shadow passed over their improvised tablecloth. With the speed of a striking snake McLaughlin dropped to his left in a crouching movement, his gun in his right hand directed at the head of one very frightened man. The fast reflex action of McLaughlin, conditioned by years in his past occupation, startled his pal as much as the stranger looking down the barrel of a revolver with both hands in the air. As Peter remarked afterwards, 'You frightened the hell out of me so much, I pissed myself on the spot.'

'Who the hell are you?' McLaughlin asked.

'Please, there is no need for that,' pleaded the stranger. 'Please forgive me, I had no intention of startling you, I shouldn't have come up on you like that. Please put that gun away.' McLaughlin could see he was unarmed and returned the gun to its holster. 'My name is Henry Comstock, I—'

'You'll never know how close you came to being a *dead* Henry Comstock,' interrupted O'Reilly.

On regaining his composure he said, 'It was thoughtless of me, but to be shot on my own land for such a trivial offence would leave Mr Comstock the laughing stock, if you'll forgive the pun.'

The two men instinctively looked at each other in surprise and McLaughlin turned to Comstock. 'My guess would be that after God this land belongs to the Shoshone.'

'That may all be very well,' said Comstock, producing a large buff-coloured envelope from an inside pocket of his jacket, the type lawyers file property deeds in. He produced official-looking papers from the envelope, stiff, parchment-like and faded. He did not hand over the papers but hunkered down beside the men, excusing himself for butting in on their meal, and spread the top sheet out before them. 'Here, gentlemen, you can see some claims were filed years ago by two brothers: here are the dates,' an index finger pointing to the dates 1843 and 1844, 'and here are the names.' The signatures were illegible and the printed names by the signatures almost as vague, but the document did appear to bear the stamp of officialdom.

'What are the names of these two brothers?' Peter asked.

'Grosch,' was the reply. 'They were two old bachelor brothers who lived in a cabin in the Washoe for many years. There wasn't much those fellows didn't know of the Sierra Nevada. Lived a hermit existence. They had a notion there was mineral wealth here in Six Mile Canyon; went through all the legalities with lawyers and surveyors. Here are some maps drawn up by the surveyors.' He pulled out several maps drawn on paper now faded with time. The whole contents of the envelope had a faint musty smell, which to McLaughlin and O'Reilly gave it all an air of authenticity.

'I guess the old guys have long gone,' asked Patrick.

'They both died a few years ago, not long after each other. The younger of the two had an accident with a pickaxe. He drove it into his foot through the shoe leather. They were out there on their own. When help finally got to them he was too far gone. The older brother stayed on. No one could persuade him to leave, including myself. He died the winter of that year.'

'How do you come into the scene?' Peter asked.

'I knew them from a long way back. One night in their cabin over a friendly hand of cards they asked me if I would look after their affairs saying I was the only friend they had and the only one they could trust. I was aware of their plight and agreed but something like that must be made legal – talk can get around. So, with their consent it was all done legally and I was given power of attorney to act on their behalf.'

'I see there is a Mr Penrod here. Who is he?'

'Boy, you guys sure ask questions, but I guess it's only right you should know. Mr Penrod was and is a friend. He signed there as witness. He and I have a small business partnership.' He began to gather up the papers.

'We can offer you some coffee, Mr Comstock, and you are welcome to share our food but you must accept we are a bit rough and ready,' said Patrick.

'I would appreciate a cup of coffee but I'm all right for eats, thanks.'

'I guess you will want us to shove off,' said Peter, handing him a mug of coffee.

'Hell no, I'm not here to chase you

Henry Tompkins Paige Comstock, namesake of the fabulous Comstock Lode. (Courtesy of the Nevada Historical Society.)

boys off. I have a horse that is given to running off at every opportunity and he has just done it again – bolted on me over that hill when I dismounted to attend to a call of nature. Bounded away from me in this direction; you haven't by chance seen him?'

'No,' said O'Reilly, 'but tell me, do you usually go a-riding with all your legal documents?'

There was a deathly silence and below Comstock's heavy black beard, his face must have turned to crimson. 'Are you boys miners?' he asked.

'You could say that,' answered Peter. 'Are you in the mining business?'

'No, but I sure would like to have a crack at it. Did a bit of placer stuff down along here when the brothers were alive and found nothing. But then I guess I never was any good at fishing either.' He sipped the coffee. The other two allowed themselves a smile. If Mr Comstock was fishing for answers they were not forthcoming.

Henry Comstock appeared to be in his late thirties or early forties, of medium height and slight build. His hands were not hands that had been used much in toil, certainly not those of a miner, but his clothing, rugged with trouser knees well worn, indicated a man in some kind of manual employment. Throughout his visit he never looked directly at either man. His pale green characterless eyes indicated a weakness in the man, but the face was one devoid of guile. He sipped his coffee looking into the fire-blackened tin mug which he cupped in both hands. There was a pause. Patrick gathered up the utensils that he had jettisoned when he reached for the gun.

Peter re-opened the conversation. 'Now, Mr Comstock—'

'Henry,' interrupted Comstock, 'just call me Henry.'

'Fine,' continued Peter. 'Henry, I ought to tell you a few facts you may not be aware of. I've been through every scrap of documentation there is at the Land Registry Office back in 'Frisco and never were there any government grants issued to anyone or to any company in this territory at any time, and government grants come from Washington. Now, without a grant from Washington, you don't own a square inch of this canyon. And remember, this territory is not a state; not yet anyway.' O'Reilly paused to allow what he had said to sink in. McLaughlin stared the visitor in the eye, driving home the message with the unspoken question, *Who do you think you're kidding?* Comstock fidgeted with the now empty mug, feeling that his mouth and his papers had landed him in a dangerous situation. A man could be shot and buried out here in this lonely land and the world would never know.

The two men took a fiendish delight in watching him squirm. It was Patrick who broke the awful silence when he felt their uninvited guest had had enough. 'Would you like a little more coffee, Mr Comstock?'

'Henry – yes, I would, that's real nice coffee.'

Peter took the mug from a shaking hand and filled it, then continued. 'Henry, this is a whole big territory out here.' At that, Henry glanced around nervously as if looking for an escape route. 'Now, as Pat has said, this land belongs to God and the Shoshone and neither is interested in what we think you have in mind. I'm talking about gold, Henry. Do you live around here?'

'I have a dwellin' place over towards Mount Davidson.'

'Then you must know this area pretty well.'

'You might say that.'

'And the canyon here?'

'Every inch of it.'

'Well, Henry, you could be as useful to us as we could be to you.' Henry relaxed a little. 'Now we have staked a claim, right here,' his finger pointing towards the ground beneath him, 'and that claim has been publicly announced. Do you know what that means, Henry?' He paused for his question to sink in. 'It means, Henry, that in a very short while miners are going to be swarming all over this whole canyon like bees over a hive. Experienced, hardbitten miners who didn't make it on the Californian fields and many who did and are just greedy for more. All searching for the noble metal, just like we are.' O'Reilly sat back against his saddle, stretched out his legs and rolled and lit a cigarette, taking his time. Patrick sat watching the nervous man, inwardly amused.

'Now here is what I would like you to do. You could have convinced us as to the ownership of the place, so, if you nearly convinced us then go a bit further and convince the others. Now, you see that lawyer friend of yours and get a land warrant drawn up.'

'But I have already got that.'

'That was in the name of the Grosch brothers, you—'

'Listen, there is no necessity. There is an addendum to the warrant, before the brothers passed away, authorising the stewardship of the land be passed on to me. Here, let me show you again.' He reached into his jacket pocket to produce the wallet, but Peter stopped him by holding up his hand.

'All right, Henry, you can be convincing. Look, my partner and I will take a stroll down by the river and have a chat about it all and come back and let you know what we think. Help yourself to coffee and there is plenty of chuck there, just help yourself. We won't be long.'

The tension was eased. A relaxed Comstock placed a few sticks on the fire saying, 'I might just take you up on that; I guess I am feeling a bit hungry.'

It was obvious to Patrick that Peter had a plan. He rose and followed him, saying as he went, 'You just help yourself, Henry.'

Peter picked up a few small pebbles and pitched them into the water as they walked slowly around the bend of the river and out of sight of Comstock. They walked past his horse, grazing on tufts of lush grass. 'Well, he won't make a run for it while we've got his horse in view,' observed Peter. 'What do you make of him, Pat?'

'I think he's a four flusher, but you've called his bluff.'

'Yeh, but now his bluff has been called, he could be useful to us. You know, and I know, that bundle of papers he has in his pocket are not worth the ink that's on them.'

'Are you planning on taking him in as a partner?'

'I think that's what we should do.'

'I don't trust him, Peter, I just don't—'

'Look, this place is rich, we both know that and we both know that where we have staked is most likely where the best of the lode is. Soon there will be others, the pick-and-shovel brigade, and there will be geologists, surveyors and the engineers close on their heels. Now, if Comstock first convinces the pick-and-shovel boys that the land is his, they don't go asking for proof. He can allocate the area as he thinks fit and let them all stake their claims. If he were to distribute two-thirds, retaining for himself the remaining third with our stake in it, then three of us can divide that third again which would leave Comstock with an enormous one third of a very productive gold mine and you and me with one third each of the claim. But wait,' he held up his hand to prevent Patrick interrupting, 'you say you don't trust him and neither do I, but if at any time he tries anything stupid, you and I together hold two-thirds of our mine – his, yours and mine – the controlling interest, m'lad.' He gave Patrick a slap on the shoulder to drive home the message and then continued, 'And that area we have staked out is where we start. Just believe me, Pat, I have seen all this before and I can tell you, before the boys with the theodolites get here, no one will know who owns what and no one will care. This place will be bedlam gone berserk.'

Patrick thought for a moment, rubbing his chin and staring into the river. He thought long and hard, watching the rivulets of clear water flowing over the rocky bed. Then he turned to Peter and said, 'All right, I'm in agreement but I tell you, Peter, I distrust that guy. We will not be able to hold him, not because he's dishonest but because he is a fool. You can watch and deal with a rogue, Peter, but you cannot watch or deal with a fool.'

As they walked slowly back to the site, Peter voiced a further reason why he felt Comstock should be involved. To isolate him would antagonise him, and they, total strangers to the area, could discover that Comstock may not be the loner he appeared to be but could be in a position to muster a few friends to his aid – and there were only two of them. They turned the bend to find him taking a keen interest in the flecks of gold dust among the sand in the apron of the rocker. So intent was he in his inspection of the gold-speckled sand that they were upon him. Startled, he wheeled around, pitching the dregs of coffee from his mug. He opened his mouth to speak but words failed him. 'There ought to be enough in these hills for all of us,' remarked Peter.

'Yes . . . yes, indeed,' was the startled reply.

'What do you think of our proposition, Henry?' asked Patrick. 'Have you come to a decision yet?'

'Yes, I agree if you have no objection to my bringing Emanuel Penrod in on my share.'

'Suit yourself,' said McLaughlin, 'and by the way, we met your horse around the bend. We were pleased to see he had the good sense to tie himself up.'

'You boys are too hot for me today,' smiled Comstock. And looking beyond the two men facing him he announced quietly, 'I guess I better be moving along, I see you have got company.'

Turning around to look in the direction he had indicated, they saw three Indians on horseback coming their way, two men and a woman. They were the Shoshone who sold the food to Patrick a few days before. They had come with more food, a lot more food: freshly baked cornbread, more cooked meats, an abundance of jerky and pemmican and a large compote of fruit which could be eaten as a pudding or alternatively used as a jam. They were friendly people and one of the men spoke haltingly in broken English. It transpired he was the woman's husband, and the second man his younger brother. It was his wife who had done the baking and the husband assured them she was an excellent cook. When Peter offered money they declined. The food was a token of goodwill and the men thanked them profusely. Unlike Henry Comstock, the Shoshones paid no attention to the rocker or its contents. In the world of the red man precious metals were of no consequence. Having brought their gifts, they mounted their ponies and took their leave.

CHAPTER 16

Peter O'Reilly was right. They came from East and West: from the East where rumours of a pending economic depression were rife; from the West, many from the mines of California, wage earners and disheartened placer miners, all chasing the rainbow on the other side of the hill.

Amongst this first rush was a man who had arrived in California in 1850 – too late by one year to be dubbed a forty-niner. For a few years he had toiled with little success as a placer miner before opening a store. When news of the strike at Six Mile Canyon reached him, he dropped all and headed there, secured a mine on the promise to pay $3,000, then charged back to California to raise the cash. His name was George Hearst. Another early arrival was an Irishman, John McKay. A latecomer to the Californian goldfields, he walked the 250 miles to the shanty town of Virginia City, and worked three years with a pick and shovel before buying out another man's claim for $500 and struck riches.

On the lower slopes of Mount Davidson, Sun Mountain to the Shoshone, tents were being erected haphazardly, many not of canvas but of potato sacks and blankets. Clapped-out wagons scattered everywhere became dwelling places. Rubbish littered the landscape. Men slept in shallow pits they had dug out of the hillside and in many cases, coyotes were forcibly evicted from their burrow and men moved in. Having secured his claim, John McKay, in the winter of 1859–60, lived in such conditions. Prospectors who had been working other sites with little or no success abandoned them and moved into Six Mile Canyon. Many of these worked claims that had been located two years earlier by James Fennimore ("Old Virginy").

In 1851, Fennimore, a teamster, had arrived with a group of Mormons in

Six Mile Canyon. He remained and joined prospectors panning the streams. Shortly after locating sites in 1857 he faded from the scene. It was generally thought that he returned to his home in Virginia. James Fennimore, or James Finney as he preferred, was a wild character, a hellraiser. Sometime around 1857, one evening on a hard-drinking spree with a few prospector boys, James intentionally or otherwise dropped a bottle of whisky on the hard, sunbaked ground in a shanty town that was being thrown together by prospectors. Looking at the shattered bottle and the lost contents, he studied it for a moment then raised his head and arms calling out, 'Fellahs, I hereby name this town Old Virginy.' And from that small scattering of shacks lying in the shadow of Mount Davidson grew Virginia City.

On 22 June 1859, immediately after agreeing with his partners to give one-third of the 1,400-foot mining ground in exchange for the horses and arrastres, Comstock took off to locate other claims for himself. Several of the locations were on the lower slopes of Mount Davidson, others on an area known to prospectors as Gold Hill and several others in close proximity to Six Mile Canyon. Greed was taking hold at the outset. On 8 July, having only days before secured 200 feet in Chollar-Potosi, he sold it for just $30. Shortly afterwards it proved to be an extremely rich seam. Henry Tompkins Paige Comstock was proving to be the loose cannon on the deck. On 23 July he sold his quarter interest in the Belcher mine for $100 which he had held for some time before meeting McLaughlin and O'Reilly. Belcher was to produce $36 million before going on the stock market for more than $30 million.

On 12 August Comstock sold all his mining interests, together with a ranch interest he had had for several years, to James Walsh for $11,130. These holdings were later quoted on the stock exchange for over $50 million. Whatever Comstock picked up seemed to run through his fingers like quicksilver. To be fair to him, he did his share of the pick-and-shovel work, when he was not elsewhere screwing things up for himself and others.

The epitome of the gold prospector was the strong, silent type, the man of few words who kept his business to himself. Not so Henry Comstock; he was as verbose as he was gregarious and given to exaggeration. His wild stories spread through the region. Many, like O'Reilly and McLaughlin, came to believe he owned what he did not and, unwittingly, he stamped his name on what was to be one of the world's richest finds, the Comstock Lode. It was ironic that a man who, through the misappropriation of papers and deeds belonging to two dead brothers, created mischief and spoiled it so ruthlessly for those who were entitled to a greater reward for this discovery and hard work. The unkindest cut of all came when he sold out, again for a paltry few dollars, over the heads of his partners, to an aggressive and well-organised syndicate who made it intolerable for the partnership to continue. Patrick

McLaughlin sold his one-sixth share on 19 September for just $3000. Peter O'Reilly may have received a similar figure, but the partnership broke up and Peter drifted off. McLaughlin remained for some time trying to reorganise.

In the spring of the following year, after a very severe winter of 1859–60, Emanuel Penrod, the last partner in the original discovery, sold out for $8,500. That mine, in which George Hearst had a considerable interest, became known as the Ophir Mine and proved to be the richest of them all. When the heavy blue-grey sticky substance, which miners at first found so bothersome, was assayed and discovered to contain high-grade silver ore, shares in the mines shot through the roof and continued spiralling upwards.

In two months towards the close of 1859, George Hearst and his team extracted from the Ophir thirty-eight tons of the highest grade ore – and that was just the start. All thirty-eight tons of it were loaded on sled-like contraptions and dragged by mules the 250 miles across the plain and over the mountain pass to San Francisco and the smelter where the bluish-grey gooey stuff was transformed into gleaming white bars of silver bullion. At George's behest, it was paraded on open ox-drawn wagons through the streets to the bank where it was placed on show to the public. The Ophir Mining Company was incorporated in April 1860 with a shareholding of 16,800 valued at $300 per share. By April 1862 these shares changed hands for $1,225 each and by October that year the price had risen to $3,800 a share.

Sometime in 1860 Hearst returned to his homeland in Missouri where he met Phoebe Apperson, an attractive nineteen-year-old teacher. He remembered Phoebe as a child before he left for California. They now saw a lot of each other, fell in love and two years later married. Until she arrived in San Francisco she had no idea that George, twenty years her senior, was an extremely wealthy man. In 1863 they had a son, their only child. In the 1920s and '30s the world knew of the newspaper tycoon William Randolph Hearst. His sway in the newspaper world was omnipotent. Many feared him but few challenged him. His opulent lifestyle constantly made headlines, such as his luxurious yacht lying at anchor off Cannes or Monte Carlo, with the wild parties on board. He was the jet-setter before the jet.

WR Hearst displayed all the idiosyncrasies of the self-made man and he made no effort to dispel the fallacy. But it was his father, George, the miner, who, on a hillside in Nevada, rolled up his sleeves, spat on the palms of his hands, dug a deep fortune and sired a dynasty. In the years following that significant discovery in Six Mile Canyon, George Hearst and John McKay went from strength to strength, locating yet more productive sites. Messrs Ralston and Crocker, founders of the Bank of California, started out "digging dirt on the Comstock". Leland Stanford, William Flood and many others made large fortunes from the Comstock mines. The day of the panner was over, at least in Nevada, for the real wealth of the Comstock lay deep in the earth.

In an indefinitely long period of time past, when a hot spinning ball in the universe was cooling down, metamorphic changes were taking place that would determine for all time the structure of the earth's formation into its three component parts: solids, liquids and gases. Resulting from an earthquake deep in the earth or a volcanic eruption, an enormous rock was cleaved along a natural grain. The fissure was some four miles long by nearly 300 feet wide and plunged to over 1,500 feet. From underneath, hot springs shot boiling steam up this gigantic fissure bringing with it silver in an emulsified form and other elements. As this was happening, huge rocks were breaking away from the surrounding mountains and falling into the fissure, thus sealing off the earth's treasure where it would remain until disturbed by man.

The treasure of the Comstock, as the area became known, proved tantalising. If men wanted it badly enough they would have to dig for it and dig deep. New machinery was designed, built and transported to the Comstock, backed by huge investments. Technology in mining had to change. Hydraulic and steam-operated equipment replaced the pick and shovel. Steam power, that could blast away tons of rock and clay, changed the landscape. The arrastre gave way to steam-driven pulverising plants, crushing the quarried rock being fed into them twenty-four hours a day. Miners delved deeper than they had ever done in the Californian fields and lives were often lost. Mining engineers from England, mostly from the tin mines of Cornwall, and other parts of Europe were made welcome, for the Comstock was posing new problems in mining that were challenging the American engineers.

The Civil War was making inroads on the Union's coffers and the eyes of Washington turned to Nevada, not yet a state within the Union. In Nevada, bankers, businessmen and those jockeying for political positions were courting Washington, but Nevada's population was well below that required for application to statehood. Notwithstanding this handicap, but for her contribution to the wealth of the nation as a whole, a grateful President Lincoln, on 31 October 1864, embraced the new state of Nevada into the Union.

Henry Comstock sold off all his interests, always at the first opportunity. In total they came to the sum of $70,601. He opened two mercantile supply stores, one in Carson City and the other in Virginia City, but went broke due to the extent of credit he allowed his friends who could not, or would not, repay. In 1862 he drifted away to Idaho where, it was reported, he was working a claim near Boise during the summer of 1864. Obviously nothing of it came to fruition for the next that was heard of him he was working as a guide for hunting parties before drifting on to Montana, turning up

124

President Abraham Lincoln's proclamation declaring Nevada admitted as the 36th member of the United States of America in 1864.

penniless in a place called the Sweetwater District near South Pass in 1868. The South Pass was part of the Oregon Trail and favoured by the guides who escorted the overlanders to their destinations in Oregon over the quarter of a century of the great migration westward. By the time of Comstock's arrival at South Pass the migratory traffic had finished, so any motive he may have had of making financial gain from the overlanders came to nothing.

On 20 September 1870, near Bozeman, Montana, the body of Henry Comstock was found in some woodland area. In his right hand was a .45 heavy Colt revolver. A neat hole at the right temple indicated where the bullet had entered. There were those who said he was waylaid by highwaymen and murdered for his money. If that were so, the assailants were not very selective in their choice of victim.

In June 1875, Comstock's sister, Mrs Silvian Clark, arrived in Virginia City to investigate his property holdings. She was to discover that her brother owned nothing and had left Nevada having only laid claim to one of the locations he so loudly boasted of owing. It was her belief that one or other of the partners had caught up with and murdered him but she was on her own in that line of thinking. The simple truth was that on a crisp September morning, a penniless and disturbed soul went for a walk in the woods armed with a loaded pistol and took his final wrong turn. In Bozeman cemetery he was laid away in what is now known as the pioneer section. A large black granite headstone stands at the head of his grave. In 1915 it was purchased, and engraved, by a subscription fund raised by some Nevadans who admired him but never knew him.

The only humble memorial to the two young Irishmen who, through their enterprise and endeavour, located the most prestigious gold and silver lode the world has ever known has now, through the pages of this book, been written.

Patrick McLaughlin, after being paid out in cash, rode to San Francisco where he deposited the bulk of the $3,000. The pass over the mountain, at that time, was a haven for highwaymen but he rode alone, preferring his chances with the robbers there to the risk of bedding down with those who travelled frequently with the mule trains. He returned to Virginia City, re-equipped and set about locating new footage but, with O'Reilly gone, it all seemed futile. He was sullen, withdrawn and easily provoked.

What prompted O'Reilly's departure was never known. It was likely Patrick blamed him for insisting Comstock should be given a partnership; after all, he had warned him. They certainly had quarrelled. At times McLaughlin would wander back to the site where he and Peter had made their find. It had a name now: it was called the Ophir. The whole area had changed out of recognition in a few months. The little stream where they first had panned was no longer there. In its place was a dam and beside it a steam-driven pumping station and nearby, two huge pulverising plants, each producing 100 tons at every stroke. Old worn-out equipment was rushed in from closed-down mines on the Californian fields and given an extension of life on the Comstock until replaced by more up-to-date, powerful mechanisms.

On the other strikes the same was happening: the Belcher, the Yellow Jacket and the Chollar-Potosi. Over on Gold Hill the scene was the same. The stillness was assailed and shattered by the noise of industry. The sweating crews operating the machinery, and wielding the shovels and pickaxes, had no time to stop to answer the questions Patrick put to them. He was a stranger amongst them, an onlooker, one come to gape and stare. It was time for him to move on.

The rooming houses of boom-town Virginia City provided more than beds and hot meals and strong, steaming, hot coffee twenty-four hours a day; they were the communications centres. It was in these quickly thrown-together wooden structures that word got around. Whatever information a man sought, he only had to walk up to the makeshift counter, order a hot pie and a mug of coffee, select his table and sit down.

The dining area was merely a large three-sided tent attached to the main wooden structure that was the dormitory. This was partitioned off into twenty small cubicles, ten either side of the corridor that ran the full length of the building. Each cubicle was fitted with two single beds, with a locker box under each bed. On the small table between the bedheads was an oil-burning lamp firmly anchored to the middle of the table, the only means of fire prevention in evidence. No chairs were provided. In the dining area, along the wall that separated the dormitory from the makeshift canteen, were two large wood-burning stoves, the top of one providing constant hot water. On top of the other, pancakes, flapjacks, doughnuts and so on were being turned out to meet the constant demand. The two large ovens provided the hot, crusty, meat-filled pies. The counter was basically three long tables laid end to end on trestles and two smaller such tables at either end. A doorway, used by staff only, led into the main building and a storeroom.

All cash transactions were done at the counter, including room bookings. Unlike the wooden floors in the dormitory, such luxury did not extend to the adjacent tent. Save for much-needed duckboards for those serving behind the counter, the rest was well-trodden hard earth. Small apertures in the canvas allowed adequate daylight to penetrate and, by night, oil-burning lamps, hanging from beams supporting the canvas roof, burned dimly over the tables.

Patrick moved towards a table occupied by three men, put down his plate of flapjacks covered with hot molasses and his mug of coffee and sat on the bench seat at the end of the table. None of the occupants took any notice of his arrival; they were too engrossed in their own conversation. Three empty plates lay in front of them and all three were finishing their coffee from the glazed earthenware mugs, the proprietor's standard equipment. Of the three, the two older men were enjoying their cigarettes with their coffee. They, the eldest two, sat facing each other, the younger one almost facing Patrick and slightly to his left but within earshot of the newcomer.

Each had his elbows spread on the table and all were in deep conversation. When Patrick got himself settled, the two older men, evidently feeling he was uncomfortably close, edged away and motioned to the youth to do the same. 'Don't worry, lads,' said Patrick, not turning to look at them while wiping some sticky molasses from the sides of his mouth, 'I have no need to listen into the problems of others, I have enough of my own.'

'What problems might that be?' the man nearest to him asked.

'Just lost a million dollars a while back,' was the nonchalant answer and he sipped his coffee, stared at his plate of flapjacks and continued, 'maybe more, maybe a whole lot more; no one will ever know.'

Having just left the Ophir he had to talk to someone, anyone. If his opening remark had been regarded by the strangers as being said in jest, then the inflection he placed on the last words left them in no doubt as to the stranger's seriousness. Patrick broke the silence.

'Would you boys know where I could offload my equipment? I've got four mules, a wagon and all the tools a man needs to get himself started and that includes an arrastre. The horse is not for sale.'

The man sitting second on his left rose, picked up his mug and sat on his right. He took a sip of coffee and placed the mug on the table with some deliberation, then inhaled a long deep drag from his hand-rolled cigarette and spent as long over the exhalation, then looked at Patrick and said, 'Tell us, stranger, all about it, nice and slow like. It does a man good to talk sometimes.' Patrick excused himself for his hunger and finished the remainder of the flapjacks, followed by some coffee, and continued. He experienced a feeling of relief that at last someone was prepared to sit and listen.

'My name is McLaughlin—'

'Not Patrick McLaughlin?' the other interrupted, showing no sign of surprise.

'You know, then?' said Patrick.

'Look, my friend,' and he waved a hand slowly around indicating the men seated at the tables, 'ask any one of these guys here if they have heard of Peter O'Reilly and Patrick Mc . . . Here, I'll prove it to you,' and he stopped a miner walking away from the counter, plate and mug in hand, to join his pals who were settling down at a table further along. 'Here, tell me something, now I don't know you nor do you know me, but have you heard the name McLaughlin mentioned around here?'

Immediately the miner answered, 'Aye surely, McLaughlin and O'Reilly, the two that were sucked in over the Ophir where I'm working.' The man who asked the question gave a wink and a nod and the miner looked down at Patrick saying, 'Christ, you're not one of the two who fell for auld Pancake's tricks?'

'Pancake?' Patrick queried.

'Aye, that's auld Comstock's nickname, always stuffing himself with pancakes. The auld bastard should be strung up and left hung out to wither.'

It occurred to Patrick that everyone on the Washoe looked upon himself and Peter as two half-wits without knowing the facts and there was no way to redress the issue. Here was a man, a passing stranger, whose dialect was that of his own, living with the erroneous belief that one of his countrymen had allowed himself to be taken for a fool. He would like to have vindicated himself but the miner was anxious to join his pals; he made his commiserations to Patrick on his bad luck and moved on.

'Why are you so anxious to sell your equipment?' the man on his right asked.

'I came all the way over here from Texas a few years ago to try my luck, started in California where I met up with O'Reilly.'

'Where is O'Reilly now?'

'I don't know, we split up.'

'What did you do for a living down in Texas?'

'I rode herd for a couple of ranchers.'

'If anyone had ever offered me a job like that I would never have gone mining, but then there are no ranches in Cornwall.'

'You're a Cornishman?'

'Been in the tin mines since I was thirteen; thought I might as well try for gold on my own rather than risk my life digging out tin for somebody else. So I came to California. I've been at it six years and I haven't struck anything worthwhile yet, but I will. What do you reckon on doing when you sell your equipment?'

Patrick thought for a moment, 'I don't know, I just don't know.'

'How do you move that arrastre around? Have you got a cart or something?'

'I have an old Conestoga in real good condition considering its years. Took a whole family to California, across the California Trail, fourteen years ago. Hasn't had much work since. I picked it up in Carson a while back for, well, just a few dollars.'

Patrick's newfound friend stubbed out his cigarette in an improvised ashtray and looked directly at him. The other two also appeared to be interested in this man. 'Four mules won't take a Conestoga very far.'

'No,' said Patrick, 'but then I don't intend to be going very far.'

'If we put four more mules to your harness would you change your mind?'

'What have you in mind?' asked Patrick.

'I'm John Tyler,' said the man, shaking hands with Patrick.

The Irishman remarked, 'Wasn't there a president by that name?'

'That's right,' said John, 'back in the early forties, before I came to America.'

Turning to Patrick's left he introduced Colin Church, the only American in the little group, and across the table a fresh-faced youth who Patrick guessed could scarcely be out of his teens. 'And the lad here is Herbert Langsfeld. We just call him Herbie, and no swearing when Herbie is around. His father is a Lutheran minister back in Germany.'

Herbie corrected him as he shook hands with Patrick. 'St Louis, my family came to America when I was vierzehn . . . Please excuse, I mean fourteen years old.'

'How old are you now, Herbie?' Patrick asked, thinking the boy should still be at home with his parents.

'I am twenty, just twenty.'

'How do you say twenty in German?'

'Zwanzig,' came the reply.

'Well, Herbie, you are a German Lutheran and I'm an Irish Papist and I don't tolerate any goddamned swearin' either so I guess we're going to get along just fine.' If Herbie experienced a sudden shock, the twinkle in the Irishman's eyes set him at ease. Turning to Tyler again, Patrick asked, 'Are you boys intending to cut out?'

'Cut out?' remarked Church. 'We haven't even had a chance to cut in.'

'Colin and I have worked the California fields together for a few years,' said Tyler, 'mostly placer stuff. Worked underground for a few companies. Herbie volunteered to join us, so we rigged ourselves out and headed over the pass.'

'But we're too late,' said Colin. 'There is not a foot of ground left.' John began to explain how big money had been rushed in and how the stock market was booming as a result of Comstock shares. All quite unnecessary, for McLaughlin was au fait with all that anyway and displayed his impatience.

'Tell me,' said Patrick, 'these four extra mules you mentioned; what have you in mind? Do I hear a proposition?'

'It could be,' said Tyler. Herbie got up from the table at that moment, volunteering to replenish the coffee. 'You have a Conestoga, four mules and a fair bit of equipment. We are not short ourselves. Would you like to team up with us and make one more go of it, Mac? What do you say; in for a penny in for a pound?'

'Well, you're not thinking of moving west, so it has to be east.'

'North-east.'

'Where?'

'The Dakotas,' came the short reply.

Patrick emitted a long, low whistle through his teeth, thought hard for a moment and said, 'That's long distance.'

'There is gold there, Patrick, and it's still unexplored territory.'

'It's also Sioux country and the Sioux don't like anyone moving in on their territory.'

Herbie returned with three fresh mugs of coffee. Patrick stubbed out his cigarette and, nodding his thanks for the coffee, he continued. 'Have any of you given thought to the distance? The desert and the heat and whatever amount of water you will carry will not be enough. Tell me, John, when you arrived in this country from England, where did you land?'

'New Orleans,' said John.

'And is that where you started your journey west?'

'No, we took the steamer to Westport and joined the wagon train from there.'

'Then you know what you're letting yourself in for. What draught animals did the train work: mules or oxen?'

'Oxen.'

'How many oxen to a Conestoga? I would guess some Conestoga were still working the trails.'

'There must have been at least eight to a yoke.'

'And at least two in reserve,' Patrick reminded him. 'And if you had a choice of mules or oxen to take you across the hot deserts and the mountains and the plains, which would you have?' All three agreed on the oxen. 'Now,' continued Patrick, 'I've got a Conestoga, an absolute beast of a thing and only four mules. Do you think another four would move us all that way over sand and prairie, to say nothing of the mountains?'

'I take your point,' said the Cornishman and he reflected on it while he sipped his coffee.

Patrick went on to drive the lesson home. 'If we were to use enough mules to draw the beast I've got, we would need twelve in yoke and four in reserve and for every extra mule your water will be at least another ten to fifteen gallons per animal to see you across the desert, and we will not have the pulling power with mules to move all that weight.'

'What if,' suggested Colin, 'that is, if you have decided to join us, we had a wagon, say half the weight of yours and nearly the carrying capacity of your beast, as you call it? Would that help?'

'It sure would,' Patrick replied, 'but if you are thinking of a Prairie Schooner we could get away with just another six, eight in yoke and two spares. Yeh, that would do. What pulling power have you boys got?'

'We have two mules and a farm wagon,' said John. Turning to Colin, sitting on Patrick's left, he continued, 'Tell him the rest of it, Colin.'

Colin took up where he left off. 'There is a team digging over on the Yellow Jacket with a neat little Prairie Schooner who would be pleased to change it for a Conestoga or something like it. If we could do a swap with them, would you exchange your Conestoga and join us? We need a man like you and we'll make up the shortfall on the mules and whatever else. And what's more, we will find gold aplenty and there will be no Pancake Comstock to get in the way.' Colin Church laid emphasis on the "will".

'How do you feel about it, young fellah?' Patrick asked Herbie. 'Do you think you will be up to it?'

'Yes, I think I will come through.'

'You'll have to, for it ain't going to be any kindergarten.'

'Ja, I know,' the young man answered in his accented speech.

It looked like a way ahead for Patrick, for there was no way back and his name was shot away for ever in Virginia City; Pancake Comstock had seen to that. 'Well, if you fellahs will have me, let's get started. Colin, if you can see about the exchange of the wagons, I'll set about selling my horse, and as you say, John – in for a penny, in for a pound.'

CHAPTER 17

The Desert, a Vast Wilderness
An Endless Sea of Scorching Sand
Where its Ally the Sun, Hangs Forever
Burning out the Souls of Men.
(Anon)

In a compound just north of Virginia City and a few miles south of the
California Trail, four men, in their insatiable quest for gold, were making
final arrangements for a trek that would take them over a thousand miles
across a continent's most hazardous terrain. It was Monday, 5 March 1860
and at first light on the morrow they would steer their small caravan of one
Prairie Schooner, a farm wagon and fourteen mules, ten in harness and four
in remuda (remounts in reserve) north onto the California Trail and then
turn north-east to Fort Hall where, still following the trail, they would take
the new cut-off known as the Lander Road and continue eastwards to Fort
Laramie, a distance of 1,200 miles.

The route they had chosen was well trodden and the decision to take it
was logical. The time of year, coinciding with their departure, could not
have been better, for the snows on the South Pass, 855 miles ahead of them,
would be well gone. They had ample provisions and a good supply of water
and, if parsimonious in their use, they and their mules should withstand
the desert. For arms they carried four .45 calibre Colt revolvers and four
rifles with ample supplies of ammunition. They were Henry repeaters.
These were the arms later favoured by the men who rode shotgun on the
wagons carrying the silver from the Comstock. The Henry repeater, in its

rate of fire, was deadly and its motto was apt: "Load on Sunday, fire all week."

Patrick McLaughlin had charge of selecting the weaponry and it was his hope and prayer that the occasion to employ them in defence would never arise, for he was the only man in the party conversant with their use. Before setting out it was agreed by all four that, of each week, one day would be set aside for rest and that day would be Sunday. This was proposed by Herbie and all readily accepted that a day's rest each week would be of benefit to man and mules alike. With an average of fifteen miles covered each day this would equal ninety miles each week and, assuming their journey was uneventful, they would make Fort Laramie by early June – a good time to rest up for a few days, get the lay of the land, stock up and head for the Black Hills.

Their departure that Tuesday morning was not entirely a closely guarded secret and the purpose of it was questioned by those who knew of it: four men heading off into the wilderness in search of gold while leaving behind what, within less than a year of its founding, would prove to be one of the nation's greatest strikes. With hundreds rushing towards Comstock, here was this little band going off in the opposite direction. It defied logic.

Colin Church was born in 1835 in the Sacramento Valley. His parents were among the first settlers there, encouraged and assisted by the United States government in its effort to populate that region with its citizens. At the time, Mexico had a feeble tenure on the area and England was biding her time to wrest it from her, hence the urgency for Washington to tighten its grip. When the boy was ten his mother died, largely due to the excesses of a brutal and drunken husband. When his father died shortly afterwards as a result of a drunken brawl, Colin was taken in by an elderly couple who eked out a living from the land. The old man, when not foraging for a living, would be off somewhere along a stream busily panning. Even before the death of his parents the boy spent more time with the old couple than at home and was a source of company to "Grandad" as the child had come to accept him. Those were perhaps his only happy childhood days, fishing the streams and helping Grandad pan for gold. And he learned many exciting tales from Grandad, for in his youth the old man had travelled far. The stories of the great tribes of Indians away to the north and to the east who roamed the vast prairies at will and the buffalo hunts became stamped indelibly in the child's memory. And he listened with the keen young ears of a child as the old man told him how he and some friends found gold, lots of gold, in mountains that he called the Black Hills in somewhere called Dakota.

On one hot and inert afternoon, as the two were lazing on the riverbank, the boy looked up into Grandad's weather-beaten face and asked, 'Grandad, can you tell me again about the time you and your pals were chased by the Indians when you were on the mountains looking for gold?'

The old man smiled and took from his teeth the straw he was chewing. He hesitated for a moment, staring into the sandy shallows and leaning on his elbow he turned to the boy. 'Son, we were not looking for gold,' he said wistfully. 'We had found it, all seven of us.' Here he paused briefly, 'Or was it eight? I don't remember. But I tell you, son, every man of us was carrying in our saddlebags more than a king's ransom. For that while in them mountains we were all rich men.'

'What happened to it, Grandad?'

'How old are you, son?'

'Eight.'

'Let me see, you were born in 1835. In 1833, that was two years afore you were born, we all went to the West; we were all from the East you see. Well, we scoured them hills high and low, panning every river and gully we found and keeping out of sight of the Indians. Often we went without a hot drink or food for fear of lighting a fire and drawing them to us but in the end we found our gold. Each man filled a saddlebag and we were coming away, making our way home, when they attacked us. You know, son, I have thought about it ever since; we were in there well over a year and never saw an Indian until we were coming out. You know what I have thought ever since?' The old man rose from his elbow to a sitting position and rubbed the numb arm and waited for an answer from the boy.

'What did you think, Grandad? That they were watching you all the time?' The astonished Grandad looked down at the small face of wisdom and just nodded and the boy continued, 'They were not going to let you take it away.'

'They didn't let us take it. We paid a high price for our hour of glory.'

'What happened to the others, Grandad?'

'They were all killed, son, and their ponies. All I lost was my pony and my pouch. The last I saw when I looked behind me were three young warriors scattering the contents of our saddlebags into a river, back from whence it came.'

A tug on the little boy's fishing rod was a welcome break to a poignant silence. To a child of eight a man of forty-seven hiding behind a thick black beard is an old man. When Grandad went to the Black Hills in 1833 he was just thirty-seven years old.

Thirty-four years were to pass after that conversation on the bank by the stream in Sacramento Valley until an article appeared in the *Black Hills*

Times. In 1877 the paper published a story following a discovery by one Louis Thoen who uncovered a stone near Lookout Mountain, South Dakota. Carved on the stone slab was the date 1834 and almost indistinguishable were the names of seven men and underneath the names was the cryptic message:

Came to these hills in 1833 Seven of us All ded but me Ezra Kind Killed by ind beyond the high hill Got our gold June 1834 Got all the gold we could carry our ponys all got by the Indians I have lost my gun and nothing to eat and Indians hunting me.

Some of the names were traced by letters from relatives to the *Black Hills Times*. All the envelopes bore eastern postmarks confirming the men "went west" but, of the men and their gold there was never a trace. Still on display in Deadwood is the Thoen Stone. And to the north of the town is the cemetery, where lies its first occupant, the legendary Wild Bill Hickok. Inscribed on his tombstone is his epitaph by Captain Jack Crawford, poet scout of 1879. It reads:

*Rough in his ways? Yes
But kind and good-hearted;
There wasn't a flaw
In the heart of Wild Bill.
And well I remember the day that he started
That graveyard on top of the hill.*

Close by lies another of Deadwood's colourful characters, Calamity Jane.

Around the time of the discovery of the Thoen Stone, evidence of other mining activities was turning up. Nine shafts, long abandoned, were uncovered by the new surge of prospectors that began moving in around the middle to late 1870s. An old Colt pistol was uncovered from bedrock in a disused placer mine. The manufacture of the pistol was traced back to 1853. A broken rifle butt pierced by bullet holes indicated a fierce battle. Could the owner of the weapon have employed it as a club in the final throes of a hand-to-hand fight? All these pieces of the jigsaw and more, most reported by the *Black Hills Times*, would indicate that white men were in those hills, rooting and tearing for the elusive metal as far back as 1833. And perhaps it was the old man's reminiscences by that trout stream in the Sacramento Valley in 1843 that unwittingly planted a dream in the mind of the young Colin Church that would obsess him throughout his life.

On the evening of the sixth day, just north of a place known as Big Meadows, they made camp. From Virginia City they had come 130 miles and it required little reckoning to establish that their distance run was an average of twenty miles per day. This pleased them and boosted their confidence for it was good progress. When they set out from Virginia City, several factors were in their favour, such as that their mules were fresh and the terrain under them was firm and that it was early March with a light westerly making pleasant going. A study of their maps showed them that from their position, the trail arched away to the north and to the south in a huge bend to a place marked Emigrant Pass and from there it straightened out running north-east for 250 miles to Fort Hall, from whence they could take the recently opened Lander Road cut-off.

By leaving the trail at Big Meadows and heading east across the desert to Emigrant Pass they could make a short cut of some fifty miles. A few intervening hills should present no difficulty and, with their compass to steer by, there was not much to go wrong. Of the four, three decided upon this plan. Herbie, the youngest and least experienced in desert travel, showed reluctance to leaving the trail but he was outvoted three to one. In the morning, having tanked up their water containers, they would head directly east to Emigrant Pass and from there continue on the well-trodden California Trail.

John and Patrick led in their Prairie Schooner with eight mules in harness and two in tow. Colin and Herbie in the farm cart with two sturdy animals in harness followed close behind. If they encountered any hilly ground ahead they may be required to double up with their two in reserve.

Away to the east, the sun which, had not quite breached the horizon, threw a panoply of colours along the desert rim and the air clung to the chill of the night. This was the time for desert travel and if a respite was needed by midday, so be it. Travelling into a rising sun made forward vision very restricted and they were upon it without warning. The falling tongue of a wagon, smashed away from its main body and the neck yoke torn from its tip, lay partly buried in the sand. Further ahead, the wreckage of a wagon lay on its side, remnants of its linen bonnet fluttering from a couple of bows that were still in evidence.

The little caravan came to a halt and the four travellers clambered down from their wagons to make a closer inspection. It was obvious to the onlookers that this wagon had come to grief long ago, perhaps in the years when the great migration was at its height. It was an old Conestoga with damage to its front. Down the years the sand had drifted over it, piling higher upon it as if nature itself was unable to bear this scene of tragedy. In the well of the vehicle were two skeletons partly covered by sand. They faced each other in a close embrace. One frame was longer than the other. Only the high-buttoned boots of different sizes told the stark story of horror to the stricken men: two females, mother and small daughter died locked in each other's arms during their last agonising hours. Scattered around were so many personal effects, cooking utensils, tools scattered from the jockey box, kicked open by the oxen in their frenzy brought on by thirst.

None of the remains of the animals was found. Having kicked themselves free of the wagon, they could have run in all directions, parts of the harnesses still attached, until they finally dropped. Two human skeletons were found, probably father and son, their bones bleached in the desert sands. Their rifles, old Hawkens, the barrels caulked with sand, lay near them. This would indicate that no white man or Indian had passed that way before, for the rifles would not have been there.

In silence the men buried the remains of the family close to the wagon. Colin took the falling tongue which had been broken off at its base, disconnected the double tree and lashed it neatly to the tapered end near the top, thus turning two lengths of timber into an ornamental cross. The spare wheel was laid flat on the sand at the head of the grave. This, with its iron tyre, would provide a sturdy base. The broad base of the cross was wedged firmly into the hub. And, from a few timbers salvaged from the wreckage, the artistic Colin Church erected a tall and elegant memorial to a family who had set out in search of their Utopia but found death, because someone had ignored the law of the desert.

Those that smoked, and that was all except Herbie, sat on the farm wagon and rolled their cigarettes in silent thought. Little lizards scurried about in the sand or lay motionless, basking in the sun. Each man's thoughts were on the family, who, years before, had obviously made the same mistake that these four were embarking upon. Had one of the men a map and compass, and with confidence and perhaps some arrogance, left the west-bound trail at Emigrant Pass, ignoring warnings, and within three miles of cool, life-giving water, brought about his death and that of the rest of his family?

When the smokers had finished, Herbie rummaged through some of his belongings in a canvas bag, drew out a small German translation of the Bible and began reading from it at the grave. The three on the wagon looked sheepishly from one to the other and quietly moved beside Herbie, who was silent in prayer. Patrick made the sign of the cross and half mumbled, half whispered a De Profundis, almost forgotten, while Colin and John stood with heads reverently bowed. Herbie, when finished, returned his Bible to his holdall, pointed to the north-west and said quietly but firmly, almost as if giving a command, 'That is the way to the trail.'

Three days later at the bend of Lassen Meadows they rested. Mules were given a good look over and the wagons and wheels checked and the axles greased. The next section of the trail to Emigrant Pass would take them over hilly ground and it was as well to be prepared. They had lost some of the time that had been made in the first week but only a few hours and that would be made up. The land around them, from horizon to horizon, was desolate but as yet there was water along the trail and their supplies were plentiful. Often they would make a short stop where there was shrub vegetation by the trail and allow the mules to graze. This was a huge saving of the fodder they carried. They were lucky here for they had not yet met wagons coming westward and their mules had first servings of the spring vegetation. Ruts dug by the wagon wheels over the years made the going hard and wheels required constant inspection.

On the evening of 26 March they arrived at a junction aptly known as City of Rocks, a desolate place. A few granite boulders marked the Salt Lake cut-off which ran south for about 150 miles to Salt Lake City on the south-east shore of the Great Salt Lake. From Lassen Meadows they had met several wagon trains but with little contact; the occasional wave from some of the women and children, which was returned, was about all. There was never any stopping. That would slow down the train or part of it. All the travellers looked lethargic, drawn within themselves, a ragtag collection of assorted humanity weary from a long and hazardous journey. Undoubtedly many had buried close relatives along the way. The four heading east were witness to the small wooden crosses by the trail from Emigrant Pass. It was said by someone that the Oregon to California Trail was the world's longest graveyard.

'Why are you limping?' enquired Patrick.

'It is nothing,' replied Herbie as he refilled his coffee mug.

'It has to be something. No one limps for nothing. Now get that boot off and let's have a look at that foot,' John Tyler demanded and went on to give Herbie a lesson on the importance of the care of the feet and especially in the conditions in which they found themselves. Reluctantly Herbie began to remove his left boot, explaining how a wheel from the farm cart rolled over it the previous day.

Patrick inspected the boot as Herbie tenderly coaxed the heavy sock away from the blood-caked big toe. 'The upper of your boot has been sliced,' remarked Patrick. 'How did that happen?'

Herbie explained that he had stopped the wagon for a moment and got down to secure a part of the load that was beginning to move due to the oscillation of the vehicle over the rutted ground. As he was standing in front of the rear wheel, the cart, due to the involuntary movement of one of the mules, moved forward. His left foot was just in front of the wheel and as it moved it took his foot down into a rut and the edge of the heavy iron tyre sliced through the leather. The big toe was bruised and discoloured and there was a laceration of the flesh just below the toenail.

'This needs watching,' said Patrick and he went to the wagon and returned with a fistful of salt in a basin. He poured hot water into the basin, rolled it around a while, helping the salt to dissolve and then tempered it down with some cold water. 'We are no surgeons,' said Patrick, as he began to bathe the boy's foot, 'but this treatment is about as good as you'll get.' He upbraided Herbie for having concealed the injury and told him to take care of it, keep it clean and walk as little as possible on it until it healed. Colin found a fresh pair of socks for him. They moved on north-east towards Fort Hall some sixty miles away. There they would replenish their supplies and, with luck, Herbie would get medical treatment for his injured toe.

The weather was hot and the sands desolate. *Why*, they wondered, *did Brigham Young ever decide to found a city here?*

CHAPTER 18

Fort Hall, 1,162 miles from Independence, Missouri, by the south route, was established early in the era of the great migration westward. Independence and Westport, both on the banks of the Missouri river, became the main starting points for the overlanders. Fort Hall, like Forts Kearney, Laramie and Casper, was founded strategically along the California Trail. Of these staging posts, Fort Laramie, 617 miles west of Independence and established in the land of the Sioux nation by a treaty signed there in 1868, would be best remembered.

Before 1848, America had laid no claim to the Oregon Country as it was then known. The Oregon area was huge, stretching to the Alaskan boundaries. The British Empire had designs on this vast area until the 1840s, when American settlers began moving westward in ever-increasing numbers, thus leaving the British in control only of the northern part of the Oregon Country, now part of Canada. No state of war existed between the two nations over this region: it was just a case of who got what first, but chicanery – initiated by the British – carried on for years.

Fort Hall became the place where the two trails split, the California overlanders taking the trail south-west, the Oregon-bound heading north-west. In other words, Fort Hall became the fork in the road. At Fort Hall, in the early days of the Oregon Trail, British agents of the Hudson Bay Company were planted to persuade Oregon-bound travellers to turn south-west, away from the hazards of the bleak Oregon wilderness, and choose instead the golden land of California. Their ruse was simple and they had some success – it was to steer the American people away from Oregon, delay the settlement of the land and protect their lucrative fur trade.

There was little activity around the fort when the four lumbered in about mid-morning on Tuesday, 3 April 1860, having travelled the 530 miles from Virginia City. Everywhere people moved about their business at a steady pace. Nowhere was there the appearance of fortress life except for a few soldiers casually strolling about and looking as if they had no right to be there. There could have been no more than a platoon. Only a few buildings – living quarters, cook house, stores, stables and so on – bounded a large square. There was no stockade and no sentry posts, but then there did not seem to be any need for them either.

Patrick may well have provided the answer when Herbie remarked on the absence of Indians. 'What self-respecting Indian would find himself in a place like this?' It was, nevertheless, an oasis in the desert for which they were grateful. No wagon trains were passing through at the time and they had the undivided attention of the keepers of the fort. There was no doctor at the fort just then, but they were told that a young army doctor was on his way from Fort Laramie and should be arriving in a week or two. The medical centre was manned by two army medical orderlies. Herbie had his toe inspected and dressed and Patrick was commended for the salt-water bathing. The medic was concerned about the laceration below the toenail and advised Patrick to see to it that it was taken care of.

They remained at the fort all that day, attending to the mules and generally resting, and in the evening, having thanked everyone for the food and hospitality, they moved on, taking the Lander Road cut-off. This cut-off had opened in 1858, only two years earlier. From the east it started from the South Pass running west to pick up the old trail at Fort Hall. The Lander Road ran parallel to the earlier Sublette cut-off which lay further to the south. The original California Trail turned south for about 120 miles just after the South Pass, then turned northwards in a great bend to a point where Fort Hall was to be sited. This route, to the early overlanders, was circuitous and hazardous. At the most southerly point of that bend, Fort Bridger, one of the earlier posts, was established. The fort was named after Jim Bridger, one of the early mountain men, Dan Boone among them, who blazed the trails across the mountains. By taking the Lander Road cut-off, the four men would save themselves a tortuous 102 miles around the mountains to the South Pass.

At noon on the ninth day out from Fort Hall, they pulled over on the pass for rest and some food. They were still using eggs they had bought back at the fort. Their progress had slowed down, for it was now all uphill travel. They were no longer sure how far they had travelled since Fort Hall. Herbie, seating himself beside Patrick, appeared to have lost his appetite. He did not look too well. Patrick, shaking a pinch of salt on a hard-boiled egg, turned to him asking if he was all right and was answered in Herbie's first language, 'Ich fuhle mich nicht wohl. Ich habe einen kopfschmerzen.'

'Now that sounds real serious,' answered the laconic McLaughlin. 'Is that the medical term?' Colin and John, sitting on Patrick's left, enjoyed a good chuckle at the Irishman's dry humour.

'Please. I sometimes forget, my apology. I said I have a headache and do not feel so good.'

'The best cure for a headache is to let plenty of cold water pour over your head and neck,' said Patrick. Pointing behind him, he continued, 'Now, if you have finished eating you get down there to that wee waterfall and get your head and shoulders under it until your headache has gone.'

'Yes, I go now. You will wait for me?'

'We'll be half way to Laramie by the time you get back up here,' smiled Patrick, and calling after him, 'and when you get back I want to have a look at that toe. You haven't had your goddamned boots off since Hall.'

It was discovered that the gash in Herbie's foot had allowed dirt to infiltrate the wound. Patrick cleaned and redressed the wound with lint impregnated with a healing balm and wrapped it from a roll of bandage, all given to him by the medic. The bruise showed no sign of clearing and there was still blood oozing from the laceration, but what concerned Patrick, and indeed the other two men, was a thick purple line which appeared to be moving up the foot. It was tiny but it was there.

Neither Patrick nor his two companions discussed their concern in Herbie's presence. He had stoically accepted the pain, irritated only by the handicap of the difficulty of walking. He was transferred to the comparative comfort of the Prairie Schooner, put into his slippers and made to rest. Patrick remarked in a low tone when out of earshot, 'Where ignorance is bliss.' The three men felt uneasy about him; it was obvious to them that they had a potentially sick man on their hands. Had they been anywhere that a doctor could be found, there would have been no problem for, as yet, he was not too bad, but they were in a mountain wilderness.

From their position they were 160 miles from Fort Casper, maybe more for they were now guessing. Thanks to Colin, who kept a calendar, at least they knew what day it was: Thursday, 12 April. The road was long and tiresome. Where was that doctor who was coming to Fort Hall with the relief troops? Then it occurred to them that the column would have gone by way of Fort Bridger on the original trail and they, being on the cut-off, would miss them. All the way to Fort Laramie and no doctor. It was hope and pray and make haste for Fort Casper. They would push on now seven days a week, regardless of Herbie's Sabbath day of rest. At an elevation of over 7,500 feet above sea level it was asking much of men and mules. The nights were cold and the wind soughed mournfully down the hills. They were out alone and each man questioned his own and the other's wisdom, but South Pass and Devil's Gate were behind them now and tomorrow that great milestone to so many, Independence Rock, would be within sight.

John and Herbie could recall clearly their sighting of that landmark when they had travelled westward. Patrick, shortly after his arrival in the New World, headed for Texas on the Santa Fe/Cherokee Trail and when he left Texas for California he travelled on the Fort Smith/Santa Fe Trail. That night, within sight of the Rock, they shared their travel experiences, talking into the early hours. And from Colin Church they heard, in full, of the old man whose stories of gold in the Black Hills were more than a little responsible for them sitting around a camp fire in the shadow of Independence Rock. At noon, three days later, they rolled into Fort Casper.

The doctor strongly advised that Herbie should not travel on to Fort Laramie immediately, but rest at the fort for a few days. 'There is an infection in that foot,' he told the other three, 'and his temperature is over one hundred.' The men looked at each other but before any objections were sounded he let them know they had no say in the matter. The doctor was in change. He would lance the toe and apply a poultice which would be changed regularly. Herbie would be put to bed in the sick bay and, there he would remain until his temperature had dropped and he showed an improvement. The doctor was asked if he had any idea how long their pal would be laid up.

'Fort Laramie is two weeks from here. If I were to keep the young fellow laid up for a week he should be fit to travel then. Let's say I keep him . . .' and he studied the calendar on the wall, '. . . until Sunday, sixth of May. You move out Monday seventh, that would put you in Laramie by – say – last week of May. How does that sound?'

'We didn't expect to be in the Black Hills before the middle of June anyway,' replied Patrick. The others nodded their agreement.

And the doctor asked, 'Why the Black Hills?'

The Irishman answered, 'Gold, doctor, just gold.'

And from his desk the doctor studied them, each man, from above his half-moon spectacles and spoke in a gentle, warning tone, 'Gentlemen, you are braver than me.' He then rose from his desk, bidding them an enjoyable stay at Fort Casper.

'That foot is coming along fine,' remarked the medical orderly, applying a fresh dressing. 'Another four or five days and we'll be sending you on your way after that gold.' This was disappointing news. True, the doctor had decided to keep him there until Sunday. It was Wednesday now and he felt fine, just fine: well rested and ready to go.

'But can I not leave now?' he asked. 'I am feeling good and the pain has gone.'

'You may well be,' replied the medic, 'but we have only finished with the poultices yesterday and neither that gash nor the incision the doctor made has fully healed yet. Better to wait a few more days. The gold can wait; it has been there a mighty long time.' But Herbie was adamant, promising to take care of it and to change the dressing regularly. 'All right,' agreed the medic, 'I'll put your point to the doctor and if he agrees to release you that will be his decision but don't be disappointed if he says no. That would be my answer.'

'So you feel you would like to be moving on, young fellow?' the doctor inquired as he lifted the end of the bed covering to look at the leg and prod at it.

'Ja, Herr Doktor. Please excuse, I sometimes forget.' The doctor smiled and waited for Herbie to settle himself. 'Doctor, I must thank you for everything you have done, for what you all have done for me, but I now feel very good, no pain in foot. I can walk now.'

The doctor stopped him as he was about to get out of bed to demonstrate. 'Quite so,' agreed the doctor, 'but you are not sufficiently healed yet. However, if you must insist I can only release you, but you must be very careful. Do as little moving around as possible and your dressings must be changed regularly. You promise you will do that?'

'I promise.'

'All right,' said the doctor, 'you rest up for the remainder of the day and tomorrow you can be on your way.'

Early the following morning, Thursday 3 May, they set out with strict orders from the doctor that Herbie was to report to the medical centre on arrival. Without incident they would be there in ten days but they allowed two weeks considering Herbie's handicap. The worst was behind them now and when they would get onto the gentle grasslands of Wyoming it would be heavenly – plenty of fresh meat off the land and good grazing for the mules. The rest of the trek would be a vacation.

And it was – for the first few days. Herbie, disregarding the doctor's advice, was undertaking too much of the work and was limping. He refused to allow Patrick or either of the others to look at his foot. On the evening of the fifth day from leaving Casper he was feverish. They had no thermometer but they knew he had a raging temperature for his forehead was hot to the touch. Patrick insisted that the boot must come off and it did, with assistance from John and Colin holding him down. And when the boot was forced off and the bandage removed, the sight and smell shocked them. The foot was swollen and discoloured up to the ankle and it stank.

After the initial shock, the feeling for the boy was a mixture of anger tempered with pity for he, through disregard for his own wellbeing, had put them all in danger. Yet he was no more than a boy, more than eager to play his part and whose feeling for others was never in question. And how he had stood in prayer at that humble graveside in the desert, holding his well-thumbed Bible. Now, within a few days of the security of the main fort, he was in grave danger. Not one of his three companions was capable of performing an amputation and that might be the only action that could save his life.

They made haste and they kept to the trail. They saw no one – no red man, no white, no one – only buffalo. Only Herbie occupied the Prairie Schooner. The rest slept in their bedrolls under the wagons. Sleep did not come easily but when it did it was the deep sleep of the exhausted.

It was Herbie who heard it and raised the alarm by firing a shot through the top of the canopy. John and Colin were first up. Patrick in sleep-starved confusion looked into the wagon thinking that Herbie had ended it all. But Herbie was alert and from his prone position was pointing and shouting, 'The mules! The mules!' Someone was running in the darkness shouting, 'Stop!' A volley of shots rang out; flashes from the gun barrels spat flames in the dark. A rattle of chains mingled with the harsh rasping sounds of the mules in protest drifting away into the night and from the distance came a few whooping shouts from the triumphant raiders. The acrid smell of black powder hung in the dark night air.

Their rifles lay by their bedrolls from where they had sprung, their brains befuddled and their eyes unfocused in the black of the night. In defence of their mules, it was their immediate reaction and John and Colin died instantly in a vicious fusillade of bullets. The Comanche raiders had all the advantages for their eyes were accustomed to the dark. But in their haste to Laramie and the resultant lack of sleep, the four prospectors had neglected to post a watch. And to add to the irony, four alert men, each equipped with a Henry rifle, would have had the power to repulse a formidable attack. For the second time within a year, Patrick McLaughlin, in his search for gold, had drawn the short straw.

The remainder of that night was an eternity and the moon threw no light. Without help, Herbie was unable to get down from the wagon. There were mules out there, so not all had been taken. They heard their sounds but Patrick would not risk looking for them lest he stumbled over a fallen comrade. That would be too much. If the mules were there then they were tethered, so it could wait until dawn. And when two animals became silhouetted by the first chinks of light, he went to them and he instinctively knew they were two of his own four, the only two left, and he hugged them around their necks each in turn, sobbing uncontrollably. His loaded rifle was close to him. He was not going to lose his two remaining mules. If any Indians were to return for these two he was prepared to kill or be killed in defence of his friends.

It was a desperate situation in which the two survivors found themselves: Patrick, left with the awful task of two dead comrades to bury and perhaps a third soon to follow; Herbie, almost delirious and running a temperature, unable to help himself or his friend. It all fell on Patrick's shoulders. *How, he thought, did Herbie deteriorate so rapidly?* Several times in his life had he not bruised a toe without any devastating effect? Admittedly Herbie had received a flesh wound and had disregarded the advice of everyone, especially the doctor's. Had the doctor detained him, this would never have happened. No, the doctor could not have held a man against his wishes; that would have been imprisonment. And he cried out aloud, 'God help me. Why? Why?' And he threw himself against the bonnet of the wagon and covered his head in his hands.

Before the sun had reached its zenith Patrick had wrapped his two dead friends in their bedrolls and placed them side by side in a shallow grave where every sun-hardened sod fought each stroke of the pickaxe. He was weary and weak from lack of sleep and food, and his mouth was parched. For a while he just sat and sipped water, just sipped and it tasted good. Then he attended to the needs of the sick boy. Herbie, he was pleased to find, was more conscious and it would seem his temperature had dropped. He was coherent and Patrick was thankful for the opportunity to explain to him what needed to be done and how much help he could solicit.

'Herbie,' he explained, 'we have to move on. Now listen. I am going to move all the heavy stuff off the farm wagon and when I have done that I am going to take the bonnet off the Schooner and fix it on the cart. As soon as I have done, I will move only what is necessary from here into the cart and that includes you, and with the two mules we will move off as light as possible. Now, can you help yourself from here into the cart when I am ready?' Herbie smiled and said he would. 'Good lad,' said Patrick, 'and I'll get your arm round my shoulder, but we must hurry. Can you eat something, Herbie?'

'Yes, I am a klein hungry.'

'That's good. First we eat,' and he gave the boy a pat on the left shoulder that made him cringe as in pain. Patrick was surprised but carried on with getting some coffee going and rustling up some food.

All the equipment associated with the procurement of gold, except for a pick and shovel, was jettisoned from the farm cart. *What a find,* thought

Patrick, *for some migrant family going westward with gold in mind.* This would surely be read as an omen of good fortune. His smile was private and cynical. Before undoing the bows that held the canvas taut, he took a light quilt from the Yankee Bed and covered Herbie from the sun to which he would soon be exposed. Herbie was clutching his small Bible but seemed asleep, so he worked quietly and quickly around him. The whole canopy came away easily and he was pleased to find the bows still had excellent tension. They would make for an easy transfer to the sides of the cart. Why did Herbie flinch when he touched his shoulder? He would have to look at that.

Transferring Herbie from Schooner to cart was arduous but required doing without delay, regardless of pain. No time now to look at that shoulder or foot. As soon as Herbie was as comfortable as was possible he hitched up the two mules, his friends, and moved on from that awful place. From the sun's position it could only have been mid-afternoon and with the reins in one hand and a chunk of rye bread in the other he urged on the mules. Without stopping, he looked back with a heavy heart at that place where no cross or stone marked the spot and he thought how soon wagons, rumbling westward, their occupants filled with euphoria and hope of riches beyond the Rockies, would be rolling over a young man who had come all the way from Cornwall and a boy from Sacramento Valley who had come in search of gold and who died under a hail of bullets trying to defend their mules from a band of brigands.

Towards evening, Patrick stopped and unhitched the mules. He would not make camp for the night, not while there was light to allow him to see the trail ahead. It would be a short respite. It seemed Laramie was further away. How far it was in time and miles he had no idea. He had Colin's calendar and compass, but what was the point? Perhaps he should keep a note of the day and date. The date was 13 May 1860, the day Sunday. He had neither pencil nor pen but luckily Herbie was able to direct him to the small valise in which he kept all his writing. Not surprisingly, Herbie had been keeping a comprehensive and up-to-date diary. There were other writings in the case, many others, and family correspondence. Patrick took one of the many pencils and closed the case quickly for he felt like an intruder. He got a small fire going from dry grass and some buffalo chips; plenty of these items but little else. He would attend to Herbie's foot and investigate that shoulder – but after they had eaten a few slices of salt bacon followed by rye bread and jam and some hot sweet coffee.

'Let's have a look at this shoulder, Herbie.'

'It is not my shoulder, it is under, here.' And he indicated with his right hand. His voice was weak.

'Your armpit?'

'Yes, my armpit, that is where it is, but it's not hurting now so we will leave it. My foot is a little painful but I think we will leave it. I feel I should sleep now. Thank you, Patrick. You are very kind. You find pencil?'

'Yeh, I did, Herbie. Thank you.'

'You must rest today,' said Herbie.

'Why?'

'It is Sunday. That is what we agreed upon when we set out.'

'Things are different now,' Patrick reminded him.

'I think we should both rest today. You have been working so hard on my behalf. I cannot thank you enough. When I meet my parents I must tell them of you. No, better you come and meet them when we get to St Louis but I would like to sleep now.'

It was early morning and far ahead Patrick saw what he thought to be a tree line. 'Herbie,' he said, 'can you see over there?' Lifting the boy's head from the improvised pillow and pointing ahead to the east he continued, 'Can you see that line of trees?' Herbie nodded his head. 'Well, if I yoke up the mules and we get moving we could make it there by noon and then we can rest in the shade of the trees for the rest of the day. What do you say?' Herbie smiled and nodded. 'But first,' said Patrick, 'I am going to take a look at that foot and see what's bothering your armpit.'

There was a huge swelling under the arm and the sight of the foot, or as it was now, the leg, frightened Patrick and the smell was the smell of death. Without touching it Patrick could detect the heat emanating from it. The leg, up to the knee, was bluish grey and swollen and tinged with purple. And what oozed from the open wound was darker than the leg itself, and it looked to Patrick like the blue-grey sticky substance that men were struggling with in the caverns of the Nevada Hills, the stuff they called silver which would be forged into sword handles and plaques and cutlery to adorn rich men's tables. Patrick redressed the leg and made him as comfortable as possible. 'Would you like your Bible, Herbie?' Patrick picked it up from the floor where it had fallen. 'Tell me, Herbie, why does a German carry an English Bible?'

'It was the last thing my father gave me before I left. "Herbikin," he said, "not only must you speak English but you must also read it and reading your Bible is just as good in English as in German."'

'All right, you just make yourself comfortable there and I'll get you to yon trees as soon as I can.'

Driving into a rising sun Patrick was unable to see much ahead, nor did he bother much. The mules kept up their steady pace. He could have done with the other two in harness but that could not be. *What did Indians want with mules anyway?* he asked himself. His mind wandered on all the happenings of the past week. Herbie was not talkative and he thought it might be good to get him talking. Turning to him he remarked on the valise with all the writing material and complimented him on his good handwriting. Herbie opened up a little, telling Patrick that he had studied journalism and instead of joining a newspaper he intended to travel around and gather material for his writings. This made sense to Patrick for Herbie did not come over to him as the prospector type. *Poor lad*, thought Patrick, *if only his father had insisted on that newspaper office.*

'Herbie,' Patrick suddenly called out with subdued excitement, 'looks like we've got company.' Herbie, with effort, raised himself up on his right elbow and managed a weak smile. Four, perhaps five, miles ahead was a wagon train heading towards them.

'Your young friend looks in mighty bad shape,' whispered the wagon master, taking Patrick aside. 'God, man, you sure have a problem.' All twenty-six wagons were now stopped on Herbie's behalf and a group of the adults gathered around him, a pathetic sight lying in the old farm cart under an improvised canopy. Several women began ministering to him.

'What are his chances of making it to Laramie?' asked Patrick.

'Friend, you say you're ten days out from Casper and if that is so, you've only been doin' about eight miles a day. Laramie is eighty miles from here.' He pointed an index finger at the ground to emphasise his point. 'You're just half way with ten days ahead of you.' Patrick felt dispirited. 'Now,' continued the wagon master, 'if you can keep that boy comfortable and you make sixteen miles a day there is a good chance he could make it. And at Laramie you'll get all the help you need. When you left Casper you took the north cut-off. It's called Child's Cut-Off. You're on it. Did you see a river on your right as you left Casper?'

'No,' said Patrick, 'no river.'

'Then you came out a bit further to the north. That's no matter, for you will pick up that river when you get to yon trees.' He pointed to the line of trees towards which Patrick was headed. 'Now stay with the river all the way to Laramie. There is a Sioux village back there about twenty miles or so but they won't bother you none; just give them a friendly wave and pass on your way. Could be they will be gone by the time you get there. The Sioux move about a lot. Now if these good ladies can fix this young fellah up somehow and get some hot soup into him, I reckon you have a good chance of making it. We left St Joseph on Sunday, fifteenth April. Now that's well over five hundred miles to Laramie – about twenty miles a day, maybe a bit more at times. So far we've been lucky but we just can't afford to stop too much. From here we have over a thousand miles to the Sierra Nevada and we've got to be over them mountains before the snows of October set in. If you get caught in the snow in them hills, that can be death to the whole train, my friend. No, Sirree, I don't want my charges endin' up like the Donner–Reed party.'[1]

'We didn't see a train going west since before Fort Hall.'

'I'm not surprised,' said the wagon master, 'so many cut-offs have been opened over the years you could travel the whole trail, any trail, from east to west and see no one.'

One of the women who had attended Herbie interrupted them. 'Your young friend,' she said, addressing Patrick, 'is very ill. We have done what we can for him but it is my opinion he will not make it much further, poor boy. What's his name?'

'Herbie,' answered Patrick.

'Well, I'm sorry to have to tell you, Herbie has got septicaemia.'

'What's that?' asked Patrick.

'It is blood poisoning caused by bacteria or, if you like, dirt that got into the wound. I have seen so much of this. My father was a doctor in Philadelphia where I grew up. My advice to you is to make it to the shelter of those trees,' pointing in the direction. 'There is a river and plenty of shade. Just rest up a while and keep him comfortable. The rest ought to do you some good. You look like you could use it. I regret to say it but with a temperature running over one hundred and the condition he is in, I don't think he is going to last too long.' She cast her eye over what she could see of his belongings in the cart and asked Patrick, 'Have you got plenty of tools and all that?'

And Patrick answered, 'And all that, yes, Ma'am; I have a pickaxe and a shovel.'

She lowered her eyes. 'It is difficult to say it directly.' She then turned and walked to her husband and children who were waiting by the wagon, stationed three or four down the line.

'Son,' confided the wagon master, 'that lady is sure worth listenin' to. Since leaving St Joseph she has been administerin' to the sick, young and old alike. I reckon she will have her work cut out before we reach Sutter's Fort.'

'You're California-bound?'

'That's right.'

'Then,' said Patrick, 'back there along the trail a day or two you will find a

---

1 In 1846 a group of overlanders, later to be known as the Donner–Reed party, took an ill-advised short cut near Great Salt Lake. The resultant delay left them caught in the snows of the High Sierras with horrendous consequences. The few that survived did so as a result of resorting to cannibalism.

Prairie Schooner. That's the bonnet of it.' He pointed to the lopsided canopy atop the cart. Patrick went on to tell the man of the attack and how he had buried his dead comrades. And the wagon master listened sympathetically. 'If anyone can use all that mining equipment they are welcome to it and the wagon, for I won't be needing any of it now.'

The wagon master nodded and no words came. He had seen all the cruel hands life can deal but he had never got case-hardened to it. 'They were Comanche,' he said, 'They were goddamned Comanche. You're on the boundary of Comanche and Sioux territory and a day or two on you will be in Sioux land but you should get no more bother. Your pals would have been all right if they had not raised the alarm. They just wanted your mules but I guess a man needs his mules.'

The "Good Samaritan" lady returned with some friends bearing fresh bread and a jar of honey and real butter, for along the line several families had their milk cows in tow. The bread was laden not only with butter but also with jam and a can of hot sweet coffee. They stayed with Herbie, helping him to take some food and fresh milk to which he would repeat, 'Danke.'

'He is German,' explained Patrick, dispelling their bewildered expressions. 'He is saying thank you.'

'Oh bless him,' said one and she may have said it for all of them for he had the sympathy of all. Patrick was provided with foodstuff for several days ahead for which he was most grateful.

It was mid-afternoon when Patrick unharnessed and tethered his mules and began setting up camp. He looked in on Herbie wrapped in his bedroll and thought how right the lady was. No use pushing it any more; he would just wait.

The land around him was spectacular; between mountain and plain. For his site he selected a rise on the ground encircled by a ring, or copse, of tall trees, a good shelter and one that offered some camouflage. Beyond the copse more trees studded the land on all sides and below him to the east where the ground rolled away, a river tumbled over a rocky bed, hurried along its course, a tributary, one of the many, of the mighty North Platte and the one the wagon master had mentioned. But Patrick was unaware of that for he had no knowledge of this land.

He wasted little tine in getting down to the river's edge with some cans for fresh water and to his delight he saw the river cascading over black granite boulders into a dark swirling pool. It was inviting, too inviting to resist, and he stripped off his sweat-soaked clothing and plunged into the cold refreshing water. As he immersed in the pool with the crystal clear water dashing down upon him, rejuvenating flesh and sinew, he thought how Herbie could benefit from these healing waters, but alas that could not be.

And if John and Colin had not met with their untimely end, how they all would have enjoyed a sojourn. That would not have happened for, in their crazy quest for gold, they would not have deviated from their course but charged on without ever knowing that such a beautiful place existed.

Herbie was quite lucid when Patrick returned from the river. He put aside his small Bible which he had been reading. Patrick listened as he told him how the cawing of the crows reminded him of his boyhood days in Duisburg on the Rhine. There were always crows around the trees beyond his house and he liked the sound, especially now, for it brought him close to home. He spoke of his parents and his sister, now attending an American school. 'One day, Patrick, you must come and visit my family in St Louis. They will like mein Katholik friend.'

Patrick nodded, 'I *am* your friend, Herbie, and I'm sure your family and I will get along fine.'

'In my writing case you will find my parents' address in St Louis, will you please—'

'You are not going to die, Herbie. You have a bad infection that will clear and when it does the fever will clear with it and when that happens we will both forget about gold and head for St Louis. Meanwhile we stay here and rest. All that rocking around in that auld cart was not helping you much. How does that sound to you?'

'That sounds real good.' It was an effort for him to speak.

Patrick smiled saying, 'You're beginning to talk like a real American. Here, have a sip of water and get some sleep.'

Patrick led the mules by a circuitous path to the river to a place where there was no bank and access to the water was easy. Walking with a mule either side of him, he thought, *if only he could meet some Indians with a kindly disposition to their white brothers he would ask their help for Herbie.* All these people had their own medicines handed down through countless generations. They had the antidotes to counteract the venom of the rattlesnake and so many other maladies that nature visits upon man. He had only heard such stories, mostly in Texas, but he had never known the Indian at close quarters. That opportunity never came his way and if it should it better come soon for Herbie.

As the mules saw the water they tested his strength so he let go of the head collars. As the mules drank, he sat on the grass, rolled tobacco into a cigarette and lit it. As he smoked, a stab of guilt pierced his conscience, for it was not his tobacco he was enjoying but that of his dead companions. How he wished they, all of them, could be sitting on the grass enjoying their cigarettes while watching, not two mules, but sixteen refreshing themselves by the riverside.

Patrick could see no point in continuing with further dressings to Herbie's foot, or rather his leg. To do so would have been distressing to the patient and to no avail. He had stopped eating several days ago and the only fluid that passed his lips was a little milk offered by one of the ladies from the wagon train. Herbie was dying. Patrick sat with him with a foot supported on a shaft of the cart, mopping his face with a damp cloth.

Evening was drawing in: a large flight of passenger pigeons crossed overhead, momentarily throwing their collective shadow over the site and stirring the family of crows hovering above the trees. *Strange,* thought Patrick, *how Herbie, earlier in the day, enjoyed their cawing and how their sounds took him back to his home town on the Rhine.* And Patrick recalled the sounds of the large colony of rooks that nestled in the tall elms below his town in those far-off boyhood days, and like Herbie's Duisburg crows, his rooks, too, were music to his ears. Without opening his eyes he uttered something unintelligible to the Irishman's ears. Having repeated it several times with Patrick prompting him to speak louder and speak English, the words came as: 'Der Sonntag . . . diesem Sonntag. It is Sunday Morgen.'

'It is Sunday morning,' repeated Patrick, firmly establishing the words in his head.

'Ja, it is Sunday . . .' and before he said morning, stopped. To Herbie, Sunday morning it was and Patrick's German was improving. 'Die Glocke, Kirchen,' murmured Herbie and in his delirium he got his message through by simply adding, 'ding-dong.'

'Ah!' exclaimed Patrick, 'church bells, Sunday morning and the crows, I see.' And with a satisfied smile Herbie closed his eyes again. Church bells and rooks, familiar sounds associated with those bright Sunday mornings. Duisburg on the Rhine and Maghera lying in the shadow of the Sperrin Hills shared affinities. Herbie Langsfeld was nearing Duisburg.

That night Patrick, tucked in his bedroll, lay looking at the stars as he smoked his last cigarette for the night. *If only he had a good guard dog,* he thought, *how contentedly he would sleep. A big hairy dog curled up beside him, what better company?* But sleep he did and when he awoke he was pleased to see his mules grazing nearby. This would be a long day and much to be done.

Herbie's breathing was laboured and irregular. Patrick sat on the grass planning his day over a mug of sweet black coffee and a cigarette. He would be leaving soon without his patient whose personal effects he would have to put together. The farm cart would be abandoned and only essentials would be securely packed to be carried on the mules. Three Henry rifles and a sizeable amount of ammunition would require careful packing so the weight would be evenly distributed. His own rifle would be carried where it should:

loaded and slung over his shoulder. The other three and ammo would fetch good money, for these guns were so new they were not yet in full production. He would head for Laramie, on foot, leading his mules.

At forty-five, Patrick was too old to start an army career. Ranches were starting to flourish across the West and Midwest and there may be a place for him in that field of work; after all, he had not been long away from it and he would not have to go all the way back to Texas. There was Colorado where cattle men were getting established with the aid of huge investments from England, and also here in Wyoming. But firstly he had an appointment he must keep in St Louis.

The day was hot and the site that Patrick had chosen, ideal for concealment, was a sun trap. The tall trees and other small foliage contained the heat within the copse and on that day no breeze blew. This added to Herbie's final discomfort. Patrick delayed his planned departure move and sat with Herbie, applying damp swabs to his face and wrists. Close by a bee buzzed around, its noise cutting out intermittently as it alighted on each wild flower to extract the nectar. Butterflies fluttered lazily and from somewhere high on a tree bole, a woodpecker tapped out his message that he was in search of food. Patrick left his unconscious patient. He was hungry and had to eat something, anything that did not require cooking, and a large mug of coffee. Afterwards he stretched his bedroll out on the grass in the shade of a tree and slept. It would be a long night.

A cooling breeze wafted over Patrick's face and his tree threw a long shadow across the grass. He stirred from his bedroll and went around to the rear of the cart and from an untidy bundle he took his small shaving mirror, unused for some time. Herbie's hand was cold to the touch but still supple. There was no pulse and the mirror that he held to his face remained clear. Herbie, Patrick guessed, had not long gone.

A cool breeze moved gently through the copse from the south-west, lifting the hot still air in that suntrap where Patrick had bivouacked. Overhead a golden eagle circled on the early evening thermal. Upwards, effortlessly upwards, it soared in regal silence, its primary feathers altering pitch to adjust for bank in the turn. Away to the north it rose, staying with the bubble of warm air which had broken free from that stifling site now far below. Patrick watched until it was a mere speck. Then it dipped and swept away down the sky towards a gold and crimson sunset.

With his tenon saw, the one Colin used in the desert, a memory now, Patrick removed the shafts from the cart and with his saw and an old blunt chisel he managed to rebate the short cross-piece to the main body of the cross with a tight-fitting joint. The perpendicular section was the full length of the shaft and laboriously hewn into the hard glazed wood, deeply indented to be forever remembered, was the following: HERBERT LANGSFELD, AGED 20, DIED HERE MAY 14TH 1860.

Patrick would remain at the site all day Tuesday, packing his belongings into four panniers in order as to what would be required on his journey and what would not. Packing panniers for mule transportation was a skill in itself and he was well practised. The rifles and revolvers with the ammunition would be stowed first with other heavy items not immediately required. Distribution of weight was an important consideration. Thought had to be given to food and water containers.

In the evening he returned to the grave, under a tree with a generous spread of foliage, where he had placed his friend in the early hours of the previous morning. With a large stone, one of the many strewn around, he hammered the cross into position; the sharp end, encased in its brass ferrule, proved helpful in driving it into the hard ground. The stones, gathered from the surrounding area, he selected and placed in a rectangle on the grave. That finished, he took from his jacket pocket Herbie's treasured possession, his small Bible, his last gift from his father. Of all the saints in the firmament above, Luke must surely have been his favourite and Patrick felt it would be right and fitting that he should read from Luke, Chapter VI – the beatitudes and woes – for that was where the little pocket Bible fell open. And he read aloud:

'Blessed are you who are poor, for yours is the Kingdom of God
Blessed are you who hunger now, for you will be satisfied
Blessed are you who weep now, for you will laugh
Blessed are you when men hate you, when they exclude you and insult you and reject your name as evil
Because of the Son of Man
Rejoice in that day and leap for joy, because great is your reward in heaven
For that is how their fathers treated the prophets
But woe to you who are rich, for you have already received your comfort
Woe to you who are well fed now, for you will go hungry
Woe to you who laugh now, for you will mourn and weep.'

He slowly closed the book and returned it to his pocket and, remembering his other companions who had neither stone nor cross to mark where they lay, nor relatives to whom he could return their possessions, he quietly recited the Lord's Prayer and finished with the sign of the cross.

At first light he strapped the panniers to his mules, belted the .45 Colt to his hip and shouldered the heavy Henry, and with a mule on either side of him he led them to the riverside so they all could drink their fill before setting out. Before dropping over the hill, he stopped and turned his head for a final look. Two young martens, frolicking on the stones over the grave, stopped simultaneously and looked directly at Patrick as if they were saying: 'He is with us now, you may leave.' An owl swept in from the darkness that was still behind him and landed silently on the bough that overhung the grave. It appeared to glower down at him; then it ruffled its feathers and emitted two loud hoots that sounded to Patrick as if it was shouting an urgent message. And to Patrick the message came over to his ear as: 'Go, go, you have little time.'

The cross stood tall and erect and some way off there was the old farm cart, its shafts sawn away and its bonnet, cannibalised from an elegant Prairie Schooner, tilted at a crazy angle. An abject monument to failure through adversity.

CHAPTER 19

What was it the man said? Patrick asked of himself. *If you can make sixteen miles a day with that buckboard, you should make Laramie in five days.* Well, he had no buckboard now and in the late evening of that first day on his own he reckoned on having covered twenty miles. Another three days at this rate and he would be in Laramie.

The immediate problem was his dwindling food supply. There was plenty of fresh meat on the hoof but having shot it, what was he going to do with it? Patrick McLaughlin was no butcher. And solid fuel was not in any great abundance. All very well brewing a pot of coffee or turning a few pancakes on the pan but roasting a leg of antelope over a fire of buffalo chips could have stretched McLaughlin's culinary ability. One thing was certain: with plenty of lush green Wyoming grass his mules would arrive in Laramie in good shape.

All that day he followed the river, keeping it to his right as the wagon master had advised, and it was easier going than walking the hard rutted trail. Patrick, his long legs made for walking, strode along easily. Either side of him his bearers, uncomplaining, kept up their lively little gait hour after hour. He had always treated his horses and mules with the respect that is customarily expected of a civilised man, even with a little kindness, but beyond that they were there to serve him. Alone now for the first time in his life and without a goal in mind other than survival, he was seeing these willing little creatures in a new light. These little fellows, moving effortlessly and with passive acceptance of their burdens, were now his friends and to his surprise they would return his affection by nudging their heads into his chest when it occurred to him to pat them and tussle their manes. And no longer was he leading his mules. All three were walking side by side.

At the close of that first day's march since leaving the copse where Herbie slept, Patrick was at peace with himself. He could not reproach himself for having neglected Herbie. He had done all he possibly could for him. Time and Herbie's deteriorating condition had not allowed him to tarry at the place where he buried John and Colin. His regret was that he had no address or name of any relative of either man. Perhaps that was the way they would have preferred it. At Laramie he would report the deaths to some official body and leave it at that but now the terrible helplessness had gone from him. He was alone now, but not lonely.

He tethered the mules close by his bedroll. The Henry rifle he tucked inside the roll, placed the Colt under his improvised pillow and turned in for the night. At daybreak he would breakfast on the last of his food supplies, the last of the bread, now stale, given to him by the Samaritan ladies on the trail. The jars of honey and jam would have to sustain him to Laramie. His last thought before sleep took over was that they would have a safe and uneventful crossing of this wild and untamed continent. 'Bless them,' he whispered, 'they will need all the luck they can get.' From the branches of a cottonwood tree down by the river's edge an owl hooted and from further down the river its call was answered. Somewhere to the north a wolf howled to the stars and close by there was the chirp of crickets in the grass. Patrick was at peace with himself and with nature.

To rise with the sun and see the thin, almost translucent, mist hanging lightly over the dew-laden grassland; to sit a while to gather one's thoughts and allow the aroma of the sweet-scented grassland to suffuse the senses, can only be compared to heaven itself. If Patrick entertained such thoughts they were tempered by the realisation that he had a forty-mile march ahead of him to be done on a chunk of stale bread and a jar of honey. The thought of fishing the river was soon dismissed. His fishing tackle was packed away. The search for that would waste time, added to setting it up and waiting for some obliging fish to come along while he, Patrick, was all the while losing his, already over-taxed, strength. No, he would lead his mules to the river, then load up and go on with what he had and hope to sight a wagon train en route.

It was a hot day and throughout the earlier part, walking into the sun's dazzling glare was trying. Flies tormented his mules and Patrick was constantly swatting them with his hat from the animals' eyes and ears. If the poor things had had the gift of speech they undoubtedly would have thanked him. His scorched and chapped lips did not miss the attention of the ubiquitous pests. The sun ascended to its zenith and slowly, never ending, continued on its downward path across the heavens.

Patrick was relieved; he could now see ahead and, more importantly, to his right across the river to the trail where, with any luck, he may hail a west-bound wagon train. He could see the trail away into the distance but no wagons were to be seen. Onward he plodded, inexorably onward, almost like a man possessed. From the pouch hanging from his belt he took the jar of honey and dipping a finger in the sweet sticky substance he licked it. A further invitation to the flies. This he did without stopping for he feared if he stopped he would sink to the ground and move no more. And if so, what would happen to his two friends; would they walk the plains forever carrying his burdens? He replaced the honey jar, swatted the flies from himself and his mules and uncorked his canteen and drank from it without stopping or breaking step.

A gentle south-westerly carried a faint and pleasant smell towards him. It was the smell of burning pine logs. And as suddenly as it came, it was gone. Was it in the wind or was it in the mind? Yes, it was in the mind for it had gone. It was happening to him; he was hallucinating. It had happened to others, many others; why should it not happen to him? In his situation he was a candidate for that kind of end.

First the smell of pine fires, next it would be the sweet smell of the peat fires of his own native land. And then he would have a woodland scene before his eyes, or a lake. If it be a lake, thought Patrick, *let it be Lough Neagh. Yes, that would be the way to go, standing somewhere on the Carntogher Hills looking across the valley to Lough Neagh on the horizon. Better that then being shot in the gut by a low-down dirty scoundrel in some filthy smoke-filled saloon.* Months, years from now his frame would lie on the plains of Wyoming, bleached by the sun and storm. Before he would fall he was determined to release his friends from their burdens – his burdens – but that was not yet. There was more distance left to cover. Another whiff of pine fires reached his nostrils, more pungent than before, and this time he lingered.

Before him the land fell away gently, giving him an extended view of the horizon and away in the distance to his right, where the line of cottonwood trees hugged the riverbank, wisps of pale blue smoke lifted lazily into the air. It emanated from several positions in close proximity. It could only be the Sioux encampment, or a village, that the wagon master had mentioned. *Twenty miles or so from there,* the man had said. *God, another forty or more to Laramie, I'll never make it unless I get help from that village. After all, the man said if I give them a wave and pass on my way, no one would bother me and he should know; he took his whole wagon train past here. That's it, I'll go in and ask for food.*

Outside the village a little boy, playing with his dog, stopped running. He stared in utter bewilderment at the bearded and bedraggled man walking between two pack mules coming towards him. As he came closer he smiled and waved to the boy who looked towards his village for assurance and down at the little dog. Patrick thought he was brave, for he did not run and yet that seemed to be his desire. Patrick kept smiling and asked the frightened boy to take him to his chief but the youngster just stood dumbfounded. Patrick, in exasperation, began waving his hands wildly indicating exuberant headdress and all the while uttering gibberish.

'Big chief . . . many feathers . . . plenty wives, you take me.' Suddenly he stopped, realising how ridiculous he must have seemed and sounded. The child waved the stranger in the direction he wished him to follow. There was little activity in the village, but it was just after midday and perhaps the Indians, like the Mexicans with whose habits he was more familiar, also had their siesta while the sun was high.

The boy waved him in the direction of the river, past some trees and towards a circle of white tipis. These tipis or lodges had multicoloured paintings, mostly of horses and buffalo. Beyond the first circle was another with an open arena-like area in the middle. The lodges were opened up for ventilation with the inhabitants relaxing inside. Pennants hung limp from the poles projecting through the tops. The absence of scalps dangling from them gave Patrick some relief. He was viewed with suspicion but no hostility and undoubtedly his guide was constantly questioned as to where he was taking the stranger. The fragrance of good rich cooking pervaded the entire area and strangely fused with the smell that one associates with horses, though none was evident.

From the open grassland Patrick had, as it were, been led by a child into a strange and alien world, like a dream from which he must surely awake. Or had he died somewhere out there on the prairie and this child, now leading him, could he be his conductor? Yes, that is what it is; they say that everyone, when they died, is sent a conductor or guide to smooth the way for the spirit in the transition from one life to the next. *They were clever*, mused Patrick, *those who thought this one out; what better than the calmness of a child to lead me in? Did they reckon that if they had sent an adult after me he would have found McLaughlin a whole lot more troublesome? And the mules; how did they get here?* His mind was addled and his physical strength on the point of exhaustion.

At one of the tipis in the second circle the boy stopped and signalled to Patrick to wait. The tipi looked no different from the others, no ostentatious embellishments that Patrick would have associated with a chief's lodge. The entrance flaps were folded back for ventilation but there was no visible sign of movement from within. Patrick assumed the occupants were all resting. He stood in a state of high anticipation between his mules as the boy disappeared into the darkness of the interior. Standing between his mules the wait seemed interminable, and realising he was too close to the opening, he backed himself and his mules away a little to give his host space without cause for offence.

Suddenly the figure of a tall man, as tall as Patrick himself, filled the aperture. This surprised him for most of the Indian population he had come into contact with were Shoshone and they were notably short in stature. This man was majestic and must surely be the chief although there was no large headdress. He wore a headband and brightly embroidered patterns, and attached to the back of it, two eagle feathers hung carelessly lying on a mane of raven-black hair parted in the middle that swept over his left shoulder to lie on his chest. The hair was held by a tight band above the shoulder which appeared to be of the same material and design as the headband. A buckskin open-fronted jerkin covered his torso and the tight-fitting trousers of the same soft skin came just to the calf of the leg. Buckskin moccasins covered his feet, fitting comfortably around the ankles. On his upper arms and wrists were leather bands beautifully decorated with bright multicoloured stones. He carried no weapon but stood with arms folded gazing at Patrick with his mules and baggage with the expression of a successful man who is suddenly met on his doorstep by a long-lost, down-at-heel relative who has, without invitation, come to dwell.

Patrick was lost for words as he faced this powerful silent man whose complexion glowed like the sun. When he finally mustered up sufficient courage, all he said was, 'The cookin' sure smells good around here,' and immediately he thought what an inane remark to make. And still his host stood, arms folded, expressionless. Patrick, dazed from fatigue and hunger, felt he was witnessing something unreal. This was a never-ending dream, a bad dream from which he must surely awake. In his confused state he had a fleeting reflection that the face before him was familiar; that he had been in this very situation in a distant time. The French, he knew, had an apt expression for it but he could not remember it.

And as the déjà vu feeling slipped away the Indian spoke, not in the native tongue of the indigenous North American but in a distinct Ulster accent. And loud and clear, the question he asked the stranger was:

'How are they all in Maghera?'

And Patrick, his head buzzing, almost hysterically called out:

'Jaysus, Willie, is that you?'

CHAPTER 20

Of all the Plains Indians – those, mostly nomadic, tribes that ranged from the Mississippi in the east to the Rockies in the west, and from the Canadian border to near the Texan boundary – the Sioux nation was undoubtedly the largest. In the Dakotas, their stronghold, together with their allies, the Cheyenne, they were a dominant force.

The word Sioux is synonymous with Dakota or Lakota. Their nation was, and still is, divided into seven tribes or clans, each with strong family connections. These clans, known as the Seven Council Fires, are the Oglala, Teton, Yankton, Miniconjou, Santee, Bruelé and Hunkpapa. Of these, the Oglala were the largest. Although they were territorial, if the Santees were to be found populating an area east of the Missouri river and the Oglala territory was designated west of the river and away to the south, there were no demarcation rules.

There was free interchange between the clans, or family groups. This was noticeably so at trading fairs and on more solemn occasions such as the Sun Dance, which can be held from late spring through to the end of summer, when many thousands would have been assembled. Often whole villages would have "upped stakes" and travelled great distances to muster at some predetermined place. Throughout each year many huge trading fairs were held at Laramie long before a white man's fort was established there. It was on such an expedition that a large number of Sioux, en route to Laramie, had sited their tipis by the little river, the one Patrick was following, in the shadows of the Laramie Mountains.

'We must find you a good horse, Pat, and some decent clothes that any civilised Indian wouldn't mind being seen in.' Patrick turned his head from

Willie, who was sitting cross-legged on a bundle of rugs, and looked with revulsion at the garments he had so long been clothed in, now scattered on the rug-covered ground beside him where he had discarded them. They stank, especially his worn-out boots.

Patrick, after a substantial meal the evening before, had slept soundly throughout the night and most of the following morning. He stretched out an arm and dragged the jacket towards him and from the pocket he fished out a silver-encased pocket watch. On the back, in miniscule block, was engraved "Robert A. Fitzroy and Son, Jewellers" and underneath "St Column Minor, Cornwall". He was seeing this for the first time and reflected on it. *St Column must be a very small place,* he thought, *for a business man to have no need to add a street name.*

He gave the winding mechanism a few turns and suddenly experienced a pang of guilt for the watch had been a cherished possession of John Tyler and the elementary but useful little pocket compass, now in one of the pockets of the same jacket, had been the property of Colin Church. He felt like a grave robber, that he had stolen from his dead comrades. He snapped the cover open and the black hands showed clearly against the white face: 11.50, ten minutes to midday, and he would still have been asleep had Willie not roused him. Scrolled on the inside was the name of "John J Tyler", just that. There was no "With love" or "To my son" – just the name, beautifully inscribed.

One thing was certain, thought Patrick, *no man ever walks into a jeweller's shop, selects a watch like that, and has his own name engraved upon it. This watch had been a present from a girlfriend, or a parent as a parting gift to a son.* But Patrick would never know the story. Comfortably wrapped in the soft buffalo rugs and well rested, he turned to Willie and told him how the watch came to be in his possession.

'Stay wrapped up there for a while,' Willie commanded. 'There will be someone coming in soon—' and as he spoke the lappet was flung open with considerable authority and into the tipi strode a woman of middle years but with the looks and grace of one half her age. She wore a buckskin tunic and skirt, the seams of the arms and skirt fringed. Her long black hair reached the small of her back, about level with the end of the tunic. A decorative soft leather band encircled her head. She carried a wickerwork basket that seated comfortably on her left hip. She strode past Patrick's rug-covered feet, her gaze constantly upon him and her eyes displaying mischief. Each item of Patrick's garments she picked up gingerly by finger and thumb and delicately placed them in the basket. When the last two items, the worn-out boots, were placed in the basket she pinched her nose in mock disgust and turned towards the opening. As she passed Willie she looked at him, then to Patrick saying with a cheeky smile, 'Poor boy.'

Patrick turned his head towards an amused Willie saying, 'Aren't women just women the world over? One of your lady friends?'

'Her name is Red Wing, daughter of Chief Two Rivers and wife of Oitancan Wakinyan,' said Willie.

'Wakinyan is a lucky little Indian,' was Patrick's comment.

'Lucky big Irishman,' replied Willie.

Patrick looked at him square in the eye, 'Your wife?' Willie nodded with a smug smile. 'And that name you mentioned, what is it again?'

'Oitancan Wakinyan,' Willie replied. 'Oitancan means Headman and Wakinyan is Thunderbird, or a bird of thunder. The Thunderbird is in Lakota folklore; it represents the natural world of space and thunder and lightning. The Thunderbird is a symbol of power.'

'And pray tell me,' asked Patrick in good-humoured fun, 'why should this honour have been conferred upon Willie McKay?'

'When I was under attack and all my friends around me were dead I was fighting for my life, these people rescued me. They thought I had put up a good fight. Chief Two Rivers felt I ought to have an Indian name. At the time of the attack a thunderstorm was in full fury overhead, so Thunderbird it was. I came fighting with thunder. Wakinyan, that has been my name ever since.' Observing Patrick about to make some facetious remark, he added sharply, 'And I like it.'

Patrick nodded in acquiescence but in his mind found it difficult to separate the Indian man squatting on a buffalo rug before him and the schoolboy with whom he had played games; with whom he sat at the same school desk; the boy he attended Mass with on Sunday mornings and with whom he sang in the choir in the little chapel in the glen. Now he had assumed another name, another language and no doubt another religion. This land and her people had claimed William John McKay . . . forever.

Willie stood up saying he would be back shortly and suggested that Patrick remain in bed until he returned, an unnecessary suggestion since Patrick's clothing had been removed. It became clear to Patrick that Willie, and whoever else shared his tipi, had vacated it, leaving the guest to himself. He did not remember turning in that evening; he just slept. He marvelled at the strange reunion and the train of events that brought it about. Would he ever have made Laramie had he not stumbled into this camp and of all people in the whole world, Willie McKay? *Hell! Whatever that fancy name he calls himself now, Willie McKay is good enough for me.* He looked around for his packs but could not see them and assured himself that they were all right. The mules, they must be grazing with the horses. He could hear horses moving and voices and from somewhere a dog barked. The luxury of lying in bed until midday, stretching the aches out of his bones was luxurious.

From his bed at ground level he began taking a mental note of his surroundings. Lying in an Indian tipi within an Indian village was a new and strangely unsettling experience, worlds away from all that was familiar to him. Patrick was no newcomer to living under canvas, or under the stars for that matter, but the structure and the contents of this Indian home caught his imagination: the concept of a mobile home, the basic structure of which was merely three or four long poles. The structure, he observed, was strong and designed to withstand the fierce surface winds that frequently swept the open plains. His thoughts were suddenly jerked back to the present by the lappet being flung aside and Willie's huge frame filling the open space holding two large towels over his arm.

'I never thought Indians used towels like these,' remarked Patrick, as he sat upright against the wickerwork backrest Willie had placed behind him.

As he fingered the soft fluffy cotton bathrobe Willie said, 'When you are with us a while you will discover what the Indian women are capable of making, but to answer your question, no, when we get to Laramie you will see where we find all these things.'

'You haven't lost any of the language,' said Patrick.

'And again when we get to Laramie you will know why, but for now let's go down to the river and have a good wash.'

Willie stripped off, wrapped the bathrobe round him and led the way; Patrick similarly clad, followed. Walking bare footed, and with only towels covering them, Patrick recalled the night when they were returning home late from a local dance. Willie took up Patrick's anecdote, 'Aye, when we took that short cut over the shough[1] at the bottom of Crilly's meadows and the auld kesh[2] gave way on us and we both went in up to our necks.'

Patrick, chortling at the memory, continued, 'And there was nothing for it but to strip off, shoes and all, and leg it out all the way home, stinking like a pair of polecats. Just as well it was dark and two in the morning when we walked up main street in our bare pelts with our stinking duds under our arms. Wasn't it just as well the girls weren't with us?'

Willie paused in thought, then, with a peal of laughter, also recalled, 'That would have been a procession for the good citizens of Maghera.' The laughter subdued as he turned to Patrick with a note of nostalgia, 'That was long ago, Pat, that was long ago.'

The chill cleansing water that raced along its stony bed from its source in the Laramie Mountains was invigorating. The pool they stood in was about four feet deep. The black granite boulders, washed smooth down the centuries,

---

1 Shough: a waterlogged ditch.
2 Kesh: an improvised bridge for walking over a bog area.

provided a lively swirl to the water due to their natural distribution. The water reflecting the dark boulders was darker here and a light froth whipped up by the whirlpool danced merrily around the water's edge. Patrick was suddenly reminded of the last time he had taken a bath, for the pool and the boulders were similar. He dismissed the morbid thought immediately, for he felt he deserved this bath and he was going to enjoy it. Willie, splashing in shortly afterwards, handed him a block of what appeared to be a lump of cake with dark green flecks throughout. 'What is this?' Patrick asked.

'Smell it,' said Willie, 'and now rub it all over your mule-smelling body.' Patrick found the mild fragrance pleasing but had difficulty in producing a lather from it, but as the water was so soft, soap was almost unnecessary. 'That is something else Indian women make when there is nothing else to do. It is made up from fats and herbs and some wild flowers but I never found out what they are.'

'It sure smells good,' said Patrick.

They lazed a while on the grass by the riverbank and talked. There was much to talk about: reminiscences, how Willie's brothers may be managing the land, the future, if any. 'You must be hungry, Pat.'

'Now that you mention it, I am – I could eat a buffalo.'

'Half will do you, I'll have the other half; let's get back.'

'Have you been here long?' asked Patrick.

'About a week,' said Willie. 'We will break camp tomorrow morning at daybreak and make Laramie by sundown and when we have eaten we have to find you a good horse.'

'It will be good to get into a saddle again,' said Patrick, but Willie reminded him that he may find the Indian saddle somewhat different. 'I thought Laramie was more than a day's ride away.'

'No,' said Willie, 'the wagon master you met on the trail was right, he was measuring your walking time and you have been walking for a longer time than you imagine. That is why you were drained when you found us.'

'How long do you intend to stay in Laramie?'

'Only as long as it takes to do our bargaining. Laramie is not a place to hang around longer than we have to these days.'

'Why?' Patrick asked.

Willie stopped in his tracks, turned and pointed to a stand of trees some way off to the south and close to the river. 'Do you see that big tree standing out from the others over there?'

'Yeh,' said Patrick.

'This place is called Cottonwood Creek. Six years ago the Miniconjou were camped here; they were a small party. Before they went off scouting they left a fourteen-year-old boy to look after the camp. A troop of soldiers happened to find the camp. They killed and scalped the boy. They were sighted later on the south side of the Platte. The sergeant in charge had the boy's scalp dangling from his horse's bridle. That tree you see there is where the child was given a tree burial. There has been unrest here since that time when a young inexperienced lieutenant, straight out of West Point, charged into a camp with a troop behind him and shot mostly women and children and one old chief, who only tried to make peace with him and offered to pay for the cow.'

'The cow?' Patrick looked puzzled.

'A cow had broken away from a wagon train heading for Oregon; it ran amok through the tipis and one of the young braves could do nothing but shoot it. The owner of the cow reported it to the garrison and the young upstart felt he knew how to deal with Indians. He got himself and his troop killed after he had opened fire on women and children and old people. It has never been the same since then; always trouble, and it's spreading.'

In 1851 a colossal assembly of the Sioux, Cheyenne and Arapaho nations, the largest gathering of the Indian population ever to have been witnessed, assembled on the plains of Laramie for the first signing of the Treaty of Laramie, the treaty drawn up to guarantee the red man freedom to roam at will over his native land without let or hindrance, in exchange for allowing the white settlers the freedom of trespass across his land. Years of hope, frustration and hard work, on all sides, had gone into the preparation for that meeting only for the Treaty to be shattered three years later by a young and inexperienced officer who did not know what he was doing.

A pleasant surprise awaited Patrick when they got back to the tipi. As he drew aside the tipi flap, with Willie just behind him, there, neatly spread out on a rug, was a smart buckskin outfit with moccasins laid at the trouser ends. The only original piece of clothing was his hat, all cleaned and smartened up and placed deliberately at the head of the tunic. It was all laid out to represent a man recumbent on his back. Beside the tunic was a roll of dollar notes, a pocket knife, pocket watch and compass, a small pocket Bible and a tobacco pouch – all his belongings retrieved from his confiscated duds. His revolver and cartridge belt were close by and, in addition, there was a knife with an elegantly carved handle of bone and leather protruding from a well-polished leather scabbard. Patrick was moved by such kindness and instinctively looked around to thank Red Wing, but was nudged by Willie saying, 'You can thank her later,' as he chivvied him to get into them. 'Let's see if you measure up to a plainsman.'

Patrick measured up all right. The shirt of buckskin was soft and light, the most comfortable he had ever placed against his skin. The trousers and jacket with their fringed seams were a striking fit and the moccasins, that clung comfortably above the ankles, could have been made for him.

'I've long wondered why Indians and white plainsmen have fringes on their sleeves and trouser seams,' said Patrick. 'Maybe you can tell me?'

'And around the bottom of jackets,' Willie continued. 'The plainsman learned from the Indian, Pat; it is to strengthen the seams. Buckskin is hardwearing but will tear at the seam easily without the fringe. But, man, aren't you just the picture of sartorial elegance?'

'Hell, Willie, who has been filling your head with all that fancy stuff?'

'It was said to me once and when you come back with us to the Dakotas you'll meet the man who said it.'

'Would you like me to go back with you?'

'Suit yourself, Pat. When we get to Laramie you may decide otherwise but I would like you to come to the Dakotas and stay a while and get to know these people. They are lovely people, my friends. And, Pat, now that the gold fever has gone from you and all the damage it has done, maybe a change of scenery and a restful life for a while will do you some good. You might be pleased to learn that the Indians are not always on the warpath and taking each other's scalps.'

There was a brief pause; Willie had said his piece and his old friend could read into that wistful smile that Willie had rediscovered a part of his history and he wanted to hold onto it as long as he could. Patrick visualised nights of good conversation around the campfires, of songs and recalling of times long past, of a hunt or two and fishing and he looked Willie straight in the eye and gave his answer. 'Willie, luck has just dealt me out a good hand and I'm going to play it.' Both men shook hands warmly and with their free hands drew each other together in a brotherly embrace.

'Pat, let's go and get some food and then find you a horse.'

CHAPTER 21

Willie and Patrick rode abreast, Willie towing his travois and Patrick leading his pack mules, their reins in his left hand. He would rather they were wound around his saddle horn but Indian saddles were not equipped with such extraneous items of equipment. The stirrups, all leather, with no means of adjustment, he found a little short for his long legs but not uncomfortably so. In the course of the journey he would let them dangle free from time to time to exercise his feet and legs.

The horse they had chosen from the remuda, a big roan gelding; Patrick found it comfortable and well behaved under him considering that no one knew how long it was since he had been ridden or by whom. He was, as Patrick had learned, stolen in a raid on a Crow camp perhaps as long ago as half a year.

Red Wing rode close behind her husband's travois which bore the bulk of their tipi furnishing, all securely bound inside their tipi canopy. Beside her on close rein was their pack pony.

Such was the order of the cavalcade as the horses moved at a brisk pace. They would not maintain this pace but with fresh horses, the riders would take advantage of the cold morning air and make distance before the sun had a chance to warm the prairie.

For the first hour of the journey no one spoke throughout the long file that stretched out over almost 1,200 yards. The riders, well spaced, kept to their little family groups. Any sounds that arose, such as the occasional yelp of a dog or snort of a horse, were dampened by the light grey mist that blanketed the prairie. The muffled swipe of the flexing travois poles over the lush Wyoming grass, further lubricated by the morning dew, added to the ghostly scene.

Patrick was first to speak, as the veil of mist lifted from the rich grass and purples of the hills away to the east and around to the south of them.

'Is it because you are the chief that I am allowed to ride at the head of the column?'

Willie did not answer for a moment; he was considering the best approach to the question. 'Pat, I am not the chief, never was and never will be. I was born white. No white man has ever become chief of an Indian tribe. Chiefs are chosen from within the tribe; they must be of the blood. You will meet chiefs and elders when you come north with us and you will learn how leaders are chosen and for what purpose. I am a headman and for a white man that is in itself a great honour.'

'Will you ever go back home, Willie?'

Willie gave him a long hard look, smiled and said, 'When we get back to the Dakotas I will answer that question.'

They would reach Laramie before noon. Patrick tried to work out how he had become so confused over time and distance since the death of Herbie. Willie had it right: Patrick had walked longer than he had known, in a stupor. Had he not had the mules on either side of him for support he may never have made it to Cottonwood Creek. 'My guess, Pat, you had an arm around the neck of each animal. You were being half carried and half walking. I've known it happen and in that way a man can cover a lot of ground. Could be you were walking that way well into the night at times.' Patrick turned round in his saddle and looked at his little passive beasts of burden that were instrumental, on more than one occasion, for having saved his life.

Willie, riding on Patrick's left, pointed across to the right, 'That's the Laramie river.' At that moment an osprey, hovering in the still air over the river, dropped and splashed heavily into the water. They watched, all three of them, as it struggled clumsily to get airborne with a fat fish firmly clutched in its talons. The bird rose as it had grabbed the fish, tail first, and the travellers watched as it passed its catch from one set of talons to the other, until the head was facing in the direction of flight. They had all seen this before but still marvelled at the wonder of it.

'We must get in a few hours' fishing, Willie; it's been a long time since we trod a riverbank together.'

Willie turned in his saddle to Patrick and assured him, 'We will, Pat, we will.'

Before they reached the bridge just north of the fort, two mounted soldiers, a sergeant and a trooper, rode out to intercept their convoy and escort them off to the left to an area suitably large enough for their tipis and their horses to be picketed. This placed them about half a mile walking distance from the fort but due to the multitude assembled, to get any closer was impossible.

The sergeant, a man of about forty-five years and with all the attributes of a weathered frontier soldier showing, kept a close eye on Patrick as the party circled their travois into position. Patrick became uneasy and the sergeant, seeing this, rode over to him and put him at his ease.

'That rifle you've got there, Sir, that wouldn't be one of the new Henry rifles, would it?'

'It sure is,' replied Patrick, proudly slapping the butt of his rifle.

'Hell, man, where did you find that?' the sergeant asked, getting all enthusiastic.

'I bought it over in Carson City, I . . .' He stopped in mid-sentence and changed the conversational course, thinking better of it, for he was about to say he had three more in his packs. 'I was lucky,' he continued, 'they're not on the open market yet.'

'I know,' said the sergeant, 'but will you not have difficulty getting ammo for it?'

'No trouble,' replied Patrick as he, and the two cavalry men, walked several paces to a quieter spot to continue their discussion. 'The shells are .44 rimfire and the 216-grain bullet is lighter than any of the hunting or military ammunition at present; 26-grain black powder charge will produce a muzzle velocity of twelve hundred feet per second.' Patrick was getting carried away by his own enthusiasm as he slipped the rifle from his shoulder and handed it to the sergeant for his inspection.

Patrick continued, 'Benjamin Henry is Oliver Winchester's senior designer. This is a follow-on from some of the earlier Winchester models.'

'Well, I'll be . . .' said the sergeant, fondling the piece of rare equipment.

'And here is the Henry cartridge,' said Patrick, plucking one from his cartridge belt and pointing to the "H" stamped on the head of the cartridge. 'The cartridge and gun designed by Ben Henry.' Patrick was proud of his acquisition. It had been his intention, after the death of his friends, to sell the three surplus Henrys in Laramie, but speaking to the soldiers, he had changed his mind.

'But I still can't see that the ammunition will be in any great supply,' said the sergeant, handing the cartridge back to Patrick and the rifle to the trooper for a further inspection. Patrick assured him that some of the existing Winchester ammo was of the same calibre. 'And how the hell, man, were you lucky enough to get your hands on it?'

'I was in Carson City last year when a small shipment came into a supplier stamped "Priority". It was rushed west from the makers in Connecticut. I happened to be there at the time and knew the dealer. I bought . . .' Again he nearly said four but hesitated, accepted the gun from the trooper, said thanks, then continued, 'I bought this one and a few hundred shells.'

'Well, I envy you; you have a gun there.' The trooper agreed. Neither the sergeant nor the trooper could have guessed the role the gun they envied would play in their country's destiny in a few years for in April of 1861, only eleven months away, the nation would be pitched into a bloody civil war.

'I better leave this rifle back here,' Patrick said to Willie. 'It's getting too much attention.'

'That will be all right,' Willie assured him. 'There will be plenty of people here to take care of it and leave your belt with it. When we get the horses picketed and the camp set out we will have something to eat, just some jerky and cornbread and tea. The tea is our own brew but we will get our new stores at the fort. We will be here for a few days and we will make the best of it.'

Red Wing volunteered to take charge of the rifle. Patrick was beginning to observe his new travelling companions – the men, the women and the children – and he found them a happy and carefree people. They were unlike those of the stories he had heard in California: stories about the Apache, the scourge of the white man. But then he found the Shoshone a most agreeable people.

Something he did discover very soon was that the women did most of the work. Already he had witnessed them dismantle and erect the tipis, load and unload the travois, cook and look after the children. Anything, any little task to be done was handed to one of the women, and with Willie in mind, he could well imagine how an Irishman could easily fit into such a population.

On the ride south a thought constantly bothered him. The end of the travois poles which must also serve as the main frame of the tipi must wear down very quickly and, on land where long straight trees are not always available, how was this problem solved? The buffalo again provided the answer: good sturdy leather ferrules, between two and three feet long, tightly fitted with the stitching uppermost. When the leather would wear a new ferrule would replace it.

It looked like the world and his wife had descended upon Fort Laramie. Patrick, with Willie and several other men, made their way slowly through multitudes towards the bridge that spanned the Laramie river on the north side of the fort. Directly below their allotted encampment area was a huge gathering of Mormon immigrants in transit. There were perhaps 120 wagons, their oxen and many milk cows, some wandering uncontrolled amongst the wagons. Many of the wagons were crammed with unnecessary and cumbersome furniture – even pianos could be seen to protrude from the slashed canvases.

Willie remarked, 'They have hauled this worthless stuff at a dear price to the oxen all the way from the East. When the poor oxen start to die, all that rubbish will be dumped by the side of the trail.' Then in disgust, and to Patrick's astonishment, he vented his anger: 'Whites, agh!' he spat.

'Why are they stopped here?' Patrick asked.

'They are not allowed to travel further on the Oregon Trail without a military escort and that is what they are waiting for. It often takes time to get a big escort together. Settlers heading to Oregon are trespassing across our best hunting lands in contravention of the 1851 Fort Laramie agreement. Now there is a young fellow of twenty-five, John Bozeman, who is talking about blazing a trail, with all the forts that it would take, all the way to Montana. Chief Red Cloud has already got wind of it and he is not a man to be angered.'[1]

They walked on through groups of Indian traders, Willie pointing out who was Cheyenne, who was Arapaho and so on. Often tribes could be identified by how their hair was dressed. There were soldiers, too, some on foot, some on horseback, most taking note of the tall man in the smart plainsman's outfit surrounded by a band of Sioux.

Ahead of them and to the right as they were coming off the bridge, a voice thundered out over the heads of the crowd, 'Wakinyan, Wakinyan, ici.' Heads turned in the direction from whence the sound came and the Lakota-speaking pedestrians could not but be amused for the roar that emanated from the throat of the bearded giant was like a rattle of thunder. Wakinyan in Lakota being "Thunderbird" added to the hilarity. He stood out from the crowd, an enormous man in a glazed buckskin shirt. A florid face, what little was exposed of it, glowed from behind a silvery beard. A shock of snow-white curly hair shone against the afternoon sun.

'Pierre Dubois!' Willie called, throwing up his arms in salutation. Pedestrians moved aside as the two giants closed to embrace. 'J'ai entendu dire il y a longtemps qu'un Pawnee vous ait tué pour votre scalp,' said Willie.

'No, no, I enjoy much life, make plenty mischief for everyone.' The twinkle in the steel-blue eyes confirmed the statement.

---

1 In 1860 Red Cloud was elected chief of all the Oglalas. The military and civilians alike paid a dear price for the introduction of the Bozeman Trail. Forts were razed and wagon trains attacked. When Fort Kearney was burned to the ground with heavy losses to soldiers and civilians, the trail was discontinued. In 1868 Red Cloud put his signature to the second treaty of Fort Laramie. John Bozeman had been killed the previous year in Montana by the Indians. He was just thirty-two years old. Migrants, still hell-bent on populating Montana, discovered a new route. They trekked a northerly course turning west and crossing the Missouri river north of the Mandans. The new route to their promised land was almost identical to the one mapped out in secrecy by Captain Oskarsen, Oskar Haug, the cartographer, and the officials from Washington in Oslo, all those years before.

They embraced like two grizzlies. Willie was forced to break his embrace to extract a tuft of Pierre's beard from his left ear and give it a good scratch.

'Pierre, mon vieux copain, comment allez-vous?'

'Très bien. Where are you camped?' Pierre asked.

'Half a mile from there on the right, just above the Mormons.'

'How long for?'

'Three or four days, maybe five; then back north to the White river.'

'I'll come and visit you all. Is Red Wing with you?'

'She is, Pierre.'

'Then I must come and speak with her. And Wind of the Wolf?'

'He is chief now.'

'That is good, I am pleased, good man. And Chief Two Rivers?'

'He is fine . . . just sits with the elders now.'

'Fine man, very wise. Give them all Pierre's blessing.'

'I will, Pierre; that I will.' Willie took his old friend by the arm and turned to Patrick. 'Pierre, you must meet an old friend, a school friend; we grew up together. Patrick taught me to fish.'

'And Willie taught me to shoot,' said Patrick.

'A good arrangement, and what is your line of country, Patrick?'

'He's a gold prospector,' Willie volunteered.

'Gold prospector, bad business. Too many poor gold hunters, I've seen.' Pierre returned to Willie and stated that he would be paying his lodge a visit that evening with two others of their old friends from the trapping days, armed with their musical instruments.

Fort Laramie, standing at the confluence of the Laramie and the mighty North Platte rivers, was the nerve centre of all the lands west of the Mississippi to the Rocky Mountains. A military fortification and trading post, it was where white men and Indians met to trade and where purveyors of poteen came to sell their produce to all.

Before the mass migration westwards, four men, employed as trappers with the American Fur Company, built a small fortification on the site. Except for one, Robert Campbell, all were of French descent. They were James Bourdeaux, William Sublette and the fourth, who joined later, was LaRamee, a first cousin of Bourdeaux. The site was then known as Fort William but there are historians who claim that it was called Fort John.

In 1835 Campbell and Sublette, joint owners, sold the site to The American Fur Company but continued working there with the others. Sublette and trailblazer Jim Bridger, after whom Fort Bridger was later named, became agents for the fort. The following year, 1836, Bourdeaux, LaRamee and several other trappers built a sturdy stockade around the site and erected more substantial log buildings within the compound. That was done in the winter of that year and from spring through to November they trapped and hunted, travelling sometimes as far as Wind river. In November tragedy struck. LaRamee, working the streams alone, was killed by a band of Arapahos. When he failed to return, his cousin and three or four others went out in search and found him. The arrows embedded in his body identified the assailants. In honour of his memory, Jim Bridger and William Sublette rearranged his name to read Laramie and Fort Laramie took its place in history.

Willie skilfully piloted Patrick through the crowds and around many of the stalls, pointing out whatever he thought would be of interest to him. Patrick's main interest was why they were all here. He had always found it tiresome to wander aimlessly around bazaar stalls with no intention of buying. "Buy what you want and get out" was his motto. *Why,* he mused, *have all these people travelled two hundred miles to wander round bazaars for a few days only, then repeat the same tedious journey home?* It had not occurred to Patrick that the Sioux were a nomadic race whose home was their tipi, or lodge, and the lodge was designed to travel. But there was more to their being in Fort Laramie, as he was about to discover.

'Are you going to buy something, Willie, or like Queen Victoria, are you above carrying money?'

Willie dropped a hand on Patrick's shoulder and with his free hand waved in a sweeping motion. 'All this craftwork you see is made for the white market, the settlers passing through and the soldiers at the garrison. When the soldiers are returning home they buy a lot of this stuff to take back home as presents. There is no end to the demand but that is not why we are here.'

'I didn't think so,' said Patrick.

'Look,' said Willie, sweeping his hand again, 'there are quite a few of our party in there among the crowd; maybe you don't recognise them?' Patrick confirmed that he had not. 'Now, like myself, you will see they are buying nothing. We are all here on the first day to make contact with our traders. They will come to where we are encamped tomorrow, or the day after, and buy from us there and provide us with all our needs. At Laramie we get better prices for our goods than if we waited for the traders to come to us. Much better.'

'What do you have to sell?'

'Pelts, Pat, the best quality: beaver, musk, marten; buffalo rugs finely worked; buckskin and moccasin. Most of the travois you have seen have carried up to a year's work – all sold here and taken straight to St Louis by teamsters and shipped out to Europe.'

'I thought,' said Patrick, 'the fur trade had long finished.'

'Finishing,' corrected Willie. 'There is still a good demand but the end is in sight.'

Willie went off with several of his companions to make arrangements with their traders, leaving Patrick at a predetermined spot where they would meet later. For the following hour or more, Patrick walked aimlessly around, talking to Indian traders and admiring their craftsmanship. A company of soldiers marched past him heading towards what must have been the main barrack block, their NCO barking orders as they went. Patrick was unimpressed with their general bearing but then, this was the frontier. Everywhere there were soldiers on horse, ox-drawn wagons and everywhere dust. This was a world away from Market Street, San Francisco.

As he stopped to admire yet more Indian craft, Willie dropped a hand on his shoulder. 'Come with me, Pat, there is someone I would like you to meet.' Patrick followed to where a wiry, athletic man was standing. He was of medium height. His face was suntanned and freckled and under an unruly mop of ginger hair were two piercing blue eyes that seemed to be constantly following everything that moved. The sharp, beaklike nose complemented his entire features. In fact, the man resembled a bird of prey. His attire was not of the mundane beings around him. It was simple and of good quality: a light multi-coloured woollen pullover with the sleeves tucked up to the elbows; a checked open-necked shirt, the large collar wings resting lightly on the open-necked pullover; no heavy serge trousers for this man but breeches of the finest white cotton that ended below the knees to fit snugly into the tops of stockings of a fancifully decorative pattern. The shoes were of soft calf and polished to perfection.

He had obviously been briefed by Willie as to who the tall man in the fringed plainsman's outfit was, for as they approached he was standing beaming a welcome, a hand outstretched. 'If you're a McLaughlin from Maghera, you're welcome,' said the man with a hearty handshake for Patrick. 'I'm damned but aren't you a fine-looking fellow and isn't it just great to witness Maghera being so well represented out here in the Wild West?'

The man was a compulsive talker and before he got into full flow, Willie intervened to introduce them. 'Pat, I'd like to introduce Thomas Gribben, all the way from Kilrea.'

'Rasharkin,' corrected Thomas, 'the other side of the Bann.'

'Tom,' said Willie turning to Patrick, 'does the best still in the whole of Wyoming.'

'The whole of the West,' Tom interrupted. 'Mine is the only alcoholic beverage permitted to grace the tables of the officers' mess hall over there,' nodding his head in the direction of the huge barrack blocks.

'Now here is a man I can do business with,' Patrick said, addressing Willie.

'No need,' Tom said. 'Willie has already taken care of that.' Having spoken the word Willie, he put a cautionary finger to his lips. 'I must be careful, he is not known by that name around here.'

Patrick smiled. 'It's all I ever called him since we were wee lads and I'm damned if I'm gonna change now.'

'Where is Kurt? Is he not here today?' Willie asked.

'Not today. He is away for stores, brown sugar and . . . Ah, but there I go again, giving away all my secrets.'

Patrick grinned as he thought, *no chance of this cunning man giving away any of his secrets.*

'He will be back tomorrow,' continued Tom, 'and you'll meet him when we go up to camp to make our deliveries. He is a grand lad. Comes from Frankfurt in Germany. He is my partner in business.'

The mention of Germany jogged Patrick's memory. 'Willie, I have got three deaths to report while we are here.'

'That will be in the admin block, I'll take you there.' Tom, judging that Patrick had some urgent business to attend to, took leave of the two men, looking forward to meeting them on the following day when he might learn from Patrick tales of interest from the Californian goldfields.

'That man makes no idle boast about his liquor,' said Willie, as they walked towards the administration block. 'His still is the best: smooth, and it even has the colour of whisky but that could be a small amount of sweetened tea. You and I know, Pat, how the poteen makers set up their stills when we were boys – far out in the bogs where the bailiffs could never find them . . .'

'And,' continued Patrick, 'where the smell from the stills was overpowered by the oily peat mingled with the perfumed heather. Even the bailiffs could never detect the smell.'[2]

---

2 Thomas Gribben emigrated from County Antrim, Ireland, in the middle of the nineteenth century to America, where, in Philadelphia, he met Kurt, a young German of his own age. The German, eager for any new idea that could be converted into silver dollars, was fascinated by the Irishman's recipe and skill, learned and perfected in a County Antrim bog. To set up a still and purvey poteen in Philadelphia would very soon have landed them in jail and subsequent deportation. So the boys packed their bags and headed west where whisky there was none and a business alliance was established that would last for many years.

Gribben's liquor, described as Nulli Secundus, second to none, was indeed mellow and, in his own words, graced the tables of the officers' mess. A blind eye may well have contributed to the success of their industry. The financial side was left entirely to Kurt. Shortly after the end of the Civil War in April 1865, the two wealthy bootleggers returned to Philadelphia where they set up a brewery, licensed and legal. They each married Irish girls and on the advice of their legal experts they set up their homes in New Jersey but ran the business in Philadelphia – an advantageous tax move.

The author is well acquainted with the story told here as the flamboyant Thomas Gribben was his great-grandmother's brother.

The two men laughed at the memory and made their way to the administration block before retiring to their tipi.

It was a restful night. All the traders had done their business with the Sioux. The Sioux had got good prices for their pelts and other commodities. Thomas Gribben had quenched a few dry throats and equally his thirst for knowledge of the Californian goldfields had been sated sufficiently to judge that he was on a safer and more productive seam than gold and silver might offer. Trading had been good. Tonight they would sleep well and tomorrow, perhaps, they would break camp in a leisurely manner and with their travois heavily loaded, head towards the Cheyenne river region 200 miles to the north. Patrick would travel with them. Strange, the twists and turns that life throws at us however much we plan; he would now make the final leg of the journey far from the way it was originally planned.

Earlier Red Wing had prepared her tent. It was agreed she would sleep there that night, leaving her husband and his old friend to their reminiscences. Willie had forgotten Pierre's promise to grace him with his presence but that was yesterday and he did not turn up in the evening. That was Pierre. Since their astonishing reunion, the two Irishmen had not had the chance to sit down for a good long chat about old times and all the circumstances that had determined each of their lives. There would be many long nights by the Cheyenne and Red rivers to tell and re-tell their stories, but tonight it would wait. From somewhere within the outer circle of the tipis there came a bull's bellow: 'Wakinyan! Wakinyan!'

'Ici, Pierre,' called Wakinyan, opening the tipi flap and waving.

Out of the darkness lumbered Pierre, followed by Louis, Francois, Jean-Paul and Andre, each carrying a bottle and an instrument of music, or perhaps torture to the ears of the Mormons. These Frenchmen were old and valued friends of Wakinyan, come to do him homage. 'Entrez,' Wakinyan called, holding the flap open and greeting each one in turn with a hearty embrace as they passed through the opening.

Handing the bottle and the violin to Patrick with the indifference of a paying guest passing his coat and hat to the porter, Pierre flung his arms around Red Wing, kissed her on both cheeks and swung her around, bellowing, 'Comment allez-vous, Red Wing? Long time since we last met. Is this Thunderbird looking after you well? You have always been too nice for that Irishman. It is good to see you again, Red Wing.' He released her from his bear-like hug and whirled around to introduce his friends to Patrick. The whirlwind embrace left Red Wing momentarily speechless and short of breath. When the conversation and the whisky flowed, she slipped away quietly to the tipi of friends to organise the preparation of food for her husband and his guests. There was every indication it was going to be a long and rumbustious night.

They were fine men, these half-French, half-Americans, thought Patrick: *loyal to their friends, good hearted and noisy – they were his kind of company.* As their stories unfolded they recalled memories of their trapping days along backwaters of the Cheyenne and Powder rivers and the Belle Fourché, their treks up the creeks of the Bighorn to set their traps, the comradeship around their fires that burned long into the night and their trading with the Indian population. These men, all from the New Orleans French Quarter, respected the Indians – the Sioux, the Cheyenne or whoever – and in return that respect was always reciprocated. And they learned to speak the other's language. He was impressed by his old friend's fluency in French as well as Lakota; the boy who sat beside him in the little schoolhouse in Falaleigh so long ago.

Much of Willie's past since they each went their own way was unfolding before him and not in a tedious monologue of conversation but in the lively recall of these interesting men's memories. Willie and his Indian companions, he gathered, had been invaluable to the trappers in those days when fur was in great demand. They guided them to the best trapping grounds along the remote creeks but the most useful service of all was that they often had prepared for them the best quality pelts. And the trappers would return from St Louis, their canoes laden with merchandise, woollen blankets, cooking utensils – so much that helped towards making life a little more tolerable in a wild and unforgiving land. The tea, sugar, coffee and tobacco were all goods cherished by the Indians. The men were not just trappers but long-distance grocers. And, yes, they provided guns and shot and black powder. It was not uncommon, though not the general rule, that a man with his spouse in St Louis would winter up in the Dakotas with his Indian "wife", an arrangement that suited both parties, especially as wife and girlfriend never met.

A canoe all the way down the Missouri river to St Louis. That could be the way to travel, thought Patrick. He would suggest it to Willie when it was time for him to go. Red Wing and two of her friends now entered with small baskets of food, pieces of meat, bread and such, and having placed the refreshments strategically around the tipi, they departed silently as Pierre tuned up his violin. Taking their leave was a good tactical move. Six large men in one tipi was crowding it a little and the noise that was soon to follow would be ear-splitting.

Andre and Pierre tuned up their violins. Francois tried out a few tentative notes on the mouth organ. Louis and Jean-Paul on their melodeons added to the cacophony. Patrick filled his cup and held it up in salute to the musicians. Pierre and Andre on the violins led off with the favourite "Alouette". Francois contributed with the mouth organ. Willie, Patrick and the two melodeon players fell in giving a rousing rendition. Even Patrick knew the words of "Alouette". It was unfortunate for the Mormons that they were downwind, and with the lappet and all ventilation flaps of the tipi open, the sound to the sleeping Mormon camp was horrendous.

A pause for refreshments, rude jokes and boisterous laughter followed by a further round of "Alouette" but this time Pierre led them out and around the outer circle of tipis in a jig-jog procession. Those not playing an instrument, Willie and Patrick, brandished their well-plenished cups. The procession picked up a number of young Sioux men and Willie got anxious lest they decide to join the party in the tipi. The French trappers had a unique way of livening up those around them and the young Sioux required little encouragement. A shot was fired in the air in protest from the Mormon camp but only added to the hilarity. Willie found it necessary to call order and to return to the confines of the tipi, and peace descended.

How one blast from a Mormon shotgun could bring order, many in the Mormon camp must have been thinking, unaware that the best was yet to come. The boys, after a little respite, more bawdy jokes and further refreshments, worked up to that best-known of the trappers' songs, "Billy Oh!" A tentative note stole quietly from the violin of Pierre Dubois to be encouraged by Andre's instrument as the two violinists tuned up. Willie, familiar with the air and the original French lyrics, hummed the tune and with his tenor voice, pleasing to the air and to the accompaniment of the two violins, carried off the first of the many verses of:

Billy oh! Billy oh!
C'est la saison des chasses
Partout dans l'Aska.
Remuez vos carcasses,
Il faut partir les gars,
Billy le blafre.
'Que le diable l'emporte'
Il faut nous preparer
Un claquement de fouet,
Allons en route tout est prêt.

Of all the songs that rang throughout the woods from the canoes of the French trappers, "Billy Oh!" must surely have been among the first and certainly the most protracted. In their heyday, wherever men followed the beaver, their songs rang through the woods from Canada to Colorado as they paddled their canoes mile after mile after mile. Their songs were as much their salvation as their coffee and pemmican and the warmth of their camp fires and, yes, their whisky. Tonight Pierre Dubois and his comrades were with friends who shared with them some of those memorable years and as the chorus rang out, 'When the moon is shining, when the day is dying,' this night was for celebration.

Quand la lune luit,
Quand le jour s'enfuit,
Les trappers gaiement s'enforcent dans la nuit.
Les chiens esquimaux
Tirant le traineau,
Et dans le ciel noir
S'envole un doux chant d'espoir
Billy oh! Billy oh! Eh! Oh! Oh!
Defiant le vent,
Le traineau tout blanc
Glisse dans la nuit silencieusement.

And as the lyrics glided not so silently into the night, the monoglot McLaughlin could only raise his filled cup towards Willie in salute to his multilingual friend.

At first light, the clatter of a hundred horses' hooves, the rattle of wagon wheels and the harsh shouts of command shattered the silence that had only a short while before fallen upon the Sioux tipis and the wagons of the overlanders. The escort for the latter had arrived, all brisk and military-like, without knowledge or sympathy for those deprived of sleep. Spent and scattered around on the rugs of Wakinyan's lodge, blissfully asleep and snoring heavily, lay the culprits. No one would be stirring from that lodge, or many of the others, in any great hurry.

CHAPTER 22

It was late June when the party, their travois laden, arrived at the place where Cherry Creek joins the Cheyenne river – not their ultimate destination but a predetermined rendezvous with others of the Sioux councils. They would muster there for the buffalo hunt, due within days, when the herds would be passing through to fresh pastures. Following the hunt would come the skinning and drying of the hides and preparation of the meat. Celebrations would follow and thereafter their most sacred of rituals, the Sun Dance, when solemn vows would be taken.

Patrick McLaughlin, the only white man present – for Willie was not considered white – was soon to be witness to scenes which, at that time, few white men had ever seen. On the 280-mile trail from Fort Laramie he was astonished at the ease and speed with which the women could unload the travois, erect the poles around the bundles on the ground and throw on the sheeting, thus securing the goods within the confines of the tipis and giving cover for their menfolk and themselves for the night. While the women were engaged in making camp, the men would be hunting or fishing one of the many rivers or creeks. It was desirable, wherever possible, to make camp close to water.

Their party was not the first to arrive. Along the north bank of the Cheyenne small villages were already established. Having crossed the river shallows just below the confluence with Cherry Creek, they turned west and in single file moved slowly past the earlier arrivals until they found space. Along the banks of the river and the creek, tall willows leaned to the water and the ubiquitous cottonwood trees were, well, everywhere. The site chosen was a picturesque oasis in a sea of grass. It was midday when they arrived; plenty of light in the day to set up camp, see to their horses and get settled in. The whole place was alive with activity and the smell of cooking, which permeated throughout the campsite, was inviting to the hungry newcomers. And their hunger was soon satisfied, for scarcely had the new arrivals dismounted than they were offered food and drink by those already eating.

Patrick had just dismounted and turned around to find himself towering over a small girl holding up to him a bowl of soup. 'Icu,' she said. Then, as if to reassure the giant before her, she smiled saying, 'Ayuco.'

'She is saying take, it is good,' said Willie. Patrick accepted the bowl with wooden spoon, a little at a loss for words. 'Say pikila . . . that is thank you.'

Patrick said, 'Pikila,' and took a spoonful of the meat and vegetable soup and expressed his approval. The little face beaming up at him said it all; the tall bearded plainsman had found new friends.

The setting sun had moved behind the two adjacent lodges of the chiefs, its gold and crimson rays softly bathing the white tipis, with their painted animals and eagles, in a hue reminiscent of the glows of autumn. But this was not autumn; this was early June, the threshold of summer, and as the two friends walked towards the chieftains sitting in front of one of the lodges, bedecked in all their finery, Patrick's inner eye captured the scene with stark reality. He had already seen the gathering storm clouds rolling in from the east, that must roll ever westward with no let up until the last glows of autumn were extinguished.

Willie sat down on the grass in a cross-legged position, his wrists resting on his knees, hands relaxed. He was comfortable and at ease. Patrick, looking down, studied the ground and rotated a few times like a large dog preparing to settle in a confined space. Chief Two Rivers was quick to spot his discomfort and with a wave of his hand and an indication as to what was necessary, a woman appeared from seemingly nowhere with a wickerwork portable backrest chair and placed it behind the chiefs' guest.

The two chiefs, with all their trappings of office on display, looked impressive to Patrick, somewhat awesome. Yet all their regalia was composed of simple, everyday things. Their conversation was light and covered many subjects. The older chief, Two Rivers, contributed little to the conversation but understood everything. He had a keen brain and showed every indication of being a wise leader. The younger man, Wind of the Wolf, proved something of an enigma to Patrick. His command of English was superb and could well have been the product of a first-class English school. Willie had spoken of his friend, Chief Wind of the Wolf, but with little account of him. This bright modest man, capable of conducting himself with ease at the court of Queen Victoria, had taken him aback. Patrick was as intrigued by the man, as he was interested in his colourful clothing.

'You appear to be impressed by our formal attire,' remarked Chief Wind of the Wolf, smiling.

'I am,' said Patrick. 'It is most impressive yet so . . .' He stumbled for a word that was less likely to embarrass.

The chief, reading his thoughts, smiled and spoke the word that Patrick had stumbled on. 'Simple, and yet so simple. You are right. Simplicity in all things is our way of life. What surprised you, Patrick? Was it the absence of gold and silver?' Patrick nodded in agreement. 'No, the Indian has no use for what the white man speaks of as precious metals. They are, in fact, the white man's folly. Where gold is, deceit, envy and avarice are not far away.'

Patrick remembered Comstock and was beginning to feel uncomfortable. *Was he having his own case history read out before him?*

'Of the seven deadly sins,' continued the chief, 'avarice, or if you like, greed, must be the most deadly. Greed spreads like an infection, like the cholera the white man spread amongst our people. Our buckskin clothing and garlands are simple things, skins of the antelope, the elk and the buffalo; feathers from the eagle, porcupine quills and flint from the earth's surface; things borrowed from the earth and that, like ourselves, will be returned to the earth. Gold and silver and diamonds taken from the earth will never be returned. They are the earth's own treasure chest coveted only by white men. When a man comes in search of food, or that which will clothe him, he is coming for his needs. When a man comes in search of gold or silver or diamonds, he is coming to take these things away for ever. He is a robber coming to steal. Many years ago a party of white men from the East came to our Dakota Mountains in search of gold. They found it in our streams but they did not succeed in taking it away.'

Patrick was listening hard for what he was hearing was uncanny. 'Did they all leave without the gold?' he asked, fishing for answers. The answer that followed was to stun him like a bolt of lightning.

'No,' said the chief, 'they all died, all but one. He got away but without his mule and the gold. He may have thought himself lucky in his escape but he was allowed to go so others could be warned. Chief Two Rivers remembers the incident well. He has always maintained that instead of the warning intended, his story, when told, would be a challenge to others to try again.' Chief Two Rivers smiled knowingly. His nephew indicated with a wave of his hand towards the Black Hills. 'Yes, one day they will return, the robbers will return.'

'What happened to the gold they found in the streams?' Patrick asked, knowing the answer that was coming.

'The sacks of gold they had taken from our streams were returned to our streams.' A chill ran down Patrick's back. A child's voice spoke from within his head. It was saying, *I think, Grandad, they were watching you all the time.*

The sun had gone some time without notice of its going. A chill breeze crossed the prairie, a gentle reminder from nature that conversation must come to a close. Chief Two Rivers leaned towards his nephew and spoke to him in Lakota and his nephew nodded and turned to Willie and his friend and, speaking in the fluent English he had used throughout the evening, he announced, 'Gentlemen, my uncle feels it is getting late and tomorrow will see many preparations that cannot wait. He thanks you both for a most interesting evening and invites you to join us in his lodge tomorrow evening with some elders and perhaps we will smoke the calumet.'

It had been agreed that Patrick would use the tent for storing his baggage and sleeping during their stay at the Cheyenne river and for the remainder of their journey. On arrival at their destination they may think again. The tent, meanwhile, was sufficient for all his needs.

On returning from their visit they discovered that Red Wing was missing from the lodge and it was assumed that she was visiting. They had the lodge to themselves and Willie began re-kindling the dying embers in the middle of the tipi where the earth was uncovered. Over large cups of hot sweet coffee and oatmeal fruit cookies, a purchase from Fort Laramie, Patrick told his story of the little boy fishing with his "Grandad" on the riverbank. Red Wing's return interrupted the conversation. Willie beckoned her to sit and listen. She poured herself some coffee and sat with them by the fire. Willie prodded a few more small logs into the centre. The flames flickered, throwing three shadows against the taut skin walls, and Patrick began again, this time starting with Peter O'Reilly and Six Mile Canyon.

The coffee in their cups had gone cold. The fire had returned to smouldering embers and a chill suffused the lodge's interior. Patrick had talked and his listeners had listened. Silence prevailed for several awkward minutes. Red Wing, daughter of Chief Two Rivers, was first to speak. Placing the cup of cold coffee close to the embers, she took Patrick's right hand in both of hers and, looking directly at him, stated what must be done. 'My father has invited you both to join him and the elders in his lodge tomorrow evening. He suggested that the calumet would be smoked. Do you know, Patrick, what the calumet is?'

Patrick shrugged his shoulders saying, 'Isn't it a pipe of peace or something?'

'A pipe of peace and more,' came the reply. 'To our people the calumet is a sacred symbol. No man, no Indian that is, must lie having smoked the calumet.'

'Like a Christian being witness in a court of law,' said Willie, 'he swears on the Bible, the Holy Book.'

Patrick felt he was getting into something too deep. Why did he say anything even to Willie and why should he be trusted now? Better he had just packed his mules and moved on. 'Does this mean I am to be dragged before an Indian tribunal and made to confess?'

They both smiled and shook their heads. Again it was Red Wing who spoke. 'No, Patrick, that is not what we are saying. Setting out with the intention and carrying out that intention are not one and the same. In the eyes of my people you have not committed any crime. What I suggest you do is go with Wakinyan to the meeting tomorrow evening, smoke the calumet and afterwards tell them of your intention on setting out and how you see it now.'

'I have had it in mind for some days,' said Patrick, 'to give the chiefs and yourself each a present. Tonight could be as good a time as any.' He thought for a moment then looked at Willie, saying, 'If you will bear with me, you can have yours in a moment or two. I'll just get it.'

It seemed an age since he had gone. Red Wing had rekindled the fire and prepared fresh coffee. Then the fold of the tipi was flung open and for a few moments Patrick stood between his friends, squatting by the fire, and the starry sky. In one hand he was holding a box-like object of about six cubic inches and in the other what immediately appeared to be his own rifle. 'A wee present for you, Willie,' said Patrick, trying to sound as nonchalant as possible as he knelt beside Willie, placing the rifle on the rug. 'And there are some shells to start you off.'

'But, Pat, why are you giving me your own rifle?'

'I still have mine. That is now yours and I have two more. They are mine to do with as I please. I provided the guns and the Prairie Schooner and some of the mules. When John and Colin were killed and Herbie died later, the equipment was mine to reclaim. It was my intention, before meeting you, to sell the lot in Fort Laramie; oh yes, and the revolvers.'

'If you had sold any of this stuff to the Indians,' said Willie, 'you would have been arrested.'

'Like that, is it?'

'Like that. Pat, this is a wonderful gift, thank you. The chiefs will appreciate such gifts.' Red Wing, squatting on her heels, enjoyed her husband's antics with his Henry rifle like a mother watching over her child with a new toy.

Chief Two Rivers sat in the circle at the back of the lodge, that is, facing the fold or lappet that opens to the outer world or closes it away. On his left sat his nephew, Chief Tateyanpa Caksi, meaning Wind of the Wolf, known to Willie simply as John. On the left of John sat three elders of the council. Willie took his position on the right of Chief Two Rivers with Patrick McLaughlin, the guest, to the right of Willie. On McLaughlin's right were three young members of the council: ten men in all, each occupying a backrest sitting in a part circle.

The opening, as did all tipis, faced south, therefore the chiefs faced in that direction. Around the framework was hung a rail between four and five feet from the ground. This served a dual purpose. Firstly it served to hang the many accoutrements of plains living, such as bows, arrow quivers, shields, cooking utensils and so on. It also carried sacred signs and symbols. Folded neatly around the periphery were parfleches or storage bags. Secondly, in cold weather when the night can be minus thirty degrees, an inner wall or curtain of buffalo hide was hung from the rail, thus giving greater warmth to the occupants. A tipi could be a comfortable abode on cruel winter nights. In the centre of the floor, or ground, was a ring of stones, all selected for their oval shape. These were built up about three courses high and in the centre of these was the fire. A small fire of wood was all that was necessary for the duration of the meeting but in the cold weather, or when cooking was in progress, more heat was required and the greater the heat from the fire the more the thermal energy conducted to the stones.

Hanging on the rail directly behind Chief Two Rivers was the most sacred of their symbols, the Hoop or Sundance Circle, more reverently referred to as the Medicine Wheel. The circle itself represents the outer limits of the Earth, the ever-changing sequence of life and death. Intersecting the centre of the Circle are two lines, one vertical, one horizontal. Where the lines cross indicates the centre of the Earth, where man stands to pray. Usually an eagle feather is attached to the centre representing the Thunder-being who flies among the thunderstorms.

It was a large lodge, that of Chief Two Rivers. For the basic structure, tipis would normally have three, perhaps five, main vertical poles with their supporting lighter framework. The chief's tipi had seven mainstays and Patrick, making a mental calculation, guessed that thirty buffalo hides had gone into the covering, as against the average twenty. Initially the conversation was in their own language, leaving Patrick's idle mind to wander.

It soon became evident to Patrick that he was the subject of the conversation between the chiefs and elders and, noticing his discomfort, John addressed him and brought him into the chat. 'My uncle and elders have learned of your hazardous trek from the West and the unfortunate loss of your companions and they are interested to know why you have chosen to come to the land of the Lakota. They think you were searching for your long-lost friend.'

Patrick shook his head, saying, 'No, I came to steal your gold.' Noting the surprised expression on John's face, it occurred to him that he had spoken in haste and since he had done so, the best course, he decided, was to charge on and be damned. He told the story that he had told Willie and Red Wing, starting from the discovery in Nevada. John and Willie acted as interpreters. Chief Two Rivers and his elders sat listening with faces of stone. The younger men, sitting with Willie, conversed among themselves whilst Patrick spoke, but listened with interest to the translations, frequently casting looks at him. He finished by purging his soul and promising to atone for his sins. The old chief and his elders went into a huddle of quick chatter, then turned and stared at Patrick who froze to his backrest.

John smiled and broke the ice. 'My uncle and elders speak highly of your honesty and they are extremely interested in the story of the grandfather and the small boy. They often wondered if the man whose life they spared had survived.'

The old man rose and, smiling, walked the few paces towards Patrick who rose to accept his handshake. The other members followed and when they were all again seated, Patrick produced a long object wrapped haphazardly in hessian that had until that moment been lying on a rug close to his backrest chair. He placed it on the rug before the two chiefs and slowly unfurled the sacking, revealing two of the most coveted pieces of equipment by either white or red men west of the Mississippi.

Apart from Willie, everyone in the lodge drew his breath in astonishment at the shining new repeater rifles, the most up-to-date of their kind anywhere to be found. Almost ceremoniously Patrick placed the first one in the outstretched hands of Chief Two Rivers who accepted it with grace, inspected it and, smiling his appreciation to the donor, passed it on to his elders for their inspection. Chief Wind of the Wolf accepted his present saying, 'Thank you, Patrick. We shall always be indebted to you for such wonderful presents.' He then passed the rifle on to the young braves waiting anxiously just to handle this deadly piece of craftsmanship.

As they spoke in their short, staccato bursts, fondling every inch of the rifle, Patrick reflected on what wrong he may have done. How many of his own race may one day fall before these guns? *My God*, he asked himself, *what have I done?*

CHAPTER 23

On the morning of the following day preparations were being made for the most sacred of the Sioux ceremonials, the Sun Dance, or, as it was known to the Sioux, the Sun Gazing Dance.

A large circle of ground was designated between the north bank of the Cheyenne river and Cherry Creek. In the centre of the circle a pole cut from the trunk of a cottonwood tree was being stripped and polished by three Santee-Yanktoni Sioux girls. At the very heart of the circle, a hole was being dug to receive the end of the trunk; that would be the centre pole on which the offerings would be placed. Near where the centre pole would stand, four other trunks were being prepared, making five in all. Around the centre pole, a circle of some fifty feet in diameter was scribed and around the circle these poles would be placed to indicate the four corners of the earth. The point indicating south was different in that two adjacent poles would be placed here, standing only five or six feet apart. All the cottonwood trees were prepared by young women, as was the custom.

When the poles were stripped and smoothed, thick buffalo-hide ropes were affixed to the top and a Wicasa Wakan, or priest, would paint the upper halves with a red paint procured from the earth. The poles would then be set firmly in the ground and the remainder of the timbers given an application of the red ochre. An altar of earth was built close by. The Sioux, as with other tribes, were children of the earth. This area was sacrosanct.

Throughout the day the crowds gathered: warriors on their spirited pintos, old and young travelling on the travois, many with their dogs. All day, drum-beat and chant filled the air and would continue long into the night until a thousand campfires smouldered before the first light on the eastern horizon.

The whole prairie reverberated to the thunder of hoof beats and war chants as the young warriors played their war games. The free people of the Oceti Sakowin (the Seven Council Fires) were mustering for their annual Sun Dance celebrations and the buffalo hunt that would follow. Under a blue Dakota sky, by the banks of the Cheyenne river, a spectacle of awesome beauty was being enacted without interruption, as it had been for centuries of their history.

Theirs was a simple undemanding religion, not called by any name; it was there. Nor was there need to set aside a day to be called holy for all days were holy. All things belonged to Wakan-tanka, the Great Spirit, and all things given by Wakan-tanka must be returned. A vow made to Wakan-tanka was a solemn vow.

The Sioux were self-governed and well organised, with emphasis placed on the importance of the family unit. Children were cared for and never lacked attention, not only from parents but from all members of the family. Uncles were addressed as "father" and aunts as "mother" as were the parents. Chiefs were not leaders as in the warrior sense, but peacemakers or advisors within the clan. The Sioux were inherently a generous people, not only among their own but also with the stranger. Often white trappers and traders, as a result of weather or other circumstances, finding themselves as their guests, sometimes for months, discovered them to be the most generous and warm-hearted of people they found anywhere.

No man ever sought wealth for there was no need, therefore crime within the clan was uncommon. The murder of a clansman was as reprehensible as it was rare. When such a crime did occur, consideration was given to the victim's relatives. Unless restitution could be made, the murderer would be banished from the tribe, a severe punishment comparable to the gravity of the crime. To survive alone on the plain was almost impossible.

Before sunrise on the third day, those young warriors who were to offer themselves freely in a form of sacrifice before the Supreme Being had already assembled in the centre ring around the cottonwood tree that represented the ever-present Wakan-tanka. They had taken neither food nor drink from the day before.

As the sun rose, a Wicasa Wakan offered the peace pipe to each participant to the chant and drumbeat from the assembled throng. For the occasion the pipe was festooned with eagle feathers and weasel fur. The young warriors around the central pole had incisions on their chest, some on their back. These cuts were of an inch in length and about the same distance apart. Wooden skewers were then thrust under one cut and pierced through the flesh to appear from under the other, similar to an awl being worked on leather. All the while the evidence of blood was not lacking. When the "pilot" holes were opened, the loose ends of the thongs attached to the top of the pole were laced through the flesh, and the participants, all the while gazing towards the top of the pole, would dance and pull on the ropes, at the same time making their own personal vows and giving thanks to the Supreme Being.

Standing between the two poles and facing south, one young warrior who was to pledge total allegiance to Wakan-tanka and his tribe had similar wounds inflicted on him but a bit deeper than the others had received. For him, the skewers would be driven under muscle of the upper chest. Here the skewers would remain and the leather ropes attached to them. Slowly he would be raised by ropes attached to his wrists until his toes were just off the ground. There he would remain staring at the top of the centre pole until sunset or until it was considered too dangerous to continue. In this excruciating position he would pray to Wakan-tanka for his sanctification and that of his tribe. More often, before the sun had come over the cottonwood pole, its zenith, the participant would have ceased to feel pain and would have gone into a state of hallucination. Often in this state, it was said, he would have a vision of his destiny. Those who survived the ordeal – and most did – were considered among the bravest of their tribesmen.

'When you return to Ireland, Patrick, will you tell them of our savage ways?' Wind of the Wolf asked.

'I shall tell them . . .' he hesitated and looked at Wakinyan with a knowing smile. 'I shall tell them,' he continued, 'that Willie McKay, my old schoolmate from Maghera, is considered by the Lakota people to be among the bravest of the brave.'

'What are you blathering about?' asked Willie.

'The day we bathed in Cottonwood Creek.' Willie appeared puzzled. 'The day we stripped off and scrubbed our hides in the water—'

'What about it?' Willie interrupted.

'The scars, Willie, the four wee scars on your chest, two either side, just above your nipples. At first I thought they were from arrow wounds and then I thought, no, they are too neat and anyway, four arrows to the chest would have left you dead.' He stopped talking and looking straight at Willie, a smile of admiration broke over his face. 'You did it, Willie, didn't you?'

It was evening on the first day of the Sun Dance ceremonies. More often the lodges of the chiefs were places where, at evening, men assembled to talk and smoke the calumet. Tonight, in the lodge of the younger chief, only three sat in conversation: the chief, Willie (Wakinyan) and Patrick. Unbeknown to Patrick, this was furtively arranged. Patrick would be leaving them soon and, lest he should leave with some preconceived notions, some aspects of Indian beliefs might be better explained.

'The Sun Dance,' said Wind of the Wolf, 'is sacred to all Indians and especially to all the tribes of the Sioux nation.' He paused for a moment. 'It is so sacred that we find it difficult to talk about it. Many Christians find this with some aspects of their own religion.' Patrick gave an understanding nod. 'When we speak of Wakan-tanka we speak of the Great Spirit. God is called in many names; Wakan-tanka is just the Lakota.'

Patrick fidgeted in his backrest. He was afraid he could be in for a conversion course. After all, look at Willie, sitting cross-legged on a rug with a feather in his head. When it came to his own religion, Patrick was never accused of being gospel greedy. To take on another one at this time could be a bit demanding, especially if it required applying the razor to his chest.

'Everything that man receives comes to him from Wakan-tanka, from God,' the chief continued. 'Everything. We see the changes of night to day; the seasons, the sun making these changes as it moves around our earth giving life and energy in light, and rest in darkness. There are those who now say that the earth moves around the sun and like the sun and the stars it, too, is round. What is round has no beginning and no end—'

A suppressed smile on Patrick's face interrupted the lecture. Wind of the Wolf hesitated and the scowl that crossed his brow indicated that Patrick must avert a difficult situation.

'No, Chief,' he exclaimed as he raised his hands, palms towards the chief in an expression of mea culpa. 'No disrespect to your beliefs, and I am interested, but I must explain; an amusing thought occurred to me.' He hesitated for a moment, thinking how best to explain his indiscretion. 'Believe me, Chief, you have my interest. I could see for a moment you, with your fine command of the English language and your persuasive ways, standing on a soap box on the corner of Market Street, 'Frisco, converting all those goddamned white heathens.' He reflected for a moment, 'And in that place they sure need some kind of converting.'

'Soap box?' The chief turned to Willie for the answer and when Willie explained in Lakota, the chief pondered the ludicrous situation and then burst into a loud guffaw that trailed off to a wistful smile. 'No, Patrick, that could never be.' Patrick's sense of humour could not but pervade even the stolid mind of a Sioux chieftain.

'The white man,' the chief continued, 'does not understand the Indian or his ways. The Indian's ways are the ways of nature. There is a universal law that governs all things. That law is the unspoken law of nature, the law of Wakan-tanka. Natural law is Wakan-tanka and Wakan-tanka is natural law.' Patrick shuffled in his backrest for a more comfortable position; he was listening with interest to this erudite man. 'When the Indian speaks to Wakan-tanka he speaks to the wind that sweeps across the prairie, to the breeze that breathes gently on the young leaves on the cottonwood tree, for that is his voice. When the Indian speaks to the plants he is speaking to Wakan-tanka, for it was He who sent them and the plants will nourish.

'When the Indian walks barefoot upon the dew-laden grass as the sun is rising, he sees and feels the power that can only come from Wakan-tanka, the Supreme Spirit. That is why the Indian will always sit on the ground rather than a chair for on the ground he is close to Mother Earth. The white man chooses to sit on a chair or lie on a soft bed. The further a man moves from nature the harder his heart becomes and the more he loses respect for his fellow man and all other creatures. The white man shuts himself away in tall houses and as he does he moves further from nature. He becomes soft and is often unwell for he has hidden himself away from the sun and the clean air that is so vital for life. The Indian has no wish to covet the white man's hand-made luxuries when he has so many of his own given to him by the Supreme Spirit. And how do we thank Him?'

Patrick noted how he referred to the Supreme Spirit as "Him", just as Christians would.

'We pray in thanksgiving, in our chant and in our ritual dance. We pray to Wakan-tanka through our sacred symbols such as the cottonwood tree and our sacred stones. We are never slaves to our symbols like the white man has become to his stones that he calls diamonds and his gold and silver that he is prepared to murder for. In our thanksgiving we make sacrifices. And how do we make sacrifices? A man's body, Patrick, is his own, given to him by the Great Spirit. If he feels he must return something to God, to Wakan-tanka in thanksgiving, he may give a horse to his neighbour who has not got one, or items of clothing. This is a token gesture to Wakan-tanka and in giving he feels good but it is not himself he is giving. How does a man give himself, his all?' He paused and looked at Patrick in the vain hope of an answer, then continued.

'By inflicting pain upon himself. The Indian, in making a solemn vow to the Supreme Being, offers his flesh. During the time he is suspended, he prays to Wakan-tanka, gazing over the top of the cottonwood pole while the sun moves from east to west. He prays and he knows that Wakan-tanka is listening. Soon his prayers and his pain will cease and he will float, as it were, into a world of calm. In this state of profound peace he may not hear the continual chant and drumming of a thousand feet, as they pound ever harder the sun-baked earth. And, as the sun leaves the sky, he is lowered carefully to the ground. Soon he will regain consciousness and within a few days, and with the help of Wakan-tanka, his wounds will have healed and never again will that brave know fear as he faces danger, even death.'

No one spoke in that tipi for some little time and from without the chant and the drumbeat filtered through the buffalo-hide sheeting. Patrick was oblivious to the sounds of the celebrations whilst the chief spoke. He was, in a strange way, suspended in an artificially, near hypnotic, contemplative mood induced by the speaker. As the sounds drew nearer, rising to a crescendo, Willie broke the silence within the tipi. Smiling, he asked, 'Pat, would you like to join in the fun?'

'What is it?' asked Patrick.

'A Sioux wedding,' said Willie, 'a whole line of weddings. Come on.'

Just beyond the outer perimeter of the lodges and close to the riverbank stood three tipis. They were smaller than the average family-size tipi and spaced a generous distance apart. The land dropped away to the river, giving Willie and Patrick a good view of the procession making its way towards the isolated bridal tipis. The three bridegrooms were being carried shoulder high at the head of the procession to the sound of chanting warriors and the rhythmic beat of a drum.

'We have missed the wedding ceremonies,' said Willie, 'but, if you are with us at the end of the summer, you will see a big one when up to a hundred couples get married in one ceremony.'

'When Red Wing and you were married,' asked Patrick, 'was yours one of the big affairs?'

'No, it was just like this one, just ourselves and two other couples; just here at this very place and at the same time of the year.'

As the procession reached the vicinity of the brightly decorated bridal tipis it broke into three groups. Outside each tipi a groom was lowered down and the young man ushered inside to a tumultuous roar from without. Patrick turned to Willie and asked, 'Where are the other halves: the brides?'

'They are already there, each clad in a fine robe, a Sioux custom. The robe, for generations, was of the finest skins and beautifully decorated with porcupine quills and coloured beads. Now the bridal gown is a soft woollen blanket of many colours introduced to us by the trappers all the way from St Louis. When the groom enters, like the eagle spreading its wings, the Indian maiden will open her robe to receive her chosen warrior.'

'And you,' asked Patrick, 'you and Red Wing, can you remember—'

Willie's smile cut across Patrick's question, 'Red Wing still has her finest pte-ha-sla tawelaha[1] with its porcupine quills and a thousand coloured beads – a bridal gown befitting a chieftain's daughter.'

The clamour subsided and slowly the crowd dispersed. From far beyond the river a warm summer breeze carried with it a hundred perfumes of the prairie. The Cheyenne sparkled like a silver thread, and above, a waxing moon hung high in an azure sky.

---

1 Pte-ha-sla tawelaha: a light summer robe made from treated buffalo hide.

CHAPTER 24

T he buffalo hunt had been a disappointment. There were fewer than in preceding years and they came in small straggly herds. Although the hunters killed sufficient for the needs of the community, they were perplexed at the fall in numbers. But it was early summer and there would be another hunt three moons hence. That would be further west, beyond where the Little Missouri flows and where for hundreds of miles the rich grasslands had always supported the countless herds.

When the surplus meat had been preserved and the hides scraped and sun-dried the clans began to disperse. Some, the Isanti/Santee, would travel east beyond the Missouri river; the Titonwan/Teton to the west; the Brule/ Sicangu and the Oglala to Pine Ridge and Rosebud; and the Hunkpapa would journey away northwards to Standing Rock and Wood Mountain. The host clans, the Miniconjou, the Itsipco/Sans Arc and the Oohenupa, all within their territory, would next year be the travellers. These were some of the clan names of the then Great Sioux Nation.

The party to which Willie belonged would travel west with the Titonwan/ Teton for 110 miles. There they would join the main body by the banks of the Belle Fourché, about thirty miles east of the Little Missouri. They would camp there until the last buffalo hunt of the season, before returning east, or more correctly south-east, to where the White river empties into the Missouri. There they would make winter camp.

They travelled in much the same formation as when they made the journey to Fort Laramie but on this occasion John rode up front with them. Chief Two Rivers, the old man, rode behind them in the comfort of a travois. The springy frames of the travois absorbed the shock of the rough ground. The simple travois was in fact a comfortable means of transport.

'When do you figure on getting back to the Missouri?' Patrick asked, not directing his question to anyone in particular.

John answered, 'The big hunt will be about the end of August. When the hides are scraped and dried and the meat dried and made into pemmican and jerky it will be into the first week of September. The meat is the first job in hand. When the skins are dried, they will be worked; that will take, together with the hides we have here, up until mid-October. Winter camp, mid-November.'

'You are in for the summer of your life, Pat,' said Willie. 'Plenty of lazy days in the sun, fishing along the banks of the Belle Fourché and the Little Missouri and—' From far behind a shot rang out and two riders could be seen galloping off to retrieve the quarry. 'And as I was about to say, plenty of time to get used to our Henry repeaters.'

'I sure am looking forward to all that,' said Patrick, but he did not have to wait to get there. The land they were passing over was a hunter's paradise. Everywhere elk and antelope bounded in the grass and, at any time, wild turkey could be brought down from the sky. No need for these people to plough and sow and harvest. They knew where to find wild turnip and other root vegetables and wild sage and parsley. It was always there. *A land*, thought Patrick, *made by God, an Eden yet untouched by man*. And he inwardly anguished over the changing scene of that once-beautiful Six Mile Canyon, sleeping in the shadow of Sun Mountain, now Mount Davidson, and he felt in no small way responsible for the wreckage that the white man's hand had brought upon it.

The small girl ran towards Willie, arms outstretched, calling, 'Father!' Willie, the first to dismount, lifted her high and held her close to him in silence for what seemed a long time for an embrace. All the while he patted her on the back while the little hand repeated the same motion on the back of Willie's neck. Willie then spoke quietly in her ear, and released her to her mother. Patrick, to avoid embarrassment and to allow the family some privacy, busied himself with his horse and his mules. 'Our daughter,' Willie exclaimed as Red Wing lowered her to the ground.

Patrick smiled down at the tiny child from his great height and instinctively viewed Willie and Red Wing, who could read him doing his mental arithmetic. Suppressing a smile she gave him the answer to his calculations: 'I was just sixteen when he married me, and I am ten years younger.' Willie, releasing the lightweight saddle, was not privy to what caused the spontaneous burst of laughter.

'What's your name, young lady?' Patrick asked, hoisting the child aloft.

'We call her Ciara,' said Red Wing.

'Ciara,' Patrick repeated. 'Now where did you find a real Irish name like that?' In the parents' absence, Ciara was left in the care of Red Wing's sister and husband whom she also addressed as mother and father. There were other members of the family whom Patrick would get to know in the weeks ahead but now it was time to get settled into the summer camp.

The cavalcade continued rolling in for the most part of the day. The Titonwan/Teton had been well represented at the festival. The main party, of which Chief Two Rivers and his family were part, had arrived at the Belle Fourché river, at a point near where the town of that name now stands, just two days earlier. How these clans could travel such long distances and rendezvous at predetermined points on the prairie with such precise timing mystified Patrick. Like migrating wild geese, it was uncanny, and the indigenous people of the plains were not going to tell.

They were lazy, carefree days in that summer of 1860. Not since he and Willie, as youths, had walked the Sperrin Hills with their dogs and their guns or fished the mountain streams had Patrick known the contentment he experienced as a guest of the Sioux people. He roamed freely among the communities, asking and answering questions and learned what lessons the young Sioux were prepared to teach him about their hunting skills. Often he sat on the shaded side of their lodges listening with interest to tales of the old warriors. And as Willie promised, there was plenty of hunting and fishing. These pleasant activities were just everyday tasks to the Sioux.

It was arranged one evening, in the lodge of Chief Wind of the Wolf, that in the morning he, with Willie and Patrick and a youth of seventeen years whose name was Ojlaka Huya Ista, or Young Eagle Eye, would go off for a day on an antelope hunt. Willie and the two Sioux men would each take a spare horse as a pack animal. Patrick would take his two mules. By taking the mules not only did he have two experienced pack animals, it was also giving them an interest as idle mules get bored easily. They would all take their Henry repeaters – any excuse for trying out their new rifles. Young Eagle, Patrick remembered, was one of the youths who had shown a keen interest in the guns on the evening he had made the presentation to the chiefs. Patrick assumed he was a family member.

They set off to the west for a few miles, then turned north. Other hunting parties were abroad that morning but they kept well clear of them – no need to draw attention to the new firearms. The plains were alive with deer, antelope and elk. It was decided that there would be no hunting until they had made good distance from the other parties. If there were any camps further north they were not aware of them. Also, it was their plan to make a full day of it for which food was well provided. With the abundance of game, they guessed that those already out would start hunting early and deer and antelope being no small quarry, there would be a limit to the capacity their pack animals could carry, and therefore an early return to camp would be necessary.

Their guess was right. From away to the south of them, isolated rifle fire punctured the morning air, their sharp metallic cracks, unimpeded by any trees or other surface obstructions to wind or sound, carrying far across the grasslands. Soon the four would be alone with their powerful new weaponry. At evening, four weary hunters returned to camp, their horses and mules laden. Tomorrow, Willie and Patrick would fulfil a promise; the day would be spent on the banks of the Belle Fourché fishing, just fishing.

'That Young Eagle fellow can put us all to shame when it comes to shooting,' remarked Patrick, referring to the hunt of the previous day.

'He is uncanny with a rifle,' replied Willie. 'That is why he was using the old chief's Henry. The chief is letting him get used to it for a special job in a few days time.'

'What special job?' asked Patrick, remembering how keen the young man was to get his hands on the gun that evening in the chief's lodge. 'He isn't going to kill someone, is he?'

'He's not going to kill anyone – or anything, Pat,' said Willie, trying to assure him.

'Then what?'

'Wait and see,' said Willie.

There the subject rested and they turned their attention back to the fishing. Never since his youth had Patrick enjoyed his fishing as he did that afternoon. Sure, he had fished in California and along the streams in Nevada with Peter O'Reilly but that was when they were placer mining and there was a difference, for then they fished to eat. Here, on the banks of the Belle Fourché, it was just the pleasure of being there.

'When we move to your winter camp, Willie, I guess it will be time for me to be moving on.'

'Where?' asked Willie. 'What have you in mind?'

'Well, I was figurin' on making it to New Orleans and working my fare to England or Ireland. But then I have that money tied up in the bank in San Francisco, the share from the Ophir seam. I could leave that making interest for—'

'Pat, to hell with the money in the bank. You have already paid dearly for it. You are happy here and, well, I know it hasn't escaped your notice that there are more than a few Indian maidens ready to entrap you.'

'That's a nice word, Willie – entrap – and you could not have said it better. If I allowed myself to be entrapped, as you put it, and it would be so easy, then I would be committed and I cannot allow myself to be committed—'

'Pat,' Willie interrupted, 'you're a forty-five-year-old man!'

'And, Willie, that is just the point I'm coming to. When you were taken in by these people you were twenty-six years old, a mere boy, young enough to learn and grow into their ways. Ask yourself if at forty-five could you do it now? Think, Willie, before you answer.'

Willie slowly raised his improvised fishing rod and drew in his line. As if for an answer he looked a while towards the sun about to settle in for the night and then turned to Patrick. 'Pat,' he said, 'it's getting later than I thought.'

'Willie,' said Patrick, gathering up his things and his catch, 'I have only one regret.'

'What is that?'

'That I wasn't with you that day when you crossed the Missouri. We were both twenty-six-year-old bucks then.'

Willie smiled a wistful smile. 'Pat, together we might have saved the lives of my friends.'

'Willie, you're damn right we would.'

Back at Willie's lodge, space was at a premium. Red Wing's sister, Eik-ala, or Little Elk, was there with her two children and the older sister to Ciara. No one had made any mention to Patrick of this one. He assumed that the children were cared for by whatever member of the family the child chose to be with at the time. This girl was about eight, about four years older than Ciara. Her name, he was told, was Tara. The Irish father's influence was evident when it came to issuing names to the girls. When asked if there were any more of his progeny around, Willie proudly proclaimed that they had two sons, the older, Helkiaka Sapa, or Black Elk, now eighteen and destined to succeed Wind of the Wolf as chief. 'These two fine Irish boys,' as Willie put it, Patrick would meet in due course. *Red Wing,* Patrick reflected, *was only seventeen years older than Black Elk.*

The women, kneeling on the rugs, were busy with some kind of needlework. Patrick marvelled at their ability to kneel so long and remain comfortable. Red Wing rose, holding a section of buckskin and, indicating to Patrick to turn his back to her, placed the ends of the skin across his shoulders and here and there made a few markings with chalk. She was unable to speak for she held between her teeth some implements of her trade. Little Elk then asked him to produce a foot for measurement. Patrick was being tailored for a new outfit and a wave of embarrassment stole over him, for he was unable to see how he could repay the kindness of these warm-hearted women.

Outside the opened-up lodge, a rider reined up his horse and beckoned Willie to him. Leaning down over the horse's neck he spoke to Willie in a tone obviously not intended for the ears of others. Willie listened to what news the man had to impart, gave a nod and what appeared to be an approval. The rider straightened up and moved on, with Willie giving the horse a friendly slap on the rump.

'That's a fine outfit the girls are making for you,' said Willie. And before Patrick could reply, he continued, 'It should be all ready for you when you get back.' Patrick was taken aback. This had something to do with the horseman who had passed by.

'Back from where?' asked Patrick.

'Before light tomorrow morning we will be off. You don't have to come but I would like you to.'

'You're not taking me on a war party or a horse-stealing mission?' Patrick joked.

'No; there could be a horse involved but we are not stealing. We should be away for most of a week. I'll explain all in a while but I've got to talk to the chief.'

That evening a small, hand-picked group was summoned to the lodge of Chief Tateyanpa Caksi. Old Chief Two Rivers was also there. The younger chief firstly addressed the group, informing them that he would be brief since they were to have an early start. Then, in English, he spoke to Patrick.

'You'll have no doubt wondered why the superb rifle you presented to my uncle found its way into the hands of this young man here.' Patrick nodded but made no comment. 'Young Eagle,' the chief continued, 'has sharp young eyes, a keen brain and a steady hand. Each year at this time a herd of wild horses that have been living in the hills south of here come down and cross the plains to the north-west. They always return about early October but last year they were late, returning in early November. Our guess was that they had gone further afield, very likely to Montana. No one has ever paid much attention to them for they are . . .' he snapped his fingers searching for a suitable word.

'Scrawny,' said Patrick.

The chief smiled and repeated the word. 'When they returned last year they brought a stranger with them and this one does interest us. He looked no more than a two-year-old. His markings are well known: black or dark brown, a white flash on the nose and the rear end—'

Patrick's knowing smile stopped the chief in mid-sentence and Patrick finished it. 'White with black or maybe dark-brown spots?'

The chief smiled and said, 'Appaloosa.'

'How do you intend to catch your Appaloosa?' Patrick asked.

'That is where we rely on Young Eagle and your Henry rifle. That is why he has been practising.'

'You don't intend to shoot the colt?' Patrick was startled.

'Yes, Patrick, we intend to shoot the colt but not to kill him. The part of the body we intend to aim for is that length of tough muscle that runs along the top of the horse's neck below the mane. We think that if Young Eagle can put a bullet clean through that, it would stun the colt just long enough—'

'Good God, man, that is about a one-in-a-million chance,' exclaimed an exasperated Patrick.

'And when it comes to marksmanship, Young Eagle is also one in a million,' said the cool Sioux chieftain, 'and with your Henry rifle we will have an even better chance.'

The soft gentle breeze barely rippled the grass, just enough to let the hunting party know it was coming in from the south-west and show them where to position to be downwind of the herd, assuming the herd would follow the same track as in previous years. That was, they would come down into the grasslands just below the big bend of the Belle Fourché. There they would stop to water before crossing the shallows and heading out west or north-west into the lush green grass of the prairie. Mustangs were nomadic; they loved to range far and wide and, like the pigeon, always knew their way home.

The men posted themselves on the west bank of the river and just by the end where there was adequate natural cover. The wind, they knew, would hold in that direction for quite a few days and perhaps weeks. As soon as camp was set up and breakfast finished, a lookout set off into the hills and took up position where the whole pass was laid out before him. Since the party were positioned away below him to the west, signalling would be done by mirror. This was an advantage since smoke signals could attract the attention of the horses but at no time could they be distracted by the flashing mirror. Mustangs were constantly on the lookout for human activity.

That first day nothing stirred but they were prepared for it. The lookout returned by moonlight. Tomorrow a fresh volunteer would take his place. Tomorrow would prove just as futile. On the third day, before the fresh morning smells had lifted from the prairie, a signal flashed from the hills. They were coming, about twenty to thirty, but the Appaloosa colt was not with them. It was disappointing news. What could have happened? Was he no longer with the herd? Perhaps he had not survived. Nothing for it now but wait for the lookout and go home. Saddened, they began to gather up their ropes and the rest of the tackle when a second signal was flashed.

Twelve more horses had appeared – twelve horses including the Appaloosa.

They emerged cautiously from behind the avenue of black granite boulders that flanked the pathway to the hills, sniffed the air and, having scented nothing that could indicate danger, charged at full gallop across the greensward to the inviting waters of the Belle Fourché.

In the "hide", two men, each holding the looped ends of two long ropes, were crouched in readiness. A third man, his hands free, was close beside them. There were no slip knots but the loops were measured to drop over a horse's head comfortably with little slack. To the right of them, behind a rock, Eagle Eye knelt on one knee with rifle at the ready. He had only one shell in the breach. The magazine was disconnected. It was one shot and only one shot, and there was no need for the additional weight. Several squeals were vented as flanks were struck by flying hooves. The wild horses were having a bout of robust fun before drinking the water. Had the watchers not been in a high state of tension, the scene being played out before them would have been entertaining. Only one of that party was relaxed: the seventeen-year-old who would fire the shot.

The herd was too tightly bunched. It was of concern to Eagle Eye for if the twelve that were due to appear got entangled with the main body, getting a shot in would be difficult if not impossible. And if the shot were to make its mark, the chance that he would bring down another horse would be very likely. 'Kahayeya,' the youth kept repeating in a whisper, 'kahayeya – go away; leave.'

The wait for the twelve seemed endless. A signal flashed from the lookout indicating that they had tarried in the pass and that they were now on their way, moving at a brisk pace to catch up with the others. The delay was an advantage to Eagle Eye for the main body of the herd had spread out across the grass. On seeing the signal he made a slight alteration to his position but otherwise his limbs were loose, his breathing moderate and his eyes alert. He was like a mountain lion, at ease, waiting for his quarry to make its fatal move.

A pounding of hooves and the twelve had cleared the pass and were heading for the water. Several of the horses, quietly grazing, raised their heads and whinnied as horses do. It seemed as if they were letting the latecomers know they were pleased to see them, or asking, 'Where have you been?' These twelve were all young horses, the next generation, and like children they preferred to be with their peers. Of the entire herd, the young Appaloosa stood out not only for his remarkable colouring but also for his size, beauty and elegant movement. The main body had now spread themselves out. This was considerate of them for they left the youngsters space to drink by the riverbank.

Every man in the hide held his breath. A difficult situation was arising. The Appaloosa was drinking with two horses between him and the marksman.

Should those horses move and expose the Appaloosa to a shot, Eagle Eye would still have to hold his fire if the target remained drinking. With the horse's head down to the water a shot from above would pierce his neck. Luck was to be with the hunters when the horse next to the Appaloosa gave him a nudge. The colt wheeled around and walked away, his head held high. Eagle Eye was looking down the sights. For one brief moment the horse's position was perfect for the shot. He placed his tongue firmly against the roof of his mouth, the tip resting behind his teeth. He did not breathe but sucked air through his teeth and held it. Simultaneously his right forefinger was taking first pressure on the trigger and then a gentle squeeze. The colt hit the ground like he had been pole-axed, his hooves flailing the air. And the herd scattered like chaff before the wind.

Before the blue-white smoke had drifted from the gun barrel, the two men with the ropes were either side of his head and the others close behind to man the ropes. As the colt struggled to rise, two loops were slipped over his head and a team of men on either side took control. By prior arrangement, Patrick and Willie took the ends, looping the ropes diagonally across their backs and over their shoulders, two good anchor men. Memories of the days of their youth were rekindled, when they had pulled for their local tug-of-war team.

Before the colt was on all fours, four men were on either rope but the anticipated struggle with the powerful three-year-old came to little. The young Appaloosa, after a token gesture of resistance, surrendered to his captors. The first tentative pat on the head caused him to flinch and back off, but it soon became apparent that this young horse had until the previous year been close to humans. Those who thought that the herd had wandered as far west as Montana could well have been right, for the Nez Percé had always favoured the big spotted horse and the Nez Percé roamed Montana.

Eagle Eye accepted the congratulations with modesty. He was a shy youth. But on his return, the adulation he would have bestowed on him would be overwhelming. Whether spoken in Lakota or in English, that shot had truly put the stamp on his name and the Henry repeater, like its predecessor the Winchester, would in years to follow be a much-sought-after firearm.

The little hole, drilled so neatly through the colt's neck by a hot spiralling bullet travelling at over the speed of sound, would soon heal and have no lasting effect.

For the horse himself, no saddle would ever be thrown across his back; no brave would ever ride him into battle or on a hunting expedition, He would be the pride of their stock, ranging freely among his concubines, and the progeny would greatly increase the quality of the herd, not only in looks and elegance but also in the bone.

Following the Pueblo Indian revolt of 1680 when, together with the Apaches, they successfully threw the Spanish out of Mexico, the withdrawing Spaniards left behind many of their horses. To the victor went the spoils and it is reasonable to assume that these two tribes were the first of the North American Indians to discover the freedom that the horse would bring them.

Large numbers of these abandoned horses roamed wild, increasing and multiplying, and soon vast areas of the continent were populated with mustang herds. In their wild state much of the quality, so valued by the Spanish, was lost down the years due to their feral environment. Nevertheless, in the early years of the mustang era, some Indian tribes, among them the Apache and the Shoshone, appreciating the quality, fostered and preserved it. By the 1700s, the horse had reached the north-west. Until the arrival of the horse in Idaho, the tribe in that area was sedentary, dwelling mainly around the banks of the Salmon and Snake rivers. The supply of salmon from these rivers and the vast waters of the Columbia was inexhaustible and constituted their main diet. The early French trappers who came down from Canada dubbed them the Nez Percé (Pierced Nose). The name outlived the fashion. With the horse, the lifestyle of the Nez Percé changed forever. They would now reach the buffalo and range far and wide, trading and making war, for they were a belligerent race.

In their 1804–06 expedition, Lewis and Clark, in their trek westward to find the Pacific coast, found the Nez Percé most helpful, and on their return found them waiting to provide fresh horses and guide them over the mountains. Considering that the haughty attitude they displayed to the Sioux had raised more than a few hackles with that population, one must assume that by the time the explorers had reached the Nez Percé they had learned a little diplomacy.

Meriwether Lewis, himself an aficionado of equine form, could not but be impressed by the horses of the Nez Percé. In his diary dated of 15 February 1806 he wrote: 'Their horses appear to be of an excellent race; they are lofty, elegantly formed, active and durable. Some of these horses are pided with large spots of white irregularly scattered and intermixed with black, brown, bey or some other dark colour.' No doubt this gentleman officer from Virginia and friend of President Jefferson was knowledgeable about horses but the nicety of spelling had escaped him.

How these horses acquired their extraordinary spots was never discovered. Spain, at the pinnacle of her power, favoured the Arabian-bred horse and the Appaloosa shows clear evidence of Arabian blood. The origin of the name is easier to trace. The early European settlers in that region associated the horse with the Palouse river and it was referred to as "A Palouse Horse".

From that, it became the "Palousey", then "Appolousey", before people finally settled on Appaloosa.

It was incumbent upon Eagle Eye to name his colt, for it was unanimously decided that from that day onward the captive Appaloosa would be in his sole charge. He deliberated over it for some time, stroking and patting the young horse and praising his good looks. Then, unintentionally, he stumbled upon it as he repeated to himself, 'Wan wawascuscuke.'

'That would sound simpler in English,' Tateyanpa Caksi announced.

'What is it in English?' Patrick asked.

'A dandy,' the chief answered. So Dandy it was to be, then.

As the party prepared to make for home with their precious catch, Willie, mounting up, beckoned Patrick to him. 'Pat,' he said, 'we'll catch up with them later. I would like you to come with me: there is something you should see and there is a question I have to answer.'

CHAPTER 25

They followed the track between the hills until the land opened up before them: a small valley bounded on three sides by hills, with the river away to the left. Away ahead of them lay a pass and that was where Willie made for, with Patrick riding alongside him. The ground they passed over was cropped of grass, and horse droppings were everywhere, evidence that it was time for the mustangs to find fresh pasture. Through the pass the land opened up again into a long narrow strip bounded on all sides by hills. It was a place of natural shelter for animals such as horses. Again the grass was over-cropped. Forty or more horses can demand much acreage.

As the riders entered this long "field", Willie turned right, bidding his pal to follow. They dismounted and led their horses up a steep winding track between the rocks to the top of the hill. The hills were not very high, just 300 feet at most, but they gave a commanding view of the land around.

Holding his horse's reins in his right hand, Willie made a wide sweep with his left, saying, 'Look at it,' with muted pride in his voice as if he were showing his friend what was his own. And it was, for he was in every way, if not in blood, a Lakota, and every Lakota owned this land.

'Look at it, Pat,' Willie repeated and he pointed to the vastness below them. 'You have seen a country rich in rivers, soil, food and timber. A land with a thousand reasons telling me I'll never go back to Maghera. On our way to Fort Laramie you asked me if I would one day go home. Back in Maghera, what would I be? A small man in a small place: someone who would gossip and be gossiped about. And if I brought my wife and children they would laugh at me there because they all would know me not as a Sioux warrior but as Willie McKay who went to school with them and grew up with them and would die exactly like them. But here in this land I am a king, a Lakota, as every Lakota is a king in his land, and as a Lakota I shall die.'[1]

Having spoken his piece he stood there beside his horse, a carved image hewn against the skyline, his countenance poker-like, emotionless, jealously protecting the innermost secrets of his Irish heart.

Far away, beyond the Little Missouri river, the mustangs, now only dots on a sea of rich green grass, could just be seen heading north-west without their adopted youngster. As the two friends mounted and turned downhill, Patrick called from behind, 'Willie, all that Gribben special we brought from Laramie, I think it's time we broke open a bottle or two.'

'Tonight, Pat,' Willie called back, 'tonight we celebrate.'

A feeling of gratitude strangely tinged with guilt and sadness swept over Patrick. Folded neatly on a backrest in the tipi were two sets of the finest quality buckskin outfits, fringed and superbly tailored. On top of each suit was a pair of the finest moccasins, the soles of thick buffalo hide, for long-lasting wear, laboriously hand-stitched to soft buckskin uppers. Folded neatly away between the suits were fine buckskin shirts and cotton underwear of the kind worn by European men, the latter having been surreptitiously purchased in Fort Laramie.

Red Wing did not hesitate to let Patrick know that her sister, Little Eagle, and the girl kneeling on a rug sifting busily through the contents of her sewing bag, had all helped with the tailoring. The young woman smiled

---

1 Years later, Patrick McLaughlin met Louis Walsh, a hotelier in California and a native of Magherafelt, a town eight miles south of Maghera. A variation of this conversation was presumably recounted to Louis Walsh. Louis later sold his business and returned home. He bought premises in Main Street, Maghera, which he opened as a hotel. His son, John Walsh, became a pharmacist and established his business in Maghera. Louis's grandson, Eoin, studied law and practised in the town. As a little boy, his grandfather had told him about the two local boys who had gone to America: one found gold and silver and the other supposedly became a Sioux chief.

The lawyer, from boyhood, was always intrigued by his grandfather's story and after some research wrote a narrative entitled *McKay*. This was included in a compendium of short stories under the title *Famous Men of Maghera,* published by *The Irish News* in the 1950s. The author, in his research, has met Fr John Walsh, Eoin's son, who was most helpful in explaining his ancestry.

Patrick McLaughlin and Peter O'Reilly are mentioned in Louis L'Amour's best-selling novel *Comstock Lode*, published by Bantam Books.

coyly without raising her head when introduced. 'Her name is Oh'anyan C'apa,' said Red Wing. 'That is Busy Beaver.'

Patrick thought the name fitting as he bent down and kissed her cheek. 'Oh'anyan, that's a nice name, Oh'anyan,' he repeated. 'That's easy, even an Irishman can say that.' He thanked all the women, fumbling with words to express his gratitude and all the while feeling that something clandestine was going on between these three females and that he was the focal point. Oh'anyan was a pretty woman who, Patrick thought, could only be in her late twenties or early thirties and he asked himself, *if she is not attached, why not?* He was about to learn.

Little Eagle told him that Oh'anyan C'apa had been widowed two years before. Her husband died in an engagement retrieving stolen horses from a band of thieves. She explained that had he charged in and attacked rather than engaging in an attempt to collect accolades by touching coup, Oh'anyan would not now be a widow. 'Touching coup – what is that?' asked Patrick and he learned from the two sisters about the belief that for a brave to ride up to the enemy and actually touch him with his hand is a courageous and contemptuous act which merits commendation.

Patrick's sympathy was with the girl but for the moment he would pretend to be ignorant of the trap awaiting him. With profuse thanks he collected his gifts and went off to his tent to deposit them and, armed with a towel, walked down to the river for a swim. Tonight, refreshed and in a smart new outfit, he would join Willie, and whoever else wished to turn up, in a little celebration.

'You used to be a good man with the melodeon,' said Patrick as he poured the first cup of the night.

'I've got one but I have never played it.'

'Why?'

'It was Brunduif Lillegard's, one of the Norwegian team. Brunduif was a reporter for a newspaper in Norway who wrote novels and travelled the world. His melodeon and a few farrier tools and a set or two of Chuck's shoes and nails was about all I saved from the wreck. They were fine men, all of them, every one a singer or musician. Man, we had great nights on the prairie.'

'And we'll have a great night now, Willie, so you just get Brunduif's squeeze-box out and let's wind up.'

Willie rummaged through some of his things and came up with the melodeon. As he was settling down to try a few notes, Red Wing threw open the flap and entered with the two girls. It occurred to him that it was the first time he had held a melodeon in her presence and a tune to her would seem appropriate. He ran off a few bars of a traditional Irish melody by Thomas Moore called "Believe Me If All Those Endearing Young Charms". In all its years of idleness, the little instrument had lost none of its tone, nor had Willie, as his clear tenor voice flowed in, softly at first, then lifted and carried beyond the bounds of the lodge to please the ears of those around with one of the most beautiful of Irish melodies.

Believe me, if all those endearing young charms,
Which I gaze on so fondly today
Were to change by tomorrow and fleet in my arms
Like fairy gifts fading away;
Thou wouldst still be adored as this moment thou art,
Let thy loveliness fade as it will;
And around the dear ruin each wish of my heart
Would entwine itself verdantly still.

Patrick was about to join in the vocal rendition, but stopped on seeing the ecstatic faces of two small children and their mother transfixed by the sounds of Willie's magic. This was their moment, their song, and he contained himself as he stretched his legs across the rugs, tilting his hat over his eyes, and reached for the cup.

It is not while beauty and youth are thine own,
And thy cheeks unprofaned by a tear,
That the fervour and faith of a soul can be known,
To which time will but make thee more dear.
No, the heart that has truly loved never forgets
But as truly loves on to the close;
As the sunflower turns on her god, when he sets,
The same look which she turned when he rose.

As the last note trailed away, Tara, the older of the girls, sidled up to her mother and whispered something in her native Lakota. 'What did she say?' Patrick asked of Red Wing, but she was too emotional and left it to Willie to explain.

Willie, not looking directly at him, interpreted his daughter's question; 'She asked why father has never sung to us like that before?' The bellows of the little melodeon fell away from his knee and he turned his head towards it, for his eyes were misting over.

The children were touched by something they did not understand and they felt that they, too, must observe this strange silence that had fallen upon the lodge. Patrick, taking the cup from his beard-encircled lips, was the one to shatter the silence. 'Jaysus, Willie, this man from Rasharkin does a good still.'

'The best,' said Willie, grateful to Patrick for crashing in with the comment. 'Nulli Secundus, that's what the man said, second to none.'

Patrick, determined to create a diversion and keep it all on a light note, led Willie off with the first line of the "Minstrel Boy" by Thomas Moore, and the pair were off.

> *The Minstrel Boy to the war is gone*
> *In the ranks of death you will find him;*
> *His father's sword he hath girded on,*
> *And his wild harp slung behind him;*
> *'Land of Song!' said the warrior bard,*
> *'Tho' all the world betrays thee,*
> *One sword, at least, thy rights shall guard,*
> *One faithful harp shall praise thee!'*

The fast rousing theme soon attracted an audience. Young men and old alike slipped quietly into the lodge and curled up, making themselves as small as possible. Eagle Eye was among them. The music stopped briefly to allow for the arrivals to get comfortable and a bottle was passed around. Eagle Eye and some of his peers declined the "fire water". Knowing what was needed, Red Wing quietly slipped outside and opened up the lappets to their fullest extent on either side. She then took the children and went off to the lodge of her sister. Old men with weather-beaten faces and fresh young fellows squatted side by side to hear, for the first time, the battle hymns of another defiant people.

> *The minstrel fell! But the foeman's chain*
> *Could not bring that proud soul under;*
> *The harp he lov'd ne'er spoke again,*
> *For he tore its chords asunder,*
> *And said, 'No chains shall sully thee,*
> *Thou soul of love and brav'ry!*
> *Thy songs were made for the pure and free,*
> *They ne'er shall sound in slavery!'*

Bottles were passed around, the cups replenished. Conversation in two languages was lively and Eagle Eye was the focus of attention. And the night passed on.

The Minstrel Boy will return, we pray;
When we hear the news we all will cheer it.
The Minstrel Boy will return one day,
Torn perhaps in body, not in spirit.
Then may he play on his harp in peace
In a world such as Heav'n intended,
For all the bitterness of man must cease
And ev'ry battle must be ended.

When the last notes of the "Minstrel Boy" ended and the young Sioux warriors called for more, the Irish tenors did not fail to provide them with some stirring stuff, dredged from the depths of a turbulent Celtic past when Malachi wore the Collar of Gold which he wrenched from the Proud Invader; when Celtic hordes vanquished for ever the warring Vikings at a place called Clontarf.

The pine-log fire, the main source of heat and light, smouldered to a cosy glow. Some of the travellers had gone. The chill air that infiltrated the lodge failed to cool the ardour of the singers. At intervals Patrick would call for some favourite of his to be played but always it landed on deaf ears. 'Here's one that will get them going,' said Willie. A few bars were run off. Patrick forgot about his favourite tune and gave voice to Willie's choice.

Proudly the note of the trumpet is sounding,
Loudly the war cries arise on the gale;
Fleetly the steed by Loch Suiligh is bounding,
To join the thick squadrons in Saimear's green vale,
On, every mountaineer,
Strangers to flight and fear,
Rush to the standards of dauntless Red Hugh!
Bonnought and gallowglass
Throng from each mountain pass!
On for old Erin – O'Donnell abu!

It was a fast and fiery song. Old men who did not know the words, but understood, sat stolid faced, remembering bygone battles, and young men became restless beating time to the rhythm. And the singers, carried away by the sound of their voices and Gribben's elixir, were oblivious to the effect their battle hymns were having on young Lakota blood.

Princely O'Neill to our aid is advancing,
With many a chieftain and warrior clan;
A thousand proud steeds in his vanguard are prancing
'Neath the borders brave from the banks of the Bann –
Many a heart shall quail
Under its coat of mail,
Deeply the merciless foeman shall rue,
When on his ear shall ring,
Borne on the breeze's wing,
Tir-Conaill's dread war-cry – O'Donnell abu!

Patrick, comparing the boisterous merriment to a good céilí night, raised his cup and emitted a loud whoop, and the young Sioux, encouraged by their elders, gave vent to their own whoops and shrill war cries. And the man with the melodeon played on.

Wildly o'er Desmond the war-wolf is howling,
Fearless the eagle sweeps over the plain;
The fox in the streets of the city is prowling,
All, all who would scare them are banished or slain.

Over to the east, atop a rocky knoll, a gray wolf sat, silhouetted against the first chink of light of a new day. He cocked his ear to the sound emanating from the lodge and throwing back his head gave vent, followed by his entire choir on the grass below him. From the lodge, the plaintive notes of a strained little melodeon mingled with the chorus of a wolf pack and the tenor tones of two drunken Irishmen, still in full voice, rose in concert and in volume to meet a Dakota dawn.

CHAPTER 26

I t was a dark and ominous place without definition. The floor, or surface, and the wall that bounded the area were both of a dark charcoal colour, a sombre and foreboding pit. In the centre, two scorpions, stingers arched over their backs, their heads locked together, gyrated in a strange dance that resembled something between a tango and a square dance. They were not engaged in a deadly duel but in a display of courtship for that is the way that scorpions perform. Their dance was not a pleasing sight. Unlike the splendid display of peacocks or the aerial ballet of eagles, it was ugly and malevolent, for scorpions are ugly and malevolent.

As the dance continued, the enthusiasm intensified and the little creatures locked head to head became oblivious to all else around them. From a cavity where floor and wall met, a forked tongue flicked, sensing the area. With deadly intent the serpent slithered towards its unsuspecting quarry. When within reach, it coiled and struck with lightning speed, then turned away and the scorpions were no more; the amorous arachnids had danced their last tango.

Patrick was aware of a persistent tapping on his forehead, gentle but persistent. He shot up, sweating, from beneath the rug that covered him to see the reassuring face of the smiling child who had awakened him from a bad dream. It was the kind of dream that is often dreamt by those who have met with trauma in desert lands, especially when sleep has been fuelled by potent alcohol. Ciara was holding out to Patrick a large multicoloured bathrobe and pointing in the direction of the river. She spoke a few laboured words she had obviously been versed to say: 'Father gone to river.' Before he could thank the child and congratulate her on her newfound language, she ran off.

The message was obvious: Willie was down by the river and would like

Patrick to join him, prepared for a morning swim. He stripped off what clothing he had fallen asleep in, wrapped the bathrobe tightly around his waist and made for the river. He found Willie sitting, bare skinned, on one of several flat-topped stones on the riverbank. There was no morning greeting. Both were suffering from their folly of the night before. Patrick, having folded his bathrobe, was about to place it on the stone but was stopped by Willie.

'No, Pat, no cushion, just sit on stone. Always sit on stone. Indians always sit close to the earth – Mother Nature's best healer.'

Strange, thought Patrick, *why this broken English so suddenly?* And then he dismissed it as a result of the effects of the alcohol.

'Headache, Pat?'

'God, it's throbbing.'

'No worry; it will soon be gone.' He began to show Patrick some exercise movements in association with his breathing and instructed his pal to follow. This was followed by focusing on a point in the riverbed and listening to the sound of the breath while relaxing the body part by part, limb by limb, until the entire body was supple and completely relaxed. Then with fingertips, Patrick learned to massage the scalp, the neck and facial muscles, followed by more prolonged breathing and relaxation. Patrick was astonished at the power of the "Indian magic".

'Now, let's have a swim in the cold clear water,' said Willie, 'and then I must talk with you.'

After an invigorating dip, followed by a brisk towelling, Willie indicated the stone slab for Patrick with the aplomb of an attentive host offering his guest the best seat.

'Pat,' Willie began, 'I have noticed you of late. Am I right in thinking that you're getting a bit restless?'

'You could be, Willie.'

'Still feel like going back home?'

'As you know, I have a few thousand dollars in a bank in San Francisco. Over and above my share from the Ophir seam, Peter and I were putting away a little now and again from our pay and what we picked up from placer mining. All in all I could be worth about six and a half thousand and then there is a bit of interest accruing. Not much for a man who discovered what could yet turn out to be the largest gold and silver deposit ever.'

'But you're richer than most who set out for gold. You have more than enough to buy a cottage and small holding back home.'

'You're right, Willie, I should count my blessings. And just think, if I had made it rich with Peter in Six Mile Canyon, our chance meeting would never have happened. You know, Willie, these last weeks living with the Sioux have been among the most contented times of my life. I envy you.'

'You envy me but you must still go back to the white man's wilderness.' Willie picked up a chip of wood and tossed it into the river and, deep in thought, watched it as it drifted away. Then, pulling his mind back to the present, he continued. 'Pat, I may have some good news for you, depending on how you see it.'

'I'm listening,' said Patrick.

'There is a trader coming through here in three or four days from now. He travels with five or six mule teams. A French Canadian; an old friend of Red Cloud and well trusted by the Sioux.'

'Fine,' said Patrick, 'but where do I come in?'

'He will be making his way along the track we came on from the Cheyenne river but he and his team go on to the steamer point on the Missouri, where they pick up their supplies from St Louis and sell on what they buy from us.'

'Steamer on the Missouri?' Patrick queried, and it occurred to him that a steamer could be preferable to a canoe.

'Yes, Pat, steamboats have been plying the river from St Louis for a good while now. From St Louis you can take another to New Orleans and then a big ship home. Anyway, Pat, you have a few days to think it over but now, let's go and get some good hot coffee and something to eat.'

Until 1862, all tribes living north of the Platte were relatively free of the white man's interference but to the south, the encroachment of the settlers, backed by military protection, was a cause for concern. Overlanders on the California and Oregon Trails were contemptuous of the "wild Indians" or the "savages" as they called them. Their haughty attitude towards the indigenous people of the land did not go unpunished and many innocent white travellers suffered for the guilty.

Almost from its beginning when Fort Laramie was set up as a trading post, Indians from several tribes established camps around the fort. Their purpose was to trade with the white man and for years good relations existed between Indian and the genuine trader. Then came the bootleggers and the unscrupulous white traders. Many Indians were robbed. Many succumbed to the white man's "fire water". All this and the endless jeers and taunts from the wagon trains, mostly from women and children, and the fire of hatred and destruction that would sweep the plains for years to come was kindled.

As they walked back to the circle of tipis, Patrick felt that he had outstayed his welcome, for Willie, having giving him the option to leave, was silent and withdrawn. *What could he have done to cause offence?* And he put the question to Willie.

'No, Pat, you have not outstayed your welcome. A short while ago I mentioned a man's name who is an old friend of the trader who will be here in a few days' time.'

'Red Cloud, I think you said.'

'Have you ever heard of him?' asked Willie.

'Not until you made mention of him.'

'Red Cloud is a powerful chief of the Oglalas. We have just learned that he has been elected supreme chief of all Oglalas.'

'What has that got to do with my hasty departure?'

'Look, Pat, let me explain. Let's take a walk along the river.' They turned back but instead of walking along the embankment they returned to the flat stones and sat down. A hungry red-tailed hawk circled overhead.

'Pat, when we were at Fort Laramie you must have felt the tension.'

'I could hardly have missed it,' said Patrick.

'And, Pat, did you see all those parties coming in from south of the Platte?'

'Well, I can't say that I took much notice of all the traffic.'

'Most of them were not there to buy or sell as we were; they were in for their annuities.'

'Their what?' Patrick snapped, wheeling around to look directly at Willie.

'That's what I said, Pat, annuities, yearly payments, not in cash but in kind. You may have seen them come in with empty travois for they had nothing to sell and if you think back on it, none of them went near the traders' area. No, they loaded up at the stores depot and went back south.'

'Do I understand that they are on some kind of handout?'

'United States government handout. For promising to be "good little Indians" and to keep the white man's peace they will be clothed and fed.'

'For handing over their homeland and their freedom,' Patrick added.

Willie nodded saying, 'That's right.'

'And where does Red Cloud come into all this?' Patrick asked.

'Between twenty-five and thirty years ago, some white traders persuaded many Sioux to move south to Laramie. About one hundred lodges did, led by a powerful Oglala chief. His name was Bull Bear and his followers were known as the Bear people. Another Oglala band moved south about this time under the leadership of a chief called Smoke. For the Oglalas this was a permanent move away from the Missouri river. Together with the Brules who had moved south later, they held sway over a large area of the land from Nebraska to Wyoming's Wind River Mountains. They could hold their own with the tribes that were there long before them, mostly the Pawnees. Fort Laramie grew and prospered with good feeling between the white traders and the Indians, and many of the traders married into the Indian communities.'

Willie paused from his narrative to reflect while he pitched a few pebbles into the water. Patrick, now wrapped up in the story, had forgotten his hunger. The red-tailed hawk turned into wind and hovered for a while, then side-slipped away toward the long grass. It had selected its nourishment.

Willie continued: 'Then quarrelling broke out between two of the factions, those of Smoke's party and some from the Bear people. The story goes that it all started in a drunken brawl and ended in the murder of Chief Bull Bear. The killing of Bull Bear was done by a small group who were never punished for it. Among them was a young hothead of only twenty. His name would become known throughout the plains to the red and white man alike. In the years that followed, Red Cloud would be known as a great leader and a chief well able to hold his own in the white man's council. Now he is beating the drum for unity, not only with all the Sioux tribes but with the Cheyenne as well and for good reason. There are many within the Sioux nation who have never forgiven him for the killing of Bull but he is a good leader in rallying the troops and he is well able for the white man.'

That evening Patrick was excluded from the meeting hastily convened by the chiefs and elders. From a soot-blackened pot hanging from the tripod over a ring of heated stones, Red Wing poured two cups of coffee and, taking the lid off a canister beside her, spooned into each cup several teaspoons of dark brown sugar. She carried them the few paces to where Patrick was sitting on a backrest and, handing him one, knelt down in front of him. Clutching her cup with both hands, she sipped from it before speaking.

'You must be confused by all that is happening and so suddenly.'

'I am and I don't see that I am in any immediate danger from the cavalry or anyone else for that matter.'

'Pat, no one is forcing you to go and as you say, you are safe enough here at present. But if you leave it until we move for winter camp it will be too late. If, on the other hand, you leave with Claude Du Prez you will be in safe hands all the way to the Missouri.'

'Willie tells me this Frenchman, or French Canadian, is a boozin' pal of Red Cloud.'

'Red Cloud is no man's "boozin' pal". He detests alcohol in every form, but, yes, they are good friends; they respect and trust each other.' *And what better friendship is there than that?* Patrick asked of himself as he raised the cup to his lips. 'Red Cloud is a clever man and a good leader,' continued Red Wing, 'but he is an irascible man and—'

'God, that's some word for an—'

'An Indian woman.' Red Wing was quick to interrupt and the hurt showed.

'I'm sorry, I just . . . well, tell me what it means,' mumbled the apologetic Patrick.

'My cousin was never mean with his education. He shared with those he felt would appreciate it.' She did not speak the word again but went on, 'Red Cloud may be a good leader but he is known to be quick tempered – a hothead – and my father and many others think that he may be acting too soon and bring the attention of the military to us.'

'Your cousin, now he is the kind of man well suited to dealing with the military.'

'He may well have to one day.'

'And your husband Willie?'

She shook her head. 'He would just be regarded as a renegade. And the rifles you gave to my family: if they were to be found they would be traced to you, and you, in their eyes, would become a gunrunner and collaborator with the enemy.'

'I see. You paint a dark picture,' said Patrick, and with a knowing smile, curiosity prompted him to probe for an answer to another question on his mind. 'Well,' he sighed, 'there goes my future with Busy Beaver.'

Red Wing smiled, 'You have been taking notice.' And then with some kind of inner wisdom she shook her head, 'No, Pat, it would not succeed. You are of different worlds.' She took Patrick's empty cup and moved towards the ring of stones and from the neatly stacked pile of firewood she kindled up the dying fire. As the flames flickered and sparkled from the sweet-smelling pine, an elation, strangely tempered with sadness, came over him for he felt free to go on his way but would be leaving behind forever a life and a people he had come to love.

Red Cloud may have been premature in beating the drum, for most of the lands north of the Platte were to enjoy a relative peace for another twelve years or more. In late 1874, a gold-prospecting party moved into the Black Hills and hastily erected a fortification against an Indian attack. This was a blatant contravention of the 1868 Laramie agreement. The military pursued them and moved them out but by the summer of the following year, miners in ever-increasing numbers were infiltrating the hills and valleys. There was "gold in them thar hills", lots of gold, and a United States government, having come out of a gruelling civil war less than ten years before, left the miners and the Indians to sort it out for themselves. But the nation's treasury needed gold and gold there was aplenty, and when troops were sent in again it was not to protect the Indians, or the Treaty of Laramie, but the miners.

There is an irony here. Had Patrick McLaughlin and his three companions reached their intended destination in June 1860 and, with the fire power they had, repulsed any attack, they may well have succeeded. But had they found gold and the news of their find had got out, the Yankee army would not, and could not, have interfered for it was soon to be caught up in a civil war.

Claude Du Prez intended to make good headway to the Missouri. He had only one call to make and that was with the No Bows people by the Cheyenne river. There would be nothing to detain him between the Belle Fourché and the Cheyenne. He and his team had five wagons, all heavily laden, but Patrick was made welcome and an extra driver would be helpful. Patrick, anxious that he would not burden his host and aware that most of his baggage was surplus to his needs, distributed most of it amongst those who could make use of it. Only Herbie's personal effects did he retain in a bag separate from his own essentials. In his breast pocket was an address written in bold capitals on a piece of brown wrapping paper. It had long since become unnecessary, for the name and address of the Reverend Langsfeld were imprinted on his memory. That would be his first call on arrival at St Louis.

The farewell was a protracted and emotional affair. Old Chief Two Rivers, a tear visible rolling down his cheek, was overcome, for he had taken Patrick to his heart as he had taken Willie into his family. Willie rode alongside the little convoy of wagons talking to Patrick and telling of so many things he must do and so many people he must be remembered to back home. When the circle of tipis lay far behind them, Claude Du Prez halted his wagons. Willie dismounted and Patrick, having secured his rifle behind the seat, leapt from the brake. They wasted little time in their farewell – there was no need; it had all been said. They shook hands and clasped each other's shoulders. 'God go with you, Pat,' called Willie as he swung into the lightweight saddle.

'And with you, Willie.'

Patrick watched as he rode off at speed, the eagle feather fluttering above his long black hair, and it just then occurred to Patrick that Willie (Wakinyan) no longer rode like a white man. At some distance off he reined up his horse and wheeled around in the way a tribesman of the plains would do and gave the red man's salute. Patrick reciprocated, then he wheeled away and was gone.

On the return trip to the Cheyenne river, Claude Du Prez took his teams on a trail that lay further south to that which his party had travelled when heading west. Hills showed up away to the south of them and stayed with them for the best part of two days, varying in height as the wagons rolled eastward. They were not black but blue, changing with the sunset to deep rich green. It was the first, and last, time Patrick would see the Black Hills of Dakota and the nearest he would ever get to them.

At the steamer point, having said his farewells to the traders and before boarding, he had one last sad parting. His two mules, hitched to the rear of the wagon in which he had ridden, each were patted and hugged. They had come a long and dangerous road together and without them he would not have survived. He was leaving them in the knowledge that they would be in good care with their new master.

The New Orleans waterfront was busy that morning. Every berth along the wharf was taken up by a ship tied up alongside and others, lying off, riding at anchor, awaited their turn to put alongside. Tugs, now powered by steam, prowled the waterway waiting for a signal to "shift ship". From every ship alongside, two gangways extended from ship to shore, one for crew and others on ship's business, the other for loading. Teamsters with their long-bodied four-wheeled carts jockeyed for position by the loading gangways. Cotton bales, in a never-ending flow, moved on the shoulders of chanting slaves, and out on the waterway, anxious tug pilots reminded everyone of their presence with constant blasts on their foghorns.

Patrick, dodging teamsters' mules in harness and other life-threatening obstructions, made his way almost the full length of the long wharf, scrutinising every ship for a name and referring frequently to the slip of paper he was given at the dingy little shipping office. Almost where the wharf ended, with only a few ships lying ahead of her, he found the one he was looking for, a big three-masted merchantman. The large white letters stood out against the black painted stern. Her name was *The Devonshire Yeoman*, and below in smaller letters was Bristol. He checked against the paper which read: "Ship's name, *The Devonshire Yeoman*, port of register, Bristol, ship's master, Captain Kneil."

Unlike the other vessels along the line, there was little activity around the *Yeoman*, certainly no evidence of cargo being moved, and the cargo gangway had been taken away. At the top of the remaining gangway, Patrick, as he stepped on the deck, asked the first man he met where he could find the captain.

The man was standing, hands on hips, looking up at what seemed to be the top of the masts. His shirt sleeves were rolled up to the elbows. His shirt, open-necked, was collarless; a pair of braces held up a pair of heavy corduroy trousers, too slack at the waistband even for a man of his girth. The man was of Patrick's height but of greater bulk. He turned to Patrick with a good-humoured smile beaming from a red weather-beaten face. A pair of lively blue eyes twinkled with mischief as he took stock of the man who had just boarded, hoping to work his passage. This newcomer was about to learn that ships' captains come in all shapes and sizes and not always in neat square-rigged naval uniform.

'I'm Captain Kneil,' the man said, and held out his hand to him. Patrick was somewhat taken aback by his informality and from the handshake he instinctively knew that this man had no trouble with command. 'You've come from the shipping office?'

'I have, Captain.'

'And you feel you could work your passage to England?'

'I could.'

'And what is your name?'

'McLaughlin, Captain. Patrick McLaughlin.'

Captain Kneil appeared to be a man who did everything in a leisurely manner, while his mind dwelt on other matters. From one of the deep trouser pockets he took a large leather tobacco pouch, opened it and took from it a short-shanked pipe and, as if he had the rest of the day all to himself, slowly filled the bowl. Then, having returned the pouch to his pocket, he lit his pipe with a match he seemingly plucked from nowhere. Patrick stood all the while quietly amused. *Why,* he pondered, *do men make such a ceremony of pipe smoking?*

With the blue fragrant smoke blowing and a long contented puff he looked Patrick directly in the eye and pointed the pipe towards the beams where only sailors and seagulls perch and said, 'Patrick, if you're man enough to climb that rigging and get yourself out on yonder yard and get back to me without killing yourself, you've got a passage to England.' The smile on his face said, *I dare you.*

Patrick was a fit man but he soon discovered that ascending a rope ladder was an art requiring more practice than he had had the opportunity to do. Deckhands were now leaving their tasks to assemble under the yard to be amused and to poke a little fun up at this fellow in a fringed plainsman outfit. Dogged tenacity pushed Patrick upwards to calls from below that he would not find any Indians in the crow's nest, and suchlike jesting as sailors are wont to make among themselves. Patrick, when he reached the yard, soon learned that the only way to get out there was to use his hands on the yard for grip and stability while walking gingerly, one foot behind the other, on the lanyard that hung in a series of loops from the yard. His riding boots he found to be an advantage. When he reached the end a cheer and a thunderous handclap came up from below.

'Come with me,' said Captain Kneil and he led Patrick up a companion ladder to an upper deck and through a dim and narrow alleyway with closed cabin doors on either side. The passageway ended at a closed door. The captain took a small bunch of keys from a pocket and as he opened the door a shaft of sunlight beamed down the alleyway. He beckoned Patrick to follow and indicated a chair by a desk affixed to the bulkhead under the window which faced over the ship's stern. The captain's cabin was small, compact and neat. On the right, as one entered, was a bunk with a curtain drawn across it. On the left and against the aft bulkhead was the ablutions area, again a curtain with a matching pattern to the one concealing the bunk drawn around it. The wardrobe stood against the bulkhead on that, the left side. To the side of the wardrobe, hanging on hooks, were oil skins and other heavy-weather gear with heavy rubber boots underneath. Under the bunk was the large sea chest. By the desk were two chairs; no room for more.

When Patrick was seated, he filled the other chair and sat facing him. It was not necessary for a sea captain to invite passage-working personnel to talks in his cabin but Captain Kneil was curious about this man and wished to know more. This plainsman intrigued him. Above his desk was a three-tier rack of polished hardwood shelves, secured to the bulkhead. Each shelf had a series of holes varying in diameter to safely hold the glasses and bottles when at sea. When his guest was comfortably seated he reached up and took down two small tumblers and a bottle of Scotch and poured a liberal measure into each. He then returned the bottle to the security of the rack and pushed a glass across the desk to his guest, reminding him that, once he had signed on, this cabin and this area of the ship would be out of bounds.

Captain Kneil had a canny way of getting the best out of people and the story that came from Patrick was an interesting one. 'You sound like one of my friends who was killed on the trail,' remarked Patrick.

'Was that the Cornish miner?' asked the captain.

'That's right, John Tyler.'

'I'm a Devon man, next-door neighbours,' said the captain, 'born for the sea. In the early days of the Californian gold rush a good many Cornish miners took passage with us. They all felt they could better their lot and I'm sure a good many did. Our company has, for a good few years, carried passengers out and cotton home, cotton for the mills of Lancashire. Outward bound we carry machinery in the lower holds. Heavy cargo keeps the ship down in the water. Cotton is light cargo. Your ship can pitch around a bit with that stuff in the holds. I like my ship well settled in the water.' He quaffed off the last drop in the glass and with a heavy hand placed it on the desk, a clear indication that the informal meeting was over.

'Well, Patrick,' said Captain Kneil, 'you have a story that will enthral your grandchildren. Now, why you are here is just this. This vessel sails on tomorrow's evening tide. Five of my hands have jumped ship. It's unlikely they will show up at this late hour. The cargo is in and the hatches are closed. It's possible they have gone off in this big country on an adventure such as yours, but I doubt it – more likely the rats are holed up in one or other of the bordellos down there in the French Quarter. If that is the case, they'll be standing on the quay, all sorry for themselves, when our next ship is due in. Now, if you get yourself on board tomorrow morning with your baggage and report to the bosun, you'll find him—'

'Captain,' Patrick interrupted, 'at the rooming house where I have my bags, I also have a rifle and a revolver and some ammun—'

'Don't bring those damn things on my ship!' the captain roared. 'Get rid of them! Take them to the kitting-out station where you will get a good price for them from some of the migrants. They are the ones who need them.' Patrick nodded his agreement.

Captain Kneil rose from his desk and walked out onto the deck with Patrick following. 'Now, maritime law states that all crew members, on joining a vessel, must sign what is known as Articles to the captain. Articles can be binding for two years but cease when the ship pays off at her port of destination. Now, whether you sign on as a deckhand or a doctor taking passage for just that trip, you are, under the terms of maritime law, known as supernumerary crew and, as such, your pay will be one shilling per calendar month. This is paid on completion of the voyage or part thereof should the voyage end before the twenty-eight days are up.' He looked directly at Patrick, smiled and said, 'But we never split hairs over it.' Then he pointed to the top of the tall mast saying, 'Tomorrow morning there will be a small square blue flag with a small white square in the centre flying from the top of the mast. That is the "Blue Peter" and it will be flying up there telling a story and that story is that on the day it is flying, if you are not on board by the next tide, you have missed the boat. But as soon as you step on that deck tomorrow, m'lad, you're homeward bound.'

Epilogue

Captain Kneil set sail without me for I was unable to comply with his order to give up my arms before joining his ship. I was not prepared to surrender my rifle and Colt 45 to any man; not then, not now. As long as evil men bear arms, good men need theirs. And if I were to have walked off the ship at Bristol with a rifle slung over my shoulder, I would not have got far before being arrested and having my rifle confiscated, for I would have been committing a crime. What was it Willie said? 'A small man in a small place.' But Captain Kneil, bless him, did unwittingly point the way for me when he suggested I should take my arms to the fitting-out depot and sell them.

It was there I arrived the next morning, instead of the ship, and bought myself a steamboat ticket to Independence, Missouri. After all those years I was surprised to see the old depot still selling merchandise to the newly arrived immigrants before they boarded the steamboat.

St Louis, once known as the gateway to the West – first to trappers and then to the first rush of immigrants – had long since ceased to provide for the overlanders. Westport, St Joseph and Independence, between 200 and 250 miles west of St Louis on the Missouri river, were the chief starting points on the trails westward. St Louis was growing all the time with land constantly in demand.

When I passed that way before – let me see now, that was 1833 – I headed straight for Texas on what was to be known as the Santa Fe Trail. Not this time. I was heading all the way to California and for two good reasons. My account in that bank in San Francisco would give me the independence I needed, and more than enough to start out in any direction that suited me. The other good reason was that on the steamboat to Independence I met my future wife. She was travelling with her nine-year-old son, and other members of her family, from Dorset in the south-west of England. They had decided to pull up stakes and emigrate after her husband died as a result of an agricultural accident.

At first I think she felt secure with the big plainsman in the buckskin outfit and the thought occurred to me of the young widow who helped with the tailoring of it. The summer of 1860 was my season for meeting young widows, but this time I was not running away. Anyhow, until Independence we were in the same boat together. Her parents and sister were grateful for what help I could give, and her son, Steven, idolised me. I thought it prudent to keep my distance, for I was well aware of the long months we would all have under canvas at Independence for no wagon trains were going to move until next year's spring when grass would be green again and the snows had gone from the High Sierras. Could be the long wait at Independence and the onward journey were the healing time she needed.

By mid-July the following year, with the blessing of her family, we were married at the little Franciscan mission in Sacramento. That was fifteen years ago. We bought some land, with government help, a few miles south-west of Sacramento. A river runs by it on the east side. I have often wondered if it is the same river where a small boy once fished with his adopted "Grandad" and learned of a faraway place called the Dakotas where rivers flowed with gold. I will never know.

As I said, that was fifteen years ago, and our piece of land has grown some. Our ranch has become known through the land for the horses we breed. That's right – Appaloosas. The horses came first; the land was there for the buying. We bought some good breed stock from an old Shoshone shortly after we arrived. He was a man who knew good horseflesh and offered us a deal we couldn't refuse. We bought the stock from him and then went out and looked for land. My stepson, Steven, has little to learn about Appaloosas, or any other horse for that matter. In the early days, when he was just a boy, we ranged far and wide, searching for good breeding lines, while his mother and her father took care of the ranch. We have a long waiting list of customers and we are particular about whom we sell to, for our horses are special to us.

Last month I had a letter that is awaiting my reply. It was from Peter O'Reilly. I found him through the bank in San Francisco where we first deposited our money and gold. It was good to hear from him for I never forgave myself for my quarrel with him. He did what he felt was right at the time. We had a maverick on our hands by the name of Henry Comstock and there is little one can do with a maverick. It was good news from Peter. He is married and living in Montana with two sons; the oldest is thirteen. They bought some rich arable land from the proceeds of his gold ventures. Yes, he found his gold.

Shortly after our split, Peter, with other prospectors, joined up with that other Irishman, John McKay. That's right, the John McKay who got in too late on the Californian rush and was in on the first rush on the Comstock. The John McKay who physically evicted a coyote from his den on a foothill of Mount Davidson and with his spade and shovel extended the poor creature's only piece of real estate and moved himself in, bag and baggage, from the fall of 1859 until the spring of 1860 when he struck gold, or rather silver.

John McKay and George Hearst, now wealthy and organised and with their Comstock claims still oozing from the earth riches yet untold, mustered together the most experienced miners and headed to Montana as soon as news had got out that gold had been found there, in a place known as Alder Gulch. That was 1864; they are still there. From Peter's letter I gather he is not long finished with mining. I wish him well with his farm, a healthier occupation than mining for whatever substance that is down there.

Seems they love Montana. There is a passage in his letter that reads: 'If God made any place more beautiful than Montana, he kept it to himself.' I don't know where he found words like that. Like myself, he was always a bit heavy with words. I guess he took time off to attend night classes, or married a school teacher. When I answer his letter I have a lot of questions to ask.

As I write, it is towards the end of June 1876, America's centennial year, and there is other news coming out of Montana to blunt the edge of the nation's celebrations. On a hillside by the name of Little Bighorn a young Oglala chief known throughout the Sioux nation as Crazy Horse has vanquished the 7th Cavalry, led by one Lieutenant Colonel George Armstrong Custer.[1] The Sioux, together with the Cheyenne, have defeated the nation's best and the nation stands stunned.

And when a shocked nation begins to recover, and recriminations fly, this will not be seen as a victory for men fighting for their homeland, a hard-pressed people provoked beyond endurance taking a last stand against the aggressor. And the young chieftain, only thirty-four years old, I learn, rallying his warriors with his battle cry, 'Come on, Lakotas, it's a good day to die,' will not be remembered as a military leader but a renegade savage. The red man has won a battle but not the war.

I fear the white man's vengeance and his propaganda will prevail. I fear for Willie and Red Wing, their family and all the families I had come to know. Many, like old Chief Two Rivers, are undoubtedly gone. But Willie, he is only sixty-one, my age – an age when a man has no right to be on the

---

1 At the Battle of Little Bighorn, Custer's rank was Lieutenant Colonel, not General as commonly believed. He was promoted to General posthumously.

battlefield. But I am sure that if he has to, like that day when he first crossed the Missouri, Willie will fight to the last.

And when the last battle has been fought, and Willie has found his Happy Hunting Ground, will he find himself forever thundering across an endless prairie on the back of Chuck with startled deer and antelope bounding away on either side of them? Or will he be that little boy half running, half flying, down a hillside on a sunny morning, his jacket above his head and Prince and little Screen bounding ahead? Or maybe, on a lazy afternoon, he will be resting among the heather, gazing across the valley to the north shore of Lough Neagh, musing to himself how, through the iniquitous behaviour of the bawdy Vikings, our existence may have come about.

Who knows, McLaughlin, who knows?